Praise for

## THE FAKE MATCHMAKER

"Breezy and charming, and the perfect summer read."
**Emily Giffin, bestselling author of** *The Summer Pact*

"Heart-warming, charming, and laugh-out-loud funny, *The Fake Matchmaker* by Sonya Singh is sure to please all rom-com lovers and bring the genre new fans. The small-town setting, a pro-tagonist you'll cheer for, a love interest you might be tempted to scoop up for yourself, and tons of delicious food all make this book an absolute delight. Highly recommended!"
**Holly Cassidy, bestselling author of**
***The Christmas Countdown***

"For fans of Annabel Monaghan, Namrata Patel, and Jane Austen, Sonya Singh's *The Fake Matchmaker* is an absolute must-read! This touching, fast-paced novel takes a deep dive into the love of family, friendship, and food, the complexity of romantic attraction, and one woman's search for her happily ever after."
**Amy Poeppel, author of** *Far and Away*

**Also by Sonya Singh**

*The Break-up Expert*

# The Fake Matchmaker

## SONYA SINGH

**SIMON &
SCHUSTER**

London · New York · Amsterdam/Antwerp · Sydney/Melbourne · Toronto · New Delhi

First published by Doubleday Canada, an imprint of Penguin Random House Canada
Limited, 2026
320 Front Street West, Suite 1400,
Toronto, Ontario, M5V 3B6, Canada

First published in Great Britain by Simon & Schuster UK Ltd, 2026

1 3 5 7 9 10 8 6 4 2

Simon & Schuster UK Ltd, 7th Floor,
199 Bishopsgate, London, EC2M 3TY

Simon & Schuster Australia, Sydney
Simon & Schuster India, New Delhi

www.simonandschuster.co.uk
www.simonandschuster.com.au
www.simonandschuster.co.in

The authorised representative in the EEA is Simon & Schuster Netherlands BV,
Herculesplein 96, 3584 AA Utrecht, Netherlands. info@simonandschuster.nl

A CIP catalogue record for this book is available from the British Library

Paperback ISBN: 978-1-3985-1054-8
eBook ISBN: 978-1-3985-1055-5
Audio ISBN: 978-1-3985-1685-4

Printed and Bound in the UK using 100% Renewable Electricity
at CPI Group (UK) Ltd

*For my parents,*
*who gave me the gift of laughing out loud,*
*and for Jordanian and Moses,*
*who remind me to keep joy close.*

*M*anisha coyly pushed his hand away from hers, her eyes sparkling with a teasing glimmer. She surveyed the opulent banquet hall, where ruby reds and dark golds intertwined, casting beams of light dancing across the room. Ornate floral arrangements filled with marigolds and rose petals adorned every table, while a cascade of fairy lights overhead fashioned a twinkling canopy reminiscent of the mandap in the centre of the stage. The vibrant colours illuminated the swirling figures of the dancers, their movements perfectly synchronized to the lively strains of popular Indian wedding tracks that filled the air.

Manisha nervously shifted her gaze to the Gupta aunties at table three. Relief filled her at the sight of the sisters much too engrossed in their chana masala and rice to notice her. With a satisfied sigh, she turned her attention back to the man before her. But instead of the familiar features she longed to see, the room around her dimmed, leaving only his silhouette. A thrilling shiver danced down her spine as the mystery of him heightened her anticipation.

*Who is he?*

Still, she knew better than to attract the aunties' disapproval with her flirtations. She stood to leave when his firm grip caught her sari, wordlessly begging her to stay. In response, Manisha playfully swept the red silk across his face. His still-shrouded face. She bit her lip as a sudden nervousness washed over her.

*Why can't I see his face?*

*Why don't I know his name?*

*Why is the room so dark?*

She looked around the hall as the stranger lightly tugged on her heavily beaded outfit, tempting her to sit with him. Unable to resist, she let herself melt into the scent of his cologne, a blend of juniper and bergamot that made her mouth dry with desire. After one last coaxing pull, Manisha gracefully tumbled into his lap, her long legs swinging to one side, her red-bottom heels coming to rest atop his pristinely polished Gucci loafers. She watched, breathless, as the hall glow reflected off the gold hardware. Her heart was racing in her chest. She could feel the heat from his body burning through the layers of her sari. Suddenly, the breath she'd finally found became heavier.

"Manisha . . ." he said softly.

Manisha's body quivered with anticipation as her name escaped his lips again. He was igniting within her a fire she hadn't felt in a while . . . or maybe ever. His soft lips grazed her fingertips, and waves of warmth coursed through her. If only she knew his name, she could return the whispers. She took a shallow, uneven breath. All she wanted to do was push aside the extravagant centrepiece from their table to make room for their passion.

"Manisha . . ." he breathed her name again, his voice deep and seductive as he pulled her tighter against him. The echoing "Desi Girl" lyrics fell away, his voice growing more urgent until it became a desperate cry.

A loud, piercing cry.

A loud, piercing *female* cry.

"Manisha!"

Abruptly, the heat surging through Manisha's body vanished. In its place, exasperation settled in as her waking mind placed the all-too-familiar shrill tone: her mother. Manisha opened one eye with a reluctant sigh, only to be met with her mother's disapproving glare. Standing next to the bed, hands planted on her hips, Ruby Patel exuded authority and disapproval. Manisha pulled the bedsheet over her head, desperately hoping to return to her dream and that sexy mystery man.

"I am your mother; you will need more than a chadar to protect you from me, Manisha," her mother said.

"A bedsheet is the only thing I could reach right now, Mom," Manisha said dryly as she pulled the cotton fabric down.

"Hurry up and get up!" her mom said loudly, voice echoing through the room. "We have things to do!"

"Moooom," Manisha moaned.

Here she was, a grown woman whining like a little girl, but there was something about being back in her childhood bedroom and getting scolded by her mother. Whining and complaining were inevitabilities.

Her mother raised a perfectly threaded eyebrow above her thin-framed glasses and fixed her gaze on Manisha, a mix of irritation and amusement in her expression. "Manisha, it is lunchtime. Get up and get dressed. You're like a baby sleeping in. We have so much to do today: go to the temple, clean up this room, and don't forget groceries! We need milk, butter, and I want to have a talk with you . . ."

Manisha sat up in bed, her brow furrowed. "Hold on, Mom," she said, raising her hand. "I can handle taking you to the grocery store and visiting the temple, but having a 'talk' feels like a scenario where not even divine intervention could help me."

"Leave divine, div-oon out of this and get dressed," her mother said briskly as she left the room.

Manisha groaned and buried her head back into her pillow. The abrupt end to her dream had left her feeling unfulfilled in so many ways. She flopped onto her side, picked up her cell phone from her nightstand, and began scrolling through photos from her brother Sanj's wedding last weekend. Had she encountered this mystery man there? She studied the images, but no one stood out—just cousins and friends of her brothers whom she'd known her whole life. Not that Manisha would've had the time to indulge in any secret caressing at her brother's wedding, even if her mystery man had been there; her hands had been too full with countless tasks that realistically should have been managed by a team of California's top wedding planners. Yet somehow they had fallen to her, courtesy of her mother's well-intended but overwhelming delegations.

"Have the flowers arrived, Isha?"

"Manisha, you need to pick up Uncle Junda from the airport."

"Call the mehndi lady and find out why she's running late!"

Manisha didn't mind helping—not for her brother's wedding. But now, in the afterglow of a dream that felt so real, she couldn't help but feel a twinge of disappointment at what might have been. She may have missed out on a romantic encounter thanks to her to-do list.

Her mother appeared at the doorway again. "Why aren't you up yet?"

"I'm exhausted, Mom," Manisha said. "I need a few more minutes to rest, and then I'll get to all your chauffeuring needs."

"Rest? What do you need rest from?" her mother asked. She looked around the room, barely hiding her disgust at the clothes and shopping bags that littered the floor. "Oh, I know! It must be from all the shopping. Yes, yes, yes. Of course, Manisha, how tired your arms must be from going through the racks at all the designer stores!" she said. "Swipe, swipe, swipe. Please take all my money." Her mother gestured dramatically, mimicking swiping a credit card through a reader.

Manisha frowned at her but kept silent.

"Or maybe the 'rest' you need is from this collection of shoes. Your feet must be so tired from trying all these juttis." She grabbed a red-soled stiletto from Manisha's dresser and tossed it onto the bed.

"Mom, please! You never throw a Loubie like that," Manisha cried, scrambling to check that it was okay.

"Looobie the bachcha."

Manisha watched her mom navigate the chaotic room as if she were attempting to avoid triggering an explosion.

"All this money you spend on all these stupid clothes. You need to be more sensible with your money and what you buy." Her mother gestured to her own two-piece Indian suit, an ensemble she'd had specially made in India during one of her annual trips. Comfort was her top priority, so there was no fancy embroidery or beading—just a simple yet lovely light-green and mustard-yellow set.

"Shh, Mom! They can hear you." Manisha clutched the stray heel to her chest protectively. "And Loubies are worth every penny. They're called investments. Besides, you're one to talk." Manisha smirked. Practical as she was, her mother's dresser drawers overflowed with beautiful Indian garments that she brought back from her visits, some that never saw the light of day. It was no wonder that Manisha had a bit of a shopping addiction—it seemed the apple didn't fall too far from the Patel tree.

"Chup! If these Loubies are so worth it, let's see them make you aloo parathas, instead of your father."

"Mom, you know nothing can beat Dad's parathas," Manisha said, and it was the truth. Her dad's spiced potato-stuffed flatbreads were her ultimate favourite—if she ever faced the unimaginable situation of being on death row, they would be the dish she'd request for her final meal. A rumble escaped her stomach at the thought of them.

"Wait," Manisha said, perking up instantly, "does that mean you have some waiting for me downstairs?" If there was anything that would make her leave the cozy confines of her bed, it was the promise of her dad's unparalleled parathas.

"Get up, Isha, and come downstairs," her mother said. She surveyed Manisha's room once again. "Why have I been cursed with a child who behaves like an animal? A pig's style is all I see here."

Manisha had to stifle her laughter. This familiar scene had played out countless times during her childhood. Back then, she used to be annoyed by her mother's theatrics and nagging. But now that Manisha was an adult, they amused her most of the time. Her mom could be a lot, but, more than anything right now, Manisha was grateful for the love and attention that surrounded her.

"Mom, I think you mean sty. A pigsty."

"Chup. I know what I mean, and what I say is what I mean."

As her mother disappeared back down the hall, Manisha's mind drifted to why she was there, in her childhood bedroom, thousands of miles away from her home in London, in the first place. The mess on the floor was a harsh reminder of her predicament. The relentless phone calls from creditors heightened her anxiety, a nagging reminder of her deteriorating financial situation caused by her impulsive spending and mounting takeout bills following her breakup. Pushing the feeling of dread aside, Manisha swung her legs off the bed and padded over to her bookcase. Her fingers brushed the worn spines of the books she used to sneak past her mother and hurriedly read under the covers as a teenager. The stories inside had whisked her away to sun-soaked beaches and summer romances, where girls named Samantha or Carly revelled in forbidden kisses and carefree days spent with charming lifeguards named Chad and Chip.

As a young girl, Manisha had yearned to be one of those teenagers playing Truth or Dare at a distant summer camp. Instead, she was bound by a strict curfew and a firm no-dating policy—the unyielding rules that felt more like laws imposed by the more "traditional" Indian parents in Baskin, California. Her teenage hormones and desire for a pimple-faced romance didn't stand a chance.

"No, you can't go to that party unless your brothers are there."

"No, you must be home by 8 p.m."

"No boys allowed."

As soon as she was old enough to break free from her parents' watchful eyes and her community's expectations, Manisha, desperately craving the freedom to explore the dating scene like a non-Indian kid, did precisely that. After all, studying law kept her busy—as far as her parents knew, she was buried in books at the library. But the truth was quite different: by day, she immersed herself in her studies, and by night, she seized the opportunity to make up for lost time, embracing the dating experiences and playful eggplant-emoji moments she had longed for. It was ironic that she was now home, finding comfort for a broken heart with her overbearing parents.

Manisha's thoughts were interrupted by a sharp buzz. Glancing at her phone, she saw the name "Cheating Scumbag" light up the screen, accompanied by a text message. An intense rage bubbled up within her at the mere thought of her ex-boyfriend, Oliver. Her skin flushed a different kind of hot and, as though the fury within her was just too much for her body to contain, angry tears began to pool along her bottom lashes. Without a second thought, she pressed the delete button, watching with satisfaction as the message vanished into the digital abyss.

The last time Manisha had seen Oliver was nearly three months ago when their relationship—and her entire world—had fallen apart. "You'll regret this," she'd managed to utter, her heart racing as she slammed the door to their shared apartment behind her. She was a fiery Aries, and the thought of forgiving him was laughable. Oliver deserved his fate. Unlike Manisha, who certainly didn't deserve how he'd treated her.

She couldn't believe she'd let her astrologer pull the wool over her eyes, convincing her that Aries and Aquarius were some cosmic power couple destined to create a "stable and honest relationship." What a joke!

Manisha blinked back the tears and instead, desperate for a distraction, opened the group chat she shared with her brothers. Sanj had sent through some photos from his and Needa's honeymoon earlier when Manisha was still sleeping.

Hola from Mexico! Can't wait to see everyone soon.

Manisha smiled as she read the message in the chat. Looks amazing! Send more pics! she typed back. She was so happy for Sanj and even happier for her other brother, Sammy, who had finally found someone, too. From the moment she met her future sister-in-law, Manny, at Sanj's wedding, Manisha had felt an instant connection. Watching Sammy beam with happiness and witnessing their budding romance felt like living out a scene from her favourite Bollywood film. Shah Rukh Khan and

Deepika Padukone in *Chennai Express* paled compared to the magic between Manny and Sammy.

Sitting on the edge of her bed, Manisha gently placed her phone on her lap. She wore an oversized Backstreet Boys T-shirt from childhood, now snug against her frame. She could hear her mother's voice the day she first saw her wearing it. "Five men all resting their head on your chest. Someone save me from this besharam!" She chuckled, recounting that memory. She picked up her phone again and checked her work emails out of habit. They were over a month old. Nothing new would arrive since she no longer had access to that account. A wave of anxiety washed over her, leaving her throat dry. She gulped audibly.

Manisha opened the photos tab, her gaze lingering on the button of the screen as her thumb slowly traced the smooth surface of the glass. She wondered if pressing harder could erase one or more of the contents. Taking a deep breath, she opened another tab on her phone, revealing her digital vision board. It was time for a reset—not just in the digital realm, but in every aspect of her life. Manisha was determined to initiate that reset while she was here in Baskin, but first things first: her stomach was growling louder than her aspirations.

## 2

*A*fter a quick shower, Manisha slipped into her green velour Juicy Couture track suit and followed the familiar, mouthwatering scent of piping hot, buttery parathas downstairs. A thin layer of smoke drifted across the hallway into the kitchen as she skipped down the last step. Food always made her happy.

"Dad, you're burning down the house again," she teased, grinning. "The roof, the roof, the roof is on fire!" Manisha waved her hands and danced into the kitchen, singing off-key.

"Chup kar," he replied, not looking up from the stove. A smile tugged at the corners of Manisha's mouth. "Keep quiet" was her dad's unique way of saying I love you. A "chup kar" went a long way in the Patel house.

"Oh, look, our rani finally decided to get up and join the rest of the world," her mother remarked from the stove. "What a royal arrival!"

Manisha rolled her eyes, stifling a yawn. "Yes, the queen is overjoyed at her aloo paratha crown. I humbly request you bestow it upon me," she responded, slipping into a British accent.

"Do you see? She becomes a lawyer in the UK, and suddenly, she's Queen Elizabeth," her mom said to Manisha's father, who was expertly flipping a paratha onto the tava, the golden-brown side sizzling.

Her dad was a real culinary genius. He'd picked up cooking skills from his travels across the globe during his military years. He could whip up anything—from deep-fried panzerotti to flawless sushi rolls—while her mom struggled to make a simple omelette without it turning into burnt scrambled eggs. But she did have two tricks up her sleeve: she could perfectly heat a paratha and brew a perfectly spiced cup of chai. One was already waiting for Manisha on the old wooden kitchen table.

Despite owning Baskin's premier home decor and design store, Manisha's parents cared little for fancy decor in their own home. Their kitchen had yellow-stained cupboards from the '80s and mismatched kitchenware, but it was just fine for them. Admittedly, when Manisha was younger, she'd been a little embarrassed by their home when her friends came over. But now, her parents' unpretentiousness was, in a way, endearing. It showed how little they cared for impressing others and—as much as Manisha teased her mom about her now-overflowing wardrobe—how truly focused they had always been on the things that mattered.

Manisha cradled the cup of hot tea in her hands, gently blowing on it to cool it down. "Hey, Dad, you're looking like a real fashion icon in that apron. Giving Gucci a run for his money!" She gestured to the flowery apron he wore over his usual uniform of a kurta top and dark Dockers khakis. The apron was one her mom had bought for herself but never wore.

He waved at her dismissively, causing her to snicker into her cup. It was good to be home. Manisha sank into her chair and relished the sweet, creamy chai that was heavy on the two percent milk, just as she liked it.

"Ghee or salted butter?" her mother asked, placing a hot paratha on a silver plate in front of Manisha.

"Ghee, obvs, Mom," Manisha replied, taking a spoonful from the jar before spreading it on the bread, watching as it melted into the flaky cracks. Her dad's secret to the perfect paratha was to use not one but two doughy layers to sandwich the filling—in this case, spiced potatoes—in between. It was like the Quarter Pounder of parathas, with golden ghee gleaming at her.

She spooned a generous scoop of the tangy raita from the bowl on the table onto her plate, then tore off a piece of the paratha and scooped it up with the cucumber-yogurt mix. The flavours exploded in her mouth, hot as they were, making it all worth it.

"How is it?" her dad asked with a smile. "You know I prefer mooli, but I made aloo just for you."

Manisha shuddered at the thought of horseradish and its offensive aftertaste. "Gross, Dad. Why even mention mooli? This is just fine."

"Just fine? If you want fine, go to your grandmother's house for that. Okay?" he shot back dramatically.

Manisha rolled her eyes. Her dad had a knack for turning any unpleasant situation into a chance to throw shade at his mother-in-law, who was a sort of forbidden topic in their home—one shrouded in secrecy and curiosity that no one dared to unravel, especially around her dad. Manisha shrugged it off as but another twist in her favourite Bollywood movie.

*Sometimes, the less I know, the better.*

"Come on, Dad. You know your parathas are excellent—the best. I hope I find a husband who makes me aloo parathas as good as yours," she said between bites.

Her father beamed at her, and, not for the first time, Manisha was struck by how much they resembled one another. She loved being tall, and her appetite for food was something she'd gotten from him—along with the care he put into his appearance. His dark beard was always impeccably groomed, and his hair neatly slicked back. Despite this, the same wavy kink that Manisha had inherited remained ever-present. He was also a man of honour and integrity, and he'd instilled those values in all three of his children from an early age.

Her mom brought a second paratha and placed it on Manisha's plate. "Oh yes. Va, va. Did I hear right? A husband for Isha? Now, that is what I am praying for, too. I hope my youngest, smartest, sweetest, and most successful child finds a husband this year—one who can cook for her, just like I have for myself." She squeezed Manisha's cheeks as if Manisha were still a child, not a grown woman.

"Please, Mom. I'm thirty-four, not four," Manisha said, breaking free from her mother's tight grasp and then moving her head away to take another bite.

"Besides," she added, "most guys actually know how to cook for themselves and for the people in their lives—like their partners. It's a modern world out there. If I were you, I'd save my prayers for something bigger."

"Speaking of cooking," her dad chuckled, rolling out another circle of dough, "I've yet to have a meal from your mother that's actually edible."

"Me too!" Manisha cried. Her mom dashed back to the counter to chide her dad, who brandished the rolling pin like a shield, flour flinging everywhere. Laughter filled Manisha's lungs like a breath of fresh air.

"Chup, both of you, before I—"

Before her mother could finish the sentence, Manisha's soon-to-be sister-in-law walked into the kitchen.

"What's happening in here?" Manny asked, wrapping her arms around Manisha and taking in the lively scene.

"Manny!" Manisha exclaimed, turning to hug her back. "Thank goodness you're here, just in time. Now back me up, will you? I'm trying to explain to my mom that times have changed, and men actually cook now."

"Sammy just uses Uber Eats. Does that count as cooking?" Manny quipped, grinning.

"I'm trying to explain to my daughter that I understand this modern world, but once you're married, cooking and cleaning take on a different meaning. For husbands, cooking and cleaning for their wives is their way of showing love—it's like flirting."

"Mom, please—I beg you—stop there! Do not give us advice on flirting."

"Hey, I don't mind listening," Manny said, putting her hands up. "I'm happy to share this flirting advice with Sammy." Manny winked at Manisha and reached for a plate piled high with steaming parathas.

"Flirting has come a long way, Manisha," her mother continued. "Nowadays, a man reaches to fix a loose strap on your dress, and it's like Diwali. Fireworks everywhere." In perfect synchronization, the butter on the stovetop sizzled and splattered, mimicking the sound of popping firecrackers.

Manisha rolled her eyes. "And that is why I pay good money to not have loose straps on my designer dresses, so I don't have to flirt like my mom."

"Touché." Manny chuckled, and Manisha's mom joined in the laughter. The vibrant energy of the Patel kitchen was exactly what Manisha had longed for in returning home—a refreshing change from the tears and misery that had consumed her back in London.

"And now my flirting is done," Manisha's father announced, untying the apron. "I am going to tend to my garden." He patted both Manny's and Manisha's heads before leaving the kitchen.

"I think we scared him away," Manisha stage-whispered.

"Oh, he likes to be out there anyway," Manny said.

"Anyway, I had no idea you were coming by today!" Manisha said excitedly, mind alight with the day's possibilities.

"Yeah, but sadly, I can't stay long." Manny dunked another piece of bread into the raita. "I have time for a quick bite, but then I have to meet your brother at the store. Sammy asked me to grab the mail for him."

"Oh, boo," Manisha said, pouting.

"Don't worry, we'll hang out before you leave," Manny comforted her. "By the way, how long are you here?"

Manisha felt her face warm. She cleared her throat, avoiding Manny's gaze. "You know, I, um, have a lot of time off, so I'm still deciding."

"Ooh, look at you, Ms. Senior Partner, calling the shots on when she decides to work," Manny cooed.

Manisha smiled faintly, though the words "senior partner" stung a little.

"By the way, what's your law firm's name again? I was going to send the details to my cousin in London. He's looking for some legal advice—"

"No!" Manisha interrupted. "I mean, don't do that. We're so busy right now. I wouldn't want to be rude and have to string him along. Why don't I let you know when we catch a break and are looking for new clients?"

Manny shrugged. "Okay, sure. Anyway, I'm just so proud of you. Your brother and I were gushing about you the other day to our friends."

"It's no big deal," Manisha said, playing with her teacup.

"Are you kidding me? Manisha, take a minute and be proud of your senior-partner moment." Manny gently touched Manisha's hand and offered her a warm smile. "You worked so hard, and you're like the first Indian woman they've ever hired in this role."

"We all are very proud of our Manisha," her mother added from the sink, where she was washing dishes but also apparently listening closely.

Manisha released a deep breath. "Yeah, I guess so. It's just that being a lawyer, it's kind of becoming . . ." She trailed off.

Manny's phone pinged. "That's Sammy," she said, standing up. "I've got to get to the store—he's already there. Where's the mail, Auntie?"

"Over there, beta," Manisha's mom said, gesturing to a couple stacks of paper on the counter. "The other one, Manny. That first pile is for recycling," she instructed. "Let me get you a bag," she added before leaving the kitchen.

"I can't believe you're leaving me all alone with her," Manisha whined as soon as her mother was out of earshot. "She's about to give me the 'talk.' I can feel it."

"We've all experienced the 'Indian parent talk' countless times, Manisha. I'm not even a Patel yet, and I think I got the talk from your mom," Manny said with a laugh. "You've got this, Ish. Sammy always tells me that you kids have mastered the art of dealing with your mom."

Manisha's mother returned, a shopping bag fluttering between her hands. "Here. Did you get it all?"

Manny nodded, hugging Manisha's mom. "Got it. Okay, I have to head out. I'll see you soon, Manisha, for some wine time at our place. Thanks for the parathas, Auntie. Will you tell Uncle I said bye?"

"Of course, beta," Manisha's mother said, walking Manny out.

Manisha tore off another piece of paratha and slowly chewed it, contemplating Manny's words. Did she actually know how to deal with her mother? Since she'd been back from London, it had felt as though they were speaking different languages. Sighing, she got up and put her ghee-stained plate in the sink before going to the living room, where her mother was now curled up on the couch, watching the Indian news—if you could call it news. Manisha thought of it as more sensational-ized TV-tabloid updates.

She moved toward the fireplace, its mantel made of rich dark oak that harmonized beautifully with the warm hues of the room. She swept her gaze over the Indian deities and the assorted trinkets collected from the Patel siblings' travels. Her mother took great pride in showcasing these items, beaming with joy over her well-educated and well-travelled children. She painstakingly made sure everything was positioned just right from the centre of the hearth. Manisha's eyes lingered on the eclectic collection of photographs that also adorned the mantel. Their frames varied—some were metal, others wood, and a few were plastic—each telling a part of their story. There were school portraits, pictures from family vacations, candid blurry snapshots—a treasured archive of memories. She smiled, remi-niscing about how young and happy-go-lucky she and her brothers once appeared. This was home. No matter what sen-sational news was playing on the television, this space always embraced her with a familiar comfort.

"Your dad is always moving the pictures from here, there, to here. I can't keep up," her mother said, breaking Manisha's train of thought. "Come sit, Ish," she said, turning away from the TV and loudly patting the couch beside her.

Manisha sighed to herself and reluctantly perched next to her mother.

"So, Ish," her mother began, taking a sip of chai. "One wedding has wrapped up, and we're already planning another. Once that's over, I can focus on our final Patel wedding!"

"Sorry, what? I can't quite hear you," Manisha fibbed.

"Sammy and Manny are engaged," her mother said calmly, lowering the TV volume. "You are the only one left. I can't worry about you while you are in London-Shondon, running around, eating and partying all day." She kept her eyes on the TV, effortlessly splitting her attention between the news and Manisha.

Manisha shot her a glance. "Is that all you think I do—eat and party? Mom, I'm a lawyer. I work long into the night. I truly don't have the luxury of the carefree life you envision. Though I have to say, it does sound tempting," she added, her tone rising more than she intended.

"Manisha, be serious! You have your career sorted; now I think it is time for you to really start thinking about the rest of your life and finding someone to have a family with."

"Geez, Mom. Now that's some dal boiling over in a pressure cooker." Manisha unzipped her hoodie, a sudden tightness settling in her chest that intensified with each passing second.

"What dal? No dal today," replied her mom, confused. "Isha, I just want to know what your plan is. And if I'm not allowed to ask you, then who is?"

"Apparently, everyone else, Mom. It's all the aunties ever talk about, too. According to them, every single Indian kid over the age of twenty-one needs to be married, like now!" Manisha said. "Like we don't have enough pressure already."

"Well, beta, the aunties talk because they care."

"They talk because they're nosy," Manisha corrected. After

a brief hesitation, she continued, "Mom, do you care about their opinions of your single daughter? Are you bothered about what they think of me now that Sanj and Sammy are both off the market?"

"I'm not bothered," her mother said firmly. "I have my own views. Isha, I'm just saying that women experience aging differently."

"Mom, I'm thirty-four, and my body feels like it's twenty-four. That's really all that matters."

Her mother turned to her with a stern expression. "Feels like it's twenty-four to whom? Tell me the names of the people who think your body acts that way!"

*Let's start with the guy from my dream this morning.*

"Mom, you usually wait a few days into my visit before you get into this. At least, that's what I had prepared for and kind of prefer," Manisha said. She didn't need another reminder of how single she was; she was painfully aware of that. And the recent memories of Sanj's wedding didn't make it any easier.

"When will you find someone nice, dear?" one of the aunties had asked, her voice lined with concern.

"You must be so lonely!" another chimed in, nudging her playfully.

"Have you tried online dating? That is how my Mintu met her million-dollar man."

Their "caring" questions echoed in her mind, reminding her that this was the last thing she wanted to think about again.

Manisha's mother looked at her for a long moment before letting out another sigh and turning her full attention back to the TV. Manisha stood up and meandered back to the kitchen, where she noticed the earlier stack of mail waiting to be recycled. Among the pile, a gold envelope glinted invitingly in the light.

"Hey, Mom—whose wedding invitation is this?" she asked, walking back into the living room with it.

"Rohit. Rohit Khanna."

"Oh. Right. I should have known from the weight of this thing. It's probably made with real gold flakes."

"Chal, it is old news now."

Manisha carefully pulled the card from the envelope and studied its details as she recalled how the wedding news had spread throughout Baskin a year prior. It was poised to be the most extravagant celebration in the city, with Rohit Khanna marrying Lucky Kapoor, uniting two of the most influential families in town. The lavishness, the dazzling variety of attendees, and the blend of cultural traditions were all set to evoke memories of the Ambani wedding, one of the most extravagant celebrations in India over the past decade. Rumour had it that, in place of horses and elephants, rare white tigers were being flown in from Bhopal, India, for a stunning entrance at the grand reception. But that all ended abruptly a few months ago, just weeks shy of the wedding. Suddenly, the town's chatter shifted from the wedding to the scandal surrounding Rohit and his heartbroken fiancée. In fact, from what Manisha's cousin, Deena, had told her, every household was now abuzz with gossip about how Rohit had cheated on poor Lucky.

Manisha's heart went out to her. She knew her vaguely from high school, though Manisha was a year younger. But knowing all too well what she must be going through, Manisha felt a sense of kinship with her. With a scoff of disgust, she marched back to the kitchen and tossed the invitation into the garbage bin.

"It doesn't matter how old the news is; what he did to Lucky is utterly humiliating. She must be devastated," Manisha remarked. "And let's not forget about his own family."

"You know, Manisha, my mother always said there are two sides to each story."

Even when left alone, they didn't often speak of Manisha's grandmother, given the tension between her and Manisha's father. Manisha lowered her voice as she returned to her mom's side. "How is Grandma?" She had once been a revered member of the Patel family, but now she was conspicuously absent from their conversations and their home.

"Mr. Khanna visited the store last week and emphasized the importance of hearing out the other side," her mother continued, sidestepping the question about Grandma.

Manisha felt her chest tighten. "Do you always have to listen to the other side, Mom? Cheating is cheating, whether it happened yesterday, a few months, or a year ago," she said quietly. She thought about Oliver and how hurtful and embarrassing his infidelity and its aftermath had been—not just in her personal life but in her professional one, too.

"Manisha, I want to talk to you about something," her mother began.

"Mom, sorry, but I don't want to hear more about Rohit 'Cheating' Khanna and how his father is trying to clear his name." Manisha wrinkled her nose. "Once a cheater, always a cheater."

Her mom clicked her tongue. "Forget Rohit, Isha. I want to talk about you."

Manisha crossed her arms, bracing herself for more pestering about her romantic life.

"You know, I was talking to Meena Auntie, and she mentioned how modern women, with their laptops, phones, and ePads, face all kinds of challenges when it comes to having children now, her mother continued.

Manisha narrowed her eyes at the mention of Meena Auntie, the local gossip who fancied herself a master of all things "medicinal." She had a potion or pill for seemingly every ailment under the sun and boasted of curing all sorts of injuries and illnesses.

"Please don't tell me this is going to be about one of her 'miracle cures.' Mom, I wish you'd avoid Meena Auntie and her weird hocus-pocus. And it's called an iPad."

"Oh, okay. iPad, not ePad. Got it," her mother said, then paused. "Anyway, Isha, she told me all about these problems, and then, like a message from God, I heard on the Hindi radio show about freezing your eggs and how women your age should be considering such a thing."

Manisha stared at her mother, stunned. "Are you serious? Freezing my eggs? Could the message from God have waited? Do we really have to do this now?" She felt more than just a little uncomfortable, taken aback by her mother's unexpected openness. This was the woman who still changed the channel any time there was kissing onscreen, and now she was broaching fertility with Manisha.

"Yes, we do, Manisha. We have to do this right now!" Her mother reached into the side of her Indian suit and dug deep into her pocket, then held out something to Manisha with a solemn expression. "This is my last wish," she said, looking up at the ceiling.

Manisha reflexively glanced upward, too, curious. It was just a white ceiling.

"Here. Please. Take this."

Manisha reluctantly took the envelope from her mother's hand and opened it. She pulled out a slip of paper and immediately gawked. It was a cheque in the amount of twenty thousand dollars.

"Holy red-bottom shoes," she whispered. Without missing a beat, her mother lightly smacked her on the head with a rolled-up newspaper, seemingly summoned out of thin air.

"Ouch!" Manisha yelped.

Her mother pointed the newspaper at her. "This is not money for your shoes or clothes. This is money for your health. Not to feed the bank accounts of those dumbo Loubie designers."

"I've only ever heard Christian Louboutin referred to as brilliant, superb, one-of-a-kind—never 'dumbo.'"

"Manisha, please take this seriously. It is my gift to you for your future. It was not an easy time for you in London this past year. I know you . . ." Her mother trailed off.

Manisha held her breath. She'd never shared the details of her breakup with her family, but her mother had a sort of superpower intuition that kicked in when her kids were away from her. She always knew when something was wrong. Even though Manisha's sudden and longer-than-expected trip home had left most of the family bewildered, her mother never questioned it.

"Listen, Isha, while you are staying here with us, I was hoping you could make an appointment with Dr. Rocky. He's a fertility doctor and an old family friend. My friend."

"A *male* family friend?" Manisha raised an eyebrow. "Do tell, Mom!"

A second smack on the head landed; this one was thoroughly deserved. Manisha couldn't move fast enough to avoid it.

"What a bandari I raised," her mother said, frowning. "Don't act foolishly when you meet him. He is a well-respected man in the community."

Manisha sighed. This wasn't something she wanted to do, but her mother's insistence paired with her generosity was enough to make her at least consider the idea. She was getting older, and maybe her mother was right. Maybe it was a good time to start planning for a family, even if she wasn't in a relationship.

"Go and meet with him. He will help you set up everything for freezing your eggs."

Manisha stared at the cheque in her hands, thinking of her friends and colleagues in London who had opted to freeze their eggs in recent years. At first, she had thought they were out of their minds. But as time went on and life got busier in her role as senior partner, she came to understand the importance of scheduling everything, including motherhood. And now, the thought of putting an end to the awkward conversations with her mom about starting a family was also incredibly appealing. Still, she couldn't shake the feeling that it was too significant an amount of money for her parents to be spending on her.

"Mom, I appreciate your offer, but using your money for this feels wrong. I have some savings I can dip into." Manisha's voice quivered as she considered her less-than-empty savings account. She took a deep breath to steady herself.

"No," her mom said firmly. "It is my gift to you. Before I die. Please, Manisha."

"Mom, you're not dying," Manisha said, exasperated. Her mom was being especially dramatic this morning. "Let me check my schedule and see when I can fit in this Dr. Rocky." She made a show of grabbing her phone and opening her calendar, even though she knew it would be utterly devoid of any upcoming events, especially work ones.

"Manisha, I am not as educated as you are sometimes. I know I didn't attend the big fancy university, but I know that raising three beautiful children was the greatest joy of my life. That was my education. Learning from all three of you. I want you to have this joy one day, too."

Manisha gave her a soft smile. "I get it, Mom. You're truly the best. And just so you know, you don't need to have attended any prestigious university to be smart." She wrapped her arms around her mother affectionately. "In my eyes, you're the smartest woman I know."

"I know you work hard, Manisha, but I want to make it a little easier for when you are ready to have your own family with this extra step."

"I appreciate that, Mom."

"Oh, I looked up the procedure, and it is straightforward. Bang, bang, shoot, shoot, and you're done."

Manisha burst into laughter. "Bang, bang, shoot, shoot? I really hope those aren't the actual medical terms Dr. Rocky uses. Okay, Mom, I'll go see him."

Her mother clapped her hands in delight. "Oh, that's wonderful news! Of course, I don't want to push you, but Manisha, this is important. It's time to stop the nonsense. You're older now. So yes, I'm putting some pressure on you."

"But you just said you weren't pressuring me."

"I changed my mind. I worry about you."

Manisha sighed, her heart heavy with the weight of her mother's concern. "Mom, you don't have to stress over this. I really mean it. I promise I'll follow through." Her gaze shifted to the cheque in her hand, where her mother's handwritten amount stood out starkly, a reminder of the responsibility she had taken on.

"Please put this toward the temple or local Indian community centre, or I don't know, something for yourself." She pressed the cheque back into her mother's hands. "I'll handle the egg freezing, but just please keep your money."

"See, I raised a good daughter," her mother said, beaming. "A good daughter who will be a good wife and then a good mother, too. Thank you, God." She looked up at the ceiling.

"In between watching all your Indian tabloid news, yes, you did manage to raise a good daughter, Mom." Manisha smiled.

"Chal, I will save this for your wedding then." Her mother folded up the cheque and tucked it back into her pocket. "A big fat Indian wedding. Shall we make a guest list now?"

"I've already agreed to freeze my eggs, and now you want me to whip up a guest list for a wedding that's only happening in your imagination. Nope, this sounds like a great time to make a swift exit to my room for some quality time with Netflix," Manisha said, spinning on her heel like she was in a dramatic Bollywood movie, strutting toward the stairs.

"You can Netflix and chili later. I need a ride to Uncle Parm's store. The milk and butter are on sale." Her mother looked at her expectantly.

"Mom, it's Netflix and chill, not chili. And Uncle Parm always seems to have a sale on milk and butter. Can't it wait?" Manisha glanced at the clock on the wall, reminding her it was hardly noon. "Besides, you know how to drive!"

"I know, but I prefer to sit back and watch, and you take the big wheel," her mother said, a barely detectable note of longing entering her voice.

Manisha met her determined gaze. To her mother, "I prefer to sit back and watch" was code for her desire to spend more quality time with her daughter. Manisha changed course for the foyer.

## 3

*T*he chimes on the door of Uncle Parm's grocery store jingled in harmony as Manisha and her mother stepped inside.

"Come in, come in! Big, big, the biggest sale today," the tall man with a perfectly sharp moustache said. He smiled at them and went back to chatting on the phone in Punjabi.

Manisha looked around. It had been years since her last visit, and the store looked the same. It was a treasure trove of Indian delights: enormous bags of yellow lentils and kidney beans lined the aisles like giant pillows while a medley of familiar scents—mothballs mingling with spices—filled the air. Shelves overflowing with every condiment and traditional Indian remedy seemed to spill into the aisles, creating chaos that only Uncle Parm knew how to manage.

"Mooli, ugh," Manisha muttered under her breath as the sharp scent of horseradish reached her nostrils.

"Hurry, Isha, before it's all sold out," her mother urged, gently nudging her toward the back of the store, where a vibrant red SALE sign made of flimsy bristol board dangled unevenly from the ceiling.

"Mom, there is literally no one in the store but us and Uncle Parm." Manisha eyed the red-and-white milk jugs and the many boxes of salted butter in the refrigerators. Her mother opened the refrigerator door and handed three jugs to Manisha.

"Here. One more," her mother said, practically throwing a fourth to her.

"Mom, these things are ridiculously heavy! I only have two arms, and there's not even a cart in sight! And look at Uncle Parm—he's just yapping away on the phone." Manisha glared at the store owner. "Hey, Uncle, can you give us a hand over here?" She exaggerated the struggle of holding the milk, hoping to catch his attention, but the only response she got from Uncle Parm was a casual wave from the front of the store, where he was still engrossed in his conversation.

"Pretend like you are at the gym weightlifting. Look—like this." Her mom pretended to do an arm curl with a jug of milk dangling from her hand. Manisha was surprised—these things were heavy.

"Hilarious, Mom. They're not dumbbells," she snorted.

"Manisha, you are a dumbbell," her mom said, brushing past her as she walked to the checkout, one arm loaded with milk and the other with butter.

"Ah, Manisha! Welcome back," Uncle Parm said, wrapping the phone cord around his neck. Manisha could hear the person on the other end of the phone chattering away. Uncle Parm took in Manisha's outfit. "Vow. I like your style. Very powerful, strong Indian woman." He pumped a fist triumphantly before turning his attention to ringing up her items.

"Thanks, Uncle." Manisha attempted a half fist back out of courtesy.

"So, when is the next Patel wedding? Are you next in line, Manisha?" Manisha gnashed her teeth. He had lasted all of ten seconds. She couldn't help but wish the phone cord would tighten a bit around his neck.

Her mother stepped in. "Soon, Parm. But first, Sammy and Manny will marry next year."

"Oh, vow. So exciting."

Manisha opted for avoidance over violence and pulled out her phone to scroll through Instagram.

"By the way, Parm, you must have some potential suitors in mind for our Isha?" her mother asked casually.

Manisha widened her eyes. "You have got to be kidding me," she grumbled quietly, slowly inching away from the conversation.

Uncle Parm nodded vigorously. "You know, funny you mention that. Aman was here this morning—Aman Basara."

"That ancient uncle?" Manisha blurted out, earning a fierce glare from her mother. "I mean—uh, that very respected ancient uncle?" Blushing, she turned her attention to the selection of chocolate bars and picked out a Mars bar.

Manisha's mother frowned and shook her head. "He's too old, Parm! We need someone younger—fit, well-educated, a journeyman."

"A journeyman?" Manisha muttered under her breath, opening the chocolate bar and taking a bite.

"He has to be able to keep up with our Isha. Who else do you have in mind?"

"Alright, let me think," Uncle Parm said, rubbing his chin. "You know, you are right. He must be the perfect man for our beloved lawyer Manisha." Suddenly, he snapped his fingers. "I've got it! What if we put up a large picture of her?" He gestured toward the wall behind him, plastered with tattered posters of

Bollywood icons—Katrina Kaif, Aishwarya Rai, Alia Bhatt. "On this very wall! It's like online dating, but on-wall dating!"

Manisha's mouth dropped open. "Uncle Parm, you can't put me on that wall."

"Manisha, there is no shame in being single," Uncle Parm said.

"I'm not the shame, I'm not ashamed—I mean—" Manisha stumbled over her words.

"What she means is that a picture is a bit much, Parm," her mother interjected, rummaging through her wallet.

"But discussing my relationship status in the middle of an Indian grocery store isn't?" Manisha sassed, taking another bite of the Mars bar.

Her mother ignored her. "But perhaps something else. Not too obvious, you know?"

Uncle Parm nodded. "Okay. Let me think about another idea!"

"Please, take your time," Manisha said with more than a hint of sarcasm. She glanced at her phone, silently hoping it would ring and rescue her from this agony.

"Oh, I have something!" Uncle Parm exclaimed as he ducked below the counter. He soon re-emerged, placing a medium-sized lemon tree on top.

"What's this for?" her mother asked, intrigued by the peculiar offer.

"Lucky lemons! Lucky man! Lucky wedding," he chimed cheerfully.

"Lucky me," Manisha added dryly, rolling her eyes. "Mom, are you almost done?" She crumpled the wrapper of her chocolate bar and stuffed it into her Louis Vuitton bag.

Manisha's mother shook her head. "Oh no, we don't need this kind of luck, Parm. We have our own luck. We have the Patel Blessing. That's all the luck we need."

"Patel Blessing?" Uncle Parm and Manisha said in unison.

The store was suddenly enveloped in an eerie silence, pierced only by the faint hum of the ugly fluorescent lights. Manisha leaned in closer to catch her mother's words. "You see, I met her father and fell in love in just over two weeks. Both her brothers found their partners and got engaged in exactly sixteen days. Now it's Manisha's turn. The Patel Blessing is to be passed down to her now."

Manisha scoffed. "I had no idea that this Patel Blessing existed until today," she remarked, rolling her eyes.

"Very, very interesting," Uncle Parm said, looking thoughtful. "Tell me more . . . and can I sell this blessing here?"

"Alright, I've had my fill of this Manisha Matchmaking special," Manisha declared. "Mom, I'll go get the car." As she started toward the door, she glanced back with a playful smirk. "Oh, and Uncle Parm, thanks for the free chocolate bar! Lucky me!" She flashed him a bright smile.

"Hain, free?" Uncle Parm said, confused.

⌒

Manisha banged on the horn. "What the hell! You've got to be kidding me!" Her voice reverberated in her car, louder than the music blaring on the radio.

Despite her furious honking, the offending yellow convertible's engine cut. Mouth agape, Manisha stared dumbstruck as the driver breezily stepped out, the definition of unbothered. He was so engrossed with his phone, he didn't so much as glance back at her. Fuming, Manisha hastily put her car in park and sprang out, slamming the door behind her. One of her high heels slipped off as she stormed toward the parking spot thief, but she snatched it up, ripped off the other, and continued marching after him barefoot.

"Hey!" she called out as he strolled toward Uncle Parm's store. "I was waiting for that spot!"

"What?" the man replied distractedly, eyes still glued to his screen.

"Hello? Eyes over here! I'm talking to you!" Manisha snapped her hands firmly on her hips. "What's your problem? That was my parking spot. I was clearly waiting for it!"

"I don't have a problem, but it sounds like you do," he retorted, still tapping away on his phone.

"My problem is with your driving skills—or lack thereof! Who the heck taught you how to drive?" Manisha shot back in annoyance.

Finally, the man glanced up and chuckled, completely un-bothered. "Me? Who taught *you* how to drive? Or how to pick appropriate footwear for it?" He motioned to her heels clutched in each hand. "Look at those six-inch daggers!"

Manisha set her shoes down and slipped them back on. Damn, even with the extra help, this guy towered over her. "These daggers"—she spat, pulling herself up stick-straight—"should be digging into your front tires after the move you just pulled—like some race car maniac! That was my spot!"

"Maniac? You weren't paying attention," the man said, narrow-ing his eyes. "You snooze, you lose."

"Oh, trust me, I don't lose at anything." Manisha crossed her arms defiantly.

He rolled his eyes. "Listen, I don't see your name anywhere," he said, gesturing to the sign at the front of the parking spot: EMPLOYEE PARKING ONLY. "Unless you're an employee of

Uncle Parm's grocery store?" He gave her a smug look, and they shared a glance toward the designated parking space.

"I'm not! And neither are you!" Manisha said.

He shrugged. "Whatever. Guess I just didn't notice you," he said dismissively.

Manisha's left eye gave an involuntary twitch. She took in his perfectly combed hair, impeccably ironed shirt, sunglasses hanging from the neck, that made him look like he'd just stepped off a fashion runway.

"Probably because you were too busy checking yourself out in the mirror of your Lambo," she snapped.

"Or maybe I was just blinded by the sunlight reflecting off your gaudy Louis Vuitton bag. What's it carry—an entire child?" he retorted, eyebrow raised.

Manisha's lip curled up in a sneer. "Oh, if only there was something to protect your poor eyes. Oh, wait," she paused for dramatic effect, "what are those?" She jabbed at his shades.

"Clever," he muttered, rubbing the spot where her finger had connected with his chest. His gaze lingered on her, as if he was properly seeing her for the first time. "Wait a second, I know you!"

"I seriously doubt that. I'd remember running into a maniac like you," she replied, angling to head back toward her car. She took in a deep calming breath. "Now, can you please move your vehicle so I can park in my spot?"

"I'm not moving it. I was here first. Why don't you find another spot?" The man pointed to a space located halfway across the lot.

Manisha felt her frustration boil over again, her face flaming red. "Of course you'd expect me to move. Why would you relocate your fancy car for my humble family SUV? You're so infuriating, and so is your ridiculous car!" She glared at him, heart back to racing.

The man stepped closer, laughter breaking through the tension. "I was right—I do know you! You're one of the Patels, Sammy's sister!" His tone softened, shedding all trace of its earlier hostility.

Who was this guy, and how did he know her? "Well, I don't know you and don't care to know you," Manisha shot back.

"You don't remember me?" he asked with a devilish grin. "You know what? The spot is yours. This car has caused me nothing but headaches, and the last thing I need is more trouble in this town, like some nosy auntie recording a video of this mess." He unlocked the car and slid into the driver's seat.

Manisha's heart tripped at the mention of "recording a video" as she glanced around in panic. "You know what? Never mind, I don't want this spot anymore," she said, turning to head back to her car.

"Don't worry about it. It's all yours," he called, rolling down his window. He reversed out of the spot, adding a casual wave as he drove away. "Enjoy the parking space, Sammy's sister!" His honking only intensified her irritation.

"Get back here, you—" Manisha exclaimed through clenched teeth. She bit off the rest of her words as his car tore out of view. Flustered, she jumped into her car just as her mother burst out of Uncle Parm's store.

"Isha, help!" her mother exclaimed, struggling to carry the several bags of groceries . . . a lemon tree.

Manisha hurriedly swung the car around, slammed it into park, then rushed over to take the plant from her mother's arms. "Mom, what on earth are you doing with this? I thought the Patel Blessing was all we needed!" She glanced back at the store, where Uncle Parm was grinning, absorbed in his phone again.

"Just put it in the back of the car," her mother urged, opening the passenger-side door. Manisha wrestled the lemon tree into the SUV's back seat before sliding into the front seat herself. She buckled her seatbelt and shifted the car into drive.

"Was that Mr. Khanna's son, Rohit?" her mother asked cheerfully, gazing out the window.

"What? Who?" Manisha turned to her, puzzled.

"The tall boy you were chatting with outside," her mother clarified.

"That was Rohit Khanna?" Manisha's face twisted in distaste. "Gross."

"He's a nice boy," her mother defended, ignoring Manisha's expression of disdain.

Manisha narrowed her eyes at her. "Mom, what took you so long? And why on earth did you buy that lemon tree?"

"Uncle Parm said it would bring us extra good, good, very good luck," her mother replied. "Lucky lemons, Isha!"

"Considering how the last five minutes have gone, I'd argue those lemons are anything but lucky," Manisha whispered to herself. "Very, very, very unlucky."

"$\mathcal{M}$om, I would really prefer not to talk about my personal life in public. I have my boundaries when it comes to matchmaking and dating, and I don't want Uncle Parm involved in any of it. He's probably already on the phone with all his uncle friends who have single sons," Manisha said, navigating the busy traffic. Her driving was a bit more hurried than usual, mirroring the turmoil of her emotions.

"Manisha, he's a nice man, and there's nothing wrong with that. Stop driving so fast. You are giving me a headache," her mother replied.

Manisha gently eased off the gas pedal. To be fair, she hadn't driven in more than six months, so her footing was a bit off. In London, it was all about the Tube. She and most of her friends didn't own a car. Client meetings, after-work drinks, and date nights were more convenient via the subway.

"It's our Indian culture; you know that by now! We see a single person who needs a match, and we send a POS!"

Manisha winced. "Um, you mean SOS, Mom."

"Just let me finish! We send out a P— SOS, and suddenly, we have all sorts of potential matches showing up at our doorstep," her mother carried on, unfazed.

"Like Aman Basara?"

"Well, not every option is a winner."

"I just don't want an SOS going out when it concerns me," Manisha said firmly. "I'm sure Uncle Parm is one of the best uncles in the community, but as I said, please stop making me and how single I am the talk of the town. I am being serious."

Manisha knew her tone was strong, but she needed her mother to hear her.

"I can't help it if my beautiful daughter is the talk of the town! You saw it with your own eyes. I was just walking through the store, minding my own business and searching for the milk and butter sale, and Uncle Parm started asking me questions about you," her mother insisted.

"Right, Mom, that's exactly how I remember it going down. All I'm saying is, if you stopped talking about me being single, people wouldn't know that I'm single, and I wouldn't be the talk of the town."

"Why are you talking so loudly?" Manisha's mom said, covering her ears. "Now my ears are also aching."

"I'm sorry. It's just a lot you're coming at me with today. First the twenty-thousand-dollar cheque, then Uncle Parm . . ."

"But Manisha, you returned the cheque, so no problem," her mother said. "I know the money is like pennies to my successful lawyer daughter," she continued with a smile. "Senior partner. Va, va."

Manisha felt her stomach sink. *Now's as good a time as any . . .*

"Well, Mom, about that . . . Some things happened in London, and it was a lot . . . too much, some would say. I mean, I'm not so sure I really loved where I was heading anyway . . ." Manisha trailed off, struggling to find the right words.

Her mother studied her face and then patted her arm. "Okay, chup. You are right. Too much for one morning."

Initial relief gave way to disappointment. Yes, Manisha had avoided having this conversation with her mother, but now, when she'd finally gathered the courage to bring it up, her mother stopped her.

"Today has been a lot." She sighed. "Especially with Uncle Parm's cringeworthy wall of single shame and Rohit Khanna's atrocious driving." Her grip on the steering wheel tightened again as the memory of Rohit's smug face flashed in her mind. "Honestly, I can't understand how a grown man thinks it's okay to behave like that. In public, no less, and with such an attitude! And then he had the audacity to insult my shoes! And my purse!"

Manisha turned another corner, entering their cul-de-sac.

"Chal. Forget him," her mother said. "We don't know what is going on with him right now. You know, maybe he was having a bad morning. Anyway, we got everything we needed, and we found a lucky tree!"

"He just had such an attitude. This full-of-yourself 'don't you know who I am?' thing going on. And then as soon as he realized I was Sammy's sister, suddenly everything shifted. I hate people who act all entitled, and who treat strangers like garbage."

Manisha slowed as they pulled up to the house.

"Oh va . . . looks like we have guests," her mother said, taking in the unfamiliar car parked in their driveway. "I wonder who it could be at this hour."

"I was really looking forward to a peaceful afternoon," Manisha grumbled as she parked beside the sleek Jaguar. "What is it with everyone in Baskin and their flashy cars? First, that ridiculous Lamborghini, and now this."

"What about all your flashy tashy items? Those shoes, the clothes upstairs in your bedroom—you and Rohit might have more in common than you think, Manisha," her mother remarked as she unbuckled her seatbelt and eyed the Jaguar.

"I can promise you the only thing we *had* in common was that parking spot we both wanted," Manisha muttered, realizing she was talking to herself while her mother hurried into the house. "Sure, no problem, Mom. I'll handle the groceries and the lemon tree I never asked for. I've got it all under control. Don't worry about a thing."

Manisha entered the house, carefully juggling everything in one go. She set the bags down in the hallway, slipped off her shoes, and continued through to the kitchen with the tree, which kept swinging its branches and smacking her in the face. She found her mother busily preparing tea, moving with purpose as Manisha tried to find a spot for the tree without losing any of the precious lemons. After all, who knew which one was blessed and would bring her the promised good, good, very good luck?

"Manisha, my dear. Come here, beta." Manisha was taken aback, spinning around to see who was calling her. A lemon walloped her in the head in the process.

"Oh, it's you, Meena Auntie. I mean, um . . . I mean, it's you. Nice to see you," Manisha said, her voice laced with a hint of annoyance.

"It's good to see you," Meena Auntie said warmly. Manisha grumbled, placing the tree aside before stepping forward to hug the older woman. She knew all too well that any good Patel child was expected to do this—if not, her mother would launch into another of her familiar lectures.

Manisha had heard it all before—the expectation to greet every visiting uncle and auntie, no matter the circumstance—be it waking from a deep sleep, cramming for an exam, or handling an important call. The moment her mother called her name, followed by the dreaded phrase "Come say hi to your uncle and auntie," she had to abandon everything.

These encounters usually began with a forced greeting, followed by an inescapably long hug. Then came a relentless stream of questions about her academic performance, favourite subjects, and the inevitable "So, when do you plan to get married?" The only enjoyable visits were from Uncle Ritesh. He always slipped her a crisp $100 bill, which, thanks to her brother Sammy, she learned was his not-so-subtle way of encouraging her to marry his son in the future. When she uncovered Uncle Ritesh's real motive, she firmly decided to reject any further money from him.

Meena Auntie was dressed in a wildly eclectic style today, sporting a long, flowing dark-blue dress and wearing a seemingly endless array of mismatched, chunky bracelets that nearly obscured her henna-adorned arm. A natural beauty, she had long black hair, freckles that highlighted her nose, and full lips. Yet to Manisha, Meena Auntie was nothing more than a mysterious woman, perpetually stirring up mischief in Baskin.

As she pulled away, Meena Auntie gripped Manisha's hand tightly, leading her into the family living room. "Come, sit with me."

Manisha groaned inwardly. Sitting with Meena Auntie and casually chatting was the last thing she wanted to be doing right now. She'd even rather go another round with Rohit Khanna. She looked around for a diversion. "Oh! Where's Dad?"

"He's out in the garden, dear," Meena Auntie said, gesturing to the window. "Now, let me take a good look at you first." She inhaled deeply, her chest rising and falling in a measured rhythm; as she exhaled, her nostrils flared slightly, expelling the air with an almost primal force. Her hands were folded neatly in her lap, fingers adorned with gaudy gold rings, each positioned with meticulous precision, radiating an aura of control and calm. Fixating her gaze on Manisha, she stared unflinchingly as if attempting to pierce the very depths of her soul. The intensity of her stare was unnerving. Manisha felt a chill creep up her spine, her heart quickening as she wrestled with the weight of that penetrating look. It was as if the woman were dissecting her thoughts and emotions, leaving Manisha feeling achingly exposed and vulnerable. The room around them faded away, isolating the two of them in a moment of connection that felt both intimate and deeply unsettling.

"Relax, beta. I'm simply absorbing the beauty that you are, along with the strength, confidence, and resilience you've shown in the face of so many challenges recently." With a gentle motion, she lifted Manisha's chin, tilting it upward.

"The lemon tree wasn't that heavy, Meena Auntie," Manisha said, attempting to shake off the spell Meena Auntie might have on her.

"Hold your head high, my dear. It's been a difficult few months, but you've managed. You understand your truth now." She leaned in and whispered to Manisha, "Deep down, you've always known it."

Manisha's eyes widened. Was Meena Auntie really referencing Oliver and everything that had taken place in London? Gently, Meena Auntie pried the cell phone from Manisha's tight grip. Manisha hadn't even realized she had been holding it all this time.

"The past is behind you, my dear. It won't shadow your future," Meena Auntie reassured her. "And your future is here in Baskin. Do not worry."

Manisha remained captivated, unable to shift her gaze from Meena Auntie's steady eyes.

*Does she know what's on my phone?*

*Does she know about Oliver?*

*Does she understand why I'm in Baskin?*

"Parm has gifted us lucky lemons for Manisha," her mother announced as she entered with two cups of steaming chai.

"Manisha doesn't need luck or lemons," Meena Auntie replied, blowing on her cup.

"See? I told you, Mom," Manisha chimed in, feeling a twinge of satisfaction that she was right about the lemons and that she had also broken free from Meena Auntie's gaze.

"She needs love."

"I need what?" Manisha asked, swallowing hard. *Not another piece of unsolicited advice about my love life.*

"Love! She said love, Isha! Are you even listening?" her mother snapped back, disapproval evident in her tone as she plopped into the recliner across from Meena Auntie.

"She's searching for many things, including love," Meena Auntie continued.

"Va, va. Searching for love. Just like that show, *The Bachelorette!*"

"I don't think that's what she meant. And my life isn't a reality show the last time I checked, Mom," Manisha said, glancing around for any hidden cameras.

"Chup. You're talking too much, and I can't hear anything," her mother scolded, cupping one ear. "Please continue, Meena. We're all ears! We have so much time. All the time for you."

Meena Auntie smiled warmly at Manisha and her mother. "The Patel family holds the past in high esteem. Yet, I see a strong resistance to embracing compassion and affection for the lives you've led." She paused and zeroed in on Manisha. "We all must find a way to forgive our pasts." Her voice took on a mysterious tone as if reciting an ancient family wisdom. The weight of Meena Auntie's words struck Manisha with an unexpected intensity. Flashes of her grandmother, hazy and distant, entered her mind. When was the last time she saw her?

"Are you speaking about my gra—"

"Chup." Her mother's stern glance silenced Manisha, forcing her to swallow her words.

"This year," Meena Auntie continued, "will bring new life . . . a great deal of new life. Everyone should be prepared to start anew." She squeezed Manisha's hand, which she was still holding.

"New life?" Manisha's mother beamed at her. "A baby is new life, no?" She clapped her hands in delight.

"Mom, she's talking about Sanj or Sammy," Manisha cut in. "I think my hopes of having a baby might involve some ice."

"What ice?" her mother asked, looking confused.

"I mean, I could really use some ice in my tea . . . like iced tea!" Manisha blurted out, suddenly rising from her seat and making a beeline for the kitchen, her thoughts racing. The last thing she wanted was for Meena Auntie to find out that her mother had been urging her to consider freezing her eggs. Then all of Baskin would know before the sun set.

"Don't worry," Meena Auntie reassured Manisha's mom. "Something big is about to happen . . ."

"Oh my, maybe a big baby," her mother exclaimed, her eyes widening. "Manisha was almost nine pounds when she was born."

As Manisha filled a glass with water and gulped half of it down as if she hadn't had a drink in ages, she re-entered the living room just in time to hear Meena Auntie say, "Big, big changes are ahead for everyone."

Clearing her throat, Manisha risked her mother's wrath and replied, "That's a bit vague, Meena Auntie. I've read fortune cookies with more insight."

Meena Auntie shook her head. "No fortune. I do not see any money."

"Oh, just great," Manisha muttered under her breath.

"Don't worry, we have money, but we don't have babies," Manisha's mother said cheerfully. "Now that is my kind of fortune, right, Isha?" she added.

"I must be going now," Meena Auntie announced.

"Already? Please stay! Perhaps more chai, or Manisha can make you some of this iced tea?" her mother insisted.

"I must go do some . . . hocus-pocus. Isn't that what the kids in Baskin call it, Manisha?" Meena Auntie added, winking at her.

Manisha nearly spat out her water. "Sorry, um, I'm not sure what you mean, Meena Auntie," she stammered, struggling to regain her composure.

"Go help Meena Auntie to the car. Chal," Manisha's mother instructed, eyeing her with disdain.

As Manisha and Meena Auntie exited the house, Manisha cleared her throat before speaking up. "Um, Meena Auntie, about what you mentioned earlier, I just wanted to say I'm sorry about the whole fortune cookie thing. I was talking out of line." She trailed off, her feet dragging as they moved toward the Jaguar.

"I know, my beta." Meena Auntie stopped walking and turned to face Manisha. "Manisha, you have to believe in some hocus-pocus. Love is magic." She pointed to Manisha's heart. "You need to fill this with magic, and then you will receive everything you want."

"Magic—" Manisha repeated the word instantly.

Meena Auntie gently tucked a strand of hair behind Manisha's ear. "And, Manisha, beta, one last thing to remember: Don't lose yourself in the pursuit of making others happy. Do what makes you happy for once. Being a lawyer didn't make you happy, did it?"

Manisha was stunned. How did Meena Auntie know?

In a slow, deliberate manner, Meena Auntie placed her hands on Manisha's stomach, the warmth and weight of her touch leaving Manisha momentarily paralyzed as if time itself had come to a standstill. Just then, a sudden gust of wind swept through the cul-de-sac, swirling around the Patel driveway and rustling the freshly pruned shrubs that bordered it. The leaves trembled—or was that just Manisha's body? She felt the chill in her sweatsuit.

Manisha struggled to find her words, her mind racing with a chaotic blend of questions and emotions. "I, uh, Meena Auntie? What are you saying? I—I don't understand what you're talking about." Her voice wavered.

"You're a star, Manisha—a bright, magical star," Meena Auntie proclaimed, her tone soothing yet mystical. Manisha furrowed her brow, bewilderment etched on her face. There was something ethereal about how Meena Auntie spoke, as if she had a direct line to the hidden truths of Manisha's life that no one in her family was privy to.

Then, as though the universe had conspired to make the moment even more poignant, Meena Auntie suddenly embraced Manisha, her warm presence wrapping around her like a soft, much-needed weighted blanket.

"Here," she whispered, sweeping her hand with deliberate grace into Manisha's jacket pocket. "My shining star."

Meena Auntie slipped into her car, leaving behind only the subtle scent of jasmine perfume as she backed out of the Patel driveway.

Manisha stood still, wondering where this mysterious woman might go next and whether she would craft yet another enthralling story at the homes of the Mangat, Shivani, or Lalli families. Did she make her rounds from house to house, diligently working through an invisible checklist of Indian families with single children while spreading her unique brand of magic and mystery? Manisha found herself lost in thought, contemplating just how much chai Meena Auntie could possibly consume in a single day. She lingered alone in the driveway, feeling both enchanted and confused.

Eventually, Manisha's focus shifted to the bulging pocket of her sweater, which now felt oddly heavy. She reached inside and pulled out a small tulle bag, its delicate fabric shimmering under the afternoon sun. Within it lay a scattering of exquisite white beads, each one iridescent and luminous, glimmering like miniature stars captured.

"My shining star." Meena Auntie's voice echoed in Manisha's head.

As she peered into the bag, the golden sunlight drenched the beads in warmth, casting tiny rainbows that danced along in a mesmerizing display. Nestled at the bottom, almost shyly, was a slip of paper, its edges softened by time.

"Consume these and embrace a fresh and magical beginning," she read aloud, her voice barely above a whisper, each word resonating deep within her heart.

A new life in Baskin? Was that what it meant? She gazed at the pouch, her mind spinning with possibilities as she pondered whether its contents held the secret to what was in store for her in Baskin. Could magic truly exist? Did Meena Auntie possess the power to craft extraordinary new beginnings, turning the mundane into the miraculous with just a touch? Manisha felt the weight of these questions settle upon her as the beads felt heavy in her hands.

Suddenly, Manisha heard her father's voice behind her. "Has she left?" She turned to see him peeking out from the garage.

"Dad! Um, yeah . . . Meena Auntie had to go."

He stepped out, standing at the top of the driveway. "Good. There's just something odd about that woman. I can't quite put my finger on it. Just . . . something."

Manisha tightened her grip on the beads. "Dad, do you think she's, I don't know, magical or something?"

"Magical? I can't say I buy into that 'Magical Meena' business." He chuckled. "But your mom swears she has a sixth sense. I'm just not convinced about all that. What I am convinced of is that I lose a lot of money to her every month with these visits," he said with some annoyance.

"You're right, Dad. How could one auntie really have the power to change your life?"

*Or mine.*

"Beta, the only one who can change your own destiny and life is you," Manisha's father said, his words lingering like the comforting embrace of Meena Auntie's hug from just a few moments ago.

Her father stepped toward her. "Oh, I need to ask you a favour. While you and your mom were out, your uncle Jas Khanna came by. You know, his son is friends with Sammy." Manisha narrowed her eyes, but her dad didn't notice. "He wants you to look at some legal paperwork. Only if you have the time, of course; he purchased that old coffee shop downtown. Cali Time. It's called Chai Time now."

"Cali Time! Seriously?" Manisha exclaimed, disbelief etched across her face. She had been frequenting that coffee shop since her high school days. "Ugh, Dad. I really don't want to deal with anything related to the Khannas." Once again, she was haunted by the infuriating memory of Rohit's arrogant face.

"Manisha, beta," her dad urged, a hint of desperation in his voice. "It's just a quick visit. It's about some extra permits for renovations . . ." He extended a large envelope toward her. "Uncle Jas emphasized how crucial these are and hopes you can swing by the coffee shop today. You know how much his friendship means to our family, to me."

"Yes, Dad, I do. I know what he did for us and how much he means to you. I know that part. The part I don't really care for is where his son Rohit took advantage of the Khanna name and treated every girl in Baskin like his personal prize," Manisha said.

"Manisha," her father said sternly, "we don't know the whole story, and—"

"And there are always two sides to the story," Manisha interrupted. "Yes, Dad, I know. Mom keeps saying that. Okay, I'll look at the papers."

"That's my good beta." Her father beamed proudly at her, gently touching her shoulder.

She took the envelope, and a whisper of unease crept up her neck. Despite Meena Auntie's comforting words about what lay ahead, Manisha grappled with the guilt of keeping a secret from her parents. "I hope I always make you proud, Dad," she murmured. "I never want to disappoint you."

"Disappoint me? Never! Not once! Besides, you're my favourite daughter," her father said, wrapping an arm around Manisha.

"Your only daughter," she replied with a light laugh. It felt nice to laugh, even if, beneath the surface, she wasn't entirely thrilled about the reason for her return to town—or why she was seeking refuge at her parents' house in Baskin.

"Alright, I'm heading inside," her father declared. "It's getting a bit chilly out here all of a sudden."

Manisha glanced back at the driveway, which had just witnessed the abrupt shift in the weather as Meena Auntie departed.

"So, you'll go to the coffee shop today?" he asked.

"I'll take a look now and go right over, Dad."

As he made his way back into the house, Manisha pulled out her phone and sent a text to her cousin, Deena. Sure, she planned to visit the coffee shop linked to Rohit Khanna for her father's sake, but she certainly wasn't going to go alone.

## 5

It was a beautiful late-fall afternoon in Baskin as Manisha made her way to her past favourite coffee shop, now owned by Rohit Khanna's father. She had just enough time to slip into her trusty Smythe blazer and matching trousers, a once-favourite choice for casual Fridays at her old job. She adjusted her collar as her black Chanel ballet flats glided along the sidewalk. Despite her parents urging her to consider a possible "other side to the story," Manisha was resolved to confine her conversation with Mr. Khanna to work, and to avoid any mention of his son's infidelity.

The sun beamed brightly overhead, but the trees lining the street provided welcome shade as she walked. As she slipped her hand into her pocket, her fingers brushed against the small bag of seeds she had inexplicably decided to bring along. She quickened her pace, feeling the weight of her mother's unexpected suggestion about freezing her eggs and the bewildering discussion with Meena Auntie.

Tucked away in the picturesque upper valley of Baskin, Cali Time was a charming café that, for years, had been celebrated for its strong coffee and delectable California croissants and desserts. Manisha had spent countless hours at the cozy little tables inside the café, sharing laughter and secrets with her high school girlfriends. Their joyful giggles filled the air as they lost themselves in endless conversations about life, love, and dreams. As she approached the café's door, her gaze stopped on a new sign above the awning. The sign was in lively shades of pink, red, and gold, proudly displaying the words "Chai Time" in a stylish script. She flung open the door and immediately found herself struck by how drastically it had transformed. Gone were the faded, mismatched tables and chairs; in their place stood elegant wood furnishings adorned with intricate carvings inspired by South Asian traditions. The walls were decorated with vibrant murals depicting bustling bazaars and serene landscapes from her homeland. At the same time, fragrant spices wafted through the air, mingling with the rich aroma of brewing coffee. Mr. Khanna had truly captured the essence of South Asian culture in all the renovations.

"Manisha! Over here." Manisha looked to the back of the café and saw Deena waving excitedly from a cozy armchair. She grinned and made her way toward her cousin. They were the dynamic duo of the Patel cousins, joined at the hip since they were teeny-weeny Indian babies. With only a fourteen-month age difference between them, people frequently mistook them for twin sisters, especially when they were younger. Even when Manisha went to law school and then moved to London, their closeness never wavered. In fact, Manisha's social circle had dwindled quite a bit while she was abroad, but Deena had remained a steadfast, long-distance confidante.

"How the heck did you beat me here?" Manisha hugged Deena, looking at her watch. "I thought you were across town!"

"Actually, I was next door on another date. Before you say a thing, yes, I am back on the apps." Frustration filled Deena's voice as she slumped back in her chair, releasing an exasperated sigh.

"What happened with this one?" Manisha asked as she took the armchair across from her cousin.

"Don't ask," Deena groaned. "It was like the worst first date ever. He was really attractive, but he has a habit of spitting when he talks! I mean, saliva started gathering at his bottom lip, and before I knew it, it ended up in my coffee."

"Ew."

"It's like he was foaming at the mouth, like, like . . ."

"Like a zombie!" Manisha playfully lunged at Deena, imitating a lifeless creature's stiff, shuffling movements from one of their favourite horror movies. Deena let out a loud shriek, and the cousins tumbled back into their chairs, bursting into giggles.

"Oh my god, remember that guy I dated who was just awful in bed. I told him that having sex with him felt like sleeping next to a dead corpse," Deena said, catching her breath.

"But corpses are . . ." Manisha began.

"Dead to begin with," Deena interjected, smirking. "That's exactly what he said! You both completely missed my point!" she exclaimed, half laughing.

"Well, since you're no longer with him, let's agree to leave the dead in their graves," Manisha added as she leaned in closer to appreciate the intricate red and pink flowers that flourished against the black fabric of Deena's sleeveless top. "I am absolutely loving this top on you!"

"It's an LV bodysuit. I just bought it for that date!"

Manisha admired Deena's style. With her luscious, bouncy curls and effortlessly natural no-makeup look, her cousin radiated beauty and grace. It wasn't just Manisha who noticed; Deena's dating apps were flooded with matches. But Deena wasn't looking for casual flings. Finding a husband was her priority, one that aligned with her parents' wishes. She was a dutiful daughter; if her family wanted her to marry, she intended to do so. For now, though, she relished the luxurious lifestyle that her father's oil company provided.

"I have to say, that blazer looks amazing on you, but why are you all dressed up like you're heading to some big meeting?" Deena asked.

"I actually have a meeting with Mr. Kh——" Manisha began, but her cousin interrupted.

"Ugh. That guy messaged me! He asked if I was feeling any better. I kind of told him I had a migraine and dipped."

Manisha's eyes bulged in shock. "Deena!"

"What? He said it was 'cool'! As it turns out, he had another date lined up in an hour, so it worked out perfectly for both of us." She rolled her eyes

"Wow. It's non-stop, isn't it? I don't get how guys manage it."

"Oh, please, it's not just the guys. We women are in on the game, too. In the world of dating apps, you've got to have a backup plan or two lined up—one guy at a time just won't cut it anymore. It's one date after the other."

"Seriously? Who has the time? It's like having a second job!" Manisha inwardly winced as the word "second" left her lips.

"Ha! A job that doesn't even come with benefits!" Deena chuckled, tossing her dark curls dramatically over her shoulder, the gold buttons on her bodysuit glimmering as they highlighted her elegant neck.

"Anyways, I could really use a break from all the swiping, at least until I catch up with you," Deena went on. "Sanj's wedding didn't really give us that much one-on-one time!" She reached for her classic black Gucci flap purse to drop her phone inside, but Manisha snatched it away before she could.

"Hold on, let me take a look at what you're working with." She grabbed Deena's phone and began swiping through her potential matches. It was a parade of strategically posed shirtless bathroom selfies, gym shots showcasing perfectly sculpted abs, and an abundance of those trendy, casually tousled morning looks. Manisha grimaced. "This is just awful." She returned the phone to her cousin, cringing as if it were contaminated with a virtual dating plague.

Deena tossed it into her bag. "I told you so! So, how are you? Have you recovered from Sanj's wedding? We really danced and drank a ton, didn't we?" She chattered away at her usual rapid pace.

"We did, and it was fun! I hoped for some downtime post-wedding activities, but you know my mom. I don't think she even understands what rest and relaxation are."

"Every Indian mom is like that. So, how long are you staying? I need to know how much trouble we can get into," Deena said mischievously.

Manisha hesitated for a moment. "I'm not entirely sure, to be honest. It might be a bit longer than anyone realizes. So much has happened since Oliver and I ended things." She inhaled deeply, preparing to finally share the whirlwind of her life with someone.

"I couldn't stand him," Deena said, cutting Manisha off. "But what else is going on? Is it work-related?" Her expression was tense, concern etched on her features. "Are they okay with you taking so much time off to be here? You just became a senior partner, right?"

"I did, but—"

Deena interjected again. "You lawyers really have it made, don't you? You can just take time off whenever you feel like it—like on some fancy sabbatical or whatever those corporate girlies call it. You get to eat, pray, and love your way into the arms of some charming European guy ready to rescue you from your 'damsel in distress' life." She chuckled. "Honestly, if you ask me, it's time to get back on the Indian man train and forget about those Olivers of the world—if you catch my drift."

"I never really got off that train, did I?" Manisha said with a hint of nostalgia.

"Manisha, Oliver was white!" Deena said, enunciating every word.

"I know!" Manisha shrugged, a playful grin spreading across her face. "Let's just say I took a little detour."

"I'd call it a derailment," Deena laughed, her eyes sparkling.

Manisha felt genuine happiness course through her. Sure, she'd seen Deena at Sanj's wedding, but this one-on-one time was something she had been craving. She'd missed her cousin dearly, and the sound of their joined laughter made the world seem a little less daunting.

"You were always more of an Indian hunk kind of gal anyway. But are you ready to meet that hunk now?" Deena mused.

"That depends on who this hunk is and what meeting him entails," Manisha replied, a shiver running down her spine as she remembered the profiles Deena had shown her.

"Don't worry, I'll guide you through the dating app process," Deena assured her.

"No dating apps. Absolutely no pictures or videos," Manisha said firmly.

Deena raised an eyebrow, clearly perplexed. "Okay . . ."

"I mean, I'm a senior partner now, so I can't just casually put myself out there on these apps. People take screenshots, and things can go viral in a heartbeat. I need to . . . uphold the firm's reputation," Manisha said, her voice trailing. The words "uphold the firm's reputation" got caught in her throat for a second.

"Okay, I see where you're coming from," Deena said placatingly, though she was giving her a bewildered look.

"Sorry, it's just that a lot has happened to me since—"

"Since my brilliant cousin got her promotion, right?"

Manisha hesitated again. She was really growing tired of all the fibbing. And if the pangs in her sternum were any indication, her body was growing tired of it, too. But telling the whole truth . . . that was bound to bring her more pain. More shame . . . "Yeah, something like that," she said finally.

"Don't worry, we can navigate this. There's got to be something we can find for you and all your dating needs," Deena said, returning her focus to her phone.

Manisha threw her hands up in front of her, palms out. "Hold on! There's something else I need to take care of before I think about dating."

Deena glanced up from her screen. "If you're looking for a good waxer while you're in town, I've got one on speed dial . . ."

"No! Deena." Manisha scrunched her nose. "You won't believe what my mom brought up this morning. Are you ready for this?" She leaned in and lowered her voice to a whisper. "Freezing my eggs."

Deena's jaw dropped. "Are you serious? Like, those eggs?" She gestured to her lap.

"Don't point to them that way, Deena," Manisha replied, instinctively covering her lower half with her hands. "Anyway, she handed me a cheque for twenty grand and told me to make an appointment with some doctor here in Baskin . . . Dr. Rocky?"

"A twenty-thousand-dollar cheque? Just like that?" Deena asked, her eyes huge.

"Yup. I couldn't believe all the zeros attached to it. I made her take it back, though. I mean, save that for the wedding, right? That's what Mom said anyway." Manisha laughed weakly.

"Absolutely! Save it for your wedding," Deena agreed. "Your parents are some of the hardest-working people I know. Plus, you could probably make that kind of money in like a day."

"I also manage to spend that kind of money in like a minute," Manisha murmured quietly.

Deena waved her hand dismissively. "But seriously, what's the big deal with freezing your eggs? We're modern-day boss babes. All the goris have been doing it for ages. There's no reason us Desi girls can't hop on the egg-freezing bandwagon, right?" She shrugged casually.

Just then, a shadow loomed over their table. "Well, well, well, look who it is. Again."

Startled, the cousins looked up to see none other than Rohit Khanna.

"Hey, Deena. Long time no see," he said, placing two glasses of sparkling water on the table. Turning to Manisha with a smirk, he added, "Can't say the same to you, though."

Manisha felt her stomach drop. Of course he'd be here right now. God, how much had he overheard? The unlucky lemons struck again. She scowled at him as she took a sip of water.

"Oh, hey, Rohit! It's been ages. I think the last time I saw you was at Neena's wedding last summer. What are you doing here?" Deena asked.

"Didn't you hear, Deena?" Manisha replied, her tone dripping with sarcasm. "Rohit's dad owns Chai Time."

Rohit raised an eyebrow. "Oh, so you do know my name. Progress!"

Manisha rolled her eyes. "I was too busy dodging your rude comments and behaviour to bother with names earlier."

Rohit crossed his arms in mock anger. "*My* rude comments?"

Deena glanced back and forth between her cousin and Rohit, clearly delighted by this unexpected rivalry. "Do you two . . . know each other?" she asked, eyes gleaming.

"We had the distinct pleasure of bumping into each other earlier today." Rohit smirked.

"More like his ridiculous car had the distinct pleasure of almost crashing into me while I was trying to bring the car around for Mom," Manisha jumped in.

"Excuse me, that's not what happened," Rohit retorted.

"You're right," Manisha nodded earnestly. "You were practicing for the Daytona 500 in Uncle Parm's parking lot."

Deena blinked, her confusion deepening. "I am so lost right now."

"Let me give you the CliffsNotes version, Deena," Manisha graciously offered. "Earlier this afternoon, Rohit decided that his luxury Lamborghini had some sort of divine right to any parking spot—specifically the one I was patiently waiting for. He swooped in like a hawk, gave me a lecture on my driving skills, and then zoomed off like he was late for a race." She turned to Rohit. "Sound about right?"

Rohit stared at Manisha, his face a mix of shock and disbelief. "That's completely wrong! You accosted me, gave *me* a lecture on my driving, and threatened to stab out my tires!"

Deena laughed, shaking her head. "Okay, I think I'm in the wrong episode of this soap opera!"

"Actually, I think you're right on track with *Lawyers and the Lies They Tell You*," Rohit said.

Deena laughed until she noticed Manisha's disapproving glare and abruptly stopped. "Oh, come on, that was kind of funny."

"None of this is funny," Manisha said between clenched teeth.

"And this all just happened today?" Deena said.

"Yes," Manisha and Rohit replied in unison.

"Wow. And I thought I was having a bad day what with Mr. Saliva Lips," Deena said, taking a big gulp of water.

"Why are you even here?" Manisha asked Rohit.

"Why wouldn't I be here?" Rohit frowned.

Manisha shrugged. "I'm just surprised you're not too busy with your extracurricular activities." This time, Deena shot her a look, and Manisha blinked at her, feigning innocence.

Rohit frowned. "What's that supposed to mean?"

"Oh, I was just referring to your hobby. Luxury cars."

"Well, I'm just surprised you have such a low opinion of my cars when you clearly have very expensive taste," Rohit said, gesturing to Manisha's bag.

Manisha let out a hollow laugh. "Look, I earned this bag. I worked hard for it—went to school, took my LSATS, went to grad school, and got a job. You do know what a job is, right, Rohit?"

"Yeah, thanks, I know what a job is," Rohit said. "In fact, I'm at my job right now. Chai Time—I'm running it."

"I hope not into the ground," Manisha said under her breath.

Deena gave Manisha a warning look. "That's so great, Rohit. Liven things up in Baskin."

Manisha looked at her watch.

"Where is your dad, by the way? I'm supposed to be meeting him."

"You are? Too bad—he's not here."

"Fine." Manisha had already spent too much time talking to Rohit Khanna. She wanted to get back to gossiping with Deena. "Can you just give these to your dad?" She held out the envelope of papers. "I highlighted a few areas he should look at more closely, along with some comments."

Rohit took the envelope from her and pulled out the stack of papers. "Look, like I said, my dad's not here and won't return for a week or so. He's on a plane right now to India. Can you walk me through your comments? He's brought me up to speed."

Manisha immediately shook her head. "No, I can't," she said. There was no way she was going to spend more of her free time with arrogant, cheating Rohit Khanna.

"Why?" Rohit asked. "What's the big deal?"

"The big deal is that I don't think I'm the right person to offer you legal advice, Rohit," Manisha said. "I'm a woman with morals," she added. She couldn't help herself.

Rohit jerked his head back, then leaned forward with narrowed eyes. "Sorry?"

He looked so vexed that Manisha felt herself blush. "Moral obligations," she sputtered, "to my family."

"Oh, just help him, Manisha!" Deena hissed.

"I just don't think I have the time," Manisha said, shaking her head.

"Look, a lot was going on this morning and—" Rohit began, sounding almost apologetic.

"I'm over this morning," Manisha interrupted.

"Are not!" Deena countered in a singsong voice, a giant smile on her face.

Manisha glared at her. "I'm glad you're finding this all quite amusing," she muttered.

Rohit shook his head and stuffed the papers back in the envelope. "Whatever," he said, turning sharply on his heel to leave. He took one step before whirling back around to face them. "For the record, I have morals, too. Like treating others with enough respect to hear them out," he bit out, then stormed off to the back of the café.

"He sounded mad."

Manisha shrugged, her expression indifferent. "Of course he's mad. He's upset because we all know the truth. I'm sure he's spinning his own version of events." *Like someone else I know.* The thought of Oliver darkened her mood. "He's a cheater, Deena. That's what cheaters do."

Deena sighed heavily. "What actually happened at Uncle Parm's?"

Manisha rehashed her squabble with Rohit, sparing no detail. "And then, of course, I had to see him here," she finished, crossing her arms in frustration.

"It's hard to believe he would behave that way, especially considering the Khanna reputation," Deena said. "Just playing devil's advocate," she was quick to add.

"His last name didn't seem to matter when he was getting busy behind Lucky's back," Manisha snapped, her voice full of resentment.

"Sounds like he's back for good, though. I heard he sold his tech startup for millions," Deena remarked with raised eyebrows.

Leaning in closer, Manisha glanced around to make sure the coast was clear, then lowered her voice to a whisper. "I also heard he was involved with the CEO who took over for him—some blonde named Suzy."

"Manisha, you know how rumours can get blown out of proportion around Baskin," Deena replied, trying to temper the gossip.

"Poor Lucky," Manisha muttered, her tone dripping with bitterness as she recalled her own sting of betrayal.

"I always thought Rohit was an intelligent, stand-up guy. He's got an MBA, comes from a respectable family, and every auntie just adores him," Deena added.

"Adored. Past tense," Manisha corrected. "And I doubt he really earned his MBA. He probably just used his parents' money to pay his way through."

Deena frowned. "I heard he even studied in France . . ."

"Studied the women in France, more like," Manisha shot back.

Deena laughed, shaking her head. "True, but I bet the women were studying him, too. He's handsome."

"Ew, Deena. Get a grip," Manisha replied. But her body betrayed her, turning to get a glimpse of Rohit. He was chatting animatedly with a customer, his face alight, thick, wavy hair falling into his eyes. She couldn't help but notice his straight teeth and how taut his T-shirt was around his biceps . . .

Shaking her head to clear her thoughts, she turned back to Deena. "He's just insufferable. The way he carries himself—that's what makes him so unattractive."

"Can't say I noticed that. He's friends with Sammy, right?"

"They're the same age, but I don't remember Rohit being around when we were younger."

"I bet he was so spoiled," Deena conceded. My parents have money, but not Khanna money. I heard they're always jet-setting somewhere. But the mom apparently had a huge hand in growing the art scene here in Baskin—or something like that."

Manisha scoffed. "I doubt she passed that down to Rohit. You know, I actually can't stand the sight of him. Cheating bastard."

Deena reached over and squeezed Manisha's hand. "He's not Oliver, Manisha."

"I know he isn't, but he did pull an Oliver: lying and humiliating a woman he was supposed to love."

Deena nodded in understanding. "So, what now?"

"I'm going to make an appointment with Dr. Rocky. It's the

least I can do for my mom, and you're right. I can be a modern woman and even freeze my eggs if I want."

"Great! But what about him?" Deena nodded toward Rohit.

Manisha glanced over her shoulder, where Rohit was now staring intently at the papers. "What are my options again?"

"I'm sorry, Manisha, but you really only have one. The Khannas are like royalty around here. Our families owe a lot to theirs. Remember how Uncle Jas helped your parents and mine settle in Baskin? Then he helped your dad get Bombay Accessories off the ground. We can't just ignore Rohit; it would be so wrong. And didn't you say his dad came by your house and handed over the documents?"

Manisha nodded slowly. "Yeah . . ."

"You just have to approach this as a professional matter. Push your feelings about Oliver aside and look at Rohit as just a proxy for the real client, his dad. This is for his dad and yours."

Manisha recalled her father's pride from earlier that day. A profound sense of guilt washed over her. He would be devastated to know how she had handled the situation. "Did I mention how much I hate that you're right?" she grumbled. "If I do it, it's for his dad, my dad, your dad . . ."

"All the Baskin Indian dads," Deena chimed in, laughing.

Manisha stole another glance at Rohit, watching as he pored over the documents. He looked so serious, but confusion was etched deeply into his forehead. He was completely lost.

"Just look at him, Manisha. He's buried under all those papers," Deena murmured, her tone filled with concern.

Manisha continued to study him, chewing on her bottom lip. Finally, she winced and then expelled a heavy breath. "Alright, I'll help him," she said, pushing up from the table to stand.

Deena looked at her expectantly, jerking her head in Rohit's direction.

"Later."

With that, she grabbed her cousin's arm, pulled her to the door, and got the hell out of there.

$\mathcal{T}$he next day, Manisha sat nervously in Dr. Rocky's office, waiting for him to arrive with her test results. Her mother had arranged a "VIP visit," as she called it, proudly stating that she had leveraged connections at the clinic to secure an appointment that typically required a year-long wait. Although Manisha still felt uncertain about the idea of freezing her eggs, she had no choice but to attend this special visit—otherwise, she'd surely face endless nagging from her mom. Ever since Meena Auntie's visit, her mother had been pressing her more than ever to find a man and settle down.

Deena was right: if all the goris are doing it, why couldn't she? If Manisha were to take advice from anyone, it would be Deena— her very own dating guru! Deena had a Ph.D. in romance, with a resumé that would put any matchmaker to shame. Forget what Manisha's mom thought she knew from her evening sessions watching Breaking Indian News; Deena had the real scoop on the dating game. She knew how difficult it was to find the right man, so having a little backup baby plan wasn't going to hurt anyone. And visiting Dr. Rocky seemed more reasonable than downing Meena Auntie's white seeds, which were now tucked away in Manisha's nightstand.

Manisha glanced at her watch, realizing she'd spent hours at the clinic. What she had expected to be a quick appointment had turned into a lengthy visit. If only she had taken the time to read the emails Dr. Rocky had sent her in preparation for her visit, she might have anticipated this. After blood work and a pelvic exam, she was hit with a spell of dizziness. It might have been the blood work or perhaps the fact that she hadn't eaten since 7 a.m., and it was now well past 10 a.m. As she sat in Dr. Rocky's office, waiting for updates, her anxiety only intensified.

She surveyed the room, noting its opulence. The handcrafted fixtures and furniture exuded sophistication, and the comfortable leather chair she occupied enveloped her in luxury. A state-of-the-art Sonos system filled the air with soft jazz melodies, epitomizing wealth. Towering oak bookcases lined the walls, showcasing an array of photographs of Dr. Rocky with his celebrity friends, from musicians to actors to politicians, all framed in dazzling, diamond-studded surrounds. Her gaze shifted to the wall behind Dr. Rocky's glass-topped desk, where numerous accolades and awards proudly displayed his intellectual prowess, proving that he was as accomplished as he was stylish.

Manisha was well aware of his reputation as one of the highest-priced fertility doctors in California, but the glowing reviews she'd perused on her Uber ride over confirmed that he was worth every cent.

Manisha got up from her seat to peek at the more personal pictures on his desk. As she leaned over his desk, the door suddenly swung open.

"Manisha Patel?"

Startled, Manisha hustled back to her seat. "Here. I mean, yes. That's me!"

Dr. Rocky strode in and slid into his own leather chair with an effortless grace, and Manisha felt her breath catch in her throat. He was undeniably handsome—an Indian silver fox. His smooth, golden skin seemed to reflect a morning ritual that involved a luxurious ghee-based moisturizer. His hair, a glossy black peppered with distinguished gray, was styled to perfection, as though he had just stepped out of a high-end salon, the kind that required a battery of hot tools to maintain such a polished look.

She glanced down at her own unruly hair, frizzy and unkempt, a stark contrast to his impeccable appearance. Frantically, she tucked strands behind her ears, fully aware that it would do little to tame the wildness. Dr. Rocky's plump lips drew her gaze, and she swallowed hard, reminding herself this was her mother's friend—an uncle in the cultural sense—and she needed to act like a reasonable adult. A normal person. Her mother's stern words played over in her head: "Bandari . . . Don't act foolishly when you meet him."

Taking a deep breath to calm her racing thoughts, Manisha was hit by the intoxicating scent of his cologne, a fragrance unlike anything she had smelled before. It was rich and alluring, as if it had been bottled in a lab nestled among the Swiss Alps, meticulously crafted to seduce. She shook her head slightly, trying to dispel the haze. *Focus*, she told herself. The eggs. Her mother would kill her if she didn't behave.

"Two kids," Dr. Rocky said.

"What? Um, I've never really thought about how many I wanted," Manisha stammered. "It kind of depends on where I am, right? Am I living in Baskin, where my mom could help? And what if my husband is travelling a lot? Do we have a nanny?" Her words tumbled out in a frantic rush, and she felt the prickle of sweat beginning to form along her forehead. Did someone turn up the heat? The room felt hotter.

Dr. Rocky looked up at her. "No, I mean, I have two kids," he said. "You were looking at the pictures on my desk, weren't you?" He smiled at her.

*Busted*, Manisha thought, but quickly shrugged off her embarrassment. He'd left her waiting for nearly thirty minutes. "Oh, lovely. Two kids."

"Hop up here for a moment," Dr. Rocky instructed, rising from his chair and striding toward the examination table to his left.

Manisha clambered onto the padded surface, her heart fluttering slightly as she watched him work with a mixture of anticipation and anxiety. Dr. Rocky was methodical, his touch gentle yet precise as he monitored her blood pressure and listened to the rhythmic cadence of her heartbeat.

"Good stuff," he said, offering a reassuring smile that momentarily eased the tension in her shoulders. He gestured for her to return to her seat as he returned to his.

"So, it's just you today," Dr. Rocky noted.

Manisha paused, searching for the right words. "Well, yes. I mean, for now," she replied, her voice wavering slightly as she considered what that meant—both for herself and for the journey ahead.

"I had hoped your mother would be able to join us today," he said, looking at her with what seemed to be disappointment.

"Anyway, plenty of women embark on this journey solo," he continued, flashing her another encouraging smile. "Let's get right to your results." With that, he opened the folder, the pages rustling softly under his touch. "It's a busy day at the clinic— everyone seems to be on a quest for a baby or two. This year has been especially fruitful for twins." He winked, a playful glimmer in his eyes.

Manisha reciprocated the wink before realizing he was just attempting to remove something from his eye. She felt the weight of her nerves pressing down, threatening to unravel her composure. She cleared her throat. "Thank you for arranging this VIP . . . this very important visit for me," she began, her voice slightly unsteady. "I know it means a lot to my mom."

"How is your mother?" Dr. Rocky inquired, his tone casual yet attentive.

"She's doing great. Really great. How do you know each other again? She never really got into it," Manisha replied, trying not to sound too curious.

A flicker of something crossed his face, too fleeting to read. "Let's just say we have some history," he said, his words trailing off into an enigmatic silence.

"Oh, okay, but I'm just curious—" Manisha began, eager to delve deeper, but Dr. Rocky deftly cut her off.

"I appreciate your patience today. It's essential for us to ensure every detail is accounted for to achieve the best results," he said, his demeanour shifting to one of professionalism. "As I'm sure you noticed, our advanced facility is equipped to provide you with the outcomes you need efficiently. Those days of endless back-and-forth visits are over; we offer a one-stop solution that puts immediate results at your fingertips."

"Advanced, indeed," was all Manisha could manage to reply.

He continued, "Thanks to this technology, I have good news—we received your test results back right away."

"That's wonderful to hear," Manisha said, her relief evident. "Good news is . . . good."

Dr. Rocky nodded slowly. "Yes, good news . . . along with some other information. It all hinges on a few things." He leafed through a few more pages, eyes skirting across the results. "Tell me, Manisha, how committed are you to the journey of starting a family?"

Her head tilted to one side in confusion. "What do you mean by that?"

"I'm asking if you genuinely want this now, or if you feel obligated to be here because your mother urged you to come."

"Of course I want to be a mother. It's always been my dream." Manisha adjusted her blue Hermès skirt, wishing it was a little longer.

"That's wonderful to hear. Many women visit me due to the pressure to have children, rather than out of their own desire."

"Dr. Rocky." She waited until he looked up at her before continuing. "As an Indian woman, there's always some level of pressure. Pressure to excel in school, to marry by a certain age, and yes, there's pressure to have a baby. But I'm here because I genuinely want this. My mom and I had an open conversation about it, and that's why I'm sitting in front of you today."

He dipped his chin slowly in understanding. "You're fortunate, Manisha; not everyone enjoys that kind of bond with their mother," he remarked. "From what I've seen, these conversations aren't something many Indian mothers and daughters find easy to have." He looked past Manisha for a moment, lost in thought. "But your mother was always truly exceptional—progressive for her era, and . . ." His voice faded away.

Manisha stayed quiet for a moment, unsure whether to break the silence or let Dr. Rocky come back from his trip down memory lane on his own. "Yes, my mom is quite exceptional," she finally said. She acknowledged the truth in what the doctor had said, feeling fortunate to have such a close relationship with her mother—even on those days when her mom dragged her to a milk and butter sale.

Dr. Rocky cleared his throat before continuing. "Alright, let's dive into your results. Manisha, after reviewing everything, I believe egg freezing is a great option for you, especially if it's done sooner rather than later."

"Okay, how soon are we talking?"

"Your results indicate that your body might be aging more rapidly than expected. To be candid, freezing your eggs should take priority for you," Dr. Rocky stated.

"What do you mean?" Manisha asked, her brow furrowing in confusion. "I'm only thirty-four."

"While thirty-four is still considered relatively young for starting a family, some women in their early thirties encounter fertility challenges that might not be immediately obvious," Dr. Rocky explained. "Your blood work and ultrasound results suggest that you may need to take a more cautious approach in your fertility journey."

"Cautious?" Manisha parroted, feeling a wave of dizziness wash over her.

"Manisha, if you're considering starting a family, I recommend we act quickly to facilitate the egg-freezing process. This includes medications, regular appointments with me, and some lifestyle changes, like cutting back on alcohol."

"Alright . . ." Manisha said, trying to wrap her head around his words.

"Timing and age are crucial factors in your fertility journey. While it's common for women your age to consider egg freezing, your specific findings suggest that delaying this decision may hinder your chances of successful pregnancies in the future. Your ovarian reserve, which refers to the number and quality of eggs left in your ovaries, appears to be aging faster than what's typical for someone your age, ultimately impacting the quality of your eggs," Dr. Rocky continued.

His expression shifted to convey earnest concern as he clasped his hands on the desk. "I want to stress the importance of making decisions now. Considering your results, I recommend starting the next steps for freezing your eggs as soon as possible."

"As soon as possible?" Manisha repeated in disbelief.

"We're merely taking a few extra steps to ensure you have the family of your dreams."

Slowly, her shock made way for coherent thought. "So, what you're saying is that thirty-four isn't the new twenty-four but rather more like forty-four for someone in my situation—and that I haven't exactly reversed the aging process?"

Dr. Rocky raised an eyebrow. "Not exactly. I meant that choosing to freeze your eggs could ultimately provide you with peace of mind. As a busy lawyer, you no doubt understand the importance of having a safety net."

"Yes, I do want that safety net. That's exactly why I'm here— my mother . . . well, she emphasized the need for future planning."

"Good! Modern technology offers many pathways," Dr. Rocky continued. "And since there's no guarantee on the number of viable eggs we collect and freeze, have you given any thought to embryo freezing?"

Cue the shock again. "But don't I need, well . . . sperm for that?"

"Yes," he confirmed, his tone gentle but firm. "It's an option worth exploring, Manisha. We can provide you with a list of reputable sperm banks, allowing you to select a donor. Either option should be made a priority."

"I can't believe I'm even considering all of this," Manisha admitted, feeling lost amid a whirlwind of new information. "That was never even on my radar."

He glanced down at her patient chart. "How long do you plan to stay in Baskin?"

"Until I find a new job," Manisha muttered.

Dr. Rocky looked up, slightly puzzled. "Sorry?"

"I mean, I'm looking into a new job here in Baskin," she clarified.

He nodded slowly. "I recommend that you go home, think everything over and weigh the costs." His eyes fell on the brand-new Chanel bag in her lap. "These procedures can be quite expensive. But Ruby—your mother—mentioned that you've had great success as a lawyer and that you've recently become senior partner."

"Yes. That's right," she replied, her voice taking on a mouselike quality.

Just then, Dr. Rocky's office phone rang.

"Excuse me for a moment," he said, picking up the line.

Manisha didn't know where to focus, so she kept her gaze on him.

"Of course! I'll see her next week. And just one second . . ." Dr. Rocky began typing on his computer. "And she's all paid up! Fifty thousand dollars, correct. Can you ensure she receives a receipt for the full amount?"

Manisha's eyes widened at the mention of fifty thousand dollars.

Dr. Rocky hung up the phone and turned his attention back to her.

"Another patient of mine, someone you might relate to. She's freezing her eggs, too. Now, where was I . . . Oh, look at the time! We need to get you on your way; you've been at the clinic all morning. You've got a lot on your plate, young lady." With that, Dr. Rocky stood up, signalling the end of her appointment.

"I know that all this information can be overwhelming, but I assure you, my team and I are devoted to providing you with unwavering support no matter which option you choose." He rounded the desk and walked toward the door. Manisha stood, following in a daze.

"And don't worry; this conversation remains confidential, as it does with all my clients," he continued. "Your mom won't receive any updates from me."

She managed a polite nod.

He paused, hand on the doorknob, his expression sombre. "It's ultimately up to you to make an informed decision once you've reflected on what we discussed today. And keep in mind"—he flung the door open and stepped aside—"there are plenty of eligible bachelors in Baskin. You could find yourself a husband in just a few weeks. Who knows, maybe you'll bump into Prince Charming on your walk home." He flashed her a toothy smile.

Dr. Rocky was starting to sound like Uncle Parm.

"In just a few weeks?" Manisha shot back incredulously. "It takes longer for my couture to arrive from India, Dr. Rocky."

"Well, we aren't ordering a man from India, Manisha." He chuckled.

"Is that an option?" Manisha asked, half joking, as she dragged her feet out of his office.

"Stop by reception on your way out and they'll have some informational pamphlets on what we discussed today. Take care now, Ms. Patel."

Manisha stood at the top of the clinic steps, her heart racing and palms damp. She tried to calm the whirlwind of thoughts in her head. Dr. Rocky had delivered something completely unexpected. Instead of the straightforward "bang, bang, shoot, shoot" she was anticipating, he had dropped a string of bombshells on her: rapidly aging eggs, fifty thousand dollars, embryo freezing, sperm selection, couture husbands. The words reverberated in her mind, leaving her with little time to absorb the weight of them all. Everything was shifting at lightning speed, mirroring the transformations happening within her own body.

She glanced at her phone, struck by how much the appointment had taken out of her. All she wanted was to retreat to the comfort of her bed, but she had promised Rohit that she would meet him at Chai Time in less than an hour. Deena had made it clear that not helping him would mean disappointing many people. It wasn't just about Rohit; it was about his father, Mr. Khanna, who had always been there for her family when they needed it. She owed it to him to prioritize helping his family, even if that included Rohit.

But first, she had to speak with Deena. She quickly texted her, insisting they meet at Chai Time for what she called an "emergency."

And indeed, it was an Egg-Freezing Emergency.

## 7

*M*anisha arrived at Chai Time thirty minutes early. After receiving Deena's message that she would be late, she decided not to wait inside with Rohit. Instead, she ducked into a bar a few doors down.

It took her eyes a second to adjust to the softly lit space. A waitress gestured for her to find a seat anywhere, and Manisha saw a table near the window. She glanced around the bar, which had a handful of patrons, perhaps regulars. Who else would be at a pub in the middle of the day? It definitely felt strange to her. Once upon a time, grabbing drinks after work at the nearby watering hole had been a regular ritual with her colleagues in London, but those days now seemed like a distant echo of her life, much like so many other memories from that time.

The waitress approached to take her order. She was young, probably in her mid-twenties, with eggs aplenty.

Manisha inwardly scowled. "I'll have a nine-ounce glass of your cheapest Chardonnay, please," she said, plastering on a smile.

"You got it," said the waitress brightly.

Manisha glanced at her phone and saw three missed calls from Cheating Scumbag, prompting a frustrated groan. As if texts weren't enough, now Oliver was resorting to calls. She could easily ignore those, too—until he finally got the hint and stopped trying to reach her. Without bothering to listen to the voicemails he'd left, she refocused her attention on the pressing issue at hand: her dire financial situation. There was no way she could afford either of Dr. Rocky's procedures.

The waitress returned with her wine in hand, and Manisha immediately gulped half the glass. It tasted cheap, but it hit the spot. The egg-freezing spot.

She inhaled deeply before opening her banking app, closing her eyes as she murmured a quiet prayer. With a sigh, she opened her eyes to the harsh reality of her account summary. Her savings account was in the red, hovering nearly $5,000 in overdraft, while her chequing account barely scraped a thousand dollars—most of which was her last paycheque. To make matters worse, both credit cards were at their limits.

Staring at the bleak numbers, she desperately tried to figure out how to juggle her finances, but the truth hit her hard: There was no money to shuffle. No lender would even consider giving her a penny after seeing her recent transactions filled with lavish purchases. In her effort to heal her broken heart, she had inadvertently dug herself into a financial abyss. It wasn't until now, a realization spurred by Dr. Rocky's words, that she truly understood the depth of her predicament.

Downing the remainder of her wine, she signalled for a refill.

The waitress returned with a glass brimming to the top, seemingly aware that Manisha was eager to numb her troubles.

"Cheers," Manisha muttered, raising her glass to the waitress, then taking a long sip. "You know, I used to be like you—young, carefree, probably with an impressive ovarian reserve. Look at me now." She gestured vaguely to herself. "I'm a cocktail of designer brands, financial chaos, and emotional wreckage." Manisha took the pamphlets from her purse and threw them on the table.

The waitress blinked. "Are you guys trying for a baby?"

Manisha burst into laughter. "Ha! What guy? It's just me, darling. No Prince Charming. No knight in shining armour. Nope. Just me, staring down a fifty-thousand-dollar bill to freeze my eggs. Can you believe that? Fifty grand."

"Oh wow. I really had no idea . . ."

*That makes two of us.*

"How about a shot?" the waitress asked, trying to comfort Manisha.

"Make it two!" Manisha replied, her voice a mix of frustration and determination. Anything to numb the pain.

The waitress returned with three shots, one for herself included.

Manisha grimaced as she picked up a glass and slammed it back in unison with her new friend. She shuddered at the burning sensation. It had been ages since she knocked back a shot of tequila. Manisha immediately accepted a lemon wedge the waitress was offering.

"You know, no one tells you any of this," Manisha said. "Like, nobody sits you down and says, 'Hey, you might want to think about saving money to freeze your eggs.' No, it's not in the pamphlet at the library or covered by the work health benefits package. Do you know why? Because that would be too easy. Instead, you have to end up here, talking to a random waitress, no offence, while sipping cheap Chardonnay and doing tequila shots in the middle of the day." Manisha slammed her hand on the table, causing their already wobbly setup to tremble.

The waitress, still a little confused, handed her the next shot.

"Thanks . . . what's your name?"

"Missy," the waitress replied.

"Missy, I need you to lean in closer. I am going to do you a favour. I'm going to be your fertility fairy godmother-auntie, and

I'm telling you now. Don't take this stuff for granted," she said, pointing at the waitress. "Because if you do, you might end up like me. And I'm not exactly prime egg-freezing material anymore."

Missy forced a smile. "Thank you."

"You'll thank me later," Manisha said.

"Well, good luck. I bet you'll make a great mom." Missy turned and hurried to another table.

Manisha, feeling empowered by her tequila-soaked wisdom, raised her glass again. "I'll be the greatest mom in Baskin!" Manisha called after her. "Sure, my child . . . she . . . or he . . . may not have anything else, like a father. But guess what they will have? The finest of Hermès," Manisha slurred loudly.

"*You're* a hairy mess!" another patron yelled.

She gasped, free hand flying to her frizzy hair. "How rude. It's *Hermès*," Manisha scolded back. She took another swig of her drink. "Hairy mess." She giggled to herself just as her phone rang. Cheating Scumbag. It was Oliver, and this time, Manisha picked it up.

"What the hell do you want, Oliver?"

"Ish! Finally. I've been trying to get a hold of you, but you haven't replied to any of my texts or . . ."

"Why the hell would I?" Manisha asked, temper flaring.

"Is everything alright? Are you alright?"

"Yeah, I'm fine, Oliver," Manisha replied impatiently. "Why are you trying to get a hold of me now? I'm out of London. Isn't that what you wanted?"

"Ish, what are you talking about? Why would I want you out of London? I know I was a complete bastard, and again, I'm sorry for what happened, but—"

"What happened is you cheated on me with your law student," Manisha interrupted.

She heard a hush fall over the bar. She hadn't realized she'd been talking so loudly.

There was silence on the phone now, too.

Manisha continued, trying to calm herself. "And I need you to stop texting and calling me. It's over. You got what you wanted. You win."

"Got what I wanted?" Oliver asked in disbelief. "I wanted you, Ish. I wanted you so badly."

Manisha scoffed. He sure had a backward way of showing it. "Let me get this straight: You wanted me so badly that you cheated on me?" Each word climbed in volume.

"I tried to get you to spend time with me! You were always working!" Oliver cried.

"We lived together. I saw you every day!" She was definitely shouting now.

"But did you see me? Like, actually see who I was, who I am?" His voice cracked, close to breaking.

Manisha froze, not knowing what to say. Did she?

"Manisha, all you saw was a guy you lived with, not someone you wanted to be with for the rest of your life. We were like roommates, and I know that deep down, you were never a hundred percent in this."

That made her bristle. "Oh, really? How do you know that?"

"I think you want to end up with an Indian guy," Oliver said simply.

Manisha didn't know what to do with that. Finally, she spoke. "Okay, Oliver. Let's say that's true. Did that give you the right to cheat on me?"

"No, and I own that."

"Oh wow! Everyone, listen up!" She raised her voice. "Oliver James Horne admits he did wrong by cheating on me!"

"Is that why you're a hairy mess?" The patron from earlier shouted.

She scowled in the direction of the heckler. "H–E–R–M–È–S!" she shouted back.

"What?" Oliver gasped through the phone. "Herpes? Do you have herpes?"

"Oh my god, no!" she cried. "Hermès."

She took a gulp of wine. "Honestly, Oliver, between the two of us, if someone was at risk of having anything, it would be you. I wasn't the one sleeping with someone."

"Oh, don't I know it," Oliver said bitterly.

Manisha fell silent, stunned. When she finally found her voice, she fought to keep it even. "Just because we weren't having sex doesn't give you the right to sleep around on me. And to be very clear, you only owned up to cheating because I caught you. You made me think I was acting crazy, denying it over and over again until that night." Tears sprang to her eyes at the awful memory. "Until I saw you. I saw you with her." She blinked hard. She was not going to let him hear her cry.

"I know. I'm so sorry, Ish."

Manisha paused. He actually sounded sincere.

"I don't care," she muttered, steeling herself. "You didn't deserve me, and I don't need to sit here listening to your pathetic excuses or apologies, either. I'm going. Goodbye."

"Isha, Ish, wait—"

But she hung up, cutting him off mid-sentence. She clumsily stuffed the pamphlets back in her purse, tossed some cash on the table, and swayed toward Chai Time, wine-fuelled confidence guiding her steps.

$\mathcal{A}$fter downing a couple giant glasses of wine and tequila shots in under half an hour, Manisha's thoughts were a bit hazy as she made her way to Chai Time. She mentally shunted aside her call with Oliver, determined instead to focus on the present issue: her fertility journey and the limited, costly options she had.

Turning to her mom for financial help was out of the question; the mere idea of her mother knowing how much she'd splurged on bags and bling made her stomach churn. It would shatter her pride, especially since she'd just turned down a cheque from her. The thought of her mother's disapproval loomed large indeed.

She could ask Uncle Parm to put her photo on the wall beside Katrina Kaif's. She shook her head. No, that'd just be a reminder of her predicament, like a mugshot of a reckless spender and an indulgent brat.

Manisha sighed. The option to freeze her eggs was available, but time was running out, and Manisha couldn't afford the high fees at Dr. Rocky's state-of-the-art clinic. Even if other clinics charged half the amount, she still wouldn't have the money. She had hoped that today's appointment would mainly be discussion, giving her more time to save up for a baby fund if it came to that. Little had she realized that she needed to act quickly and begin the process immediately, or else lose out on the chance altogether.

But living a life without children . . . the idea filled her with a crushing sense of dread and self-loathing for her past splurges. More than ever, Manisha had no idea how to move forward. Personally, professionally—her life was one big mess.

She finally reached Chai Time, and with a weary sigh, Manisha eased the door open and shuffled up to the counter. Her eyes scanned the menu board, but the words wavered fuzzily before her as she fought to stand upright.

"Hey! Welcome to Chai Time. What can I get you?" the young man behind the counter said, flashing a cheerful smile.

"Eggs," Manisha replied, her mind still preoccupied with thoughts of freezing her eggs.

"How would you like your eggs?" he asked, raising an eyebrow.

"Frozen," she said vaguely, still lost in her thoughts.

"You'd like frozen eggs?" he echoed, clearly puzzled.

Manisha shook her head, embarrassment washing over her. "I'm sorry, I meant to say I don't have eggs—I mean, I do have eggs, they're just limited. So can I get your eggs instead—" She felt flustered, the wine she'd consumed making her tongue heavy. She tried to concentrate on what the employee was saying, but the words seemed to float over her head.

"Manisha? Are you feeling alright?"

Suddenly, Rohit was standing next to the employee, a concerned look on his face. "Adam, why don't I take over here? A couple of tables in the back need to be cleared."

"Absolutely, boss." Adam's relief was obvious as he quickly made his escape.

Rohit leaned over the counter, lowering his voice to a whisper. "Manisha, are you drunk?"

Manisha shot him an icy glare. *Seriously, you're such a Rude Rohit,* she thought, emphasizing both "rude" and "Rohit" in her mind.

"How about you sit down?" he suggested. "I'll grab you a coffee and some water."

She shook her head vehemently. "I'm fine! Let's just go over those papers."

"Now? Not like this," Rohit replied, his tone laced with disapproval, which only fuelled her annoyance.

"Just because I might have accidentally had a few too many drinks doesn't mean I, former lawyer Miss Manisha Patel, can't look over some legal—" She hiccupped. "Some legal documents for a coffee shop . . ."

"Honestly, today's not a good day for that anymore," Rohit countered.

"Why not? Your dad told mine this was really important."

"You're right; my dad asked your dad for a favour," Rohit said patiently. "But this can wait a day or two . . . and I think you should head home."

Manisha burst into laughter. "Rohit Khanna is kicking me out of his café!"

A few patrons turned to look.

"Uh, no! That's not what I'm doing at all," he said, glancing around nervously.

"Good, because I want to stay," Manisha declared stubbornly, plopping down in a chair. "Let's go through the papers!"

Rohit handed her a glass of water. "Look, you've had way too much to drink. There's no way you can focus on anything right now."

"Well, I'm looking at you wearing that. That's focusing, isn't it?" Manisha remarked, eyeing him up and down. She assessed his stylish purple suit paired with a light blue shirt. Why was he dressed like that?

Rohit glanced down at his outfit in surprise. "It's just a suit."

Manisha chuckled. "*Just* a suit, like it's *just* a Lamborghini." She mimicked his tone, completing the sentence with flair.

"Go home, Manisha."

"You're so . . ."

"Rude?" he interjected.

Manisha smirked. "Exactly."

Now, it was Rohit's turn to laugh. "Look who's talking! The kettle is calling the pot black!"

"It's the pot calling the kettle black," she corrected. "And I'll have you know my kettle is blue. It's a Smug. That I paid for using my own hard-earned money."

"Smeg . . ."

"That's what I just said," Manisha growled.

"You said 'Smug,'" he pointed out, frustration creeping into his tone.

She opened her mouth to counter with a mature "Did not!" but he cut in.

"You know what? Never mind. There's no point in arguing with you. I have a lot to do." He glanced at his watch.

"Are you implying I don't?" she shot back.

"What? No! I don't know what your schedule looks like," Rohit replied. "But since you seem to be on vacation—"

"Self-imposed sabbatical."

"Whatever you call it," Rohit said, lifting his hands in surrender. "Let's just do this another time."

"I'll see if I can pencil you into my jam-packed sched—" Manisha began, reaching for the waterglass.

Suddenly, Deena burst through the café doors, spotting Manisha right away. "Are you okay?"

"Deena!" Manisha exclaimed, then turned to Rohit. "Look, it's Deena!"

Deena looked at Rohit, perplexed. He chuckled. "You're welcome for taking care of your drunk friend."

"Cousin," Manisha corrected him. "We're cousins, Rude Vain Rohit." She sniggered then took a sip of water. From over the rim of her glass, she watched Deena's jaw slowly drop open.

"She's been like this since she arrived five minutes ago," Rohit informed Deena.

Deena kept staring at her, aghast. "Manisha, you're drunk! It's the middle of the day. Impressive."

Manisha lowered the glass and gave her cousin the stink eye. "I'm not drunk, Deena," she insisted.

And then she hiccupped again. "Okay, fine. Maybe I had a few too many sips of Chardonnay." In hindsight, she probably shouldn't have mixed wine with tequila. But who was she to turn down Missy's offer?

"I'll get her out of your hair," Deena said apologetically to Rohit.

"But we still need to go over those papers!" Manisha protested. She flung her arm toward the back of the café, nearly knocking over her water and untouched coffee in the process.

"Whoa!" Deena yelped, as both Rohit and she dove to steady the table. She shook her head firmly. "Not today, Manisha. How about we get going?"

"Fine." Manisha brought her hand—pinky and thumb extended—up to her face. "My people are gonna call his people."

"Right. Thanks, Rohit," Deena said, helping Manisha out of her chair and steering her toward the door.

Manisha scowled. "Why are you thanking him? In fact, someone should be thanking—"

Before Manisha could finish, a tall blonde woman swooped into the café and narrowly avoided colliding with them.

"Oh gosh, sorry about that," the woman said, slipping off her sunglasses. "Ro!" she exclaimed, looking past them. A giant smile spread across her face.

Rohit stepped out from behind them and checked his watch. "Hi, you're early!"

Manisha caught Deena's eye, who mouthed "Ro" back at her with a quizzical brow lift.

"Oh, I hope that's alright?" The woman looked to Deena and Manisha, then to Rohit, then back to them. She extended her hand with a nervous smile. "Um, hi, I'm—"

"Of course," Rohit interjected smoothly. "Where are my manners?"

"Did you ever have any?" Manisha muttered just loud enough for Deena to catch, who shot her a warning look, silently urging her to be quiet.

"Suzy is . . . well, she's, um, a business partner," Rohit announced. "Suzy, meet Manisha and Deena, a couple of my fellow Baskinites."

Deena and Manisha exchanged incredulous glances. This was Suzy—the woman Rohit had supposedly strayed with, the very reason for the much-talked-about cancellation of the Indian wedding of the year.

"Nice to meet you, Suzy," Deena managed to say, her voice shaky.

"Homewrecker," Manisha whispered into Deena's ear, slightly slurred yet unmistakable.

"Hi, Suzy, I'm a little boozy." Manisha raised a hand in the air like she was giving a toast and nearly lost her balance, swaying dangerously.

Suzy looked baffled. "Did I miss a happy hour or something?"

"Not for everyone," Rohit quickly replied, his tone a touch defensive.

"Sorry, my cousin was celebrating her, um, her brother's post-wedding excitement," Deena jumped in, trying to smooth over the awkwardness. "She might have had one too many!" She laughed nervously.

"I'm totally fine," Manisha hissed, rolling her eyes. Rohit and now Deena were really testing her patience.

"We've all been there," Suzy said, flashing a sympathetic smile.

"I bet most girls in Baskin could say that about Rohit, too," Manisha quipped with a big grin.

"Manisha!" Deena snapped at her.

Rohit raised an eyebrow but said nothing.

"I'm just saying . . ." Manisha shrugged. "We've all hea—"

"I think it's time for us to leave," Rohit said coldly. "Suzy and I have plans, and to be honest, I've had my fill of the Manisha happy hour."

"Sorry, Rohit. You know jet lag can hit hard. One drink feels like five!" Deena said with a sheepish grin.

"Jet lag? I've been in Baskin for we—ee—" Manisha started to say, but Deena slapped a hand over her mouth, holding it firmly in place.

"Regardless, you two should enjoy yourselves. I've got Manisha," Deena said. She shot Manisha a cross look before carefully removing her hand, then pulled them to the side to clear the way for Rohit.

"It was great meeting you both," Suzy said. "Let's head out, Ro." The pair linked arms and took their leave.

"See you, Ro!" Manisha called out as the door clicked shut behind them.

Deena made a weird noise, somewhere between a sigh and a chuckle. "Manisha, you're plastered," she said, shaking her head.

"Just a tad," Manisha replied, leaning her weight on Deena, who stumbled to keep them upright.

"We really need to get out of here," Deena insisted.

"Are we going to another bar? I'm starving!"

"Yeah, it's called Deena's Bar," Deena replied, a lopsided grin on her face as they walked out.

$\mathcal{M}$anisha yawned as she stepped into Deena's kitchen and hopped up on a stool.

"Well, look who finally decided to wake up—in the early evening, might I add," Deena said with a playful smile.

"What time is it? I need some water," Manisha replied groggily while rubbing her eyes. "My head," she moaned, surveying Deena's spacious loft.

Deena filled a glass and handed it to Manisha before settling on the stool beside her. "It's just after five."

"I guess I needed a nap," Manisha admitted, managing a small smile.

"You passed out, Manisha," Deena said, her tone half serious. "You crashed like a kitten after feeding time. How are you feeling?"

"Fine, I think," Manisha answered, stifling another yawn.

"Good, because now you need to tell me what the hell happened today," Deena pressed. She narrowed her eyes at her, awaiting a response.

"I just had a couple glasses of wine," Manisha began defensively. "Maybe too much?"

"I'd definitely say so. Then you strolled into Chai Time, and, well, you lit into Rohit."

"I didn't light into Rohit! You're exaggerating, Deena." Manisha frowned, trying to recall the day's events. She remembered arriving at Chai Time, Rohit not wanting to go through the paperwork, and then . . . things were blurry. "Even if I did, he probably deserved it."

"Manisha, you were so rude to him."

"Well, he is Rude Rohit," Manisha pointed out.

"Correction. 'Rude Vain Rohit' is what you called him. To his face."

"Oh." Her earlier words at the café came back to her in a flood. Colour filled her cheeks.

"Okay, I guess I wasn't the kindest. Maybe I owe him an apology . . ." she admitted. "But can we pause for a second? Did we actually meet Suzy?"

"We did!" Deena's voice rose in excitement. "I guess it was only a matter of time before we saw them together."

"Are you kidding? Rohit and Lucky were supposed to get *married*," Manisha said, drawing out the last word. "And now he's flaunting his relationship with Suzy right in front of everyone!" Manisha continued.

"Come on, Manisha. You know how it goes with Indian people. They've probably moved on to the next piece of gossip already. You and I are still sipping this spilled chai while the rest of the world moves on. Speaking of chai . . ." Deena stood, striding toward her stovetop where the kettle was spewing steam. Her kitchen was a space equipped so extravagantly it would mesmerize any chef, but for her, it was merely a repository for takeout containers.

"I'm just so surprised," Manisha remarked, still processing everything. "His family, especially his dad—they're such upstanding people. And yet here's Rohit, parading his scandalous life for the entire Indian community to see."

"Rude Rohit," they both said in unison, chuckling.

"Anyway, back to why you've been drinking midday without me. Was that what your emergency text was all about?" Deena teased, pouring tea for two—a signal that she was ready to dive into the latest gossip.

Manisha groaned, burying her face in her hands. "Ugh, today has been a disaster from the second I stepped into Dr. Rocky's office."

"The fertility doctor! You went already! How did it go? I want to hear everything!" Deena bounced up and down on her toes in anticipation.

Manisha fell silent, unsure of how to even begin.

"Wait a second," Deena said, concern emanating from her. "Is that what led you to the nearest Baskin bar?"

Manisha nodded. "Yeah, something like that." She took a deep breath. "He—Dr. Rocky had some not-so-great news to share." Manisha grabbed her purse from the counter and began pulling out the pamphlets he had given her. She placed them one by one on the island.

"What's all this?" Deena asked, handing Manisha a steaming cup of tea.

Deena picked up the pamphlets, her brow furrowing as she read the headings. "'What is embryo cryopreservation?' 'Newest in sperm bank technology.' 'Your private sperm donor.' 'His sperm, your baby.'" She looked up, her eyes scrunched with confusion. "I don't understand—why do you have all these? Where are the pamphlets for freezing your eggs?"

"They didn't give me any," Manisha replied with a shrug.

"Okay, but why do you need all this?" Deena fluttered the pamphlets in the air, her impatience evident.

"It turns out that age isn't the only determining factor in egg freezing," Manisha said flatly. "And based on my results today, Dr. Rocky recommended I explore all my options, and maybe consider a different path."

"The embryos path? But you need sperm for that. Does Dr. Rocky have any?"

"He probably does, but not for me." Manisha sniggered at her own quip, though Deena didn't share her laughter.

She sobered under her cousin's cool stare. "Sorry. Basically, these are the current sperm options he thinks I should weigh, especially given the tight timeline."

"Alright then, options it is," Deena said, trying to sound hopeful. "Look, he's right. There's nothing wrong with thinking ahead and strategizing here."

Manisha bit her lip, her heart pounding. "But there's more, Deena."

"More . . . options?" Deena asked, raising her voice slightly.

"Not exactly. The thing is, all these options come with a steep price tag—somewhere around fifty thousand dollars," Manisha added.

Deena looked perplexed. "But Manisha, I don't understand. Fifty thousand is nothing for you—it's like a mini Birkin bag to you."

Manisha winced. "It *was* nothing . . ."

"What do you mean, 'was'?" Deena asked.

"Deena, I've been meaning to tell you something else," Manisha began, her voice trembling. "I'm not as financially stable as I once was. I mean, I can't afford that kind of thing anymore."

The furrow between Deena's brows deepened. "But you're carrying around a ten-thousand-dollar designer bag right now! It's a month old. I just saw it on your Instagram!"

"Which I probably shouldn't have bought," Manisha admitted. "After the breakup, I went on a shopping spree down Bond Street. It was my version of retail therapy."

"I get that, but is it really all gone?" Deena's expression shifted with concern. She paused, her voice serious. "Manisha, I wish I could lend you that kind of money, but all my finances go through Mom and Dad, especially for something that big."

"Oh, I know," Manisha responded instantly. "I wasn't asking for help. I genuinely appreciate you considering it. And I can't go to my mom, either; if I do, she'll discover that I've spent nearly all my money this year. She doesn't even know about Oliver, let alone the breakup."

"Alright, so the Bank of Ruby and Ashok is off the table. That means the Bank of Your Brothers is out, too," Deena said, browsing through a pamphlet. "But hold on—what about a layaway plan?"

"You need some initial payment just to start that. All my accounts are drained, and my credit score is terrible."

Deena exhaled slowly, taking in the situation. "Wow . . . Hold on! You're currently on a sabbatical, right? Don't those usually come with pay? Or couldn't you return to work sooner and start rebuilding your savings?"

Time to drop another bomb. "Um, Deena, about that sabbatical. There's something else I haven't told you."

"Come on, Manisha, what more could possibly be left?"

"I can't go back to work," Manisha admitted, "because there's no work to go back to."

"What?" Deena's eyes popped in disbelief.

Manisha's heart raced as she struggled to catch her breath. After a moment's hesitation, she confessed, "I quit because they took my promotion away."

"But why?" Deena asked, frowning.

Manisha reached for her phone, knowing it was time to show Deena the video. "A few months ago, I went out with my co-workers for drinks and ran into Oliver. This was right after the breakup and right after I found out he was cheating. I might have had a bit too much to drink that night—"

"Like today?" Deena interjected, a playful smirk tugging at her lips.

Manisha flushed. "Yes, exactly like today. And . . . well, I said some things I probably shouldn't have—specifically to him."

"Okay, so you told him off like you did with Rohit," Deena guessed. "They can't fire you for that, can they?"

"You're right, they can't. But they can demote you for threatening to sue on the company's behalf," Manisha said, her voice tinged with regret. "I was furious when I saw Oliver with that law student he was dating, and I completely lost it. I shouted something like, 'The firm where I'm a senior partner is going to sue you for being a jerk!'"

She took a deep breath and took a sip of her tea, trying to keep her emotions in check. "And, of course, someone recorded the whole thing and sent it to McGuire & McLeod. They told me my behaviour didn't reflect the company's values, and that it was unprofessional for someone in my role. They offered me a consultant position, after demoting me."

"A consultant?" Deena said, incredulous. "No way."

"That's exactly what I said! No way! I didn't deserve to be demoted." Manisha sighed, rubbing her temples. "That firm became one of the most sought-after in the city because of me. Sure, my actions weren't exactly professional that night, but it was a mistake. Who hasn't had a little meltdown, right?"

Deena raised an eyebrow. "But how little of a meltdown are we talking about?"

Manisha didn't respond. Instead, she handed her phone to Deena. As Deena hit play, her expression shifted from one of dubiousness to outright shock.

"So, we're looking at a solid six and a half on the meltdown scale here," Deena said. "Seriously, did you have to punch him, Manisha?"

"I didn't actually punch him," Manisha protested.

"Manisha, you swung—"

"Into the air!" she interrupted. "I wasn't actually going to hit him."

"I get it. You had a few drinks. You saw your ex—"

"My cheating ex," Manisha amended.

"Yes, right. You saw your cheating ex having the time of his life. You had every right to lose it. I would have done worse." Deena paused, her eyes suddenly going wide. "Wait. Holy shit." She looked up at Manisha. "This video has over half a million views."

"And counting!" Manisha groaned, slumping in her seat. Despite her best efforts, she couldn't get the original taken down, let alone the dozens of copies floating around. "Now do you under-stand why I can't show my face on dating apps? The last thing I want is some guy I'm interested in stumbling across this disaster. It's already bad enough trying to keep my family in the dark."

"Your mom would kill you."

"She would," Manisha agreed, shuddering at the thought. "If she saw that video, she'd probably re-enact a Bollywood scene, and not the kind with a happy ending."

Deena studied her. "I don't get it. Why aren't you more upset? I'd be furious if this happened to me and I lost a promo-tion I'd worked my ass off for."

Manisha shrugged. "I don't know, Deena. Sure, the money's great, but being a lawyer, taking money from the poor to help the rich—it's not exactly what I imagined for myself. I didn't

want things to go down this way, but I don't think I really wanted
to stay at McGuire & McLeod. Becoming a senior partner was
supposed to feel like an accomplishment, but honestly? It was
just . . . unfulfilling."

Deena looked at her thoughtfully. "Okay, let's focus on one
thing at a time. How much money do you have?"

Manisha winced. "I have, like, five thousand dollars I could
give you."

Deena let out a frustrated groan.

"Honestly, I've got nothing. I'm drowning in credit card debt,
especially after Sanj's wedding. I can't put a penny toward any of
this. The only thing I'm glad about is that I paid my rent for the
rest of the year already!" She glanced at the pamphlets on the
table, eyes narrowing. "No money, no eggs, no sperm."

Deena's face lit up with an idea. "What about selling some of
your post-breakup purchases?"

Manisha shook her head. "I'd have to deal with consignment
shops and probably wait forever for authentication and a buyer.
And even then, most of my items wouldn't fetch anywhere near
what I paid for them."

A heavy silence settled over the room, one of those rare
moments when neither cousin had the energy to speak. Usually,
their conversations were fast-paced and animated. But not now.

Finally, Deena broke the quiet. "Manisha, remember when
we were kids, dreaming about getting married and starting families? Is that still what you want?"

"Absolutely," Manisha said without missing a beat.

"Okay . . ." Deena hesitated, then continued, "But using a
donor's sperm? I don't know . . ."

"It's not how I imagined things, either. I always envisioned
finding someone, having a big Indian wedding, then starting a

family together. Look, it's even on my vision board." Manisha pulled out her phone and showed Deena a picture of her vision board, brimming with images of the sort.

Deena studied it and then nodded. "Well, if it's on your vision board, it has to happen. We just need to figure out how."

They both sat in silence again, lost in their thoughts. Finally, Deena spoke. "What else did Dr. Rocky say?"

"I don't know. He said something about how I could just walk down the street and find my 'Prince Charming,'" Manisha said with a roll of her eyes.

"What?"

Manisha shrugged. "It was more of a joke, but he suggested I find a boyfriend, a partner . . . a guy." She set her phone on the table, the vision board lighting up again.

Deena straightened, her eyes lighting up with excitement. "How much time do we have to find this guy?"

Manisha shrugged. "I'm not sure. But given my situation, he hinted that I need to move fast. Apparently, time isn't exactly on my side."

"Don't stress. You just need to hit the gas and make this mission happen faster than expected. It's like why you're back in town—new man, maybe a new job . . ." Deena looked at her with a glint of mischief in her eyes.

"Something like that," Manisha murmured, but she could feel a sense of defeat creeping in.

Without warning, Deena jumped up and rushed out of the kitchen, returning seconds later with her laptop in hand. She settled back in beside Manisha and started typing furiously.

"Okay, check this out." She turned the screen toward Manisha. "This is a website from one of the sperm banks. It's incredible how detailed it is. You can choose based on race and ethnicity, eye colour, age, height, medical history, profession. It's like a dream come true for selecting sperm."

Manisha read through the page. "It is impressive, I'll give you that." She leaned back, a frown tugging at her lips. "But it still feels so unfair. Sanj and Sammy found their perfect matches, fell in love, and are on the fast track to babies. Here I am, picking from some strangers on a website I can't even afford!"

She dropped her head dramatically to the counter, forehead coming to rest on the cool surface. "Mom was so wrong about the Patels being 'blessed,'" she said, her words muffled.

"What do you mean?"

Manisha turned her head to the side, cheek pressed into the granite. "She always goes on about how every member of our family finds love almost overnight. She calls it the 'Patel Blessing.' Maybe I was adopted," Manisha added with a small laugh.

Deena rolled her eyes. "You're definitely not adopted. We just need to channel those genes. Channel that blessing!"

"How?" Manisha raised an eyebrow. "The dating apps aren't exactly brimming with Prince Charmings. And it could take months, maybe even years."

Deena gave her a pointed look. "It's true. I'll be the first to acknowledge that. But hear me out." She waved Manisha's phone in front of her face. "What if we had a shortcut? What if there was a Man Bank?"

Manisha sat up. "What are you talking about?"

Deena's eyes danced with mischief. "I'm talking about a matchmaking site. But instead of the perfect sperm, we help you find the perfect partner."

Manisha raised an eyebrow. "Are you serious?"

"I'm serious!" Deena's fingers were already flying over her keyboard. "Guys can send their bios to an 'auntie'—like an Indian matchmaker. But in reality, it's you and me doing the vetting. We filter through their details based on your requirements and find your perfect match. No dating apps, no embarrassing setups. Just one tailored guy who fits exactly what you need."

Manisha's curiosity was undeniably piqued. "So, no public profiles? No swiping? Just you and me sifting through resumés to find my Prince Charming?"

"Exactly!" Deena grinned. "I'll handle the website, SEO, and all the details. It's going to be perfect!"

Manisha thought about it for a moment. "This could actually work. But wait, you have to let me help with *something*. I can't just sit back and let you do everything."

"Fine. You can help with some of the admin, general query emails or whatever. No filtering profiles for you though—let me handle that. Trust me, dear cousin," Deena said.

"Okay, but we've got to move quickly. Time is ticking, and building a family has to be my priority now."

Deena's eyes gleamed. "We'll make it happen. This is the magic we've been waiting for."

Manisha smiled to herself, the word "magic" taking on a new, deeper meaning. Maybe—just maybe—this was the beginning of something.

## 10

After spending most of the evening at Deena's loft brainstorming, Manisha left feeling more energized than she had in weeks. What initially seemed like a far-fetched plan now appeared feasible—a viable alternative that was also more budget-friendly than the options Dr. Rocky had proposed.

As she strolled through the lively streets of downtown Baskin, her eyes were drawn to the many couples surrounding her, all clearly wrapped up in their love. She thought back to what Oliver had said, that Manisha was too focused on her career ambitions to give him the attention he sought. It was true that she was, at one point, driven in her pursuit of becoming a senior partner. But no, she wasn't to blame for their split. He was the one who had betrayed their relationship.

Then again . . . had her lack of interest in their romance stemmed from an underlying hesitation to embrace the kind of love she now witnessed thriving around her? Perhaps Oliver had been on to something there. Maybe Manisha had secretly always yearned to be with an Indian man. Whatever the reason, Oliver was now a chapter closed, and Prince Charming represented the promise of her future. Manisha felt a thrill that eclipsed anything she'd experienced with that cheater.

Turning a corner, she caught a glimpse of her reflection in a restaurant window and a surge of confidence coursed through her—something she hadn't felt in months.

"Move aside, lady!" A cyclist zipped past Manisha, jolting her from the moment. She let out an instinctive yelp, stumbling back.

"Oy! Take it easy!" she shouted after him, once she'd regained her composure.

"Forget you!" he shot back.

"Right back at you!" she retorted.

At that exact second, Rohit emerged from the restaurant, catching her off guard with nowhere to hide.

"Manisha? What are you doing here? I thought I heard yelling," Rohit exclaimed in surprise.

"Oh, hey," she replied, waving lamely, just as startled to see him.

"Still roaming the streets looking for another drink?" Rohit joked, his voice dripping with amusement.

"Oh, come on! Don't make a big deal out of it just because I decided to have a little fun in the middle of the day. You're probably just jealous that I can actually let loose," she ribbed back.

Rohit chuckled. "I'm not one to judge, especially when it comes to lawyers like you. You all have your special ways of having fun."

What in the world was that supposed to mean? "I really don't know what you're implying," she said, annoyance slipping into her tone.

He had the decency to look rueful, one hand sliding to the back of his neck. A sigh escaped her lips; she was getting increasingly weary of their bickering. "If you must know, I'm just heading home."

"As long as you're going somewhere safe," he replied lightly.

Manisha furrowed her brows with suspicion. "Why do you care where I go?"

"I really don't," he said, shrugging. "I was having a quiet night until I heard the chaos outside. Figured I'd capture whatever was happening on my phone just in case. You never know these days." He brandished his phone in front of her.

Manisha's eyes flared, her mind dragging her right back to the night of her viral video moment in London. Warmth filled her cheeks.

"Manisha? Hello, earth to Manisha! You alright?" He waved his hand directly in her face to get her attention.

She dragged herself back from the past, clambering for something to say. She narrowed her eyes at Rohit. "I was—until I remembered that your obsession with your phone cost me my parking spot yesterday," she retorted. "You know, you could've hit me!"

"Here we go again." His eyes rolled.

"What is your problem?" she said. "You're so—"

"Rude? You've already thrown that one out there."

"Honestly, you are!" Manisha shot back.

"Manisha, you're just as rude as I am! It's like you've got a personal vendetta against me!"

"You wish. I don't have time to think about you," she countered, lifting her chin to look down her nose at him. Well, as best as she could given his height.

"So, instead, you just happen to be trailing me?" he shot back.

"I wasn't trailing you! This is the way back to my parents' from Deena's!"

"Well, at least you're on foot and not behind the wheel."

"God, your arrogance is—"

Before Manisha could complete her sentence, the restaurant door swung open, and Suzy stepped out.

"Oh, hi! Manisha, right?" Suzy beamed at her. Manisha just stared.

Rohit cleared his throat, sensing the sudden shift in the atmosphere. "Suzy, Manisha was just—"

"Leaving," Manisha cut in, completing his thought.

Suzy's face fell, disappointment evident in her eyes. "Oh, please don't go. We're about to grab drinks across the street. You should really join us!"

Manisha shook her head, forcing a polite smile. "I appreciate the invite, but I promised my parents I'd spend some time with them tonight."

Rohit quickly jumped in. "Honestly, I think Manisha's had enough excitement for one day," he said, his tone implying he wanted to wrap things up.

"Yeah, I like to keep my drinking to a minimum," Manisha added, her sarcasm barely concealed.

"That's such a bummer! I was really looking forward to hearing more about this amazing guy from his friends," Suzy remarked with a playful nudge toward Rohit, her hand resting on his arm.

"Amazing?" Manisha replied, her eyes widening in disbelief.

"Hard to believe?" Rohit shot back with a smirk, then turned to Suzy, placing a hand over hers. "Really, tonight's not the best time; we've got so much catching up to do. Maybe another time?"

"Yeah, I'll save my incredible 'Ro' stories for another time. Honestly, there are so many that I wouldn't even know where to start." Manisha skewered Rohit with a pointed look.

"Another time it is, then. I, for one, can't wait to hear them," Rohit replied with a hint of disdain.

"You two have a wonderful date night! I'll see you soon,

Suzy," Manisha said, walking away. She cast one last glance back, muttering under her breath, "But hopefully not too soon." The sight of the two of them together irked her to no end.

She was turning onto her parents' street when Dr. Rocky's parting words popped into her thoughts. *Maybe you'll bump into Prince Charming on your walk home.*

She snorted. So far, the only guy she'd run into was Rohit—and he was far from the type of man Dr. Rocky or she envisioned for her fertility journey—or any journey, for that matter.

She pushed those thoughts aside. Soon, with Deena's help, she would find the right guy. She had to.

Feeling renewed determination, she walked the last bit home with a newfound pep in her step.

## 11

"*I* feel like we should be at home working on the website or something. Do we even have a name?" Manisha asked, adjusting the hem of a fitted black Stella McCartney blazer dress that hugged her curves comfortably.

She and Deena carefully made their way down the narrow staircase of the lively karaoke bar, the sound of their heels echoing against the polished wooden steps. The air was thick with the stale scent of beer and cheap cologne.

"I'm working on that! You'd think it would be easy to come up with a name for a fake matchmaking site, but it's not!" Deena chuckled. She was dressed in a trendy combo of high-waisted jeans and a vibrant off-the-shoulder red blouse that fluttered with every step.

"Anyway, I needed a break from the fake!" she continued and shot Manisha a pitiful look. "I've been at it non-stop for two days. But tonight is about fun! We're going to let loose." She tousled her hair, flashing a playful grin.

"Okay, fine!" Manisha relented. She bit her lip nervously as she surveyed the room. The bar buzzed with energy. Patrons devoured heaping plates of nachos and bottomless glasses of cheap wine. Laughter and cheers created an electric atmosphere, and colourful lights danced around the room, illuminating the small stage where a karaoke machine awaited its next aspiring rock star.

"Why this place of all places to have 'fun'?" Manisha asked, bemused.

"I wanted somewhere we could unwind without worrying about running into anyone we know. I want you to have a good time, Manisha! No one's going to know us here," Deena explained.

"Thanks, Deena. I appreciate you looking out for me!" Manisha said.

"Anything for my favourite cousin. Now, I need to hit the restroom, so can you grab us drinks? Strong ones," Deena shouted, her voice barely cutting through the lively chorus of "Livin' on a Prayer" resonating from the stage. With a quick wave, she vanished into the crowd, leaving Manisha to navigate her way to the bar.

She flagged down a bartender and ordered two vodka sodas, then turned to watch the performance. A nearby group clapped and shouted encouragement as their pals belted their hearts out onstage. Deena was right; they needed a night out. The past few days had been filled with restless nights and anxiety.

She spotted a flash of Deena's red blouse and waved to catch her attention.

"Is this all you got?" Deena scrunched her nose, getting there just as the bartender slid the drinks toward them. "Hey, can we also grab two whiskey shots?" she asked before he left. He threw her a wink to confirm.

Deena grabbed a glass, clinked it against Manisha's, and then guzzled it down. "Bottoms up, Manisha!"

Manisha swirled her drink in response.

"Hey, stop worrying. Surrender to the fun! Everything will work itself out," Deena reassured her, grinning. "You just have to let the universe do its thing."

"Now you're starting to sound like Meena Auntie," Manisha teased, taking a huge sip.

Deena shrugged, a playful glint in her eye. "Maybe she has the right idea."

Leaning closer, Manisha raised her voice above the couple belting out a duet onstage. "What do you mean?"

"There's just something about her. She's like, I don't know—"

"Magical?" Manisha blurted out, finishing Deena's thought.

"Yes! That's the word I was looking for. Meena Auntie is magical."

Deena thanked the bartender as he returned with their shots. "I visited her the other day, and she said some things that really made me think," she revealed.

"You did what?" Manisha gasped, her eyebrows shooting up in disbelief.

"I know, I know! But my friend has an aunt whose daughter was about to marry this guy. Turns out he was seeing someone else—and his family knew about it, too. Anyway, post-breakup with him, her daughter went to see Meena Auntie about her future—and two months later, we got a wedding invitation from her and her new man!"

"Wow! What happened to the first guy?" Manisha asked, invested.

"His other girlfriend found out and dumped him, but not before spilling that his family had been in on the whole thing over an Instagram Live," Deena added with a smirk.

"Unreal!" Manisha said, shaking her head.

"I've heard Meena Auntie's helped a lot of people with their problems, and honestly, I'm having no luck with online dating. At this point, why not give her a shot? She might be a little eccentric, but aren't we all a bit out there?"

"You're creating a website for a fake matchmaking auntie, and her only client is me. Yes, I'd say we're all a little out there." Manisha chuckled.

"Well, cheers to that!" Deena laughed, passing a shot to Manisha. A quick cheers, then they downed them.

"Two more vodka sodas, please—but make them doubles!" Deena called to the bartender while Manisha chased the shot with a sip of her first drink.

"Meena Auntie might not be everyone's cup of chai, but I have to say, I left that appointment with a sense of optimism. You should think about visiting her," Deena suggested.

"Actually, she already stopped by my place," Manisha replied, wincing at the memory.

"No way! To your house? She doesn't make house calls anymore! You're so lucky!" Deena exclaimed in disbelief.

"Seriously?"

"Absolutely! I heard she stopped visiting people because her special skills were just too intense. Some folks went into literal shock—frozen stiff like a statue, and it took them months to thaw out," Deena declared.

"Sounds like something out of Greek mythology," Manisha remarked with a smirk. "Mind you, she showed up at my parents' unexpectedly and it was odd; I felt like I was in a trance the whole time she was there."

"See, you were almost frozen like the others!" Deena cried.

"Anyway," Manisha continued, "as she was leaving, she handed me something."

She reached into her purse and pulled out the sachet of white seeds.

"Holy shit, me too! Mine are blue! Look!" Deena exclaimed, pulling out an identical bag from her jean pocket.

"Oh my god!" Manisha whispered. "Why are yours blue?" she asked.

"Well, they're customized for each customer's needs," Deena replied, slightly slurring as the whiskey began to kick in. "It's not like she just pulls them out of a candy machine. Meena Auntie makes them fresh for everyone."

"I had no idea."

"Yeah, mine are like 'destined to find me love,'" Deena practically squealed, her excitement bubbling over.

"I can't remember mine exactly, but it was something about a new life or something along those lines . . ."

"Manisha Patel! Why didn't you mention this sooner? It's like she's basically delivering you baby news!" Deena exclaimed, pulling Manisha into an enthusiastic hug.

Manisha chuckled. "Wow, you're channelling my mom right now." She took another hearty gulp of her drink before asking, "But seriously, why haven't you taken them?"

"Well," Deena huffed, "I've been a bit preoccupied, in case you forgot. And you? Why haven't you taken yours?"

"I'm just not sure . . . Aren't you at all scared of what they'll do to you? Like, what if I get high or something worse? We're not exactly in Ibiza."

Deena shimmied her shoulders and waggled her brows at the mention of Ibiza, conjuring the memory of their unspeakably wild nights of dancing and more until sunrise. The bartender chose that moment to place their two double vodka sodas in front of them, and the cousins burst into laughter.

"Okay," Deena gasped, catching her breath. "But what if you become pregnant? Manisha, what if these are meant to nurture a new life within you?"

"Deena, I hate to break it to you, but I also need sperm."

"We're working on that, remember?" Deena reminded Manisha.

"How could I forget," she scoffed.

"All I'm saying is these seeds plus some sperm, and poof, a baby." Deena gestured animatedly with her hands, emphasizing the word poof. "Baby-making through the magic of Meena Auntie!"

Manisha laughed. "You think that's how this works? If so, then poof to you finding love!"

"I just thought of something."

"What?" Manisha asked warily.

"Why don't we take these seeds together?" Deena said, pumped.

"Right now? Right here?"

"What's the worst that can happen?" Deena asked.

"Ibiza," they both said at the same time.

"Seriously though, Manisha, it's not like any temple-going auntie is going to distribute disguised ecstasy pills to a bunch of Indian kids."

"I suppose you're right," Manisha replied cautiously.

Deena poured her blue seeds onto her palm and eyed Manisha, willing her to do the same.

Manisha hesitated, but Deena was right. Meena Auntie wasn't looking to harm anyone. In fact, from their one encounter, Manisha had felt safe in her presence. Entranced, but safe.

The cousins looked at each other and quickly threw the seeds in their mouths like kids eating Pop Rocks—but now, as adults, they were washing them down with vodka sodas.

"We did it!" Deena declared. They'd done something, alright.

Before Manisha could say anything back, she heard their names being called.

"Manisha and Deena, get ready to take the stage after the upcoming song," the DJ called out.

"Deena!" Manisha looked at her in shock. "You added us to the karaoke lineup?"

"Absolutely," Deena grinned. "Let's do it."

"Absolutely not."

"There's a high probability I am not listening to you." Deena tugged at Manisha's arm, pulling her to the stage. The drinks (or maybe the seeds?) were starting to take their toll on Manisha, but she knew she had only a few seconds to get fully on board before the music started.

"What song are we singing?" she asked. Her question was nearly drowned out by the cheers and applause from the crowd as they made their way to the stage.

"'Step by Step' . . . New Kids on the Block, obviously!" Manisha began singing, the lyrics flowing effortlessly from her lips. As she stood under the spotlight next to her cousin, she felt her nerves melt away and make room for joy. With each note, she took another step toward her new life.

## 12

*O*ne night later, as Manisha nestled into her bed, she glanced at her phone, a grin spreading across her face. The memories of the lively brainstorming session following karaoke night at Deena's kitchen table rushed back to her—where laughter and bursts of creativity blended with just a touch too much vodka.

While they'd waited for their shawarmas to arrive, Manisha had joked about wanting to find a man who shared her passion for food, sparking the playful idea of "Curry and Cupid."

"And the tagline could be, 'Spicing up your love life, one match at a time!'" Deena had chimed in.

"I love it! Who wouldn't want to explore romance over a shared curry platter?" Manisha had said, excitement bubbling within her.

Just as she was about to drift off, her phone buzzed to life. It had been a long day—filled with errand-running with her mother, helping her dad around the house, and keeping up with Deena's updates about the website. Finally, Deena had launched Curry and Cupid, and the mere idea of a Bollywood-style romance blossoming sent a tingle through Manisha. Despite her exhaustion, the anticipation of what was to come pulled her out of her drowsiness and prompted her to reach for her phone.

The profiles are rolling in fast, Deena texted.

Manisha jolted upright in bed, surprised. She knew Deena had strong marketing instincts, but Manisha hadn't expected such swift results virtually overnight. It was both thrilling and a little intimidating to realize that men were actively seeking love, even if it was through a somewhat dubious matchmaking platform. But she didn't have the luxury of pondering that right now; another text pinged on her phone.

About half a dozen profiles.

Wow, that's amazing! Manisha replied.

Deena wasted no time writing a follow-up text. I've narrowed it down to two potential dates for you. Clear your schedule for tomorrow!

Two dates in one day? she typed back, incredulous.

Remember what I told you? Don't expect to be the only one on your date's radar that day, either!

Manisha groaned lightly. Alright, two dates it is! I'll manage!

We're on track with everything you wanted in your Prince Charming: strong family values, ambitious, goal-oriented, and cute.

Don't forget, MUST LOVE FOOD! Manisha typed back.

Deena replied with a playful Ha, ha! Yes!

Before she could second-guess her instincts, Manisha typed, Maybe those seeds really are working!

Told you! Never underestimate the power of a mysterious auntie, LOL... Deena replied. Sending you an email with more info.

Almost immediately, an email notification popped up on Manisha's screen.

I've attached details for both dates. Take some time to familiarize yourself with them—it's . . .

Intrigued, Manisha opened the PDF and began to delve into the profiles of her first two dates, Paul and Arinder.

Paul was a family-oriented man who co-owned a business with his sister, a venture they had nurtured from the ground up. His profile picture captured him in a lively family gathering, laughter illuminating his face and giving her a glimpse into his warm personality.

His family reminded Manisha so much of her own family.

He dedicated his weekends to volunteering at the Boys and Girls Club and organizing community events aimed at uplifting underprivileged children.

Okay, with his passion for entrepreneurship and commitment to family, this Paul was a gem!

Her heart raced when she noticed his list of interests: hiking in local parks, cooking Italian cuisine, and indulging in road trips with his close-knit family.

Paul was really setting the bar high for Curry and Cupid matches.

Next, she turned her attention to Arinder's profile. An only child, he had managed to capture a truly endearing moment in his profile: a snapshot of him and his mom, both flashing radiant smiles against the backdrop of the Taj Mahal. Arinder, a self-proclaimed foodie, loved exploring culinary delights from different cultures and often shared recommendations on his food blog, which he maintained alongside his full-time job in tech.

And his favourite wine was Barolo? He was making her thirsty!

He was also an avid chess player, regularly attending tournaments at the local chess club, where he had a reputation for being a strategic thinker. Impressive!

His weekends often involved trying out new restaurants or hosting dinner parties for friends, where he showcased his cooking talents.

Manisha was genuinely intrigued; both men had distinct qualities that piqued her interest. And from what she could glean, they would make great dads.

Still, there was one more important thing to do. She opened her Instagram and searched for Paul and Arinder, hoping not to discover any viral moments like hers. Thankfully, all she found were unassuming posts: Paul with his sister at a charity event and Arinder sharing a scenic photo of a vineyard tour. What a relief!

Deena texted to confirm, So, you'll meet Paul at 4 p.m. and Arinder at 5 p.m.

Okay, back-to-back dates. If you can do this . . . I can do this. Where? Manisha replied, her determination growing.

Everyone is doing this. Chai Time. Sweet dreams.

Manisha flopped back onto her pillow with a groan.

$\mathcal{T}$he following day, Manisha woke up brimming with anxious excitement. She spent the morning puttering around the house, helping her parents when called upon, trying to work off her nerves. But by the time early afternoon rolled around, she'd worked herself into a frenzy. Looking the part, she could handle. But how to act, what to look for . . . it had been years since her last first date.

*I need to talk to Manny*, she said to herself as she tied off the belt of her Zimmerman wrap dress.

Deena had already played her part as the faux auntie on the matchmaking site, using her marketing skills to attract potential suitors for Manisha. Now it was time to seek advice from the real relationship expert, Manny Dogra.

Manny, her soon-to-be sister-in-law, ran a hugely successful breakup agency and had fallen head over heels for Manisha's brother, Sammy, in just a week. With Manny's guidance, she'd learn to differentiate between a great guy and the type Manny usually ended things with for her clients.

An hour later, Manisha arrived at Manny and Sammy's home, where Manny excitedly greeted her before she even reached the door.

"Ish! Come on in! It's just us—your brother's out grabbing a few things," she called. Welcoming Manisha with arms wide, she pulled her into a warm hug. The moment Manny's arms wrapped around her, Manisha felt the tension in her begin to unravel. An easy comfort settled in, the kind she'd felt the first time she met Manny. Even though they'd only known each other for a few weeks, it felt like they were sisters from different misters.

"Love the dress!" Manny cooed, stepping back. "Come on, let's head to the kitchen."

As they strolled through the grand hall of their lakeside home—Sammy had recently moved into Manny's place—Manisha marvelled at the blend of rustic charm and modern sophistication. The high ceilings and large windows overlooking Baskin Lake made the house feel like a ship sailing on the water.

"Drink?" Manny asked, moving to the fridge as Manisha slid onto a sleek black leather stool at the kitchen island. "I have an open Pinot here calling your name."

"Yes, please," she answered automatically.

"So, you've decided to date while you're back in Baskin?" Manny asked. "I think that's fantastic! I used to have this Bridget Jones-like fantasy of escaping to the UK to find myself a brown bloke before I met your brother." She handed Manisha her glass. "We'd explore the Indian food scene, enjoy the theatre, and share drinks with friends. Please humour me and tell me you've had a romantic encounter that even slightly resembles my fantasy!"

Manisha laughed lightly. "Of course I did, Manny. He was, um, an Indian lawyer. I'll leave the juicy details to your imagination." In truth, he was definitely not Indian, and more of a law professor who had broken her heart. She watched Manny crack open a Diet Coke and take a sip. Perhaps she should've opted for one too before her date, but her nerves demanded a little wine to calm her.

"I knew it! Well, since you're back, you might as well keep busy. Besides, most of the men in Baskin are underrated and make fantastic partners."

"Even if you're breaking their hearts for a living?"

"I said most, didn't I?" Manny shot back with a laugh. "And you know what? I break people up because they really shouldn't be together in the first place. Once their hearts heal, they usually thank me."

"I believe it. Well, it's just a few dates here and there for me. You know, to keep Mama Patel happy. No big deal." Except she was trying to find the father of her future children.

"I wanted to ask you, Ish. What about London? You're still planning to go back, right?" Manny probed gently.

Manisha felt a tightening in her throat. "Of course I am. Like I said, I've just taken a little sabbatical from my lawyer duties. You know how it is—working tirelessly for so long can lead to serious burnout."

"Yeah, I get it. And if going on a few dates while you're here helps keep Mama Patel from nagging you . . ." Manny replied, shooting Manisha a knowing look.

"Exactly." Manisha laughed before her expression shifted to seriousness. "Manny, fill me in. What should I expect? With all those long hours at the firm, I never really had a chance to date." That was half true. Work had made it tough for Oliver and her to see each other.

"I'm curious about what it's really like out there. What are your clients dealing with? What sort of advice are you offering them? Deena keeps saying it's a jungle out there, every person for themselves." Manisha took a sip of her wine, hoping to alleviate the sudden dryness in her mouth.

"Honestly, the dating landscape is wild at the moment. It's fantastic for my business but not so wonderful for anyone searching for that perfect match. But you won't have to worry about that." Manny waved her off. "I've got some casual, everyday tips and tricks ready to share." She went to the living room, grabbed a whiteboard that had been propped against the fireplace, and brought it into the kitchen.

Manisha's eyes grew large as she examined the board more closely. It was filled with notes and scribbles, leaving her unsure where one idea ended and another began.

Was there more on the other side?

"I know it looks overwhelming," Manny said, adjusting the whiteboard for a better view.

"You can definitely say that again," Manisha mumbled.

"We're just focusing on the basics for your first date," Manny said, smiling encouragingly.

Manisha was taken aback, her mouth hanging open. "These are the basics?"

"These are the basics," Manny replied, chuckling.

"Well, we only have an hour before my date with Paul," Manisha quipped.

"If I can break people up in seconds, I can teach you Dating 101 in a flash!" Manny laughed, gesturing toward the board. "Alright, let's get into the rules of dating. Number one: Make sure you show up for your date."

"That's obvious," Manisha retorted.

"Used to be. But I don't just mean physically show up. The key is to be your authentic self and stay engaged. Put your phone away and eliminate distractions. Give your date a real chance. Meeting someone new can be nerve-racking for both parties!"

"Totally makes sense. I've seen plenty of couples glued to their phones or lost in their own worlds when they're together." Manisha's thoughts drifted to all the times Oliver had been absorbed in his phone while he was cheating on her.

"Exactly! Being present is crucial. On to rule number two: Share your must-haves and dealbreakers upfront. Not the trivial stuff, like leaving the toothpaste cap off, but what you truly value and won't compromise on."

*A baby*, Manisha thought immediately. But what she said was, "Right. Like ambition, family, and giving back to the community . . ."

"Yes! All that should be on the table early on. If a guy claims he can't stand his mom but still depends on her and has only done community service as part of his probation—"

Manisha burst into laughter. "Come on, Manny! Be for real!"

"That's actually a true story from a client."

"What!" Manisha exclaimed, shocked.

"But I digress. Now that we've covered what to do, let's go into what not to do." Manny pointed to a different section on the board. "First, don't dominate the conversation. Ask questions and show genuine curiosity. You've got a lifetime to talk over each other, but listening for cues and being interested in the other person is essential."

Manisha nodded her understanding.

"Which leads us to the last cardinal rule: Avoid being rude or disrespectful."

Manisha nearly choked on her wine at the word "rude," recalling her recent encounters with Rohit. "I wouldn't," she managed to say weakly.

"I'm serious! Remember, it's just as tough for men to make a good impression," Manny continued. "Don't be too quick to judge or dismiss. Give them time and space to showcase their best selves. It might take a few minutes."

"Alright, I suppose I can be a bit too critical too fast sometimes," Manisha admitted.

"We all jump to conclusions, but awareness is key. And that's it! Oh, but most importantly, don't forget to have fun!"

"Fun is my middle name," Manisha joked, as she tipped back and drained her glass.

"Is it? I thought it was 'Busy'!" Manny laughed. "There's more if you want another?" she tilted her head to the fridge.

Manisha glanced at the microwave clock and jolted at the time. "Oh wow, time flies! I should get going." She stood. "Thanks, Manny. I really appreciate all this."

"Of course!" They moved in for a hug, when Manny added, "Did I say that I'm proud of you for putting yourself out there, even if it is just to appease your mom? I know it isn't easy being this vulnerable."

Manisha's breath hitched, surprised to find that Manny's words struck something deep inside of her. "I— Thank you for saying that, Manny," she whispered. "I'll be the first to admit that I'm really, really nervous."

Manny pulled away and met her eyes. "You have nothing to be nervous about," she said with a warm smile. "Let me remind you, Isha is the one with that infectious laugh who doesn't let anyone get away with nonsense. She's the first to make you smile when you're feeling down, and trust me, she'll always appreciate a good meal . . . especially if it's something homemade. And you know she loves it when you dress up, but she's the first one to tell you that you don't need to be perfect to be amazing."

"Manny . . ." Manisha broke off. She swallowed a lump in her throat, wiping moisture from her eyes.

"Manisha, why are you putting so much pressure on yourself? This is supposed to fun, remember?"

If only she knew . . .

"I don't know—it's like you said. Being this vulnerable, with a random stranger . . ."

"Oh, that reminds me! I have something for you." She handed her a vibrant tube of red Stila lipstick. "It's my go-to confidence booster. And it's very appropriately named 'First Kiss,'" she said, with a flirty smack of her lips.

"You're the best. Thanks again, but I really should get going!" Manisha insisted, tucking the lipstick into her purse.

They made it to the door when her phone pinged loudly. It was an email notification from the dating site. She clicked on it, just in case it was one of her dates changing plans.

Dear Admin,

I'll admit I'm not usually one to jump on dating sites. But I came across this poster and curiosity got the best of me. Now, I'm definitely not the type to send emails to the back end of a website, but I have to give credit where it's due. The straight-up question-naire? Brilliant. And when I read MUST LOVE FOOD—well . . . that's the kind of vibe I'm all about.

Keep doing what you're doing because this feels refreshingly honest and original. Kudos to whoever came up with this!

—Sunil

"What are you smiling at?" Manny asked, her interest piqued, and leaned over to catch a glimpse of her screen. "What is this?"

"Oh, just the guy I'm meeting," she fibbed, hastily locking her phone and tucking it away.

"And he calls you Admin?" Manny quipped.

Manisha laughed, feeling a bit flustered. "It's a playful nickname that's trending, don't you know? Anyway, I really have to go."

"Thank God I'm not single anymore," Manny laughed, getting the door for her.

"Thanks, Manny! Bye!" Manisha dashed outside, ducking her head, and bolted for her car. Something about this Sunil's words had a blush creeping up her neck.

"You're welcome. You'll be great, Manisha!" she called after her. "Just don't forget your First Kiss!" The sound of Manny's tinkling laughter followed as Manisha sped off.

## 14

*M*anisha arrived at Chai Time a few minutes early, deciding to hold off on going inside until it was time to meet Paul. She wasn't thrilled about the dates happening at Rohit's workplace—something she'd definitely need to discuss with Deena later. It was evident that he wasn't particularly fond of her, and that was just fine. She could manage the situation gracefully, given the circumstances. She made the best of it, arranging to go over the legal paperwork with him at some point that afternoon. And Manisha could admit that Deena was right; it was also a relief to be away from the prying eyes of any aunties or uncles. As her cousin had reminded her, the gossip train was hot in Baskin for any single person.

Pulling up the email from Sunil, she read it one more time before considering how to respond. Finally, she crafted a quick reply:

Hey Sunil,
At Curry and Cupid, we're women who take our food seriously. It's less about preferences and more about non-negotiables. If you can't appreciate a perfectly spiced curry or enjoy a lazy Sunday aloo paratha brunch with your match, well, we definitely got your order wrong and probably need to find you a new date.

> Just know that as long as you're into good food,
> you've found the right place and are already halfway
> to winning our hearts! 🍽️ 💬
> Admin

After sending the message, she checked the time. It was now or never; lingering outside in the sweltering sun would only leave her sweaty and frazzled before her date. She took a deep breath, steeling herself.

As she imagined sitting across from Paul, their laughter merging with the rich aroma of coffee, she pictured her dress straps slipping off her shoulders, adding a playful flirtation to their conversation. She could almost hear her mother's voice, proud that her flirting tips were being put to good use.

In her fantasy, Paul would gently push the straps back up her shoulders, letting his fingers linger just a moment longer on her arm. It would be a date she'd never forget. With one last tousle of her wavy hair, she stepped inside, hoping to spot Deena already settled in.

The café was bustling, and Manisha quickly caught sight of Rohit at a table in the back. If he happened to notice her early arrival and wondered why she was there, she could effortlessly explain that she was meeting potential clients, just as Deena had advised. Finding a quiet corner table, she texted Deena to let her know her location.

She casually checked her messages as she waited, noting that her date was running a bit late. Tapping her foot lightly, she scrolled through Instagram to pass the time.

"Thought you could use one of these, or do you prefer something stronger?" Rohit teased, setting a cup of tea on the table.

"Thanks," Manisha replied, sounding reluctant, then fixed her gaze on him.

He stood there awkwardly for a moment.

"I said thanks," she reiterated, her voice clipped. What was he still doing there?

"Right, sorry . . . So, uh, why are you all made up?" Rohit asked, flustered.

"Made up? Gosh, you sure have a way with words," Manisha said, rolling her eyes. "I have a couple meetings with potential clients if you must know."

Rohit squinted at her. "So, you're back to work in Baskin?"

"Something like that."

"Speaking of work," he continued, "I guess you can walk me through the café papers when you're done with your meetings. My dad wants an update."

"Yeah," Manisha said, flicking her hand in the air.

"How long do you think you'll be?" Rohit asked.

"I don't know," she said irritably. She could really do without all the questions.

"You don't know, like you have no idea?"

"I don't know like *I don't know*," she snapped back. "Who are you, my personal timekeeper?"

His face soured, tone matching it. "I figured I'd ask to avoid either of us having to wait on the other. You're doing my dad a favour, sure, but the world doesn't revolve around you, Manisha. Some of us have our own things to do."

It took everything in Manisha to not literally growl at him. What could this walking embodiment of rich and entitled possibly have to do?

But she was the picture of grace, biting her tongue.

Rohit threw his hands up in exasperation. "You know what, Manisha, fine. The sooner we wrap things up, the sooner we can avoid each other."

"You can say that again." Manisha took a sip of tea and shot him a glare.

"Say what again?" Deena interjected, approaching the table and interrupting their tense exchange.

"Nothing," Manisha and Rohit chimed in unison.

Rohit let out a sigh. "I'm going to head back to the kitchen. I've suddenly developed a headache." He cast a pointed glance at Manisha before turning to go.

"Funny, I have one, too. A migraine," Manisha called after him.

"You have a migraine?" Deena asked, concern etched on her face.

"Yes! No. He's just so irritating!"

"Why are you two always at each other's throats like that?" Deena asked, exasperated. "Actually, forget it. Don't worry about Rohit. Focus on your dates."

"I can't believe I still have to help him with that paperwork for his dad afterward!" Manisha groaned.

"Let's prioritize your dates first," Deena suggested softly. She looked at Manisha and grinned. You look incredible . . . 'looking like a total VOW!'" Deena did a lousy job of striking a pose reminiscent of the viral Indian auntie from TikTok and her fashionable flair.

Manisha couldn't help but laugh, her earlier crankiness melting away. "You're too much, Deena. I really appreciate you always having my back."

"Of course! So, how are you feeling?"

"Honestly? I feel great! I'm excited, and you know what? I'll try not to put too much pressure on myself." She paused momentarily, then added with a twinkle in her eye, "Well, maybe just a pinch . . . but overall, I'm really optimistic."

Deena's smile grew even wider. "I'm feeling optimistic, too—especially since Paul is here!"

"Oh my god, he's here!"

"Oh, and if he mentions Leena Auntie . . ."

"Leena, as in my grandma?" Manisha raised an eyebrow.

"I know, I know! But your grandma is definitely more glamma than mine! I found this old profile picture of her online from her teaching days at UCLA that was perfect for Curry and Cupid's 'matchmaking auntie,' so I just popped it on to the site. Indian Grandmas don't go online."

"We haven't talked to her in ages. But whatever will find me Prince Charming."

"Alright, well he may be coming right up. Good luck! I'll be hanging out over there in case you need me." She gestured toward a quieter spot, giving Manisha a reassuring smile.

Manisha smiled as a man walked toward her, waving enthusiastically. His tall frame was dressed casually yet stylishly, his dark jeans complementing a well-fitted navy shirt that accentuated his athletic build. His hair fell in a way that looked effortlessly cool, and the warm smile he wore revealed straight white teeth, bringing out his dark brown irises.

"Manisha?" Paul inquired, his voice deep and confident.

"That's me!" Manisha said, rising to greet him, her eyes flitting over his assured stance. It's great to meet you, Paul."

Paul stepped in for a hug, catching Manisha off guard, but she welcomed it.

*Be your authentic self*, she heard Manny's voice saying in her mind.

He then held out her seat, exhibiting a politeness that made her smile even wider.

"Wow, this place is amazing!" he exclaimed, glancing around at the vibrant decor.

"It's been a beloved part of Baskin for many years. Did you grow up here, too?" Manisha asked curiously, noting the passion in his voice.

"You bet, but I moved to New York for my graduate studies, and now I'm back. I wanted to be closer to home. My sister and I are running a physiotherapy clinic together here," he shared, his eyes lighting up as he spoke about his work.

"That's wonderful," Manisha said, genuinely impressed. "And I can relate—I've been living in London for the past few years, but I'm also ready to return home. But I opted out of running the family business with my brothers. I couldn't work with both of them day in and day out."

Paul stared at her, a spark of curiosity flickering in his eyes. "You know, you're not exactly what I expected from a Baskin type of girl," he remarked thoughtfully.

"What do you mean by that?" Manisha asked, raising an eyebrow.

"Well, you have really great style and confidence. It's been a while since I've met someone I find physically attractive," he explained, his expression sincere.

"Thank you, that's nice. Um, I hope we share more than just physical attraction," she said with a playful smile, her heart racing a little at his compliment.

As she took a moment to appreciate how handsome he was—especially with those irresistible dimples that appeared each time he smiled—Rohit interrupted their conversation with a freshly brewed cup of coffee for Paul. "Fresh coffee. Thought you could use it for your meeting?"

Manisha scowled, about to respond, but before she could, Deena, her friend, swooped in like a superhero.

"Rohit, can you assist me with the coffee I accidentally spilled on the table way over there? You know me, I'm just so clumsy." Manisha could see right through Deena's act.

"Sure, but I just want to make sure Manisha and her guest don't need anything else," he replied, still lingering.

"Rohit, come with me now! I actually need your help right now!" Deena insisted, grabbing Rohit's arm and immediately pulling him away.

"Alright, now that's some impressive service here!" Paul said, chuckling to himself. "They really anticipate your needs—unless you know him?"

"Him? No. Not really!" Manisha replied, eager to refocus their conversation. "I think he owns this place, but let's get back to you. So, you enjoy travelling, you're a fan of Sunday night football, and apparently, you can cook an amazing lasagna."

"You read and remembered my bio. I love that about you."

*Did he just say love?* Manisha beamed at him.

"It's just that no one takes the time to get to know people, so thanks for doing that," Paul said sincerely, his gaze locked with hers. "And yes, to all those things! Could we do them together?"

Manisha could feel the already magnetic connection between them grow stronger.

"Yes!" Manisha exclaimed, her enthusiasm a cover-up for her nerves.

"So, you have brothers. Are they married?" Paul leaned forward slightly. "It can be tough when a sibling is married; all the pressure can suddenly shift to you. Do you feel that at all? The pressure to get married?"

"I'm feeling something, I guess you could say," Manisha confessed, glancing down at her hands. "What about you? Being the only son and the oldest—I think your profile said you're an uncle to three?"

"That's right, and I adore those kids. I'll be completely honest: I feel a little pressure, too, but it doesn't bother me. When I find the right person, I'll know. I'm sure it'll all happen quickly, like within a few weeks," Paul responded, a mixture of certainty and eagerness in his voice.

A few weeks? Did Paul also know about the Patel Blessing? Or maybe his family had their own luck?

Paul's gaze fixed on her, causing her pulse to race. "I just have to say, you're so beautiful, Manisha, and that dress . . ." He gestured to her outfit. "Sorry if that's too forward," he hurried to add.

*Oh, please go on*, she thought. She gave the tiniest shake of her head to reassure him.

"It's gorgeous," he continued. "It's hitting you in all the right places."

*Yes, that's why I wore it.* "Thank you," she said bashfully.

"So, will you move back to Baskin?"

"I think I'd move back here for my family and the right person," replied Manisha.

Paul beamed, his smile radiating warmth. "Maybe start your own family?" he suggested. "Raising a family here would be great."

Paul was perfect, and Manisha felt herself hanging on his every word.

"How's your tea?" he asked, taking a sip of coffee before grimacing dramatically.

"Oh, shit," he said, slamming the cup down, his expression shifting from pleasant to furious.

"What's wrong? Is it too hot? Are you okay, Paul?" Manisha asked, suddenly anxious. She'd be furious if Rohit's scorching coffee robbed her of a kiss later.

"No!" he fumed. "This coffee is literally disgusting! It's just brown water!"

"Oh, maybe it was a bad pot," she suggested, wondering why his reaction was so over-the-top.

"I hate it when people are stingy. Why open a business if you're going to sell garbage?" Paul railed. "My sister and I pride ourselves on offering the best to our customers. Not this crap."

"I doubt that's the owner's intention," Manisha said quickly, desperate to calm his rising anger. "Let's just ask for a fresh pot. Here, let me find him." She stood up, trying to spot Rohit, who was perplexingly absent, followed by a glance for Deena, who was nowhere to be found.

"Forget it," he snapped. "My tastebuds have been ruined. Disgusting."

"I think you're overreacting a bit, don't you? Can't we just move on?" she said, exasperated.

"Overreacting? Just move on?" His eyes flared with irritation. "Is that what you do when someone screws up as a lawyer? Just move on? Disgusting. I'm going online and leaving this guy a terrible review."

"Okay, well, let's not do that," she insisted, trying to inject some logic into his tirade.

"Why not? People need to know to avoid this place! Give me a minute; this won't take long," he replied, pulling out his phone.

"Paul, that's unnecessary," Manisha said pleadingly.

"People like him ruin it for all of us hard-working brown folks. Just give me a sec—"

"You know what? We're done!" she interrupted, standing up abruptly.

"What?" His shock was palpable.

Manisha sat back down, feeling the weight of the tension. "You've ruined this date by making a huge deal over a bad cup of coffee." She overenunciated "cup of coffee" to drive the point home. "Which I'm sure was just because of a small misstep, and you won't even give the guy a chance to fix it."

"For all we know, he serves this filth on purpose," Paul shot back defensively.

"I seriously doubt that. Why would anyone do that? And take a look around you," she said, scanning the very busy shop. "Honestly, it would be best if you just left, Paul. Now." Her voice was firm.

Paul stood, eyes blazing. "More than happy to, Manisha. I'll leave you to your precious café."

"This isn't my precious café!" she snapped. "You . . . coffee jerk, you!"

As Paul stormed out, Manisha sat in stunned silence. Perfect Paul was a big fat no.

She looked around for Deena, muttering, "Where is she?" Grabbing her phone for a message, she noticed a new email from Sunil.

Hey there, Admin!
You've got my full attention. A woman who can chow down? Now, that is the kind of woman who can have my heart. 😊

Lately, I've been dining solo pretty much every night, which isn't nearly as fun as sharing a plate of aloo paratha with someone who appreciates a good spice combo. I've got to say, I miss enjoying a quality meal with that special person. But is it just me or is good company hard to come by these days? I've had some serious bad luck recently. Call me a fool but I even went ahead and bought a lemon tree. Apparently, lucky lemons are supposed to lead to something sweet, like the woman of my dreams (or at least a dinner date, so I don't have to eat alone). 🍋 Who knew lemons could be so . . . romantic?"

—Sunil

A slow smile broke across Manisha's face as she read Sunil's message. It sounded as though Uncle Parm had conned yet another unsuspecting customer into taking a tree home. She was about to type out a reply when Deena blithely sauntered back.

"Where did Paul vanish to?" Deena asked, raising an eyebrow at Manisha, who quickly hid her phone.

Manisha, unfazed, replied with a sneer, "I asked Paul to skedaddle. Let's just say he had a coffee meltdown."

"Really?" Deena leaned in, curiosity piqued.

Manisha dramatically flicked open her Sephora compact, refreshing her lipstick. "That guy lost it over coffee! It was like watching a toddler throw a tantrum over a broken toy. I mean, who knew a bad brew could get him that riled up? I half expected him to start flinging sugar packets!"

Deena sniffed the cup Paul had left behind, making a face. "Smells fine to me! Disappointing, though—I was ready to book a banquet hall for your wedding!"

"Don't be ridiculous!" Manisha said. "I just can't believe he was about to leave Rohit a bad review. The gall!"

Deena raised an eyebrow. "Wait, hold on! Did you defend Rohit? Is the sky falling?!"

"What? No . . ." Manisha said. "It was Chai Time I was defending." Manisha crossed her arms and grinned.

Deena smirked, a playful glint in her eyes. "Be honest, Manisha. Don't you think you could've coaxed him back? I thought you two were about to clear the table and break into song!"

Manisha rolled her eyes, recalling her dream from the other day. "Deena, he was so over-the-top dramatic. I mean, it started so well, but then he just snapped over free coffee!"

"Okay, well, upward and onward! You've got about forty minutes until date number two with Arinder." Deena clapped her hands excitedly.

"That's me."

Both Manisha and Deena turned around, startled, to see a man with a playful grin and a vibrant green turban standing behind them. His eyes danced with humour, and he had an approachable vibe about him that instantly lightened the atmosphere.

"Oh, Arinder!" Manisha exclaimed, shooting him a smile. "I didn't realize you had arrived!"

"Well, I actually got here before you. I was watching you from the back corner," he said.

"Watching?" Deena and Manisha echoed in unison, raising their eyebrows.

"You know, just observing the scene," he replied, his tone lighthearted.

"Right. Okay, then, I'll leave you two to it!" Deena gave Manisha a look and strolled away.

Arinder settled into the chair across from Manisha, his posture casual yet confident.

"Look, I'm really sorry if you saw anything odd earlier," Manisha began, her tone apologetic.

He waved a hand dismissively, still grinning. "No worries at all. I know how these things work. It's all about maximizing your output, right?"

"What do you mean?" Manisha said slowly, amused by his upbeat attitude.

"I was also on a date. I think it went as well as yours."

Manisha giggled nervously. "Always gotta have a backup."

"Until you find the one," Arinder replied, gazing deeply into Manisha's eyes. The intensity made her squirm a bit.

"I'm really curious about you," he said, pulling out a notepad from his jacket pocket. "Do you mind if I take notes?"

Manisha raised an eyebrow at the sight of the bright-green notebook that matched his turban impeccably. "Um, no, not at all," she said, suppressing a laugh.

"Awesome! Tell me everything!" he prompted, pen at the ready.

"Well, I was born in Baskin; I'm a foodie, the only daughter, and the youngest," Manisha prattled off.

Arinder scribbled frantically, jotting down her details like he was taking minutes for an important business meeting. "Only daughter—my mom's going to love that!" He nodded emphatically, oblivious to her slight frown.

Manisha took advantage of Arinder's focus on his notetaking to shift the conversation back to him, as per Manny's advice.

"What about you? Since I'm date number two today, I'm guessing you must know what you want and don't want?" Manisha asked.

"Oh, I know exactly what I want. What my family wants," Arinder said nonchalantly. "The person I choose has to align with my family's financial and aesthetic preferences. From what I've seen so far, you definitely check those boxes."

"Are there more boxes to check?" Manisha said warily. This guy had a very archaic view of relationships!

"Well, of course, but those are the top two." Arinder shrugged, grinning as if he'd just landed a great deal.

"Looks and money?"

"Well, I have everything else," Arinder said confidently.

Manisha felt her patience waning, but Manny's advice to give her date the time and space to be the best version of himself sprang to mind.

"Arinder, I'm sorry, but we have different relationship viewpoints. You really don't think there's more to relationships than looks and how much someone earns?" She was throwing him a lifeline.

"Our family is one of the wealthiest in Baskin. We can't just let any woman into our dynasty. She's got to undergo proper training to become a Singh and, of course, sign a pre-nup." He flashed another smile.

His constant smiling was officially testing her last nerve.

"Proper training?" Manisha repeated, incredulity taking over her voice.

"Yes! She has to learn how to be a wife, run a household, and know what I like and what my family likes." He said this like he was giving her a grand opportunity. "Is that clear?"

"Oh yes, perfectly clear, Arinder," Manisha said icily. "I'm sorry, but I'm not your family's pet. I won't be molded into a Singh or become part of your dynasty."

His smile was still plastered to his face, but it had morphed into a haughty smirk. Manisha's hand itched to make it disappear.

"Honestly, I couldn't care less about your wealth. We want

different things. You're looking for your next project, and I'm looking for a husband," she stated matter-of-factly.

Suddenly, an elderly Indian woman appeared at their table, her nose wrinkled in disapproval.

"This one talks too much," she declared to Arinder, her voice dripping with judgment. "Not suitable for us."

Manisha's jaw dropped. "Is this your mom?"

Unperturbed, Arinder puffed his chest a bit. "Yes, I brought my mom like you brought your friend." He got up and stood beside her, exuding pride and boyish charm.

"My cousin Deena? That's not the same thing!" Manisha retorted.

"And her voice is loud. No, no, no, beta. Not for us," Arinder's mom added, shaking her head so hard, Manisha feared for the woman's updo.

"I'm sorry, Auntie, but with all due respect, you and your son are way out of line. It sounds like you're looking to groom someone!" Manisha responded, crossing her arms.

"Let's go, beta. This is wasting our time."

As they turned to leave, Arinder paused for one last quip. "What a shame. Almost all the boxes were checked, too."

"You and your boxes can leave now!" Manisha cried, pointing dramatically toward the door, her eyes ablaze.

He lifted his chin defiantly. "I know what I'm looking for, and I don't pretend otherwise," he said with a smug grin. "Here's some free advice for your next date: Drop the attitude. If you're genuinely seeking love or whatever, maybe take a long hard look in the mirror. Because right now, we're exactly the same, you and me, boxes and all." And with that, Arinder swaggered away with his mother.

Manisha flushed so hot with rage at his words, she was actually trembling. How dare he offer unsolicited dating advice! She knew she had her goals, but finding a genuine connection was all she truly wanted.

The only box that needed ticking in her book was love.

## 15

*A*fter back-to-back disastrous dates, Manisha and Deena took the time to seriously revise their questionnaire, adding more detailed and targeted questions.

"I'm sorry the dates didn't go as planned," Deena said, offering Manisha a sympathetic half smile. "But once I input these new prompts, that should rule out anyone looking for a group date with his mom or a coffee critic," she continued, attempting to lighten the mood.

"If you say so . . ." Manisha replied, her tone uncertain.

"Oh, come on! It was just your first two dates. Honestly, they were better than any I've had recently."

"Thanks, but that's not much consolation."

"I know you're feeling disappointed," Deena said, glancing at Rohit, who was waiting for Manisha. "But you've got this. And so do I.

"I'll message you later," Deena added, attempting to sound hopeful. "And don't worry—plenty more dates are out there."

"Let's hope so!" Manisha quipped, managing a slight grin.

With Deena gone, Manisha stayed behind, waiting for Rohit to finish closing the café. As she waited, she tapped out a response to Sunil.

Hey, Sunil,

Sounds like you've crossed paths with our good friend,
Uncle "Lucky Lemons" Parm! 🍋 Whatever it takes to
get you closer to that perfect plate of aloo parathas—
though, between us, at Curry and Cupid, we like to
keep those delicious APs to ourselves . . . or maybe we
just haven't found "the one" to share them with yet. 😊

On that note, why the stroke of bad luck? What's been
keeping you lonely at meals? You strike us as someone
who knows what you're looking for. So, what are you
hoping those lucky lemons will bring your way? 😊
Cheers,
Admin

Why not have a pen pal on the same mission as her? She
heard the kitchen door open. Looking up, she saw Rohit appear
at the front counter.

"Are you ready?" she asked, going over to join him.

"Yeah, I am," Rohit replied, picking up a stack of messy
papers from beneath the counter.

"What happened to those papers?" Manisha asked, raising an
eyebrow.

"Sorry, I was reviewing everything this morning and—"

"And you thought it would be a great idea to turn it into a
mess?" she teased.

Rohit scowled at her. "Come on, Manisha."

"It just means more work for me to organize all of these
again, and I'm pretty short on time," Manisha added.

"Look, I accidentally tripped," Rohit said defensively.

"What do you mean, you tripped?" Manisha asked, confused.

"I fell. Yep, a grown man tripped over his own feet. I wasn't paying attention and—"

"And you fell?" Manisha said, then burst into laughter. "I'm sorry! I don't mean to laugh, but . . ."

Her laughter only grew, spreading to Rohit, who let out a low chuckle. Soon the two of them were overcome with unrestrained guffaws.

"Yeah, I fell hard," he gasped between laughs.

"I'm really sorry," Manisha said, trying to catch her breath. "It's just that I've had such a terrible day, and this is just too funny."

"You and me both," Rohit admitted. He held up a bottle of wine. "Maybe this could help?"

She smiled. "You know I'm never one to say no to a glass of wine."

Rohit grinned and poured two glasses while Manisha attempted to right the pile of papers.

"So, difficult meetings today?" he asked, sitting on a stool next to her with a glass in hand.

"I suppose you could say that," Manisha replied with a sigh.

"Well, let's toast to brighter days," Rohit said, raising his glass.

"I'll gladly drink to that." Manisha clinked glasses with him and took a sip. She hummed in appreciation at its smoothness. He had good taste in wines.

"And you?" she asked after a beat.

"You mean besides tripping over my own feet?" Rohit replied, causing them both to snicker.

"There's just a lot going on," he continued. "Moving back home hasn't been as smooth as I expected. I always knew time stood still in Baskin . . ."

"You can say that again." Manisha nodded in agreement.

"But this is only temporary for you," Rohit said. "Soon, you'll be back on the mean streets of London, leaving behind all the nosy aunties and uncles."

"Spot on about the uncles!" Manisha exclaimed. "I'm so relieved it's not just me who noticed. They've really taken over the gossip scene!"

"It's out of control either way!" Rohit remarked.

"I can't even go to the store without an uncle demanding a wedding invite," she complained.

"At least they don't bother me about that anymore," Rohit said.

"Probably because they've already gotten one from you." Manisha raised her eyebrows playfully.

"Touché," he conceded, raising his glass again.

After a sip of wine, Manisha asked the question that had been on everyone's lips in town. "So, what happened?"

Rohit shrugged slightly. "A lot happened. I don't even know where to begin."

He'd taken the words right out of her brain when it came to her own situation. "I get that," Manisha said, her expression softening some.

"It's like my story, and I want to tell it, but people have already written it for me."

"I get that, too," Manisha replied, her voice quieter now.

"I know the truth, my truth, and for now, that's what gets me through the nights," he added, his gaze distant.

Manisha tightened her lip. "What about Lucky? Don't you ever wonder how she gets through the nights?"

"Trust me, I know she's doing just fine."

"So, you keep in touch still?" Manisha pressed.

"We don't really talk, and I prefer it that way," Rohit said, his tone firm, but there was a weariness to it.

"I prefer not to talk to my ex, either," Manisha admitted, feeling a sudden vulnerability creep in. Was she really about to tell Rohit about Oliver?

"Your ex?" Rohit asked.

"Oliver. He called me a few days ago. I know how this works—he's just trying not to feel bad about what he did."

Rohit studied her for a moment. "And how do you feel?"

"I feel good—" She hesitated.

"You look great," Rohit said. I mean, you look like you're doing great."

Manisha blushed slightly, glancing down at her wineglass.

A heavy silence fell over them, both engrossed in their own thoughts.

With a small shake of her head, Manisha took another sip of wine. "It's fascinating how relationships are formed," she started up again. "You share your deepest thoughts and most intimate parts of yourself, and then sometimes, one day, it's all just used and discarded once they've had their fill and moved on. Why do people do that, Rohit?" Manisha asked, her voice sincere but laced with confusion.

"I have no idea, Manisha. Maybe people just get bored with what others find interesting. It could be as simple as that. They might be captivated, drawn to the shiny new apple," he said with a shrug.

"Is that what happened to you? Bored of the same apple?" she asked, a hint of challenge in her voice.

He turned and looked her dead in the eye. "You know, I would have taken apple pie, apple muffins, apple cake, all from the same apple. I didn't mind the same apple."

"Oh . . ." Manisha said feebly. Her eyes narrowed in thought. "It's just I heard you—well, I just heard differently."

"I know what you heard, what this whole town has heard," Rohit's tone grew sharper. "But that's not the full story . . ."

Manisha broke eye contact, focusing on the scattered papers. "Well, maybe with you being so busy here, the town will forget what they heard," Manisha added, trying to deflect the tension.

She knew that, like Oliver, Rohit would spin his version of events sooner or later—his side of the cheating story. And though she had her own opinions on infidelity, she'd learned from her viral video fiasco that it was all too easy to get caught up in the drama.

"Or maybe they'll remember the Khanna legacy," Rohit said with pride. "*Seva*. Giving back. Helping others."

Manisha watched as his eyes briefly clouded over, and then the vulnerability she'd glimpsed earlier resurfaced.

"It's like suddenly, no one wants to focus on everything my parents have done . . ."

"Continue to do," Manisha added, her gaze sweeping around the cozy Chai Time café.

"You're right. I'll keep doing what the Khannas do best. But it's tough not to hear the whispers or see the looks people give you," he sighed deeply.

Manisha nodded sympathetically. "Oh, I know. Have you ever gotten *the look* from one of the Gupta aunties? It's like a mix of disappointment, embarrassment, and 'I knew it all along,' all wrapped up in one."

Rohit squinted, raising his eyebrows and trying to perfect the infamous look. "Like this?"

"Oh my god, you've had the look!"

Both of them burst into laughter, the tension finally breaking.

"You know, one of these days, we should look right back," Manisha said with a wicked grin.

"No way!" Rohit said, laughing.

"Oh, come on! You, me . . . against the Gupta aunties. Think of the town gossip then!"

"Me and you a team?" he said, giving her an amused look.

Manisha smiled, finishing her glass of wine. "Alright, alright. Let's get back on track here." She leafed through the scattered papers. "These aren't anywhere close to being in order anymore. They're going to need a complete overhaul. How about I take this folder with me tonight, organize it, and we meet here tomorrow evening to go over everything for real?"

"Yeah, sure," Rohit agreed quickly, nodding. "It's getting late. Sorry again about the mess."

"No problem. We've all tripped up before," Manisha said, collecting the papers and grabbing her bag. "I'll see you tomorrow."

"Yeah, see you later," Rohit said.

As Manisha stepped out into the cool evening air, the heel of her shoe caught on the door sill. She stumbled, barely keeping her grip on the papers clutched to her chest.

A deep chuckle sounded from behind her.

Of course he caught that.

With a parting flourish of the hand, she threw her shoulders back and sauntered off into the night.

alking to Uncle Parm's store the next morning, Manisha's mind kept drifting back to her conversation with Rohit. They had been enemies ever since she'd come back to Baskin, clashing at every turn. Literally. But last night had been a turning point—something had shifted between them. For the first time in ages, they had dropped their defences, and instead of arguing, they had actually talked and listened to each other.

Her mother's voice echoed in her mind: "You might have more in common with Rohit than you think." But Manisha was skeptical—and, frankly, indifferent—to the idea. Like Deena had said, Rohit was nothing more than a client. Chai Time was the best spot for dates away from the prying Baskin gossipmongers, and she was still searching for her Prince Charming. If that meant running into Rohit now and then, she could manage it. But she knew they were far from friends.

Manisha pulled out her phone to check her mother's grocery list. Normally, her mother would have tagged along, as she did last time. But today she was completely absorbed in the season finale of the Indian version of *Big Brother*, *Bigg Boss*, which was just fine by Manisha. The solo outing gave her space, a little bit of peace and quiet.

Her thumb was hovering over the messages app when another email from Sunil came through. She opened it without hesitation.

> That's the million-dollar question, right? If you'd asked me a year ago, I would have had all the answers. But the truth is, I was wrong. Now, I'm not so sure. My friends keep telling me I just have to get back out there, but I have a feeling that in today's dating world, it isn't going to be as simple as that. What about you? Given that you work behind the scenes on a matchmaking website, I bet you've seen it all and know exactly what you want. So, what are you looking for . . . [insert name here]?
> —Sunil

Manisha laughed quietly to herself. Sunil was funny. And there was a steady kindness to his emails. She could already feel herself becoming fast friends with him.

She wanted to tell Sunil her real name, but she didn't want to blow her matchmaking cover. Talking to him made her feel so much less alone in the dating game. Sure, she had Deena— the dating guru who had been on plenty of dates—and Manny, with her tips and tricks—but from the few emails between Sunil and . . .

Isha.

Manisha smiled at her cleverness. She'd give Sunil the name Isha, her nickname used only within the Patel family.

On the one hand, it felt like a way of reconnecting with the person she used to be, before Curry and Cupid, before her financial predicament, before Oliver. She was free to be just Isha, the one with the infectious laugh and a knack for making people smile; the one with an incomparable love for homecooked meals.

On the other hand, this would allow her to start fresh. And there was something oddly comforting in knowing that someone else was doing the same.

Manisha had a feeling she was going to need someone to make her laugh. So far, she was zero for two with her dates. For now, Manisha figured Sunil would be her laugh break between all the dating chaos. A little humour never hurt anyone, especially when the alternatives were . . . well, less than ideal.

Manisha rounded the corner to the plaza where Uncle Parm's grocery store was located.

The scene of the crime, she thought, surveying the parking lot. She was semi-over it now. Mostly because she had other things to focus on.

Strolling past the neighbouring laundromat and convenience store, Manisha halted in front of Uncle Parm's and took stock of her surroundings. Save for a pair of seagulls duelling for a chunk of bread crust, she was alone. Under the blissfully cool shade of a dutiful palm tree, she pulled out her phone and got to composing her reply to Sunil.

> Dear Sunil,
> I guess you could say I'm looking for my "ride or die." The past year has been far from that, but I'm ready to move on. I'm just asking for the occasional Bollywood movie marathoner, a fellow wine enthusiast, and someone who also dreams of having a family. Right away.

Wait—scratch that. Too much.

~~Right away.~~
I was lucky to grow up in a home filled with love
from my parents and siblings, so it would be great to
find someone who cherishes family time, too.
Inserting name below,
Isha 😊

Her fingers flew effortlessly over the phone screen, and with a smile, she hit send. Tucking her phone back in her purse, she waltzed into the store hoping for relative quiet this early in the day. Instead, Uncle Parm's was aggressively busy. Manisha rushed to grab a red basket and began scouring the aisles for the items on her mother's list: chaat, two cans of chickpeas, ginger, coriander, masala, and, of course, her mother's favourite, Parle-G, the delicately sweet Indian tea biscuit that Manisha couldn't resist whenever it was offered to her. One by one, she piled the products into her basket, skirting around mountainous product displays and dodging other patrons.

As she made her way to the front of the store, where the Indian sweets were neatly displayed, Manisha felt her mouth begin to water. Rows of decadent barfis, gulab jamuns, and ladoos glistened under the fluorescent lights, practically calling her name.

As a child and even now as an adult, Manisha had a soft spot for sweets—especially the ones that melted in your mouth or were stuffed with rich, spiced fillings.

She picked out a few gulab jamuns, some ladoos, a handful of barfis, a couple of kaju katlis, and, as always, a few jalebis—the perfect mix of sweetness and crunch to keep things interesting. That would be enough for the week. She lined up at the checkout, the familiar greasy box of sweets heavy in her hands. She couldn't resist the temptation of sneaking just one little ladoo while she waited.

"Ready?" Uncle Parm's wife asked, not taking her eyes off the small television behind the counter. Not that Manisha could blame her; an old Bollywood movie starring Rekha and Anil Kapoor was playing. Their chemistry was off the charts. And how did her hair always look so perfect?

"Chocolate bar?" Auntie asked without looking up. Manisha blinked and looked down to see Auntie had already finished ringing up and bagging her items with impressive speed.

"I think I'm good, Auntie," Manisha replied, shaking her head.

"Gum?"

"Not today."

"How about feet?" Auntie blindly pointed to the sour, foot-shaped candy, like Manisha was still in elementary school.

Manisha couldn't suppress a laugh. "This is all, Auntie. Thank you."

Auntie sighed dramatically, still staring at the screen. "Okay. Twenty dollars even."

As Manisha rummaged through her purse, a sinking realization hit her like a ton of bricks—she'd forgotten her wallet.

Uncle Parm's wife finally made eye contact. "No money, honey?" she said, her voice light but with that unmistakable you-did-this-to-yourself tone.

Manisha sighed, sheepishly pulling her hand from the depths of her purse. "I forgot my wallet, Auntie," she admitted. "Is Uncle around? I was just here the other day with my mom. He'll remember me—lucky lemons, lucky Manisha?"

She tried to lighten the mood, flashing a smile as if it would magically fix the awkwardness. If only she could jump through the TV screen and join Rekha and Anil in some grand Bollywood number about forgetting her wallet, she thought. Bollywood movies always seemed to break out in perfectly timed songs that solved every problem with a catchy tune and a dramatic dance move.

But reality had no chorus or sparkles. And right now, Manisha had no money.

Uncle Parm's wife raised an eyebrow but said nothing, her gaze now back on the screen, completely unimpressed. Manisha could practically hear her mother's disapproving voice in her head. "How could you forget your wallet, besharam?"

"Here, let me take care of it for you," came a voice from behind.

Manisha spun around, almost knocking over a jar of Indian pickles in the process. "Rohit?"

"Don't worry, I got this," he said, pulling out his wallet like it was no big deal.

"No, no!" Manisha waved her hands in protest, flustered. "I can come back later. You really don't have to pay for me."

"You've already eaten," Auntie pointed out, glancing at Manisha's sticky fingers, which were still suspiciously covered in ladoo remnants.

"I doubt Auntie's starting a tab for you," Rohit said with a knowing smirk.

Uncle Parm's wife, who had absolutely no time for this drama, rang up the items Rohit had added and extended her hand expectantly. Palm up.

"This doesn't usually happen to me," Manisha blurted, trying to explain the whole mess, but her words were tangled. "My mom borrowed my purse last night—"

Before she could finish, Rohit handed Auntie the cash without a second thought.

"Okay, done. Next!" Auntie called to the next customer, already turning back to the TV. Rohit swept up their groceries and gently nudged her toward the exit.

"I'll make sure to Venmo you the money as soon as I get home. I haven't had a chance to add my credit cards to my phone yet," she added, trying to sound casual. "It's a whole process, transferring banking info from the UK to here."

Manisha was only half telling the truth, of course. Even if her cards were on her phone, there was only enough money left for a few essentials: cheap wine and ladoos.

"Consider it a thank-you for helping me with the paperwork for the café," Rohit said, his tone so casual it made paying for her sweets sound like a perfectly normal gesture. "Where are you parked?" His eyes scanned the parking lot.

Manisha blinked. "Oh, uh, don't worry about it—I walked. But thanks," she said, taking her groceries off his hands with a polite smile. "So, I guess I'll see you tonight, then?"

"Actually," Rohit said, rubbing the back of his neck like he was trying to massage the awkwardness out of the moment, "something's come up. Can we push it to tomorrow afternoon?"

Manisha's smile faltered just a bit. "I suppose . . ."

Before she could say anything else, a voice called out from a sleek, shiny Volvo parked nearby.

"Hey, Manisha!"

Manisha turned, forcing a smile despite the sudden twist in her stomach. "Hi, Suzy!" she said, her voice a little too bright.

Suzy waved enthusiastically from the passenger seat, her bright eyes practically sparkling with mischief. "Ro promised me a home-cooked Indian meal while I'm in town—he's making that amazing chana masala, you know?"

So that's what came up.

Manisha raised an eyebrow. "What happened to the Lambo?"

He shrugged casually. "It wasn't mine. This is my car," he said, gesturing to the Volvo with a nonchalant wave.

Manisha stared at the car for a moment, squinting like she was trying to make sense of it. "You drive a Volvo?" she asked, genuinely incredulous.

"Yup," he replied, shrugging again. "Is your Gucci bag disappointed?" He eyed her purse with a teasing smirk.

Manisha shot him a pointed look. "I just thought that, you know, you were driving your own car that day."

Rohit climbed into the driver's seat, clearly trying to play it cool as he shifted uncomfortably. "I was just returning Lucky's Lambo."

"Wait—Lucky's Lambo?" Manisha's eyebrow shot up in surprise.

He glanced at her, starting the engine. "Can we give you a ride anywhere?"

"Oh, God, no," she said, panic creeping into her voice as she took a step back from the car. "I mean, three's a crowd, right? Thanks for the, uh, money. I'll pay you back, I promise!"

Suzy leaned over with wide, encouraging eyes. "Are you sure you don't want to join us?"

Manisha's smile was tight but polite. "Nope!" she said a little too forcefully. She softened her tone. "I mean, maybe another time."

"Okay. Nice to see you again! Don't be a stranger!" Suzy called out cheerfully as they began to pull away, waving at Manisha like they were old friends.

Manisha stood there for a moment, watching them drive off, a curdling feeling in her stomach. *It's hard to be a stranger when we keep bumping into each other*, she thought bitterly.

The Volvo disappeared around the corner, leaving Manisha to sulk in her lonely bitterness. There Rohit and Suzy were—carefree, happy, and apparently enjoying the kind of chana masala that made everything seem a little brighter—while she was left standing in the parking lot, trying to scrape gooey ladoos off her fingers.

A sigh escaped her lips, her heart feeling just a little emptier than before.

It was time to kick Curry and Cupid into high gear. She wasn't going to just sit on the sidelines any longer.

## 17

*M*anisha had just finished putting the groceries away when she noticed her wallet sitting innocently on the table. She groaned. Of course it was there.

Her phone buzzed, startling her. It was an email from Sunil.

> It's great to put a name to these emails. I can tell you have good energy, Isha. You've even managed to get me a little more excited about a future partner. Not to be a bummer, but not much has seemed worth getting excited about lately . . .
>
> So, how do you plan on finding your "ride or die"?
> —Sunil

Manisha smiled, her fingers dancing across the keyboard as she typed back:

> Trust me, I get it, Sunil. It's hard to move on, and I hear it's rough out there. But I'll admit, your emails have been giving me hope that decent people do still exist after all. I actually decided to get back into dating a few days ago. I have an idea. How about we

team up? You know, Team Sunil & Isha, cheering
each other on in the wild world of dating?
Isha


She hit send. It was fun to talk to Sunil.

"Why are you standing there grinning like a checkers cat?"
her mom called from the doorway, her tone half amused, half
suspicious.

Manisha blinked, biting back a grin. "*Cheshire* cat, Mom!
Anyway, I picked up the groceries from Uncle Parm's store,
but . . . I forgot my wallet because I took it out when you borrowed my purse yesterday. So, you owe Rohit money."

"Rohit Khanna?" her mom asked, her brows shooting up
above her glasses.

"Yep. There I was, scrambling for cash, and he just casually
tossed Auntie money like it was no big deal. Total rich kid move."

"So, he came to your rescue? Like your knight in shining
armour?" her mom teased, obviously loving the drama.

"Not my knight—more like Suzy's," Manisha replied, diving
into full gossip mode. "He was with his new girlfriend—the one
he cheated on Lucky with."

"Chup. You're just adding masala to the story again," her
mom said, half rolling her eyes.

"I've seen them everywhere, walking around like a couple of
lovebirds. In his café, on the streets, and now at Uncle Parm's
store. It's like they've forgotten about subtlety."

"Beta, it sounds like someone's a little envious . . ."

"Envious of Rohit Khanna?" Manisha scoffed. "Ugh, no.
Why would I be?" *Well, maybe a little.*

"Manisha, do I need to remind you that the Khannas are the
reason we were able to afford this very house? Rohit's mother

was a dear, dear friend to me before . . ." Her mother's words trailed off.

Manisha's eyes widened in surprise. Rohit's mom was a friend? A dear, dear friend? She hadn't known that. How could she not have known that?

"The Khannas are well-respected members of our community, which means Rohit is respected, too," her mother ended with a note of finality.

"Rohit's many things, Mom. But respected is not exactly how I'd describe him," she muttered.

"There are two—" her mom began.

"Sides to every story. I know, Mom. But come on! Can you imagine how hurt Lucky must be?" she pressed.

"Maybe Rohit is hurting, too?" her mom countered gently.

Manisha exhaled sharply. "He seems perfectly fine. He's got Suzy, he's got his café. He's got his bursting-at-the-seams wallet. He's more than fine from what I got from him the other night."

"The other night?" her mom asked, her voice suddenly lighter, brows waggling.

"Mom, not like that!" Manisha's face flushed. "I was just helping him with some legal stuff for the café. You know, the paperwork Dad made me look over for Uncle Jas. I was supposed to help again tonight, but instead, he's making dinner for Suzy."

Her mom raised an eyebrow. "So, what? He is busy. He is getting on with his life. You should get busy, too."

Manisha bristled. "I'm busy! I've got plans. I'm a very occupied woman."

"Manisha, you're acting old-fashioned," her mom said. "We live in a different world now. There is no rule that says you can't bring girlfriends to Uncle Parm's store. You must stop caring so much about what other people think."

"Mom, I really don't care—especially when it comes to Rohit Khanna and his girlfriends."

Except maybe she did care, just a little. Seeing him so unbothered and smiling had left an annoying knot in her chest. Why did it bother her that he had seemed to move on so easily while she was still figuring it out?

"Oh, really? Well, you could've fooled me with all this Rohit-and-Suzy gup shup," her mom said, her tone dry but amused.

Manisha rolled her eyes. "Mom, I'm just sharing my day, not gossiping."

Manisha filled herself a glass of water and mulled over her mom's words. Maybe she *was* making too big a deal out of this.

"Maybe you're right," Manisha admitted, more to herself than anyone. "I just . . . expected more discretion. What if Lucky's parents see him with Suzy?"

"What he does is none of their business anymore."

Again, Manisha turned her mom's words over in her mind. They made sense. At some point, you had to stop worrying about your ex's family, and clearly, that time had long passed.

"Chal, let's forget it," her mom said with a dismissive wave, clearly ready to move on. "Talking about this is making me hungry."

Manisha smiled. "Finally, something we can agree on."

Her mom handed her a jalebi from the box on the counter. Manisha took it, savouring the sweet crunch. She let herself relax and enjoy the treat, realizing that maybe she had been putting too much energy into things that didn't really matter.

*Drop the attitude.* Arinder's cutting departing words echoed in her thoughts.

*Forget it. Just let it go,* she told herself, taking another bite of the sugary treat, moving on to imagining the day she could share a jalebi with her own Prince Charming.

## 18

*M*anisha had been looking forward to a quiet evening in her childhood room—the kind of peace she could never seem to find in London. Surrounded by the constant buzz of client meetings, crowded Tube rides, and the endless cycle of after-work drinks with colleagues, life in London always felt like a sprint. But here in Baskin, time seemed to stretch out, offering her a rare chance to breathe. Even with the looming "Dr. Rocky baby deadline," Manisha felt oddly at ease.

As she was starting to unwind though, her phone buzzed, breaking the calm. It was a message from Deena. Manisha had shared with Deena that she was ready to "ramp up the dating game," and it seemed her cousin had taken that request as a cue to take matters into her own hands.

*Four dates!* Manisha stared at the message, blinking a few times. Four dates in one day?

No sweat, I can totally do this! Manisha typed back, more to reassure herself than Deena, who she knew wouldn't need any convincing. In fact, she had a sneaking suspicion that Deena had probably done five, six—heck, maybe even ten dates in one day at some point. The woman was on a mission. Just like Manisha, but Deena's mission was on pause—until Manisha found "the one" first.

"You should get busy, too." Manisha's mother's voice replayed in her head. Four dates would surely keep her busy. Manisha didn't mind taking her mom's advice for now, especially because her mom wasn't giving her a hard time about returning to London. Manisha had told them her vacation was "indefinite," a statement her parents had accepted without a second thought. Like most Indian parents, Manisha's wanted their adult daughter to stay at home for as long as possible.

Manisha smiled at the thought.

She took off her watch and placed it on the nightstand, glancing at the empty baggie from Meena Auntie sitting next to it. She had taken the magical seeds only a few days ago with Deena, but so far . . .

No miracles.

No enchanted encounters.

No Prince Charming.

Nothing.

Her phone buzzed again—this time, it was from Sunil. She leaned back into the pillows, putting Deena's date schedule aside for a moment as she opened Sunil's message. He had become her favourite distraction lately. They were good at this—sharing their thoughts, their frustrations, laughing over the small stuff.

> I like the sound of that team. And good for you!
> You'll have to keep me posted on your adventures
> and I can cheer you on from the virtual sidelines.
> Rah-rah!
>
> I think you're a step or two ahead of me, though.
> A friend of mine strong-armed me into making an
> account on a dating app the other day. She had to

help me write my bio and everything, which, by the
way, was way harder than I thought it would be. Then
I started swiping . . . and swiping . . . and 30 minutes
later, my thumb was sore. My heart just wasn't in it,
you know?

Manisha chuckled to herself.
He continued:

All I saw were women obsessed with their looks (why
so many selfies?), showing off their fancy meals,
purses, cars, and vacations. Don't get me wrong,
I can appreciate the finer things in life (especially
food and wine), but I'm not about just slapping a
name on something, or going somewhere because
it's "luxury." I can't say I'm interested in dating
someone who's obsessed with appearances. So,
I deleted the app. Too much, too soon perhaps.

Manisha tightened her lips as she ran her fingers over the
underside of her phone case, grazing the double Gs. Without
allowing herself to dwell, she tapped out a reply from the heart.

There's no rush, Sunil. And I'd take a nice person
over nice things right now. I've dealt with my share
of dishonesty, blame, and a lack of accountability in
the past. You could say I carry a bit of PTSD from my
last relationship, but I'm hopeful. However, spending
half an hour swiping through dating profiles doesn't
seem appealing. I'd much prefer to put that time
toward exploring new career opportunities instead.

> I'm in a bit of an adult funk when it comes to figuring
> out what I want to do for the rest of my life. Can't
> be the admin of a matchmaking site forever . . .

As soon as she hit send, she felt a surge of exhilaration go through her. It was liberating to express her true feelings about her life in Baskin and admit that she was still in the process of figuring everything out. Just as quickly, a new message came in.

> I read your message twice, and it gave me chills.
> I can relate. You can probably tell that I'm also work-
> ing through my own PTSD from my last relationship.
> Not to overstep but I've found a bit of therapy can
> truly make a difference.

*Retail therapy*, Manisha thought guiltily as she slid her gaze over her carpet, strewn with designer clothes.

She went back to reading his message:

> Funnily enough, I'm still figuring out my own career
> goals too. There was a time I thought I had every-
> thing mapped out—like a good Indian son—but I
> realized I wanted something deeper, something that
> allowed me to give back. My parents have always
> been big on that, and I'm striving to honour them.

> Isha, I have to say I really admire your openness. And
> your assuredness in where you are in life. It sounds
> like you aren't afraid to just be and go for it. I hope
> the right guy for you comes along soon and spares
> your thumbs.

A sympathetic smile pulled at Manisha's lips. She could feel the weight of his words—the kindness, the compassion, the hope he carried with him. Something about his candour made her want to reach through the screen and give him a hug. She settled back into the bed, taking a moment before replying.

> You and me both, Sunil. I'm (im)patiently waiting
> for that special man to come along. I believe it'll
> happen, and when it does, I know it will be every bit
> as magical as I imagine.

Manisha smiled as she typed out the last part, thinking about Meena Auntie's words. She still wasn't sure if magic was real, but speaking to Sunil . . . it was as though his understanding had eased some of the pressure on her.

A new message from Sunil popped up almost instantly.

> That word, magic, is strange. I've encountered it a
> few times, but never really felt it. But call me crazy,
> I still believe in it. Speaking of magic, take a look
> outside your window. The sky is filled with stars, just
> waiting for wishes to be made.

Manisha nestled further into her pillows, gazing out the window at the stars above. Closing her eyes, she sent a silent wish for her Prince Charming skyward. When she opened them again, another message awaited her.

Anyway, red or white wine?

Red, Manisha responded instantly.

A bold choice. Vegas or LA? he followed up.

Vegas, she typed quickly, but only for the brunches.

I'm with you there. Brunch is life, Sunil replied. Deepika or Katrina?

Manisha paused. Tough one, she admitted. But . . . I'm going to say Deepika.

Team Ranveer and Deepika, all the way! he responded. She could practically see him grinning through the screen. Not literally, of course. But through his messages, she had begun to paint a picture of the kind of person Sunil was: He was an honest, thoughtful man who had, like her, been burned in the past. A man who, understandably, wasn't ready to venture back into the dating realm, but hadn't given up on love.

She chewed her lip, trying to think of where to take the conversation next.

I'm afraid of spiders, she typed on a whim.

Don't laugh, but I'm afraid of hot tubs, came his next reply.

She laughed.

It felt easy to talk to him. To share little quirks and random preferences. They spent the next few messages sharing their favourite activities—road trips, Sunday hikes, beach days with a good book, and occasional art gallery visits. Sunil was a seasoned traveller, fluent in three languages, studying Italian in preparation for his dream adventure in Italy. Manisha had a love for languages as well, and while her travel adventures were limited, she found joy in simpler things like brunches with her parents and mimosas with friends.

As the conversation went on, she noticed the contrasts between them—he was the world explorer, and she was the more homebound one. Funny that—it was almost the opposite when it came to their search for love. Regardless, her conversation with Sunil was acting as a nice confidence booster ahead of her four (four!) dates tomorrow.

## 19

*M*anisha sat at a corner table in Chai Time, her eyes flicking up to the clock that read 9:42 a.m. The café was abuzz, and yet Rohit was nowhere to be seen.

*Probably slept in with Suzy.*

As quick as the thought crossed her mind, Manisha inwardly took it back and scolded herself. Her mother's remark that she was letting envy colour her opinion of Rohit, and Suzy, rang true. They were together, sharing those little moments, while she what? Filled her time tapping away on her phone, no closer to finding her Prince Charming.

She sighed, running a hand through her wavy hair. It was early and last night, she'd stayed up late messaging Sunil and studying the profiles of today's four dates. They'd spent all that time filling out questionnaires, the least she could do was read them. Now, with her eyes still half closed from lack of sleep, she took a long sip of her coffee, hoping the caffeine would kick in quickly. Just as she settled back in her chair, her phone buzzed. She glanced down. Speaking of Sunil . . .

Good morning, Isha! You know, our conversation had me thinking. I know you said no rush, but I'm toying with the idea of re-downloading that app and giving

people a proper chance, maybe even going on a
date. Maybe I'll even send my profile to Cupid and
Curry, too!

She could empathize with Sunil's struggle to find love. Here
she was, resorting to deceitful measures to find a sperm donor
and start a family. She had created a fake matchmaking site,
weaving a web of deception to find potential donors. Some
might say it was a desperate move, but Manisha was determined
to have a baby, no matter what it took.

She couldn't shake off the guilt that gnawed at her, though.
For all her honesty with Sunil last night, she was still holding
back the truth about one major thing. But she had no time to
dwell on it right now. She quickly fired off a response.

Morning! Funny you mention that. I'm actually heading on a date right now. I'm sending you lots of luck.
We can do this!

She was pulling up the dating profiles Deena had outlined for
her when her phone buzzed. Sunil again. He was quick.

Sending you luck back! We can do this. You're absolutely right. Hey, props to you for gearing up for a
date WHILE being a great website admin and squeezing in the time to answer me. I can barely walk and talk
at the same time without tripping over my own feet!

Manisha reread the part where Sunil mentioned her working
for the site. Her stomach flipped. She needed to focus on her
actual dates, not the pen pal she was playing make believe with.

She typed out a reply:

> Here's to hoping all that tripping leads you straight
> into the arms of someone special.

"Well, don't you look cheerful! More meetings today?" Rohit's voice suddenly came from beside her, causing her to nearly drop her phone in shock.

"Oh, Rohit! When did you get here? I didn't even see you come in," she said, trying to sound casual.

"I kind of snuck in. Had a late night," he said with a wink, grinning as he leaned against the counter.

*I'm sure you did*, Manisha thought sourly, her envy getting the best of her again. But she kept it in, going for a polite "I should be free just after noon."

"Sounds good. Can I get you anything else?" he asked, gesturing to her cup.

"Yeah, how about a stiff drink?" She was only half joking.

"A drink before your client meetings? At ten in the morning?"

"Right," she said. "Clients." Not a date. Manisha had to keep up with all her stories. "I guess I'll have a refill."

"One refill coming up."

Manisha unlocked her phone again, navigating out of her email thread with Sunil and to her potential matches' profiles. Vikas was first up. He was a criminal lawyer. Even though Manisha was hesitant to meet another lawyer, Deena had made it clear that the right person was the right person, regardless of career. Next up was Nick, a doctor who enjoyed being around kids. Manisha was pleased to see that, hoping that if Nick was her Prince Charming, he'd be a good candidate to become a dad.

"I'm here," Deena said as she entered the café. "Are you ready to do this again?"

"Absolutely! I'm so excited!"

"Really?" Deena looked at Manisha with curiosity in her eyes.

Manisha shrugged. "Today feels different."

"How?"

"The guys you set me up with seem promising." Manisha shrugged. "Or maybe those seeds are starting to work . . ." She decided to keep her digital dating-support pen pal to herself for now.

"Ha, very funny. Well, guess what? While I've been working miracles for you, Gina Auntie is setting me up on a date with her grandson. So I guess my seeds are kicking in."

"That's great to hear! I'll keep you posted on whether mine start working. Given my luck, I might just have the placebo seeds!"

Deena and Manisha shared a laugh.

Manisha felt her phone vibrate in her hand. "Can you give me a few minutes? I need to review those bios you sent," she fibbed, eager to read Sunil's email.

"Yeah, sure."

Deena walked away while Manisha glanced at her phone.

> Haha. If I trip today, I don't think I can blame multi-tasking. Call me old, but we were up way past my bedtime. I'm feeling a bit foggy, almost like I have a hangover. I could really go for some aloo parathas right now.

Sunil was speaking Manisha's love language. She was about to reply, but Sunil beat her to the punch with a follow-up.

Aloo parathas give me life.

Manisha couldn't type her response fast enough.

Same here! Food gives me life. I so don't understand
the people who only eat like rabbits to fuel their
bodies. How can anyone say no to a good aloo
paratha? You will never catch me doing that!

"Hey, Manisha?" a male voice said.

Preoccupied, she blurted, "Sunil!" Then she recovered. "I mean . . . you're not Sunil. Sorry, I was sending a work email. Vikas, you're Vikas." Great, now Manisha was starting her date with a white lie.

"No worries, dude. You do you. But damn, does you doing you look good from here."

Manisha wasn't sure if she should feel flattered or violated by Vikas's words. She decided to put away her judgment like Manny had reminded her to do.

"Please, sit."

Vikas hung his jacket on the chair before settling in. His hair was impeccably styled, neatly parted to the side with a close fade that suggested he was comfortable in front of the mirror. He looked sharp, sporting a black jacket over a brown turtleneck paired with skinny jeans—a bold choice that he was just managing to pull off.

However, as Manisha's gaze drifted back upward, she spotted a price tag dangling from his jacket. She didn't want to embarrass him, so she kept it to herself.

"How's your day been?" Vikas said as he looked around for the server.

"Oh, it's been great. You?"

"Really great now that I'm sitting in front of an Indian goddess. Manisha, tell me about yourself. Leena Auntie mentioned that we have a lot in common and that we'd be a great match."

"Oh, she did?" Manisha stared down Deena a.k.a. Leena Auntie, who was watching with an encouraging grin. "Right, of course she did. Why else would we be here? You're a lawyer—we have that in common." Manisha wished she had spent more time committing Vikas's profile to memory and less time being distracted by Sunil's emails.

"Yup, I'm what you call an international lawyer. Dabble in a little bit of criminal law, too. How about you?" Vikas asked.

"Same . . . well, I'm just on a little break from law. Not sure how long that'll be, to be honest. I guess I'm still trying to figure out what I want to be when I grow up."

"Besides being a sexy woman." Vikas winked at Manisha. "I'm lucky, I love my job. There's just something about working with criminals. If you need a pair of VIP tickets to a sports or music event, or a luxury car, they have that kind of access."

"Is that a good thing?"

"Sure. Payment doesn't have to be made in cash, you know?"

The back of her neck prickled. "But you're a lawyer. It's almost like you're acting like the criminal yourself?"

He leaned across the table. "Except I'm smarter than these guys. I don't get caught," he said proudly.

"As lawyers, we take an oath. It sounds like you might be engaging in some questionable under-the-table activities."

"Oh, come on, baby girl, you don't like to do anything under the table?" Okay, this guy's words were bordering on offensive.

"I don't do that under the table," Manisha said with a firm

voice. Then she softened her tone, hoping to segue and give him another chance.

"What else do you like to do for fun?"

"I little bit of this, a little bit of that."

Vikas swiped at his nose, as if to signal he was into doing drugs. Did he really just do that? Manisha shook it off, trying to play off his cues and questions like Manny had suggested.

"Do you have any interesting hobbies?" she asked.

"Yeah." Vikas winked. "Can't wait to show you later."

It took everything in Manisha not to let her shock and repulsion show on her face. She could really use one of Rohit's inopportune interruptions right about now.

"And how about your family?" she ventured. Surely that was a safe question. "The bio said you have a brother?"

"Yeah, he's out west right now. We've had our issues in the past; probably best he keeps his distance from me." Vikas made a fake gunshot with his hand.

Or not. Manisha concealed her surprise again, and gave Vikas one more chance to redeem himself. "And your parents?"

"Meh, I don't care for my parents. I've given all I could."

"I'm sorry to hear that."

He shrugged. "It's just a money thing now. If you're lucky enough to be with me, I'll share my inheritance with you when they keel over."

This time she couldn't hide her shock. "Oh my god."

"Exciting, right?"

"No. I mean, that's awful!" Here she was on a date with a guy who was literally waiting for his parents to die so he could collect their money. "I can't believe how nonchalant you're being, especially as a lawyer."

"Okay, busted. I thought I could be a lawyer but didn't get into law school. Mostly because I didn't try."

Her jaw dropped. "You lied to me? To Leena Auntie?"

"Not lied, just didn't tell the whole truth. That's how people date these days. You tell half-truths, and later, shit comes out and you get over it."

Manisha chose not to dwell on the fact that she was no better herself—hiding her intentions, fabricating the dating site.

"I had to test the waters," Vikas went on. "I know all you Indian chicks want a doctor or lawyer, so I fibbed a little. I wanted to see how far I could take it. Look, I may not have the kind of money you want now, but like I said, play your cards right, and we could be in for a major windfall soon enough."

"That's not what I want at all! Ever!" she exclaimed. "Hold up, so what do you do for work?"

"I'm kind of in between jobs until that inheritance kicks in."

Finally, Manisha was saved by Rohit as he delivered the refill she'd ordered what felt like ages ago and put a bottle of sparkling water on the table between them.

Vikas asked Manisha, "Listen, you can pay for this, right?"

"Um, I guess," she said, glancing nervously at Rohit. "You can charge it to me, Rohit. You know how it goes. I always pay for potential clients."

She was desperate for Rohit to leave before he realized she was on a date. He looked at her funny but left without any questions. She let out a long breath.

"Potential client, huh?" Vikas smirked. "So, you like to role play?"

"No!"

"Calm down, baby girl. You were asking about my parents and the 'plan.'"

"I wasn't, and that's enough. I really don't like the way you're talking about your parents. I feel like an accomplice in some plot to . . . I don't know . . . to murder them."

"Wait, are you suggesting we kill them ourselves?" He leaned forward, interest sparking in his eyes. "I'm all ears. I've heard about these 'unsolved mysteries.' Is that what you're thinking?"

"No! That's not what I am thinking at all!" Irate, Manisha leaped out of her chair. It made an awful scraping noise as she stood, drawing the attention of neighbouring tables.

"If you don't leave now, you'll become an unsolved mystery," she hissed between clenched teeth.

"Geez, okay." Vikas took a big gulp of the sparkling water. "At least this was on you."

A low growl emitted from deep within her throat.

Vikas dropped the bottle on the table with a clunk and scurried out the door. Deena hurried over to Manisha.

"Another one?" she asked sympathetically.

"He was not looking for an ambitious, well-rounded, and down-to-earth woman like his profile said. He was looking for a partner in crime. Literally."

"Wow, this is a lot tougher than I thought it would be. I can't believe these guys. They take the time to fill out their bios and answer our questions and then . . . they show up like walking red flags. I'm sorry, Manisha."

"I don't remember this being on Manny's whiteboard," Manisha said under her breath.

Deena frowned. "Who would have thought? Even my online dating disasters are turning out to be no match for yours."

"Maybe I'm just not cut out for dating Baskin guys, Deena. They're all handsome Indian men, but they're so shallow. I know I said I'm looking for my Prince Charming, but these guys are all charm, no depth at best. What I really need is someone who's more than just charming—he should be kind, genuine, and passionate about exploring life. Isn't that what I'm putting out into the world? So why does it feel like the only thing I'm getting on these dates is attention for my looks?"

"I get it, Manisha, but it's only been a few dates. You've got to give it more time. You can't expect to find your Prince Charming in just six days. Trust me, it's not the Baskin guys—it's guys in general. I've dated in New York, Colorado . . . heck, I even went to Canada."

"Canada?"

"Yeah, Meena Auntie did say to keep all my options open. But honestly, it's no better up there." They shared a soft chuckle.

"Look, we're just getting started. Forget Vikas. Nick's up next. Why don't you take some time to go over his profile?" Deena suggested, taking Manisha's hand and coaxing her to sit.

Manisha did just that, trying her best to push her frustration aside.

"He's right on time," Deena whispered when Nick entered the café fifteen minutes later. She rushed back to her table as Nick approached Manisha with an enthusiastic wave.

He extended his hand, giving her a handshake that felt perhaps a little too eager.

"Sorry I'm a little late," he said with a sheepish smile. "Busy day in the ER."

"Oh, no, you're right on time," Manisha replied. "We could've rescheduled if you needed to."

"I'm glad we didn't," Nick said quickly. "I've been really looking forward to meeting you."

Manisha racked her brain for something relatable to say. "Uh, *ER* was one of my favourite shows."

"Ah, classic! Who doesn't enjoy a good medical drama?" Nick chuckled. "So, your bio said you're a lawyer, and I'm a doctor. Pretty much a Bollywood rom-com waiting to happen. Our parents would be thrilled."

Manisha gave a tight smile. "Well, I'm actually not sure I'll stick with law. It's—"

"Funny, I feel the same way about medicine." Nick leaned forward. "I love saving lives and all, but I've been thinking . . . maybe it's time for something more. Something different. Like owning my own business. Or retiring early and setting up in a different country. Maybe starting a family soon? I'd really love to be a dad."

Manisha blinked, her mind racing to keep up. He was talking a mile a minute. Did he just say . . . family?

"I'm lucky. I had a great dad," Nick continued. "He was an amazing role model. I want to pass that on to my kids. You want kids, right? Leena Auntie said you did."

"Yeah," Manisha said quickly, her voice a little too high-pitched. She cleared her throat. "I mean, yes. And I got lucky with my parents, too."

Nick smiled widely, reaching across the table to take her hand. His gaze locked on hers, and there was a moment of silence as they studied each other.

His thumb gently caressed her palm.

Manisha nervously bit her lip.

"If this is our version of foreplay, I can't wait to see how play-ful we get in between the sheets."

Her eyes flared, and she yanked back her hand, knocking over her coffee in the process. What just happened?!

"Okay, that's it! I've reached my limit!" she blurted, jumping out of her seat, and looking around the shop in panic.

Nick blinked, genuinely surprised. "Wait, what? You went from playful to prude in, like, two seconds."

"Maybe, but this is a first date!" Manisha cried as her face flushed bright.

Nick, undeterred, slowly stood with a casual grin. "That it is, and I was kinda hoping this first date would end at my place, just around the corner."

He jerked his thumb at the door.

"Ugh, please just go! Alone," Manisha emphasized, shoving him lightly in the direction of the door, her face a mix of disgust and second-hand embarrassment.

"Alright, alright," Nick said, raising both hands like he was surrendering. "But if you change your mind, I'm a block away . . ."

"Leave now!" Manisha practically yelled. Nick finally got the hint.

Deena came running up. "I heard the whole thing. That went from G-rated to X-rated in seconds. What a weirdo!"

"Deena, I've had my fill of dates today. I can't handle any more."

"I get it. Even I'm tired of watching your dates. They're like slow-motion car crashes." Deena reached out and squeezed her arm. "I'll cancel the others for today. Besides, don't we have to run that stuff over to the temple for your mom later?"

Manisha glanced at the counter. "Oh shoot. We do. Okay, let me just help Rohit quickly with the paperwork and then come pick me up at my house in a couple of hours."

"At least you two are being more civil to each other now."

"It was a low bar."

Manisha hugged Deena goodbye. Deena noticed the loose straps on Manisha's dress and adjusted them for her.

"Thanks, Mama Patel, for the amazing flirting advice," Manisha said with a sarcastic grin. "She told me loose straps are a perfect excuse for flirting—because a guy can 'fix' the strap and, you know, casually graze your shoulder." Manisha huffed. "That's the last time I take her flirting tips!"

"Well, we'll keep searching for that perfect man to fix your straps for you. He's out there, I promise!" Deena said, waving goodbye.

Manisha approached the counter and spotted a sign. *The Café will be closing early today.* How much time did Rohit think they needed to go through a few pages of legal jargon?

Manisha sank into her chair, waiting for Rohit. It was still early, not even eleven, so she decided to kill time by sending a quick email to Sunil.

Subject: Breaking News!
The date was a disaster!

Apparently, finding a decent guy, let alone my ride or die, isn't as easy as I thought. Here I was trying to bring my authentic self and I'm not sure they even know the meaning of authentic—seems like they're too busy spelling "sex" to spell "sincere."

Anyway, I could use a little cheering up from the squad. How's your thumb? And did you end up tucking into some aloo parathas?
Isha

Manisha hit send and stretched back in her chair, letting out a small sigh of relief. A few minutes later, Rohit appeared from the kitchen, jacket in hand.

"What's going on? I thought we agreed to meet after my meetings?" she called out, a bit surprised.

"Yeah, sorry about that," Rohit said, looking apologetic. "Something came up, and I actually need to get going."

"Oh . . . well, I guess we can meet another time, then," Manisha said, her voice trailing off. "I just thought your dad wanted to get this done sooner rather than later."

"He did," Rohit replied, running a hand through his hair. "It's my fault. I've been a little distracted lately and forgot I had something else I needed to do today."

Manisha nodded. "Okay, well, I've reorganized everything." She held out the folder containing the righted paperwork.

"Thanks," he said, quickly taking it from her and tucking it behind the counter.

She hesitated before speaking again. "And . . . before you go, here's the money from the other day." She pulled the cash from her purse and placed it on the counter.

Rohit shook his head, gently pushing the money away. "No need for that. I don't want it back."

Manisha raised an eyebrow, leaning forward slightly. "But I want you to have it back," she insisted, nudging the cash closer to him.

He sighed. "Look, Manisha, I really don't have the energy for another round of this right now. I've got a lot going on."

Manisha crossed her arms but softened, the tension lifting a little. "So do I . . ."

"Really?" Rohit said, his tone teasing. "Because from where I'm standing, all you seem to be doing is coming in here, looking all fancy for meetings that always seem to end in a hurry."

"Well, I'm a lawyer," Manisha replied with a slight shrug. "That's just how I work. Remember, it's all about billable hours."

Rohit let out an exaggerated sigh. "As I mentioned, I need to get going, and so do you." He scooped up the cash and dropped it into the tip jar.

"And that's how I work," he added, starting toward the door.

Manisha trailed behind him, feigning annoyance. "Okay, okay. I'll be on my way, too. Good grief." She turned toward the exit, rolling her eyes playfully.

After locking up, Rohit jumped into his car and sped off, leaving Manisha standing in the parking lot.

"Well, that was a fun twist," she muttered to herself, shaking her head. With a sigh, she slid into her own car, trying to shake off the lingering awkwardness as she drove away.

## 20

*A* couple of hours later, Deena and Manisha arrived at the temple, where Manisha's mom had asked them to deliver some items for the kitchen. The Khannas had built this beautiful sanctuary as a gathering place for the Baskin Indian community, and it truly felt like a home for all. While it was designed with traditional Indian temple architecture in mind, it also had a contemporary touch that made it feel welcoming to people from all walks of life. The tall white marble spires of the temple stretched into the sky, each one delicately carved with intricate patterns that sparkled in the afternoon sun.

"So Rohit just took off? I did notice he looked a little stressed today," Deena said, breaking the silence as they grabbed the grocery bags from the trunk and started heading toward the entrance. "I could see him at the counter while I was supervising your dates."

"Ugh, those dates," Manisha groaned. "Please don't remind me."

They made their way up the broad stone steps to a pair of grand wooden doors flanked by vibrant floral arrangements. Manisha took a deep, appreciative breath. The air here always smelled faintly of jasmine and incense. The lush green gardens surrounding the temple were filled with fragrant flowers and towering trees that offered plenty of shade, making it a peaceful spot for reflection.

"But you're right something was off with Rohit today," she said after some thought. "Selfishly, I just want to get this paperwork done, and then I won't have to see him as much—or talk to him as much. God, are you hearing me?" She lifted her gaze skyward.

Deena giggled, but the sound came to an abrupt stop. "Well, you might want to pray a bit harder."

Manisha followed Deena's gaze and saw Rohit standing near the back of the temple kitchen, chatting with Meena Auntie. Her eyes widened, surprised to see him at the temple.

"What's he doing here?" Manisha blurted.

"Talking to Meena Auntie," Deena said, sounding more puzzled than anything.

"Yeah, I can see that, but why?" Her brain was running in overdrive. "We need to leave. Now."

Deena raised an eyebrow. "What's the big deal? We're just here to drop off flour and milk. I'm not trying to mess with God's plan, okay?" Deena insisted, looking up at the sky like she was asking for divine guidance.

Manisha grinned. "Deena, I'm pretty sure God's plan doesn't involve us being stuck in a room with those two. Besides, you don't want Rohit to know we know Meena Auntie that way. What if she spills the beans—"

"Seeds," Deena corrected.

"Right, seeds," Manisha let out a half chuckle.

"So what? Half the brown town is probably on her list, anyway. But I get it—you just don't want her blabbing about it in front of Rohit. Okay, let's just unload the groceries, say hi to a few aunties and uncles, show them how well-behaved we are, and get out of here."

Manisha thought for a moment and then nodded reluctantly. "Alright, I guess we don't have much of a choice. But I have a feeling this isn't going to go as planned . . ."

They entered the kitchen and immediately, Rohit waved them over with a smile. Manisha was equal parts surprised and confused—after all, he'd practically kicked her out earlier at the café.

"Deena, Manisha! Over here!" Rohit called out. His smile was wide but anyone looking closely enough would see that it didn't reach his eyes, which seemed to carry a hint of something. Not the usual mischief or annoyance Manisha was used to seeing. Sorrow. "It's really good to see you both here today. It means a lot to me!"

"But we just saw you and, well, you were trying to shoo me out of the café," Manisha couldn't resist pointing out.

"Sorry," he muttered, hand shooting to the back of his neck, clearly embarrassed. "I just couldn't be late. Not today."

"We're glad we could be here. And it's nice to see you, Meena Auntie," Deena said with a knowing glance at Manisha as they started unloading the grocery bags onto the table.

Meena Auntie wrapped them both in a warm embrace. "I was just telling Rohit how incredible the women of Baskin are," she said, her voice full of affection. "It seems like God has answered my prayers by bringing both of you here."

Manisha was appalled. A quick peek at Rohit showed her own horror mirrored in his expression. How did Meena Auntie not know about Suzy?

"Thank you, Meena Auntie," Deena said, fixing Manisha with a look that said "We're being extra nice now."

Meena Auntie took a deep breath, placing her hand on her

chest. "This moment, with all of us gathered here, feels truly magical. We are planting seeds of good friendship, my dears. Seeds that will blossom in time."

Manisha and Deena exchanged wide-eyed looks at the mention of seeds. Even Rohit seemed to flinch, but he quickly recovered, his expression neutral.

"I'd better store the milk before it spoils," Rohit interjected.

Meena Auntie watched him go with a wistful sigh. "He is such a kind-hearted person," she said, almost dreamily.

Manisha smartly chose to keep quiet.

"Life's been challenging for him lately," Meena Auntie continued. "But it's so comforting to see both of you here supporting him and his family."

She cupped her hands around each of their cheeks. "I have to leave now, but I'm so glad you came to show your respect for his mother. She was such a beautiful soul. We miss her every day, but especially today."

With that, Meena Auntie drifted off, leaving behind a mystical aura.

Manisha stood still for a moment, her thoughts catching up with the conversation. "I think I know why he's been off today," she said softly. "It's the anniversary of his mother's passing."

They stood there in silence, staring after Rohit. Any annoyance Manisha felt over Rohit's earlier behaviour at Chai Time fizzled out. In its place, a mix of guilt and sympathy settled.

When Rohit returned from the fridge, Deena immediately stepped forward, pulling him into a hug. "We're so sorry about the loss of your mother, Rohit."

"Truly sorry," Manisha added, her voice sincere. To her surprise, she found herself hugging him, too. "She was one of my mom's closest friends . . . she's dearly missed."

Rohit hugged her back, his voice thick with emotion. "It's been a tough week. And this kind of came together last-minute. But all I can do is try to focus on carrying forward her legacy. Speaking of which, would one of you mind helping me in the back? I've got something I need to do, and I could use an extra pair of hands."

"Sure!" Deena immediately volunteered. "Manisha would be happy to help you," she added with a smile that wasn't entirely convincing.

Manisha opened her mouth to protest, but Deena shot her a look.

"Me?" Manisha squeaked, but before she could argue further, Rohit was already leading her outside.

"Here, you'll need these." He handed her a pair of gardening gloves and a dirt-stained apron as they made their way around to the backyard. "I hear the Patels have a green thumb."

Manisha eyed the potted plants that lined a small garden area. "My dad," she said, glancing at the greenery with a hint of admiration. "He's the one with the real green thumb."

As she slipped on the gloves, she couldn't help but wonder how much more unexpected this day could get.

"Manisha, would you mind helping me plant these in honour of my mother?"

Manisha was stunned for a moment, but as Rohit got to work, she tied on the apron and dropped to her knees to join him.

There were marigolds, carnations, roses, and all kinds of plants Manisha had never seen before. She and Rohit worked together to plant each one with care, gently unpotting and nestling the assortment of flowers and foliage into the earth.

Manisha snuck a glance at his face and noticed how serene Rohit looked. The sorrow in his eyes from just before seemed to have quieted.

"Did your mom have a passion for gardening?" she asked, breaking the silence.

"She definitely did. In fact, a few years back, your dad came by and helped her get rid of those annoying weeds."

Manisha was surprised to hear her dad had helped out Mrs. Khanna. "Yeah, my dad has a knack for that. What about you? Do you find gardening peaceful?"

Rohit exhaled deeply. "You know, I'm really trying to find peace in gardening, in the temple, in the café, in future plans," he said, his voice heavy with frustration. "It's just . . . it's hard when you're the centre of attention for all the wrong reasons."

Manisha gave him a reassuring smile. "Just give it some time, Rohit."

He nodded slowly, the weight in his expression softening. "You're right, Manisha. My mom found peace here. I just have to believe I can find it, too."

"As long as you believe, you will," Manisha said softly.

Her gaze caught on his apron, stained with sweat and dirt. Her own apron matched his, and the sight transported her back to a cozy morning just a few days prior in her family kitchen. Her mother and father working side by side in the kitchen flashed before her eyes, a strange parallel to the current scene in the garden.

She physically recoiled from the thought, rocking her weight back to the tops of her feet.

"Alright, I think we are all done." Rohit rose from the ground and offered assistance to Manisha.

"Wow, this is absolutely stunning!" Deena's voice echoed from behind them. Manisha turned to see her cousin making her way around the side of the temple. The three of them stood for a moment, taking in their addition to the garden, the quiet hum of nature surrounding them.

Finally, Deena spoke again, interrupting the stillness. "Manisha, we should probably get going."

"Of course," Manisha replied. She shed her gloves and apron, handing them back to Rohit.

"Thanks again, Manisha," he said, giving her a grateful smile. "I really appreciate your help. Suzy won't get here until later, but I wanted to get this finished sooner so that people can appreciate it in daylight."

Manisha nodded. "No problem."

As they walked back toward the parking lot, Manisha turned to take one more look at the garden, at Rohit. Maybe it was the seeds from Meena Auntie, or perhaps the power of the temple, but in that moment, she felt an inexplicable tug on her heart.

"Earth to Manisha . . ." Deena's voice called out from up ahead.

"Coming!" Manisha said, whirling back around and quickening her pace to catch up with her cousin.

## 21

When Manisha opened the front door to the Patel home, the familiar scent of her dad's cooking instantly filled her nostrils, pulling her back to childhood. The comforting aroma of spices brought on a deluge of memories: lazy summer afternoons, her dad humming in the kitchen, her brothers chasing her around the living room—the warmth of home.

"Mom, I'm back!" she called out, her words bouncing off the walls. But there was no response.

"Mom?" she called again, stepping further into the house. The heat hit her as soon as she entered, stifling and thick. Despite the scorching Baskin evening, her mom refused to turn on the AC, convinced it made her aching back worse. Some things never changed.

She heard her dad's voice drift from the back of the house, and she followed the sound. Unlatching the sliding door, she stepped into the lush garden oasis he had crafted over the years—string lights twinkling around the wooden deck he had built himself, the air thick with the scent of blooming florals and fresh herbs.

"Come, Isha. Your mother's gone out," her dad called.

She made her way through the garden, admiring the neatly tended plants.

"The backyard looks sick, Dad!" she called out as she approached him, standing on the deck where he was inspecting a small pot of basil.

"What? Beemaar? Which one looks sick?" he asked, looking up with a furrowed brow.

Manisha laughed. "No, no—sick as in awesome! You've got your own little paradise out here."

Her dad playfully rolled his eyes, the corners of his mouth twitching upward. "You and your modern slang." He gestured to the bench beside him and she took a seat, feeling the warmth of the sun-soaked wood beneath her.

They sat together for a moment, surrounded by the quiet rustling of leaves, the soft hum of the late afternoon.

"I was just at the temple," Manisha said, breaking the silence, "helping Rohit plant flowers in honour of his mom. All this time away from Baskin, I had forgotten how close everyone was to Mrs. Khanna."

Her dad nodded thoughtfully. "She was a pillar of this community. A good woman."

Manisha glanced at him, remembering something Rohit had said. "Dad, you didn't tell me you used to help Mrs. Khanna with her garden."

He shrugged, plucking a blade of grass and chewing on it absently, a habit he'd kept since his childhood on the farm. "We all helped each other. In this community, that's just how it works. I'd help her with the garden, and she'd often share new recipes with me."

"So, you were close?"

"We all were," he said, his voice softening, tinged with respect. "She was the heart of this town for many Indian families. Your mom and I—the whole community—owe a lot to her."

Manisha nodded, her thoughts drifting to her own memories of Mrs. Khanna—her kindness, the way she always seemed to have time for everyone.

"Rohit's trying to carry on his mom's legacy here. You should've seen him today, helping in the temple kitchen, then planting flowers in the back garden she'd created . . ."

She paused, stunned by the words tumbling out of her own mouth. Clearing her throat, she changed the topic. "Anyway, I'm taking care of the paperwork for the café like you asked. It looks like Mr. Khanna wants to do some renovations. A lot of permits and city regulations to navigate, but I've got it covered."

Her dad gave her a proud smile. "Good. I'm glad to hear that."

He took another thoughtful nibble of grass, his eyes scanning the garden, as though he could see more than just the plants. He always did have a way of seeing the bigger picture.

"Manisha," he said after a moment, "I know I don't have to tell you this, but Mr. Khanna . . . well, he's the reason I'm sitting here today, enjoying this garden, this house, all of it. He's the one who helped me get started—when your mother and I had nothing but dreams."

Manisha looked at her dad, her heart swelling with emotion. He had always been the steady foundation of their family, the one who kept everything together, but moments like this—when he let his guard down and spoke so openly—reminded her of how much he had sacrificed, how much he had worked for.

"He gave me the chance to build something here," he said, sweeping his arm across the house and garden. His tone was quiet but full of conviction. "By doing that, he helped me build something for all of you. For you, Sanj, and Sammy. You know, not everyone was supportive back then. There were plenty who didn't think I could make it. But the Khannas . . . they stood by me when I needed it most. I can never repay them for that."

Manisha's throat tightened. She turned her eyes to the garden, the flowers blooming in the dimming light like small bursts of hope, like the very legacy her father spoke of. This was it, she realized. The garden, the house, everything her dad had built was part of something much bigger than just bricks and mortar. It was a living testament to years of struggle and kindness, of love and hard work.

"Dad, I . . ." she started softly, her voice thick with gratitude. She swallowed hard. "Thank you. For everything."

Her father smiled, his eyes filled with a warmth that never failed to make her feel at home. "You don't need to thank me, Isha. Just . . . remember what we have here and carry it forward."

Manisha leaned back against the bench, letting the tranquil air settle around her. With her dad beside her, the familiar sounds of the neighbourhood in the distance, and the beauty of the garden, she felt a sense of peace she hadn't realized she'd been missing. Everything felt right.

"I know, Dad."

He nodded, his hands resting comfortably on his knees. "And Rohit is a good young man. Very respectful. He greets his elders in both Hindi and Punjabi. Has good qualities—integrity, kindness."

Manisha thought about her recent dates, the ones that had felt more like obligations than connections. "Qualities that are hard to find these days in a man," she replied, a small smile tugging at the corners of her lips. "Don't worry, Dad. I'll make sure Rohit and his dad get those permits filed without any issues."

Her dad smiled back at her, a quiet pride in his eyes. "Thank you, kiddo. It means a lot. But listen, I want you to be happy, too. And I know, back in London, you weren't always so happy . . . not just with work, but maybe with other things, too."

Manisha stiffened. It wasn't that she was trying to hide her struggles—she knew her family could read her pretty well. But hearing it from her dad, in such a straightforward way, made her realize just how much she'd been carrying around in secret, both personally and professionally.

He reached over and patted her head gently. "We taught you kids to be independent, to work hard for what you deserve. You deserve everything in this life, Isha."

Manisha looked at him, taking in his words. The lines on his face, suntanned and weathered by years of hard work, were now the signs of his experience—of the lessons he'd learned and was passing on to her.

"Times are tougher for you kids now," he said, his voice soft and full of quiet concern. "So many distractions, so many things pulling you in every direction. But you've got to allow yourself to be pulled back here, too." He placed a hand over his chest, his eyes meeting hers with a tenderness that made Manisha's heart swell. "You've got to listen to where it is leading you, Isha. To what you truly want, not just what the world tells you to want."

Not knowing what to say, Manisha rested her head on his shoulder affectionately.

"You know I love you the most," her dad said. She could feel his shoulders shake with a chuckle. "Don't tell your brothers, though."

Manisha laughed, sitting back up. "Dang, Sanj and Sammy got the short end of the stick."

He grinned, patting her hand affectionately. "They got your mother's long stick. That laathi is long enough for everyone to get a smack," he joked, making her laugh even harder.

"Your mother and I will always ask about your future, beta, it's in our nature. We want you to be settled, with a good career, good friends, and yes, one day . . . a good life partner. We worry, sometimes, because that's what parents do. We want to protect you, keep you safe, and ensure you're taken care of. But at the end of the day, you must follow what makes you happy. Your happiness is all that matters to us."

Manisha took a deep breath, feeling the weight of her thoughts pressing against her chest. "I know, Dad. You're right. It's just . . . sometimes, with work and with Mom constantly asking about everything, I forget what I really want. And I know I put too much pressure on myself. But . . . with Sanj getting married, and now Sammy starting his life with Manny, I can't help but wonder when it'll be my turn. And what if it never happens for me? What if I run out of time?"

She sighed, feeling vulnerable and unsure, but her father's presence gave her a small sense of comfort.

Her dad reached over and squeezed her hand gently. "Manisha, beta, please listen to me. Life is not a race. Your turn will come when it is meant to. No rush, no need to worry. You have your whole life ahead of you."

He looked at her with deep affection, his eyes full of reassurance, as though he could take away all her worries with just his words.

Manisha let out a breath she didn't realize she'd been holding. "I just wanted to make you and Mom proud," she said quietly. "I guess somewhere along the way, I lost track of what would make me proud."

Her dad smiled warmly, his eyes softening with affection. "We've always been proud of you, Manisha. And we always will be, no matter what."

Manisha looked at him, feeling a wave of gratitude fill her heart. "I'm really glad to be home, Dad. I like spending time with you and Mom. Honestly, I need more of these talks with you. Your wisdom—it's . . ."

"Sick, right?" he teased, his face lighting up with a playful grin.

Manisha burst out laughing, the weight of the conversation lifting as she caught his infectious sense of humour. "Definitely, Dad. Definitely."

## 22

*A*fter the moment with her dad in the garden, Manisha headed back into the house, feeling rather emotional. The sound of the TV murmured from the living room, and she knew her mom had returned. She found her sitting on the couch, absorbed in the Indian news channel, as usual. Without a word, Manisha walked over and threw her arms around her.

"What's this?" her mom asked, her voice warm with surprise as she hugged her back.

"A big hug for you, Mom," Manisha said, holding on a little longer than usual.

"You should go to the temple more often," her mom suggested lightly, as she pulled away, settling back into the couch.

"I should," Manisha agreed, smiling softly. "But right now, I think I'm going to head up to my room for a bit."

"Okay, beta." Her mom didn't look up, already engrossed in the latest headlines.

Manisha nodded and made her way upstairs, the familiar rhythm of her house providing some comfort. But the conversation with her dad had her mind reeling. It felt as though her thoughts were being tugged in a hundred different directions—the Khannas, the temple, her parents' sacrifices, her law career, the future—it all felt so overwhelming.

As she reached her bedroom, her phone pinged. The familiar notification appeared—an email from Sunil. She sat down on the edge of her bed, her heart lifting just a little. An email from Sunil was exactly what she needed right now.

> On behalf of men, I'm sorry you had to sit through that. Just know that any self-respecting guy would never behave like such an idiot, especially in front of someone as genuine as you. You deserve better.
>
> Sadly, no aloo parathas for me, just lots of coffee and chai. The day got away from me. And the thumb is . . . resting—I chickened out. But no rush, right?

She typed a response to him:

> I do deserve better! Maybe next time I can have you on standby to save me from having to deal with that again. Or at least remind me that I'm worthy of more. Better yet, I'm hopeful there won't be a next time, and my next date will be with my ride or die.
>
> No rush—only when you're ready.

The last thing she wanted was to pressure Sunil into anything. The world didn't need another apprehensive, uncommitted man playing the field.

If only she had the luxury of taking her time, too . . . Her thoughts whirled back to Dr. Rocky stressing how urgent her situation was. It was baffling how these past few years had just passed her by—so much time spent studying, working long hours, and for what?

Her phone lit up again.

> Good for you! I really admire your optimism, Isha.
> And it's clear that you're truly ready to find someone,
> settle down and build a meaningful relationship. I wish
> I was there, but I think my previous relationship is still
> holding me back. I have a feeling you understand how
> hard it can be to allow yourself to trust new people
> when someone you thought would always be by your
> side betrays you. I hope this doesn't come off as insin-
> cere, but I'm proud of you for getting to that place.

Manisha was deeply touched by Sunil's words. Her heart ached for him and the hurt that he was still working through.

> That means a lot, Sunil. I have total faith that, when
> the time is right, your person will show up to help
> heal your heart. Honestly, I'm not without my own
> scars. Sometimes, it feels like just yesterday I was
> shutting out the world. Have you ever been to
> Henriette's? They have the best cheesecake in town,
> and an incredible collection of books lining the walls.
> I would sit there for hours getting lost in story after
> story, devouring slice after slice. It's the ultimate
> pick-me-up.

Manisha could've gone for a slice at this very moment after the weird day she just had, but the rich, spiced aroma of butter chicken and fresh garlic naan wafted under the door. Her dad must've started making dinner, and there was nothing more comforting than that.

> No way! My parents went there all the time back in
> the day. It used to be their go-to date spot, and I'd
> get jealous because they'd usually leave me behind
> at home. God, I haven't been there in ages. Thanks
> for the throwback, Isha!

Manisha smiled softly. Now that she thought about it, Henriette's would make the perfect date spot. Maybe she'd ask Deena to arrange for her next batch of Curry and Cupid meetings to be held there.

Suddenly, her mom's voice echoed through the house.

"Isha! Beta, your father needs help with dinner!"

## 23

The next evening, Manisha's father gently reminded her that Mr. Khanna would be returning to Baskin soon. Manisha knew it was time to nudge Rohit into sitting down and sorting through the paperwork. Some of the changes Mr. Khanna had in mind for the café required city permits, and she wanted to make sure everything was in order.

She took a gamble and headed over to Chai Time to see if Rohit was available to go through the documents. But when she arrived, she found the café locked up tight. It made sense, though—it was already dark, with the streetlights casting a soft glow across the quiet street.

She glanced through the windows, but Rohit was nowhere in sight.

"Looking for me?" a voice called from behind her.

She turned, squinting through the darkness. Rohit was emerging from the side of the café.

"Rohit! Yes, I heard your dad's coming back soon, so I think we should really focus on the paperwork. There are a lot of questions about what he wants to do with the café, and it could take some time to get through the permit process at city hall."

"I'm free now. Want to come in and go through everything now?" Rohit offered.

Manisha smiled. "Sure."

As they entered the café, their shadows stretched across the dimly lit walls. She settled in at the counter while Rohit went to retrieve the paperwork. Her eyes drifted to the corner table where yesterday's disastrous dates had unfolded and she shrugged off a shudder. She would be avoiding that spot in the future, perfect vantage point and seclusion be damned.

Rohit returned and wordlessly placed the paperwork on the counter. He sat down next to her, the silence hanging heavily between them.

"Listen, about yesterday . . . I had no idea it was the anniversary of your mom's passing," she said, trying to break the tension.

She flipped through the folder for a moment, but noticed he wasn't responding. When she glanced over, she saw he was staring down at his phone, dejection etched into his features.

"How are you doing today? I can only imagine how tough yesterday was," she pressed.

He sighed heavily and set his phone down. "Well, Manisha Patel, I'd feel a lot better if I had a drink right now."

"Well, Rohit Khanna, why don't you grab a drink, then?" she replied with a smirk.

"I don't like drinking alone."

"If you think I'm going to let you drink alone, you clearly don't know me as well as you think you do," she said, raising an eyebrow.

Rohit rounded the counter, grabbed a bottle of Chianti, and poured them each a glass.

"To your mother," Manisha said, raising her glass.

They clinked glasses and took a sip. She hummed as the bold flavour flooded her palate.

"To our mothers, for raising two Indian kids who turned out pretty alright!" Rohit added, lifting his glass again with a grin.

Manisha chuckled softly. "Well, that depends on what you mean by 'alright,'" she said, her tone quiet.

"What do you mean?" Rohit asked. "You seem to have it all together, at least in the eyes of most Indian parents."

Manisha shrugged. "My mom's opinion of my professional and personal life changes depending on the day of the week. She's happy with my career, but when it comes to my personal life . . . let's just say it's been a challenge."

Rohit laughed. "The struggle is real. I think every Indian parent feels that way until their kids are married. You're not letting the pressure get to you, though, are you?"

She almost laughed out loud. If only he knew just how much pressure she felt—from her mother, from Dr. Rocky, from herself . . .

"How can I not? But maybe it's just because I'm back in Baskin . . ." she said, giving a half smile.

"Are you thinking of staying?"

She hesitated. "Well . . . maybe. It wasn't the plan originally, but you know how it goes." She decided to change the subject. "Speaking of plans . . . your dad really has big plans for this place," Manisha said.

"Not my dad, actually. Me," Rohit corrected with a grin.

Her head cocked to the side. "Oh, so you're not just running the place, you're actually creating the whole vibe?" she asked, impressed.

Rohit shrugged nonchalantly. "You know what they say—change is good. Just look at me—I went from running a tech company to developing a community hub in Baskin. Who knew?"

"Oh, a community hub! That explains why you need permits to update the front exterior. You need more room!" Manisha pulled out the blueprints that were attached to the legal paperwork.

"You're looking at it the wrong way," Rohit said, flipping the draft around. "That's the back of Chai Time." He stood up from his stool and gestured toward the door. "Come on, follow me."

"What? Where?" Manisha asked, puzzled.

"To show you the back. You're a lawyer, right? Aren't you supposed to do your due diligence?"

"Right, but I need a little more info before—" Manisha began.

"Manisha, you've been stubborn from the moment I met you. Just, for once, trust me. Come on." Rohit extended his hand, clearly not taking no for an answer.

She eyed him for a beat.

"Fine, but can I bring this?" she said, lifting her glass of wine like a treasure.

"Wouldn't have it any other way." Rohit grinned, hand still outstretched. Slowly, she placed her free one in his.

He grasped it gently, then grabbing his own glass and the wine bottle in the other hand, he led the way through the kitchen. Manisha followed, her body lightly brushing his as they made their way toward the back.

"You know . . ." Manisha cleared her throat, squinting a little in the low light. "I'm guessing there are a few violations back here. Mostly the complete lack of lighting."

"Ah, now the lawyer comes out," Rohit teased.

"Why does it feel like I'm being led to the scene of a crime? Or what will be one," she shot back, a playful glint in her eye.

"Oh, it's not a crime scene," Rohit said with a smirk. "Just a little further . . ."

"I hope this is worth it, Rohit Khanna," Manisha muttered, still not entirely convinced.

"It is, Manisha Patel. You'll see." He gave her an encouraging smile.

And it was. When they finally stepped through the back door, everything behind them seemed to fade away. Manisha found herself standing in a peaceful little courtyard. The air was still and cool, the streetlights casting a faint glow from afar. But the real magic was overhead. A sea of stars stretched across the sky like a blanket, twinkling and shining brightly in the desert night. The soft desert breeze carried the scent of earth and sage, and for a moment, Manisha forgot all about the chaos of her life.

"Rohit . . . this . . . this is . . ." She was at a loss for words, staring up at the sky.

"Magic, right?" Rohit said with a grin, clearly proud of his little secret.

"You took the words right out of my mouth," she said, her voice soft with awe.

Rohit nodded, then dropped her hand to point to a cozy little table set up under a mesquite tree, with a few lanterns casting a warm, flickering glow. "I've got a table over there. Come on, I'll show you."

Manisha took a seat next to Rohit and got lost in the view as they both sat in silence, sipping their wine. Finally, Rohit spoke up.

"My dream is to turn Chai Time into a space where artists can come, create, and practice their craft," Rohit continued, his voice steady and filled with conviction. "It's going to be a not-for-profit, something that gives back to the community. I want it to be a place where young people can feel free to explore their creativity without worrying about making a living off it. The sad reality is that Indian kids don't always get that push to pursue careers in the arts. There's a lot of pressure to go into medicine, engineering, or something more 'practical.' My mom always felt that if kids could see the value in the arts, they'd be able to break free from that mindset, and maybe even find a way to make a living doing what they love."

He paused, looking up at the stars, as if his mother's spirit was somehow still there with him. "She dreamed of a place where they could learn, create, and be supported. That's what I want to build here—something that lasts, that helps people find their voice, without the pressure to conform to what society expects."

Manisha was quiet for a moment, feeling the weight of his words. She could see the fire behind his vision, how deeply he cared about carrying forward his mother's dream. "That's incredible, Rohit," she finally said, her voice barely above a whisper. "A space like that could change so many lives."

Rohit smiled, a little shyly. "That's the hope."

"So, you're developing the new Chai Time in honour of your mother."

Rohit nodded, a little smile playing on his lips. "For the Khanna family legacy. I'm finally in a position to . . ."

"Give back," Manisha finished for him.

He turned to her, his smile widening. "Exactly."

There was a brief lull before Rohit leaned back, looking at her with a glint of curiosity in his eyes. "Manisha, if you had the chance to become anything your heart desired at this moment, what would you choose?"

A mother.

"As a kid, I always dreamed of owning my own bakery, but you got there first!" She chuckled.

"It isn't a race, Manisha," Rohit reminded her.

"Can I share my real aspirations, or will you think I'm crazy?" she asked.

"Hey, I've learned to expect the unexpected around here," Rohit said, half smiling. "Go ahead."

Taking a deep breath, Manisha shut her eyes, as though she were reliving the journey that had brought her here. After what felt like maybe too long, she spoke, her tone one of both reflection and resolve. "I used to think I wanted to be a lawyer. It seemed like the right path—the kind of job where I could make an impact, where I could help people, where my parents would be proud. But once I stepped into that world, it felt . . . too easy. The work was predictable, the challenges weren't as demanding as I'd imagined. So, I set my sights higher—I aimed for senior partner at one of the biggest firms in the UK. I thought that title would push me, would make me feel like I was truly achieving something."

She paused, her gaze distant, lost in thought for a moment. "But here's the thing," she continued, her tone shifting slightly. "At that level, you start to see things differently. We had clients— good people—who came to us desperate for help. But they couldn't afford our fees. And when I suggested that we take on some pro bono cases, the firm shut it down. No room for charity, no room for doing what felt right. It was all about the billable hours, the prestige, the bottom line. The more I saw of that, the more disillusioned I became, and the further I withdrew, until the work that had once felt like a calling just started to feel hollow. And I realized—perhaps too late—that success, at least the way I'd imagined it, wasn't worth sacrificing the kind of values I thought I'd always had."

Her eyes met Rohit's again, the light in them now tempered by a quiet wisdom. "That's when I knew I had to step away. To find something that would challenge me, but in a way that felt meaningful again."

"That makes perfect sense," Rohit said. "Your heart wasn't in it anymore. You wanted to help, but you weren't allowed to."

"Exactly!" Manisha's eyes lit up as she spoke, her voice carrying a warmth that seemed to radiate from within. "Lately, there's been this fire inside me—this longing to spread love. I know it might sound cheesy, but it's like I can't shake the feeling that I'm meant to help people find real happiness, to guide them toward the kind of love that's life changing. It feels bigger than just a wish; it feels like a calling. I know I've got something to offer, some way to make a difference, but the path is still a little unclear. I'm still figuring it out, you know?"

She shrugged, but the gesture was light, almost as if she was letting go of any pressure to have it all figured out. "But I can feel it, deep down. I know one day, I'll find the right way to share it."

And the right person to share it with.

Her words carried a quiet confidence, as if she understood that the journey was just as important as the destination.

Rohit studied her for a moment, his gaze thoughtful. He nodded slowly, as if he could sense the depth of her conviction. "I have no doubt you will," he said with certainty. "Your passion is clear. I can feel it in everything you say. And it sounds like you already know where you want to begin. Right here, in Baskin."

Manisha sighed, leaning back in her chair and gazing out at the stars. "I know it sounds weird, but it's like I was called to come back home. Maybe all the aunties up there were yelling at the universe to drag my butt back to Baskin." She laughed softly. "I didn't expect it, but here I am. Honestly, someone needs to write a handbook for people in their thirties. There have been so many twists and turns in my life lately that I can't keep up."

Rohit chuckled, a sympathetic look crossing his face. "I hear you. Not too long ago I was engaged, living in Europe, planning a wedding . . . and now, look at me. Life really has a way of throwing curveballs, huh?"

Manisha lifted her glass with a smile. "Cheers to that," she said, clinking her wine with his. "To the unexpected paths and the adventures they bring us."

"Or the ones they mercifully steer us away from, like the 'biggest wedding in Baskin history.' Wasn't that what the *Baskin Daily* called it?" Rohit replied, shaking his head in disbelief.

Manisha laughed. "At one point, they even said it could rival the Ambani wedding!"

"It was completely out of control," Rohit said, a hint of disgust on his face.

Manisha paused, then asked cautiously, "So, what made you return to Baskin after everything that happened with Lucky? It must be tough dealing with all the judgmental looks from people who were supposed to be guests at your wedding."

Rohit raised an eyebrow, a little amused. "Including yours?"

Manisha wiggled her head in a mock apologetic gesture. "Okay, guilty. I admit it—I was quick to judge. But I guess I felt some kind of connection to Lucky, you know? I could relate to what she went through. All you did was pack up and come back here, but she had to figure out how to pick herself up again."

Rohit frowned. "What do you mean?"

Manisha sighed. She was really going to do this.

"Well, my ex—Oliver—cheated on me, too. And even though I can see now that our breakup was for the best, his betrayal still stings. It's tough when someone doesn't consider your feelings at all, and then they just move on with their life, while you're left trying to figure out what your next step is."

Rohit's expression shifted, indignation colouring his features. "Wait, hold on. I'm not sure what you've been told, but—"

Manisha cut him off, raising her voice. "The same thing everyone else heard. You were supposed to be happily engaged, and then, out of nowhere, you cheated on her. You broke Lucky's heart and her family's, too—"

"I have to stop you right there. That's not what happened." Rohit spoke quickly and forcefully, in a tone she'd never heard from him before. "I'm so tired of hearing this garbage. I am not this guy everyone's making me out to be—a liar, a low-life, someone who . . . hurts people." The last words came out as a croak, as though it pained him to say them out loud. His eyes, too, blazed with so much hurt and anger, it was hard to not look away.

She was slightly relieved when he ran a hand over his face, taking a second to gather himself.

"The truth is, Lucky broke us. She cheated on me."

Manisha froze. A high-pitched ringing sounded inside her ears, and for a second, it felt like the whole world was turning in on itself.

"Wait . . . what? Lucky cheated on you?"

Rohit nodded, and, his voice thick with emotion, said, "Yeah. We hadn't been happy for a while. In the beginning, I loved her. The real her, the Lucky who cared about people, who made seva a priority and wanted to make a difference. But as time went on, I saw another side of her—the side that only cared about money, status, and appearances. And that's when things really started to fall apart."

Manisha's eyes widened as Rohit continued. "When my mom was on her last breaths, Lucky . . . she was on a shopping spree. I was grieving, and she was buying luxury cars. Do you know what else she was doing while I was losing my mom? She was sleeping with my best friend, and—" His voice faltered. "She got pregnant with his kid."

Manisha gasped, her hand flying to her mouth in shock.

"But I never cheated on her," Rohit added firmly. "I lost my mom, my best friend, and my fiancée all at once. But no one wants to talk about that. Instead, they want the juicy story, the one that paints me as the villain."

Manisha, speechless, struggled to process everything. "I . . . I had no idea."

Rohit nodded, his gaze falling to the ground. "Her parents thought the best way to deflect attention from Lucky was to spread lies about me. They didn't want anyone to know the truth—that their precious daughter had used me for money and status, only to walk away for someone wealthier."

Manisha's heart sank as the gravity of his words settled in. "And those stories . . . those are what we all believed. I'm so sorry, Rohit. I feel awful. My parents always told me to tune out the chatter around me, but I didn't listen."

"At least you know the truth now," Rohit said heavily. "I just wish more people could hear it instead of the version they've been fed. But no one wants to. It's hard, you know? Even at the temple, they're still talking about what I supposedly did to Lucky."

"I'm sorry," Manisha said earnestly, her voice full of regret. "I shouldn't have listened to gossip."

*I shouldn't have helped spread the gossip.*

"I know what it's like to be misunderstood," Manisha said quietly. "It's like carrying a weight that no one else can see."

Rohit let out a bitter laugh. "Most people in this town still don't know the full story. But that's the way it is, isn't it? The more destructive version always seems to win out."

Manisha gave him an empathetic look. "I'm really sorry for being part of that, Rohit. I didn't mean to add to your burden. I guess seeing you and Suzy together . . ."

"She's really been there for me this past year. Sometimes, I feel like she's too good for—"

"Hey, don't say that," she interjected.

He shot her a grateful look. "All I want is to focus on building something good together, you know? I'm determined to make something of this place, and I can't let the past weigh me down. Even if half the town is still whispering about me, I refuse to give up. My mom wouldn't have."

Manisha smiled gently. "And you won't, either. People are always drawn to a scandalous story. But that's not who you are. You're creating something good for the future of this town."

Rohit turned to her, his expression softening with gratitude. "I really needed to hear that. I've been stuck in the past for too long, but I can't let it hold me back anymore."

Manisha's voice was warm as she spoke. "And you don't have to do any of this alone. I'm here, and I'll help in any way I can. Consider me your friend."

The words slipped out before she fully realized what she was saying. It felt right, though.

Rohit returned her gaze with a genuine smile. "I could really use a friend."

"Well, then it's settled. As your friend, I'll take care of all the permits for this place. I'll handle the paperwork at city hall, so you don't have to worry about it. Consider it done."

Rohit's eyes brightened with relief. "Really? Manisha, you have no idea what that means to me. I was dreading the trip to city hall, especially with all the nosy uncles and aunties hovering around."

"Of course," she said with a warm smile. "I'll take care of everything—just think of it as a friend helping out another friend."

He let out a deep breath, his shoulders visibly relaxing. "I really like the sound of that."

Manisha's stomach rumbled loudly, cutting the moment short.

"Oops, guess that's my cue to go," Manisha said, laughing sheepishly. "I haven't eaten much today."

"Why leave now? I'm hungry, too, and I'd be happy to fix that for you."

Manisha hesitated for a moment looking at her phone. "You know what, I'll stay."

"Perfect! Let me whip up my world-famous grilled cheese. It won't take long, promise. And it'll pair great with this." He held up his wineglass.

"World-famous, huh? You've got big shoes to fill. My dad makes the best grilled cheese sandwich I've had in Baskin."

Rohit chuckled. "Not sure I'm ready to challenge Papa Patel for his crown, but I'll give it a shot."

Manisha grinned. "Deal. But just to warn you, my mom always says, 'If you find a guy who can cook, you've hit the jackpot.' Looks like I'm one step closer to striking gold with my new friend."

Rohit shot her an amused look. "Well, my mom always said, 'If you find a woman who loves to eat, you've hit the lottery.' So, looks like we're both rolling in riches."

They both laughed, the camaraderie between them growing stronger. As they stood to head back inside, Manisha paused at the door and glanced up at the night sky. A shooting star streaked across the heavens, and without thinking, she repeated her quiet wish from just a few nights ago. One day the universe would bring her her Prince Charming. And maybe that someone would make her killer grilled cheeses.

The thought made her smile as she absentmindedly squeezed the pocket where her phone was tucked.

## 24

When Manisha got back home, her mind was still reeling from the whirlwind of emotions she had experienced with Rohit that evening. The truths he'd shared had struck her like a ton of bricks, shattering the misconceptions she'd held for so long. No wonder he'd been so eager to escape the luxury car when they first met. It had been a painful reminder of everything he'd lost, a symbol of a past he was desperate to leave behind.

Manisha had grown up in a world where gossip was as constant as the air she breathed. Despite her parents' warnings to never judge others based on hearsay, she had, unfortunately, become swept up in the gossip mill—especially when it came to Rohit.

Hadn't her own family been victims of the gossip cycle, too? There was the time when everyone in town assumed Sanj had gotten his now-wife pregnant, and that's why they'd rushed into marriage. But the truth? They simply wanted to be together, and didn't want to waste another second before making it official. And then there was the time Manisha had fainted at the temple from the intense heat, but of course, Gurshan Auntie had spread the story that Manisha had been knocked up out of wedlock, rather than acknowledging the scorching 95-degree temperature and the lack of air conditioning in a room packed with aunties.

The whole thing had become a ridiculous game of telephone, and in the end, no one really cared about the truth.

It was a harsh reminder that the loudest voices were often the ones spouting the most damaging stories. From this point forward, she would rise above the petty rumours and focus on what mattered: figuring out her own life and finding a husband.

Although the latter quest was still ongoing, she realized that for the first time she had actually admitted to herself that practicing law wasn't something she was excited about anymore. Perhaps it was the few glasses of wine they had shared, or the serene night sky overhead, the stars twinkling like whispers of vast possibilities. Or maybe it was simply the quiet reassurance of Rohit's presence that made everything come into focus. Whatever the reason, she felt a flicker of potential that she had long kept hidden away.

But Deena's voice echoed in her mind: *One thing at a time*. She smiled softly to herself. It was true. There was a lot to untangle, a lot to figure out, but for the first time, she felt like she was on the right path. And that was enough for now.

She leaned against the doorway to the living room, watching her parents. They were engrossed in conversation, their faces illuminated by the soft glow of the lamp on the side table. She moved to join them on the couch, reaching for an apple slice off the plate on the coffee table, brushing away the bits of black pepper that her dad always added for that spicy Indian twist. The crisp crunch of the gala apple filled the room, and she savoured the sweet and tangy flavour. This was her parents' routine every night before bed. A simple yet loving tradition that united them and allowed them to connect after a long day. She hoped to share that with her own partner one day.

"Hungry? I can cook you something?" her dad inquired with a smile.

"This apple is good for me, Dad. Rohit whipped up some sandwiches at the coffee shop earlier, so I'm good," she replied.

As she spoke, the volume on the TV conspicuously lowered.

"Beta, you have been out and about all week. What have you been doing and with whom?" her mom asked.

"You told me to keep busy, so I was catching up with Deena, meeting new people," Manisha replied. "A date here and there."

Her mother sat up suddenly. "Oh, tell us more. I heard Chakar Uncle's son is back. Did you meet with him?"

"Mom! Didn't he just get back from university? He's like twenty-two! So no, it wasn't him. Geez."

"Age doesn't matter. Look at your father and me. He is seventy-two, and I am fifty-three."

"Wow, Mom, your math skills are way off. I'm pretty sure you're in your sixt—"

"Chup, Manisha."

"Anyway, it was nobody. Not even worth mentioning because it was such a disappointment."

"Because you didn't take my flirting advice."

"I tried, I swear! But there were no attempts to help me with my straps. Unless you count Deena."

"Chal, next time, beta. You know, sometimes you've got to kiss a few toads before you find your frog," her mom said, gesturing dramatically toward Manisha's dad.

"Mom, you mean prince, not frog," Manisha corrected with a snicker. "Also, Dad, just so you know, Mom just called you a frog."

Her dad, ever the jokester, shot back, "Better than the donkey she called me this morning!"

"All you girls these days are looking for Hrithik Roshan or what's his name . . . Rahul Singh? No. Hmm . . ." Her mom grabbed at the air as though trying to catch the escaped name.

"Ha! Ran . . . Ran–what? Ranesh? Ranvit? Oh, I don't know. But I do know, you all want someone like that, but do you know how many surgeries and personal chefs those people have? It's all these unrealistic expectations you kids have. No one looks like that in real life! I know the real Shah Rukh Khan, mind you, long before he became this Mister Worldwide SRK," her mom added, leaning back in her chair with a satisfied smirk.

Manisha inwardly sighed. Here it came again—the Shah Rukh Khan story. She sent up a silent plea for a quick escape.

"When I was young, hot, and happening . . ." her mother began with that familiar twinkle in her eye.

"Mom, please, don't call yourself hot," Manisha interrupted, stifling a grin.

Her mom raised an eyebrow, undeterred. "Leh, hot and spicy girl, you know what I mean?" She shot a playful glance at her husband.

"You're still hot and happening, darling," her dad replied.

"Anyway," her mother continued, oblivious to the exchange, "all these private school boys were after me, trying to tie the knot. And then—this guy shows up."

Manisha stifled a laugh. Guy? Only her mother would ever reduce Shah Rukh Khan to a mere "guy." But she knew better than to interrupt now.

"He just wouldn't leave me alone! Everywhere I went, there he was—*Chalte Chalte*, following me around India like I was his personal love interest." Her mother sighed dramatically, rolling her eyes.

Manisha shook her head, smiling. She'd heard this story so many times, but her mom always managed to make it sound like a blockbuster romance.

"So finally, I had to put my foot down. I told him, 'Listen,

I'm not interested!'" Her mother sat back, as if this had been some monumental moment in her life.

"And then?" Manisha asked, feigning curiosity, though she knew the rest by heart.

"Then, the guy walked away, heartbroken," her mom said with a mischievous grin. "But I moved on, of course. I'm very happy now. But him? Every time I see him on TV, I can still see the sadness in his eyes. Especially when he says, 'To the love of my life!'"

Manisha couldn't stifle a burst of laughter. "Oh my god, Mom, really? Poor Shah Rukh Khan. He's probably just giving speeches for his fans, and you're convinced he's still pining for you."

Her mom waved a dismissive hand. "Who knows? Maybe he's still thinking about me. After all, he never did find anyone as hot as me."

"Yes, Mom. Everyone knows you chose Dad over SRK. And after losing you, he became a Bollywood superstar, obviously heartbroken, and now dedicates all his award speeches to you. What a tragic loss for him!"

"Superstar, stupid star, I couldn't care less," her mom said, shrugging. "The point is your prince doesn't have to look like a Bollywood hero. He can look like your father and still be a good husband."

Manisha's dad, lounging on the sofa in his trusty white kurta, shook his head and got up. "I'm going to get a drink droonk while you ladies compare me to other men."

Her mom waved him off dismissively. Turning back to Manisha, she added, "You know Meena Auntie called today, na? She said she has very high hopes for you."

"Well, in that case, all is well now because Meena Auntie believes in me," Manisha said with exaggerated enthusiasm. "Sunshine, rainbows, and—"

Seeds.

"Chup! Too much talking," her mom scolded, wagging her finger.

"I'm joking, Mom! And you're right, I probably have to kiss a few frogs before I find my prince."

"Oye! Not too much kissing, ah? I don't want to hear you're out there kissing this uncle's son or that uncle's nephew. Anyway," her mom continued, ignoring her, "I'm glad you and Rohit Khanna have sorted things out."

"Well, let's not get carried away. But yes, I do think he deserves a second chance—and so does his current girlfriend."

Just then, Manisha's phone buzzed. Not even bothering to check who it was, she jumped up from the couch.

"I'm heading upstairs," she announced, gesturing with her phone. "Deena."

"Don't stay up too late, beta. Get some rest," her mom said. "More rest equals more dates."

"I don't think that's how it works, Mom."

She kissed her mom on the forehead, gave her dad a big hug, and practically skipped up the stairs like a kid with a perfect report card. As odd as it had been, today had left her with the sense that, finally, things might be falling into place.

$\mathcal{S}$he checked her phone while quickly changing out of her clothes and brushing her teeth.

Isha,
How's your day been? Mine had a few unexpected twists and turns, but I was thinking of you and wanted to check in. I miss seeing my inbox filled with your name. Hope that's not too cheesy.
—Sunil

Manisha couldn't help but grin. She quickly started typing her reply.

I wanted to write to you sooner, but I got caught up helping a friend. I was thinking about you, too, so I guess we're both fans of cheese. Although I draw the line at blue cheese. Please tell me you're not a fan.
Isha

She hit send before she could second-guess herself. But as she wiped off her makeup in front of the mirror, another message popped up from Sunil.

A ban on all blue cheese? I'm here for it.

She laughed to herself as she read on.

> It's nice to know we were both thinking about each
> other. You seem like such a wonderful friend, always
> ready to help. I've had a tough time seeing Baskin in
> as friendly a light as I once did. Maybe I'm just getting
> more skeptical as I get older. Or, I'm not too proud
> to admit that I've made some mistakes in the past.
> But I've been focusing a lot on self-improvement
> lately, and I think I'm finally becoming a better version
> of myself. Learning from our mistakes is the best we
> can do, don't you think?

Manisha's fingers hovered over her phone as she pondered his words. He seemed so sincere and perceptive.

She typed back:

> You're right. We all make mistakes, but that doesn't
> mean we should give up on ourselves, and depend-
> ing on the circumstances, others, too. I think in my
> next relationship, I want someone who will be there
> for me through thick and thin. That's the kind of love
> I believe in.

She hit send, then leaned back on the bed, her mind racing. Moments later, Sunil's reply popped up.

> You and me both. Relationships can be tough, and
> it's hard to keep going when people bail. But I want

my future wife to know I'll always be there for her.
That's how I was raised. My mother once told me
that one of the things she loved most about her
relationship with my father was how he allowed
her to be her true self. He accepted and loved all of
who she was, and, no matter her roles as a wife and
mother, he always supported her dreams and never
tried to hold her back.

I think I've inherited that mindset—life is too precious
to live anything less than fully and authentically.

Hopefully, one day, I can experience that kind of
partnership, as a husband and father, too.

Manisha smiled at his response. She loved that Sunil wanted
to model his future relationship after the values he had grown up
with. It felt grounded and real, and she appreciated that. She
might have complained about her parents more often than she'd
expressed how grateful she was for them. But lately, she was
trying to change that. While she may have gotten most of her
romantic ideas from cheesy Bollywood movies, it was her parents
who'd taught her the true value of unconditional love and family
in ways no film ever could.

She quickly typed back:

Your mom had the right mindset. Something tells
me if I ever met her, I would really like her . . .

Manisha had barely hit send when her phone lit up with
another message from Sunil.

Something tells me she would have liked you, too.

Manisha stared at the message, stunned. A wave of sadness overcame her as she thought about the loss Sunil had experienced, touched by his deep dedication to honouring his mother's memory. While her own mother could sometimes be overwhelming, Manisha felt immense gratitude for having her in her life. Her conversations with both Rohit and Sunil had made her realize just how lucky she truly was to still have that connection.

Sunil, I'm so, so sorry . . . I didn't know. I can't even begin to imagine how difficult losing your mom must have been. But I can tell by the way you speak of her, that she was an incredible woman and mother. I just know she would be so proud of the good, kind, and honest person that you are. You should be proud, too.

She hit send.

Manisha sat there for a moment, reading his last few messages over and over again. Their sweetness, their vulnerability.

Her conscience nudged her as the reality of the situation hit her. She couldn't forget the truth that lingered underneath it all—that this connection with Sunil was all built on a fabrication. A beautiful, fun one, but a fabrication, nonetheless.

## 26

*M*anisha woke up feeling as though she'd barely slept. She had stayed up way too late waiting for a response from Sunil, mind swirling with thoughts of his mother, Curry and Cupid, her own deception.

She moved through her morning routine, getting dressed, trying not to let her worry that she'd said the wrong thing get to her. The crisp morning air felt refreshing as she stepped outside, holding a steaming cup of chai in one hand. The rising sun painted the backyard garden in soft golden light, the vegetables still dewy from the early morning. She sank into her favourite cozy red chair as her phone buzzed, interrupting her thoughts. She smiled with relief as she saw Sunil's name in her inbox.

> Sorry, Isha. The long day caught up to me and I ended up passing out. But thank you for saying that. I try to carry her with me in everything that I do.
>
> On a lighter note, I'm in need of some serious caffeine this morning. Are you a coffee or tea kind of gal? –S

You and me both, Manisha thought.

Chai, all the way! I'm having some right now. How
about you?

BTW, I've got another date lined up for tomorrow.
Can I get a rah-rah?
Isha

Suddenly, the house phone rang. The automated voice
announced an incoming call from Leena Singhal.

Her dad's voice boomed from inside. "Delete!" he shouted,
as if the phone would just stop ringing at the command.

Manisha blinked in shock, then rushed into the kitchen
where her Dad was glaring bitterly at the answering machine.
"Dad, you can't stop the call by yelling 'delete' at it."

He looked up at her and sighed. "I meant, just . . . delete the
whole situation."

Manisha leaned in, intrigued. "Why do you always get so
upset when Grandma calls?"

He gave her a weary look, then softened. "It's between adults."

Manisha wasn't about to let it go. "Dad, I'm an adult, too. I'm
allowed to know what's going on. I'm not a kid anymore." Her
voice didn't sound exactly like an adult's—more like someone
trying too hard to sound grown-up—but she was determined to
get to the bottom of it.

He looked at her for a long moment, then sighed. "Beta, your
nani wasn't there for us when we needed her. Instead of helping,
she tried to drive a wedge between your mother and me."

Manisha's eyebrows furrowed. "What do you mean, 'drive a
wedge'?"

He hesitated, choosing his words carefully. "Marriage is hard
work, and your mother always knew that. No matter what came

our way, we faced it together. But, well, not everyone understands that."

Manisha was quiet for a moment. "I feel like there's more to
this story . . ."

"There is, beta," he said, his voice softening. "But that's all I
can say for now."

She offered him a small smile. "Thanks for sharing what you
could. I really admire how you and Mom have always stuck
together. It's something I truly value. Rohit even mentioned it
the other day—how having someone you can depend on makes
all the difference. It really stuck with me." Her dad looked at her
for a moment, then gave a small, knowing nod.

"Yes, the Khannas taught us a lot about that, too. When your
grandmother wasn't there for us, they were."

Manisha couldn't help but think of Rohit and how Lucky had
failed him when he needed support the most.

"There was no Google or Siri back then," her dad said, his
voice softening as he gazed into the distance, lost in nostalgia. "It
was just your mom and me, armed with a handful of English
words, trying to figure out how to get a driver's licence, a mort-
gage, and our citizenship. And Uncle Jas . . . he helped us with
everything. We didn't have a rupee to our name, but when we
finally made it, he wouldn't take a single penny back. All he
asked was that we pay it forward."

Manisha smiled softly. "That's what Rohit hopes to do with
the new Chai Time. Pay it forward. I guess the apple doesn't fall
far from the tree, huh?"

Her dad grinned. "Rohit's a good man."

"I know that now," Manisha said, thinking back to their
recent conversation. "He wants to turn the coffee shop into a
hub for local artists. Something his mom really wanted to do.

I really admire how he's giving back to the community, and the best part is, he doesn't expect anything in return, Dad."

Her dad raised an eyebrow. "Sounds like you two have some common interests."

Manisha sighed at the familiar phrase her mother had used only a few days ago. "Except he actually loves what he does for a living now . . ." She added more loudly, "But I'm just happy he found love again after all that's happened with Lucky."

Her dad nodded. "We all deserve to be happy, even after tough times."

As he bent down to pull another weed, he smiled. "I'm feeling good today. I'm going to make some Italian food tonight. You know, after the army, I worked in a few restaurants, and I met this man, Mario, who taught me how to make panzerotti."

Manisha laughed. "Oh no, not the panzerotti story again . . ."

Her dad's face lit up. "It was the 1980s! An Indian man, making panzerotti in an Italian restaurant. Imagine that!"

She chuckled. "And that's how you became the world's best chef?"

He gave her a mock bow. "Of course. All that experience made me the great father I am today. Sammy, Sanj, and you— spoiled in more ways than just food. You've all had a good life because of it."

Manisha smiled warmly. "Thanks, Dad. You've really given us everything. We're lucky."

Just then, her phone buzzed again, pulling her attention away from the heartfelt moment.

> Indian chai for the win. Actually, seeing you put
> yourself out there has really empowered me. It's
> time for me to get back out there, too. If I'm being

honest, I think I've been ready for a couple days
now, even when I said I wasn't. I was just in my head.
Nerves, you know? So rah-rah to us both!

Manisha grinned down at her screen, a warmth blossoming
in her chest, like knowing that she had brought Sunil one step
closer to finding his love had sown something deep inside of her.

That's amazing, Sunil!

Her dad shook his head with a grin. "All you kids, glued to
your phones all day long. Type, type, type. What could possibly
be so interesting?"

She smiled sheepishly. "Sorry, Dad. I was talking to a friend."

He gave her a knowing look. "I don't even own a cell phone,
and my life is just fine."

Manisha smirked. "We got you one last year, remember? But
you said it was only good for getting calls from Mom, and then
it mysteriously disappeared."

Her dad's gaze flicked away. "Oh, that's right. I think . . .
someone must have stolen it."

Manisha raised an eyebrow. "As your daughter, who knows
you better than anyone, I'm pretty sure you lost it on purpose."

He grinned. "I think I need a lawyer."

Manisha winked at him. "I happen to know one."

They both burst out laughing, the moment light and easy
between them.

## 27

*A*s Manisha pulled into the parking lot at city hall, her phone beeped. Deena was just sending through more assurance that she was being pickier now, fully committed to the plan of finding someone at least worthy of a second date.

Manisha retrieved the folder containing the Chai Time legal documents from the trunk of her car and made her way into the municipal building. Inside, the office was a bustling hive of activity. Aunties and uncles moved about, a handful waiting in line to apply for permits or renew licences, while most stood in small groups, exchanging gossip in low voices. Manisha was grateful she had taken care of the permits for Rohit's business herself; the last thing she wanted was for him to be caught up in the whispers behind his back.

She kept her head down as she navigated through the crowd, her mind fixed on the task at hand. The last thing she needed was another round of "When are you getting married?" or "Have you found a nice boy yet?" It seemed like every time she stepped foot in a room full of familiar faces, city hall or not, the same well-meaning but intrusive questions followed. So she kept her pace quick and her attention on the folder in her hand, determined to avoid the social minefield.

As she walked past the counter for marriage licences, she froze.

Beneath the large sign that read "Marriage Licences" stood the last person she ever expected to see: Lucky Kapoor—Rohit's ex.

She had certainly matured since their high school days. Now, she was the epitome of high fashion, dressed head-to-toe in designer labels. She wore a Burberry trench coat draped over a silk blouse, paired with crisp, wide-legged trousers that accentuated her statuesque frame. Manisha was simultaneously pleased and ashamed to realize that she recognized the blouse and trousers from Chanel's latest collection. Lucky's accessories were just as impressive—an elegant Louis Vuitton bag . . . but it wasn't the chic purse Manisha would have expected. Instead, it was a diaper bag, clearly packed with baby essentials.

Sparkling Cartier jewellery completed the look as did the sleek Prada heels that clicked against the floor with every confident step. Although Manisha couldn't help but be impressed by Lucky's impeccable style, for once her mother's words rang true in her mind: *stupid designers*.

Manisha's instinct was to slip away, but before she could, Lucky spotted her from across the room. With a smirk, she started heading straight toward her.

"Look who's back in town—Manisha Patel!" Lucky's voice rang out, a toothy smile plastered on her face as she neared.

"Lucky," Manisha said, her voice tight with discomfort. "You're back in town?"

"Yes, but not for long. This town reminds me of my challenging year," Lucky replied, with a deep sigh, her words dripping with exaggerated sorrow.

Manisha wasn't in the mood for Lucky's lies. "I actually have to run. Swamped with work."

Lucky's eyes narrowed as she spotted the folder in Manisha's hand. She moved closer, her curiosity piqued. "Rohit Khanna.

What's this about?" She grabbed the folder from Manisha, scanning the name on the cover.

"I'm just helping him with a few things," Manisha replied, trying to keep her tone calm while she attempted to snatch the folder back.

Lucky didn't care about boundaries. She flipped through the folder without asking. "What's he up to now . . . ?" she muttered.

"Sorry, I can't discuss it. Client confidentiality," Manisha said coldly, making increasingly more desperate grabs.

Lucky didn't miss a beat. She threw the folder back at Manisha with a dismissive flick, shot her a withering glare, and sauntered away. Gone was the supposedly wounded, heartbroken woman. "You may want to keep an eye out, or he'll betray you like he did me," she called, her voice loud enough to catch everyone's attention.

Manisha's blood began to boil. Oh no she didn't.

"Lucky, that's not how it happened," Manisha shot back, her voice sharp.

Lucky spun around, eyes narrowing. "What was that?"

The aunties, who had been chatting nearby, paused their conversations and turned their heads, intrigued.

Without missing a beat, Manisha fired back, "I said, that's not what happened. You're lying."

Lucky took a few steps closer, her voice growing louder. "How dare you? You have no idea what you're talking about," she sneered.

Manisha squared her shoulders, standing tall. "Yes, I do. Stop lying, Lucky. Rohit didn't do anything to you. He's the one paying the price for your lies." Manisha paused, glancing at the aunties.

"You're the one who left. You're the one who cheated on him."

Lucky's face went red. "That's not what . . . err . . . happened!" she stammered, clearly rattled.

"Then tell us all what happened." Manisha gestured to the crowd now listening intently. "Let's hear it."

"Shut up, Manisha!" Lucky snapped, clearly losing her cool.

"I think it's time you shut up, Lucky," Manisha shot back, her voice low and dangerous. "If I ever hear you or your family put down Rohit or the Khannas again, so help me God . . ."

Manisha noticed a faint gasp from one of the aunties, clearly shocked by her boldness.

Lucky scoffed, crossing her arms. "Let me guess," she said with a smirk. "You're his new : . . what? His little sidekick? His resident protector, here to fight his battles for him?"

Manisha steadied her breathing, calming herself so she wouldn't erupt. She wasn't about to lose her cool like she had with Oliver—not this time. She had learned from that mistake.

"Rohit's a friend of mine," she said, keeping her voice even. "He's a good guy and he actually cares about this community. You, you don't care about anyone but yourself. The way you treated him, especially when his mother was dying, is unforgivable."

Lucky rolled her eyes. "He's clearly filled your head with all kinds of stories."

"No, Lucky," Manisha replied firmly. "He was honest with me. You're the one spreading lies. And you get to walk away while his reputation here is dragged through the mud. He genuinely cares about this town, and it's about time everyone here knows that you made everything up."

Lucky laughed bitterly. "I'm out of here. I never liked this town anyway."

Manisha gave a pointed smile. "Goodbye, and good riddance." She turned to walk away, ready to finish the paperwork and escape the chaos.

But as she spun around, she took in the full effect of the room full of stunned aunties and uncles, their eyes wide. Whispers were already starting.

Manisha ignored them as she joined the lineup for permits.

The security guard standing nearby raised an eyebrow. "Not too shabby," he said, his tone dry but amused. "You know, if you're interested, we're hiring."

Manisha snickered. "Thanks, but I think I've had enough drama for at least a year."

## 28

*L*ater that afternoon, Manisha stepped into Chandan's Indian Clothing Shop a few steps behind her mom. The shop was the go-to destination for Indian clothes in Little India and usually packed with customers, but on this Tuesday, it was surprisingly quiet. Manisha took a deep breath and began sifting through the various ready-made garments on display. Her phone pinged with two texts from Deena that came through one after the other.

I can't believe you confronted her like that.

I'm proud of you, but I kinda wish I had been there.

"Manisha!" Her mother's voice beckoned her from the changeroom. She'd already tucked away to try on a few garments that had caught her eye.

I'll tell you more later, Manisha typed back before hurrying over to her mother.

"I love this pink one," Manisha said, picking up a bright outfit along the way and draping it over the top of the door to the tiny changeroom. "I think it's time for you to change this boring brown colour scheme you have worn for decades." When her mom didn't immediately respond, she asked, "Mom, did you hear what I said?"

"Yes. Boring brown. That is all I heard from you."

She heard her mother bump her elbow as she swore her way through trying on the clothes she had picked.

"I just meant; you know . . . maybe Dad wouldn't mind seeing you in something a little sexier."

"Oye. Don't say sexy inside Indian stores."

"Fine. How about foxy? You're a foxy lady, Mom. You don't look like an auntie. Stop dressing like one."

When her mom didn't respond, Manisha gave up. She leaned against the wall and pulled out her phone.

There was a new message from Sunil.

> I've been chatting with someone and, dare I say, I think we're hitting it off? I don't want to jinx it, but I'm hoping this'll lead to an actual date!

An unidentifiable knot of something formed in Manisha's gut. Envy, perhaps? That Sunil had so quickly found someone he was getting on with, in just a matter of hours? The thought of him going out on a date with this woman made the knot furl even tighter. Whatever the feeling, Manisha knew she had to be supportive of him, the same way he'd been so supportive of her.

> That's great news! I'd love to hear more about her. I'm sure she'll be thrilled if you ask her out.

She pressed send and immediately felt antsy.

"Hey, Mom, you ready?"

"Yes. I got one foxy outfit just to please you." Her mother emerged from the changeroom. With a warm smile, she handed Manisha the pink Indian suit. She playfully gave her a little pat on the backside on her way to the counter. Over her shoulder, she said,

"I don't understand you. You are on a break from work, but all day, type, type, type. Must be someone very special you are typing to."

Manisha frowned at the thought. "You sound like Dad. That's how people keep connected now, Mom."

They were interrupted by the store owner. "Any new bangles?"

"No bracelets," her mother replied swiftly. "Just suit."

"How about for your sister?" He gestured at Manisha.

"My daughter," she corrected him with a scowl on her face.

"Only suits, then."

Manisha moved to the front of the store, not wanting to linger too long and be tempted to spend money she didn't really have.

"Another Indian wedding coming up?" a voice called from the store entrance.

Manisha instantly recognized it—Rohit. She turned to see him standing there, holding a steaming cup of chai, a friendly grin on his face.

"What brings you here?" she asked, flashing him a quick smile. "And yes, isn't there always a wedding around the corner in Baskin?"

"You're right. And I was just picking up a few things for the Indian community festival next week," he replied, glancing at her mother.

"Oh, Rohit, hello!" Manisha's mother said, her voice warm as she joined them. "It's been a while since we've seen you! Look at you, always doing seva. How kind of you."

Manisha could feel the subtle judgment in her mother's words. It was almost as if she were saying *Why aren't you doing more seva, Manisha?*

"Hello, Auntie-ji," Rohit greeted, smiling at her mother.

Her mom, always a fan of a good hug, embraced him with a long one. "My goodness, look at those strong muscles! Rohit, whenever you're free from all your seva, you must come over. Uncle will make you his famous aloo paratha."

His face lit up. "Aloo paratha sounds amazing, Auntie, but . . . can he make mooli paratha, too?"

Manisha couldn't help herself. "Yuck," she exclaimed louder than she meant to.

Rohit laughed. "Not a mooli fan?"

"No one is!" Manisha shot back. "Except maybe you, clearly."

Her mother quickly chimed in. "Manisha also said you're making cheesecakes now?"

Manisha raised an eyebrow. "It was a grilled cheese, Mom. And don't burden Rohit—he's really busy."

"I'll try to come by soon, Auntie-ji," Rohit said ambivalently, turning the wattage up on his smile.

"By the way, the permit applications are all submitted. I'm hoping we get approval soon," Manisha added.

"Thank you so much. I'm crossing my fingers." His relief was near palpable.

"Me too," her mother chimed in, crossing her fingers with enthusiasm—though Manisha had a feeling it was for something other than permits.

Rohit nodded, glancing at his watch. "I should get going. Suzy's waiting in the car. But . . . I look forward to seeing you both soon."

Manisha watched him leave, her mother still standing in the doorway, waving until he disappeared down the street.

"Geez, Mom, drool much?"

Her mom shot her a playful glance. "Drool? Where? It must be this new toothpaste your Uncle Parm suggested."

Manisha rolled her eyes. "Sure, Mom. You were practically salivating over Rohit. Your eyes were about to pop out of your head."

Her mom chuckled. "My eyes are naturally big, like a cat's. They used to call me billi eyes when I was young."

Manisha raised an eyebrow. "Yeah, somehow I doubt anyone actually called you that. You've got a wild imagination, Mom."

They stepped out of the shop, the soft breeze of the quiet street momentarily easing the tension. But her mother's tone shifted as she looked at Manisha with a hint of concern. "You know, Rohit's family has been through so much. But look at him—still giving so much to the community. Helping at the temple, organizing events . . . Who else from your generation is doing seva like that?"

Manisha's sigh was heavy as she stopped walking for a moment. "I get it, Mom. But Rohit's not the only one who has a lot going on right now. I've got my own stuff happening, too."

Her mom paused, glancing at her with surprise. The strength in Manisha's voice had caught her off guard.

Manisha immediately softened. "Sorry. I didn't mean to snap. It's just . . . since Sanj's wedding, I feel like there's always this pressure on me to be the perfect daughter. I just need a little space."

Her mom looked at her, eyes full of understanding. "Okay, beta. I just care about you so much, and I want you to be happy . . . but I worry."

Manisha wrapped her arm around her mother's shoulders. "I know, Mom. But I'm doing my best. I promise, I'll figure things out. Dating is important, but . . . so is my career. I need to find something I love."

"You love law," her mother replied, taken aback.

Manisha sighed. "I do, or at least I used to. I don't know. I could just really use some breathing room, please."

Her mother smiled knowingly, though concern still touched her eyes. "Breathing room, huh? Fine, I get it. Breathing room."

Manisha perked up, sensing an opportunity to change the mood. "How about we get some breathing room at Thali Express?"

Her mother smiled. "Chal, we breathe together there. I could use some good food and some time with my good daughter."

As they got into the car, Manisha's phone buzzed. She couldn't help but hope it was Sunil.

She took a second to check: Deena, who really wanted the details on her run-in with Lucky. Manisha tamped down what she could no longer deny was disappointment.

"Come on, let's grab something to eat," Manisha said, trying to sound casual.

Her mom grinned. "Okay, I've never seen you this excited about food."

Manisha smirked. "All that typing, typing, typing makes me want to eat, eat, eat!"

They both laughed, and the weight of their earlier conversation faded as they headed for some well-deserved comfort food.

## 29

"*O*kay, okay, can you just go over it one more time? I need to picture it better," Deena said, stretching out on Manisha's bed, her legs sprawled across the comforter. The afternoon rays streamed through the window, concentrating on the bedspread, but Deena barely noticed, her attention completely fixed on the latest gossip.

"Deena, we've gone over this, like, six times already," Manisha replied, holding up a dress to her body and checking herself out in the mirror. She was getting ready for her date later, but even without Deena's prompting, her mind kept drifting back to the drama with Lucky.

Deena raised an eyebrow. "You're really telling me Lucky just stood there while you called her out on all her lies? And then she just . . . walked off without a word?" Her voice had a hint of disbelief, her eyes wide as if she still couldn't quite believe it. "I wish I'd been there. That must've been wild."

Manisha sighed, smoothing the dress as she studied herself. "Yeah, she muttered something about hating Baskin, and then— poof!—she just walked out. Like, no comeback. Nothing. Just her waving her designer diaper bag around."

Deena sat up, resting on one elbow, clearly hooked on every

detail. "And the whole crew—aunties, uncles—just stood there, staring, watching it all go down?"

Manisha paused for a second, letting the weight of the moment sink in again. "Yeah. They were all just . . . silent. And then the whispers started, of course. But at least now they know the truth." She tossed the dress onto the bed, narrowly avoiding Deena, and started rummaging through her closet again.

Deena sighed, a proud smile tugging at her lips. "Manisha, you're a legend. Seriously. And I'm so glad Rohit finally told you what really happened."

"Me too," Manisha said, her voice quieter now, a small smile tugging at the corner of her lips.

The room fell into a comfortable silence, save for the faint buzzing sound of Manisha's curling iron warming up. The soft hum was oddly soothing, but Deena wasn't done yet.

"You don't think there's a chance that maybe . . ." Deena trailed off, her eyes flickering toward Manisha with a mischievous glint. But before she could finish her thought, she quickly back-tracked. "Never mind."

Manisha spun around, narrowing her eyes playfully. "Deena, don't even think about saying it."

Deena raised her hands in mock surrender. "I know, I stopped myself." She leaned back, propping herself up on her elbows again, a teasing smile still on her lips.

Manisha shook her head, half smiling. "Rohit is happy with Suzy. And even if Suzy weren't in the picture—which she is—Rohit and I would still be friends. And that's a good place for us, considering where we started."

The room fell quiet again, except for the soft click of the curling iron as Manisha set it down. Deena gave her a long look, but Manisha didn't meet her gaze this time, silently zhuzhing her curls.

"Just making sure. What kind of matchmaking auntie would I be if I wasn't considering all possible suitors?"

"Between you and my mom, even my dad, I'm tired of hearing about it."

"Alright, fine. Back to your dates. I need you to take the next several minutes to study each of these profiles, so you don't mess them up. I got some feedback that you referred to one of the men by another name?"

"I know. I'm sorry. Going on dates back to back has been a lot harder than I thought," Manisha said, trying to justify being so distracted by Sunil's email that she called one of her dates by his name.

"Study up and it'll get easier." Deena gave Manisha a playful swat on her back as she watched her twist a few pieces of her hair.

"Oh, dear cousin, how little faith you have in me. I passed my driver's test after twenty-four hours of 'studying' time."

Deena gave her a dubious look. "You barely passed it."

"Sometimes I tell you too much," she groaned before giggling.

"We need to kick it up a notch. I'm totally serious about this now. The first few were trial and error. We were just getting warmed up."

"You're starting to sound like Vikas."

"We had so many new applications today. I swear Rohit must have handed the Curry and Cupid flyers I made to every customer that entered the coffee shop," Deena said jokingly.

"You gave some to him?" Manisha asked, surprised.

"Just a few to put around in the café and maybe hand out to some trusted customers. Don't worry, he thinks my distant cousin is launching a new dating site."

"As long as he doesn't find out we're behind it—can you imagine if he knew we were running a fake matchmaking site?"

Manisha shuddered at the thought, then held up a cute green top with a plunging neckline. "What do you think?"

Deena raised an eyebrow, studying the shirt. "Looks more like a window to your cleavage than a top. How about we show off some shoulder instead of that much boob?"

Manisha rolled her eyes but grinned. "Okay, find me something, then."

Deena dove into the closet, pulling out a red strappy dress from Reformation. She held it up and gave it a dramatic twirl. "How about this one?"

Manisha's eyes lit up. "I forgot about that dress. It's been ages!"

"It's casual but hot, and the red? It brings out the fierce woman in you," Deena said with a wink.

Manisha laughed, tugging the dress closer to her. "Maybe I should try changing outfits between dates, like they do at Indian weddings. Keep things fresh."

Deena's eyes sparkled mischievously. "I'm just hoping to have you out of clothes by the end of one of these dates."

Manisha laughed again. "As long as it's not halfway through a date, like Vikas wanted."

"Maybe I should give Vikas a call and see what he's doing later," she joked.

"Oh my gosh, Deena. Get out of here."

Deena started to make her way out of Manisha's bedroom.

"You know, that guy on your vision board looks a lot like someone we know. Someone whose name starts with an R . . ."

"Oh give me a break. It was just meant as a placeholder."

"Just saying." Deena shrugged as she headed out the door.

Manisha adjusted her outfit before reaching for her phone. Her heart stuttered when she saw a new message from Sunil—he'd gone quiet after her last email yesterday.

I have a confession to make.

Manisha's stomach did a somersault. Taking a deep breath, she read on:

> There's this woman in my life that I really care about. She's a good friend of mine and has supported me through a lot. But, well, she's come to mean more to me than that . . . I've developed feelings for her. The thing is, I'm not sure I'm ready for the possibility of being turned down. I'm worried that might jeopardize our friendship. I need your help, Isha. What do I do?

She tried her best to ignore the nagging twinge in her chest. Isha's role was to support Sunil and cheer him on. To him, Manisha didn't exist. And she never could.

Inwardly, she was kicking herself with regret for playing into the false narrative that she worked for Curry and Cupid. It felt far messier than simply bending the truth with the fake match-making site to set up a few dates. After all, the guy of her dreams was already looking for love—he just didn't know yet that Manisha was his perfect and only match. She imagined that someday, when they were happily together, she'd confess the whole scheme over a bottle of wine, and they'd laugh about it like a charming inside joke.

But her ongoing deception with Sunil wasn't the kind of thing that could easily be smoothed over with even the finest Barolo. She knew with absolute certainty that coming clean about the premise on which their connection was founded would break his trust and make her see her in a completely different, awful light.

Manisha closed her eyes and drew in the deepest breath she possibly could. With an audible exhale, she ordered herself back to reality.

Batting open her eyes, she got to reassuring Sunil.

> Listen, no girl in her right mind would turn you down. Trust me on this one. If you unleash that Sunil charm of yours, she won't be able to resist. Seriously. Just look at me—you won me over in a matter of days, and we've never even met in real life! But whether you knew it or not, you helped me work through so much. She would be a fool to refuse you.
> You've got this, S!

Manisha's eyes caught the colour-coded Dates folder Deena had left on her bed, and her heart skipped a beat back to reality. The reality was that Sunil was interested in someone else, and Manisha needed to get interested in the guys Deena had gone to the trouble of finding for her. They were putting in the effort, and she knew it was time for her to do the same. With a determined breath, she opened the folder.

Dentist. Check.

Played varsity football. Check.

Enjoys pizza, reality TV, and shopping. Triple check.

Manisha smiled softly as she read through the notes that Deena had written for her. Her cousin was thorough, that was for sure. And she really was the best of friends. She'd been poring over the details for half an hour when Sunil's answer came through.

> I'm just feeling a bit nervous about this whole thing. Maybe you're right—maybe it's time to just go for it.

I haven't felt like this in a long time, but there's something about her . . . I'm thinking about her non-stop.
I'm finally in a place where I'm really focused on my
future—on pursuing my dreams, finding someone
to share that passion with, and building something
together. I know she wants the same thing. I just
feel like I need to tell her how I feel, or I'll regret
it forever.

Manisha typed back.

Are you trying to convince me? Because I don't
need convincing. She sounds like the perfect woman
for you, Sunil.

The email brought a bittersweet smile to Manisha's face as she
wrestled with a mix of emotions. On the one hand, she was
genuinely happy for her friend, knowing he'd found someone
who made him so happy. But on the other, a part of her couldn't
shake the thought that the closest she'd come to something similar was with the very man who had filled her inbox.

She quickly pushed the feeling aside, focusing on the optimism she'd felt just moments ago about her upcoming dates. She
was committed to finding her own Prince Charming.

## 30

The warm breeze gently mussed Manisha's freshly curled hair as she strolled toward Chai Time. She scanned the packed streets around her, suddenly aware that Sunil could be any one of the men here. It was strange to think that perhaps he'd been right under her nose this whole time, and she hadn't even noticed.

*Maybe you'll bump into Prince Charming on your walk home.* She could hear Dr. Rocky's words.

If only it was as easy as Dr. Rocky made it seem. She thought back to how easy it was to talk to Sunil, how effortlessly he made her feel heard and confident in a way she'd never known before. It was clear now that someone was going to be incredibly lucky to experience all those qualities he brought to the table.

Serendipitously, an email from Sunil lit up her screen.

Well, I guess I have no choice when you put it like that . . .

She started to reply, but then another one came in.

Isha, I've been thinking about this for a while, and after a little push from a friend, I've decided to put my charm to good use. So here I am, with all the

confidence I can muster, telling you that I'd love to
meet you in person and take you out on a date.

Manisha came to an abrupt stop.

"Hey! Careful!" a woman behind her yelled, skirting around
her frozen form.

Manisha's heart raced as she quickly reread the message. Sunil
wanted to meet her. *Her!* Of course—they'd spent the past week
sharing their values, their dreams, their fears late into the night.
She'd opened up to him more than she had with anyone in a long
time. But her elation morphed into panic not a second later.
How was she supposed to explain the tangle they were stuck in,
all because of her? Manisha was at a loss for words—a first when
it came to corresponding with Sunil.

Her name being called from afar ripped Manisha from her
thoughts. Turning around, she was startled to see Suzy waving at
her across the street.

"Manisha, wait up!" Suzy exclaimed, trying to catch up
with her.

"Suzy, hi. I'm surprised to see you without Rohit."

"Oh, he's busy working at the café, and I need to finalize the
touches on our acquisition."

"Ah. Well, you two have been having a lot of fun, so I guess
it's time for a little work now."

"Are you kidding? It's been more work than fun. It's all business with Rohit."

Manisha playfully nudged her. "Better get that Indian man in
line or send him packing!"

"Not so easy to send a business partner packing."

Manisha was perplexed, her brows furrowing in confusion.
"Especially when he's also your boyfriend . . . right?"

"Boyfriend? Rohit?" Suzy laughed. "No way! He's a great person, but we're just good friends."

Manisha was speechless. After Rohit mentioned that Lucky had been lying, Manisha had convinced herself Suzy was his girlfriend.

But then, they were together all the time. Ate fancy meals in each other's company. And he cooked for her. So, it wasn't such an out-there assumption.

"I just thought because he was making dinner for you . . ."

"Well, we often work through dinner! And he has a talent for preparing the most mouth-watering Indian cuisine, which he graciously used to share with my ex-husband and me."

"Your ex-husband," Manisha said dumbly. She hadn't known Suzy used to be married . . . but then, she didn't really know anything about Suzy, did she? She hadn't allowed herself to learn. "Does he live in Baskin?"

"No, why would he live here? Oh, Manisha, you don't know who he is?"

"Is he a famous celeb or something?" she asked, intrigued.

"No, not at all. I guess I just thought Rohit would have told his friends. After all, he speaks so highly of you."

Now Manisha was utterly bewildered. "He does?"

"My ex-husband is the man Rohit's ex-fiancée cheated on him with. Rohit's best friend and former business partner. Lucky and my ex left us for each other."

Manisha struggled to process all this information. It felt like a plot straight out of a Bollywood movie, but these were real people with real feelings. Overwhelmed by it all, Manisha unexpectedly embraced Suzy.

"Oh wow . . . thank you." Suzy hugged her back.

Manisha pulled back, her hands still resting on Suzy's shoulders as she looked at her with genuine regret. "I'm so sorry, Suzy.

I had no idea. I was so awful to you and Rohit. The things I said, how I reacted . . . I was out of line, and I just . . . I feel—" Her voice wavered as she spoke, the weight of her apology sinking in. She pulled Suzy into another tight hug. "I can't believe I misjudged everything like that. Please, forgive me."

"It's alright, Manisha," Suzy said softly, her hand resting on Manisha's shoulder. "You didn't know."

Manisha swallowed, still feeling the guilty sting of her earlier judgment. She took a step back, her voice laced with genuine concern. "Are you okay, Suzy? I mean, with everything that's happened . . . how are you holding up?"

Suzy let out a slow breath, her expression thoughtful. "I'm actually alright now. The divorce settlement was just finalized. Rohit didn't want anything to do with the company, even though he helped build it. He handed over his shares to me, which left me and my ex to figure out the rest. This week, the board decided all the shares would go to me. I sold the company, and now . . . I'm giving half the money to Rohit."

Manisha was taken aback. "Why? The Khannas don't need the money."

Suzy nodded, a wry smile tugging at her lips. "No, but I didn't want it. So, I took my half and donated it to a children's charity. And when Rohit told me about the community hub he was working on, I decided the rest of it should go to him. It felt right."

Manisha's heart softened. "So, you've been visiting Rohit—"

"It's been a difficult week with the settlement and everything, but more importantly, I've been there to support him. The anniversary of his mother's passing has been weighing on him, and I wanted to be here for him during that."

The pieces began to fall into place for Manisha. Her mouth pulled to the side in understanding. "You two are really something, you know? The way you've supported each other . . . It's incredible, handling everything with such grace."

Suzy smiled faintly, a touch of sadness in her eyes. "It's been hard, but we're doing it. We're in this together."

Manisha hesitated, then spoke with vulnerability, her voice quiet. "I went through a cheating scandal of my own, and honestly, I didn't handle it with grace. There were a lot of f-bombs thrown around, clothes scattered all over the place . . . and let's not even talk about the wine bottles that didn't survive the night."

Suzy let out a small laugh. "Well, I drank those wine bottles instead," she said, giving Manisha a playful look. "It was more satisfying that way."

Manisha grinned, shaking her head. "I probably should have done the same."

"Everyone copes differently," Suzy said with a shrug. "Especially when it comes to betrayal. It's messy."

Manisha nodded in agreement, but then her thoughts shifted. She took out her phone and pulled up the viral video that had been the talk of the town in London, handing it to Suzy. "Well, there's also this," she said, her voice tinged with a mix of exasperation and resignation.

Suzy watched the video, then looked at Manisha with a raised brow. "Oh, come on, Manisha. This? This is nothing. I set my ex's clothes on fire once. Almost set him on fire, too—though I'm only half kidding about that last part."

"Wow, remind me not to mess with you!"

Suzy smirked, leaning back against the wall. "It's all part of the process, right?"

Manisha let out a small laugh, but then her tone shifted, more sombre. "Well, I basically lost my job over this mess."

Suzy gave her a scrutinizing look. "So? You'll find another

one. I have a feeling that someone who made senior partner at a prestigious firm is smart enough—no matter how much she's had to drink—to understand that there's always someone watching. Maybe . . . maybe you wanted to lose your job?"

Manisha froze, wide eyed, the words hitting her harder than she expected. She'd been wondering about that very possibility herself for months but never had the guts to voice it. Maybe, deep down, she had wanted it all to implode. "You might be right," she whispered.

Suzy gave her a reassuring smile. "Manisha, you'll figure it all out. Just . . . be kind to yourself, alright?"

Manisha nodded slowly, her eyes meeting Suzy's with new-found respect. "Thank you. And again, I'm so sorry for the way I acted. I honestly had no idea, but even then, it still wasn't okay. It was my mistake."

Suzy smiled warmly, her eyes softening. "It's alright. We all make mistakes. But now, we can all start fresh. Rohit included."

Manisha's heart skipped a beat. "What do you mean by that?"

Suzy's expression grew a little more serious. "I'm just worried that he might not want to open up to anyone again, after everything that's happened."

"I have a feeling he'll open up when he's ready," Manisha said, her voice steady. "On his own time. He's a good person, Suzy. And so are you."

Suzy smiled at her, her expression softening with a quiet sense of understanding. "Thanks, Manisha. That means a lot."

Manisha looked at her watch, suddenly aware of the time. "Speaking of time, I have to run . . . I've got a date!"

Suzy's eyes sparkled with excitement. "A date? That's fantastic! I'll be sending all the positive vibes your way, though honestly, in that dress, you're already glowing. You look incredible!"

Manisha grinned. "Thanks. I'm really looking forward to it. And I'll send some positive vibes right back at you."

Suzy chuckled. "Funny enough, I just met this woman today who claimed she could help me heal my broken heart with a bag of—"

"Seeds?" Manisha interrupted, laughing. "Oh, no, not Meena Auntie. She got to you, too?"

Suzy raised an eyebrow. "Meena who?"

Manisha waved a hand dismissively. "Never mind. You know what? We all need to have faith in something."

Suzy smiled, her eyes thoughtful. "Yeah, we do."

Manisha felt lighter than she had in days as she turned to go. It wasn't just the date on the horizon that made her smile—it was the realization that despite the messiness of life, the bonds she created, the ways she supported those around her, were the things that truly mattered.

## 31

*M*anisha stepped into the bustling Chai Time, astounded by the sheer energy and noise that filled the air. A chalkboard sign in the back read "Bollywood Trivia Night"—that would explain the crowd. She hovered next to a couple preparing to leave, then snagged their table the second they cleared their seats.

With just a few minutes to spare before Ali's arrival, Manisha took out her trusty YSL blotting powder compact and gave her face a once-over. She needed to focus, but it seemed an impossible task. Her mind kept drifting back to Sunil's email. How would she respond?

"Manisha!"

Rohit appeared in the reflection of her compact. He swept up the used glasses in front of her. "Are you here for Bollywood Trivia? I remember you saying you loved all things Bollywood."

"Looks like a lot of fun, but I have more meetings! Let's catch up after."

"Yeah, sure." Rohit was distracted by the rowdy patrons. "Better get back to this wild bunch. Let me know if you need anything, preferably before a fight starts over which brother is more successful in the Kapoor dynasty."

"Anil," she answered automatically. He flashed her a grin as he left to clear a table.

"Whoa, this place is buzzing!" Deena exclaimed, plopping down in the seat across from Manisha and taking in the vibrant atmosphere. "This is exactly what the community needed. So much energy!"

Manisha nodded emphatically.

"Ali should be here soon. By the way, you look incredible! That dress is perfect on you—strap issues and all," Deena said with a grin, reaching over to adjust one of Manisha's dress straps.

"Thanks. Suzy said the same thing, too," Manisha added, her tone a little more serious.

"Suzy? She and Rohit must really be hitting it off. Good for him. I have to say, it's nice seeing their relationship blossom. It gives me hope for the rest of us, you know?"

Manisha leaned in. "They're not in a relationship."

Deena's eyes flared. "Wait, what?"

"Rohit isn't dating Suzy."

Her jaw dropped. "No way! Honestly, I can't tell what's gossip and what's true anymore."

"Unless it's coming straight from the horse's mouth?" Manisha replied with a wry smile.

Deena's eyes went even wider. "Rohit's mouth?"

"Suzy's mouth. I bumped into her on my way here. She's only in town for business and to support Rohit as a friend."

Deena shook her head, still processing. "I'm struggling to make sense of all of this. It feels like major Indian news."

"We don't need to figure it out," Manisha said with a shrug. "It's Rohit's business to share if he wants to."

"You're right," Deena agreed. "All this gossip needs to stop. We need to have each other's back. We're the next generation of Indian kids. We should be supporting each other more."

Manisha paused for a moment, gathering her thoughts. "Well, there's more . . ."

Deena dramatically flopped back in her seat, groaning. "Manisha! You're seriously killing me with this."

"I'm sorry, I promise it's the last thing. But, um, do you ever read the emails that come into Curry and Cupid's admin inbox?" Manisha asked, trying to sound casual.

Deena's brows furrowed, concerned. "Why, what's going on with them? The last time I checked, we had one Indian woman looking for love, even though we made it clear that Leena Auntie was looking for men. I moved that into another folder, but I haven't checked in some time, I've been so busy with the bios. Why do you ask?"

Manisha studied her cousin's face, the shadow of worry that set in after her question. As prepared as she was to finally fess up to her Sunil situation and get Deena's take on things, it could wait until after her dates today. Deena had put so much effort into setting them up, telling her now would feel as though she were trampling all over her work.

"I just wanted to make sure we weren't doubling our efforts. I've been replying as the admin, so it's all good."

"Is that all? Good. I don't know how much more truth I can take for one day." She held her phone up. "The Wi-Fi in here seems to be crappy tonight. I'm getting all kinds of delays on my dating apps. Yes, I am back on them!"

"No judgment here. You know who can fix the W-Fi." Manisha nodded her head toward Rohit, who was running between tables serving customer after customer.

"He seems a little busy. It's probably all the people jammed in here anyway. Okay, Ali will be here any second, so I'm out. Good luck!"

Manisha bid her cousin goodbye. Still distracted by Sunil's message, she accidentally dropped her compact as she was trying to slip it back into her bag, causing it to break into pieces.

"Clean up on aisle five!" shouted a stocky man who'd stopped at her table, doing his best grocery store clerk impression. Then he laughed. "Hey there, I'm Ali."

"Hi, Ali, I'm Manisha. Sorry, I was distracted and, well, you can see what came of it," she said, gesturing to the mess on the floor.

"No worries, the waiter will come over and clean it up."

They shook hands, and she couldn't help but notice how small his was compared to hers.

"Sorry I was running late. Surgery on a dental patient," Ali explained.

"How did that go?"

"Great for me, bad for him—he's dead," Ali said, humorously imitating the lifeless body.

Manisha's eyes widened in shock. "He's dead?"

"I'm kidding!" Ali said with a grin as he got comfortable in the chair.

Okay, so Ali's morbid sense of humour wasn't quite a match to hers.

Right then, Rohit arrived at their table asking if he could bring them anything. They ordered drinks, Manisha going for a double vodka soda. Something told her she might need it.

"So, tell me about yourself," Ali asked when they were alone again. "What kind of stuff are you into?"

"Let's see. I'm a huge foodie! I love a good aloo paratha—my dad makes the best ones in the world."

Ali pulled a face that Manisha gracefully chose to ignore.

"I also enjoy Bollywood movies," she continued, "and spending time with my family. What about you?"

Ali shifted in his seat, his eyes roving the room. "Man, this brown jam is killing my vibe. What's up with this tonight? I love being brown but don't need a constant reminder." His fist flew forward in the air, missing the decorative Indian lamp on the table by mere inches. "Boom! Ha-ha, just kidding."

"Did you just pretend to punch someone?" Manisha's heart sank in yet more disappointment. She looked around for Rohit, praying for a record-time delivery of their drinks. "Where is that server with our drinks?"

"Thirsty? I like where this is heading, honey."

Honey?

As though she had summoned him, Rohit returned with their drinks, setting them down with a quick nod before rushing off to tend to the busy night.

Manisha, attempting to lighten things up, asked, "So, Ali, what do you like to do, besides sucker-punching?"

"Surfing. Dude, it's just so gnarly."

"I can barely stand on a board without falling off. Maybe you could give me a lesson sometime."

"Tell me more about you wanting lessons on my board."

Manisha's eyes bugged. Instead of dignifying his request with a response, she slung back her drink.

"Slow down, girl. We've got all night. Hey, can I ask you something?"

Manisha hesitated. "Sure . . ."

"Do you wear thongs? Magical thongs?"

"What?"

"You know, that stuff that tickles you in all the right places before . . . boom." He punched the air again.

Manisha had had enough of Ali—his off-putting humour, air punches, flirting—all of it.

"Okay," she said, gathering her bag. "Time to go."

"I'm in! My place or yours?"

"You are going to your place—alone."

"What? But I was having so much fun."

"I wasn't. This date isn't working for me. I'll pay the bill, and I suggest you go catch a wave or hit a boxing class or something somewhere that isn't here."

"Oh, sassy. I like it. But I feel you. All good, man. Listen, all the best, eh? Keep in touch and holla if you ever need a new set of crowns."

When he finally left, Manisha plopped back into her chair, relieved.

Rohit appeared to clear Ali's glass. "Where are you finding these potential clients, Manisha?" he asked, his tone slightly amused.

"Apparently, our hometown has some very interesting residents."

They both shared a laugh at that one before he was being called from the counter and hurried off.

Deena came over from her viewing table. "What happened?"

"Didn't you see him throwing fists around?"

"Yeah, I just thought you got him excited."

"Oh, I did, but those were something else. By the way, what the heck is a magical thong?"

"We could Google it?"

"Forget it—I don't want to know."

"Manisha, are you sure you're being open-minded?" Deena asked gently.

"Of course, but these men are living on different planets! There's only so much I can take."

A little while later, Deena perked up as someone entered the café. "Here comes Rahim. Right on time." She got up, heading back to her table.

Manisha tried to rally, giving Rahim a smile. "Nice to meet you."

"Great to meet you, too," he said, taking the seat across from her. "How's your day so far?"

"Actually—"

"Mine was brutal," he interrupted. "It was a crazy day at the start-up. I just got it going and had to make some big decisions. Ever had to let go of someone after giving them so many chances?"

"Well, last year, my intern—"

Rahim cut her off again. "Like, I really liked this gal, her work was so strong, but she was always late, just couldn't get to the office on time. That's my pet peeve; what about you? Got any?"

"Well, I don't—"

"And don't get me started on elevator hogs. When people know you're coming to the elevator but hit the close button anyway. Why make me wait when there's room for me?"

"Yeah, I guess that's—"

But she didn't get to finish this sentence, or the next one, either, as Rahim kept cutting Manisha off. By the fifteen-minute mark, she had said fewer than thirty words.

"And you know what drives me crazy," he continued after yet another monologue.

"When people cut you off?" Manisha got up—she'd had enough. "I can't take it anymore. Rahim, this date is over!"

"Geez. Alright. Must be that time of the month."

"No, it is not. I just believe a conversation should go two ways, and clearly, we're not on the same page about that."

He rolled his eyes, as though Manisha had some gall to want to speak. "Holy! Check you later then."

As he stormed out of the café, Deena rushed up. "I heard all of it. Well, all of him for the last fifteen minutes. Sorry, Manisha."

"What is going on?" Manisha said, not believing her terrible luck. "It's one bad date after another."

"Welcome to the world of dating."

"I knew this wouldn't be easy, but this difficult?" She looked and felt utterly defeated. "I thought it would be easier with an auntie."

"It will be. We're going through a bad batch." Deena nudged her affectionately with the toe of her boot. "Let's start fresh again tomorrow. Remember, you have to kiss—"

"A bunch of frogs. Yes, I know. Now you sound like my mother." Manisha face-planted onto the table.

"Well, I'm just saying it will take more than a handful of dates . . ."

"I know, and I'm not giving up," she reassured her, straightening in her seat. "Trial and error, right?"

"That's my gal! I should get going. See you at Anjali's wedding tomorrow?"

Manisha nodded, and they hugged goodbye.

When she was alone, Manisha quickly pulled out her phone, ready to write Sunil back. Between dates, she had pretended to be captivated by the ongoing trivia game, but really, she was running through the various possible scenarios in her head for how to answer him: Tell Sunil she wasn't comfortable meeting him in person. Tell him she was moving back abroad. Tell him she didn't feel the same way. Tell him she found someone else and they had to end their correspondence because her partner was jealous. Tell him . . . she hadn't been entirely honest.

It was the only option that could, against all odds, lead to what she really wanted: to go on a date with Sunil. But even if he ended up hating her after the truth was revealed, at least she could go to bed at night knowing she had done her best to learn from her mistakes and right her wrongs.

She took a deep breath, knowing she had to come clean to Sunil.

She walked over to the counter where Rohit was cleaning up as the trivia night had come to an end, the last few customers gathering their jackets and bags to head out. Manisha hoped spending a bit of time with Rohit would give her a break from the duplicitous monster she was feeling like.

"Seems like the evening was a success," she said to him. "You must be so tired."

"You know what, I'm actually feeling pretty energized. I don't really want to go home yet—being in the house without my dad is just too quiet these days. Want a glass of wine? I could really use one."

"Sure, I'll join you."

Rohit poured two glasses of a bold Argentinian red.

"Ah, that's a good Malbec," she said, recognizing the label.

"You know your Argentinian wine, Manisha Patel?"

"I do. Funny enough, I love a good asado, too, but I've never been to Argentina to actually experience the food or wine from the source."

"Well, I've been lucky enough to go, and that's definitely something to add to your bucket list. I have a feeling you'd love it there," he said.

"I'll take that under serious advisement. So, what's on yours?"

Rohit paused, thinking for a moment. "Travel-wise? Hmm . . . my mom—she always dreamed of visiting every temple in India before she passed, so I'd love to do that in her memory."

Manisha reached across the counter and squeezed his hand, offering him a small smile. A wordless exchange of understanding and appreciation passed between them.

"I'd also love to explore the vineyards in Italy. But I'm waiting for a special lady to share that with, whenever she comes along," Rohit added.

"Special lady?" Manisha said, surprised. "Feeling ready to date again?"

"You know what? Lately, I've been feeling like something's shifted inside me. I'm more receptive to love than ever, and, well, I've just got a hunch about something brewing."

"I'm happy to hear that. Umm, Rohit, I ran into Suzy today, and I owe you another apology. I thought you two were, um . . . well, I thought you were dating her."

"You and everybody else. I see the looks and hear the whispers," he added. "Sometimes, I wish I could just get out of this town."

"You can," she said. "Escape to Italy, travel the world. I mean, you can afford to."

"But why should I run away from my home? My parents built this town, nurtured this community. I love it and want to keep my family's legacy alive here. I should be able to do that, not be chased away by some BS gossip."

"Cheers to that." Manisha gazed at Rohit as he refilled her glass.

"Why did you propose to someone like Lucky?"

The question surprised Manisha as much as Rohit.

"Sorry," she said, rattling her head. "The drinks are flowing, and . . . I shouldn't have asked that."

"No, don't be. It's a fair question. I don't think anyone has asked me that before. Honestly, I didn't. I mean, not officially. We were dating for a while, having conversations about the future, and before I knew it, wedding invitations were going out. I never proposed."

Manisha gawked at him.

"I don't know how things progressed to that point, but Lucky knew what she wanted and was going to make it happen no matter what. I don't remember much of that time, to be honest. My entire world was being turned upside down as my mom's illness progressed. I don't even think I saw the actual invitation."

"I did. It was gaudy as hell, covered in real gold flecks." She slapped a hand over her mouth belatedly.

He huffed a humorless laugh. "Sounds like Lucky."

"So, she was sending out wedding invites, and then . . ."

Rohit nodded. "Then sleeping with my best friend and business partner."

"I'm so sorry." Manisha reached over again, placing her hand over Rohit's.

He looked at her, and they held each other's gaze.

"Were you engaged to that guy in London?" he asked.

"Thankfully not."

His phone buzzed on the countertop then.

"Oh man, the Wi-Fi must be back up," he said. "Do you mind if I look at my phone? I'm expecting an email."

Before Manisha could say, "Go for it," Rohit reached for his phone. She checked hers as well, but it was disappointingly blank.

"Everything okay?" Manisha asked as Rohit put his phone down, a frown marring his expression.

"Not really sure," he said, seeming preoccupied.

She cleared her throat to get his attention. "Speaking of Lucky, I should tell you something, Rohit."

"Okay . . ."

"Well, when I dropped off the applications for the permits at city hall, I ran into her."

"I know," he said.

"You know?" she said, surprised. "How?"

"She came by earlier today, and she apologized. It was the first time she even acknowledged the cheating. My ex-best friend came with her."

Manisha tried to hide her shock. "How do you feel?"

"It wasn't as tough as I thought," he said. "I think I just became numb to the initial pain, and now I truly wish them both well."

"I can't believe she came here; they came here."

"She said you really gave it to her and she needed to own up to what she did. I was shocked. But not as shocked as the day I found them in bed together." He scrunched up his face.

"I can't imagine what that felt like. It was gut-wrenching to find out my ex was sleeping with one of his law students . . . but on some level, I also felt relieved." Manisha took a slow sip of her wine. The pain of that discovery had been sharp, undeniable, and yet, beneath the sting, a strange sense of clarity had started to take root.

"Me too! It was a painful way for it to end, but we just weren't right for each other. The right person will fit into my life, not try to make me fit into theirs."

She bobbed her head. It was as if Rohit had pulled the exact words from her mind, articulating everything she had been feeling but hadn't quite been able to express.

"You know, for a while I was calm about it, but then I bumped into them when I'd had a few drinks and, well . . ."

"Funny, that happened to me, too. I saw them at a bar together, and it felt worse than catching them in bed together. Alcohol can do that to you, huh?"

Manisha eyed him with caution before giving in to her impulse with a sigh. "Can I show you something?"

"Yeah, sure."

Manisha pulled up the video of her shouting at Oliver, turning her screen for him to see.

Surprisingly, Rohit didn't appear as shocked as she had anticipated.

"So what?" he said. "He deserved it. He hurt you, and it was devastating. Of course you were going to react that way."

"Really? You're not bothered by my reaction?"

"Bothered by something I can relate to?" he questioned.

"Thanks for saying that. The video being out there has made me want to crawl into a hole and hide away in shame. What I said and how I acted . . . I'm not proud of that Manisha."

Rohit put a hand on Manisha's shoulder. "The only person that should feel any shame is Oliver."

"And Lucky. And your former best friend."

He smiled. "At this rate, with all these secrets we've shared, you may be in the running for my new BFF."

She was touched by his sentiment. "Well, you'll have to fight Deena for that title."

He laughed. "Thanks for having my back with Lucky, Manisha—I needed more closure than I realized."

"No need to thank me. Right place, right time."

"How about the right place, right time—and right friend?"

Manisha smiled back at Rohit.

"Can I show you something else?" he said, gesturing to the back. "I've been working on it for a while . . ."

"Are we going down a dark, creepy hall again, possibly leading to our untimely demises?" she teased.

"Yep. You go first. Your dress can act as a beacon."

"Oh, shut up." Manisha hopped off her stool. She poked him to lead the way, then followed him through the kitchen and down the hall toward a doorway at the end.

As Manisha entered the room, her eyes widened in awe at the sight before her. A grand stage stood on one end of a spacious hall. The broad floor was marked for rows and rows of seating. A theatre in the making. It was still in the midst of renovations but already built and beautiful enough that it took her breath away. She marvelled at the sheer size of it all.

"Wow, Rohit," she exclaimed, walking into the centre of the space. "Once again, you've outdone yourself."

"Lie down." Rohit's voice interrupted her thoughts. Without hesitation, Manisha placed her glass of wine on a sturdy box and followed Rohit's instructions, lying down on the stage as he directed. He moved behind her and the lights dimmed; the room transformed into a magical scene with twinkling stars all around.

Manisha gasped. "You've brought the outdoors inside." She was impressed by the effort he had put into creating such a mesmerizing ambience. Joining her on the stage, Rohit lay down beside her, their closeness potent in the dimly lit room.

"It's a theatre, for the community," he said.

"It's absolutely stunning," she replied. "Every little detail is just perfect."

"Well, if you ever need a place to rehearse your next fight scene, you know where to come," Rohit said, adding a touch of humour to the enchanting moment.

Manisha playfully punched Rohit on his arm. He moved in closer and nudged her, causing her to giggle. In response, she pushed him away good-naturedly and he leaned in even closer, propping his head up on one arm.

"My mom had big dreams of becoming an actress when she was younger," Rohit shared, a hint of nostalgia in his voice. "But unfortunately, there weren't many opportunities for Indian women to pursue those dreams back then."

Manisha turned to face him, a warm smile on her face. "You're right. Even now there aren't many avenues for Indian men and women to chase their dreams in the creative industry."

"But I'm determined to change that. I want to have an impact here."

Manisha was touched by Rohit's commitment. It wasn't all talk with him—he was a man of his word. "And you're doing exactly that. You're making a very positive impact."

She turned her gaze back to the night sky above. "That's the kind of person I've been searching for to share my life with." She didn't know what made her say that. Actually, nothing had compelled her to; she had simply let her guard down.

"I know what you mean," he said, his voice filled with a mix of nostalgia and hope. "Sometimes, I catch myself reflecting on all the dreams I had when I was younger."

Manisha grinned, teasing, "When I was little, I wanted to join the circus."

Rohit's expression shifted in mock shock. "No way! Me too!"

Suddenly, Rohit shot up and held out his hand to Manisha. "Shall we go now? Run away with the circus?"

"I'm afraid I gave up my clown suit when I was five."

"Oh, darn it."

Out of nowhere, Sunil popped into Manisha's head. She frowned, guilt settling over her as she thought about the precious moment she had just shared with Rohit. She wanted to be sharing it with Sunil. She wanted to be on a date with Sunil.

She surged to her feet. "I should probably get going."

"Oh, okay," Rohit said, something like disappointment in his tone. "Here, let me lead you back out."

She swayed forward, and Rohit grabbed her hand to steady her. "Easy there."

The wine had made her tipsy. "I'll call an Uber."

"Let me drive you. I've only had one glass," he insisted.

"No, no, it's alright."

"Manisha, it's raining outside. Let me take you home. I live like a block away from your parents' house."

"Alright, fine," she relented.

Outside, Rohit opened his umbrella, guiding Manisha to his car as the rain intensified. She moved closer, instinctively wrapping her hand around his bicep for warmth and support.

He fumbled with the fob, trying to unlock the door. "Sorry, it sometimes acts up," he said, mild frustration in his voice.

Manisha's gaze softened as the moonlight illuminated his rugged features, his charm more pronounced in the dim glow. Just as he reached for the door handle, the rain picked up, and without thinking, she stepped closer, wrapping her arms around him, seeking solace in his embrace. For a brief moment, time seemed to slow.

Then the car alarm blared, jolting them back to reality. Rohit quickly silenced it and finally opened the door. Manisha, her heart racing with a mix of emotions, reluctantly let go, slipping into the passenger seat.

The alcohol had loosened her thoughts, and all she could think about was being held by Sunil, craving the comfort of his arms. Not Rohit's.

They drove in silence. As soon as Rohit dropped her off and the car pulled away, Manisha didn't even make it to her bedroom. She grabbed her phone and quickly typed an email to Sunil, her fingers trembling with anticipation.

> I want to meet you, too. There's something I need to tell you, though—but I need to sleep on it first.

## 32

*M*anisha stood in the hallway of her parents' house, her
fingers gripping her phone as she reread Sunil's email
from earlier that morning.

> Isha, I've been thinking about you so much. I can't
> wait to meet you, and I'm so happy you agreed to
> give us a shot. You can tell me anything.

Her heart raced as she typed her response.

> I know I can.

She paused, her fingers hovering over the keyboard, the
weight of what she was about to say settling heavily on her chest.
Taking a deep breath, she knew that what she was about to confess would change everything between them.

She stood before the full-length mirror, assessing her reflection. She reached out to wipe away the dust that had collected
on the frame's surface.

"Oh well, I see I missed a spot for Mr. Spic and Span," her
mother said, appearing in the doorway.

"I think you mean Mr. Clean, Mom. Tell me again why we need to be there so early?" Manisha tugged on her black-and-gold sari. It was a one-of-a-kind piece she had picked up in New York at a Kynah pop-up, one of her favourite Indian clothing stores. Somehow, it felt tighter than when she had purchased it six months ago. But she took that as a sign that she was on the right path toward healing. Half a year ago, she was miserable in a love-less relationship, pushing herself too hard in an unfulfilling job. Now, she was weeks into a comforting routine of deep-fried bread and other delicious homemade food, on her way to finding love.

When her mother didn't answer, Manisha sighed and remarked, "I guess being Indian means you follow your own set of rules and never show up on time. It's either ridiculously early or shamefully late, yeah?" She watched her mother adjust the gold embroidery on her newly purchased pink two-piece suit, looking effortlessly elegant as always. The CoverGirl lipstick she wore, probably long expired, still added a touch of glamour that only seemed to emerge on special occasions.

"No! We will show up on time and leave on time," her mother declared firmly. "The longer you stay, the crazier things get. Right?" She turned to Manisha's father for some backup.

"I'll be looking for crazier things from my seat at the bar," he grinned as he stepped next to Manisha's mom.

Manisha couldn't suppress a chuckle at her mom's words. It was true—Indian events often operated on "Indian time," but her mom was determined to break that stereotype.

They made their way out of the house and piled themselves into the SUV.

"What do you mean by 'crazier,' though?" Manisha asked, buckling in and starting the ignition.

"Drinking. More drinking. Parking lot fights. And more

drinking. No way are we staying for all that nonsense. We go at the right time and come back at a reasonable hour," her mother said with finality.

Manisha raised an eyebrow. "Parking lot fights? Mom, this isn't WrestleMania."

She could hear her dad chuckling from the back seat.

"Chup, or I'll show you what is Wrestle-maniac," her mom teased, her eyes twinkling.

Manisha laughed at that, fairly certain her mom's slip-up was on purpose this time. She carefully steered the car, trying to adjust the weight of her heavily beaded outfit, struggling to get comfortable. She could never understand how women managed to look graceful in these things.

"We're running late," her mother reminded her, glancing at her watch.

"Mom, trust me. We're not late," Manisha replied with a confident smile, though she wasn't entirely sure herself.

When they arrived at the banquet hall twenty minutes later, the parking lot was unsurprisingly half empty.

"Look at how early we are!" Manisha exclaimed. She dropped her parents off at the front and parked the car around the back. As she made her way to the front of the building, her phone buzzed. Sunil.

Take your time, Isha. I'm here. Waiting patiently.

Manisha's skin sprouted goosebumps. Who needed magical thongs when she had Sunil's magical words?

Manisha didn't want to keep him waiting any longer, but she needed to figure out precisely what to do or if there was anything she could do. She needed to tell Deena.

"Manisha Patel!" a voice boomed, causing her to spin around. Dr. Rocky strode toward her with the confidence of someone who owned the world, his sleek Mercedes sparkling behind him. Dressed in a bespoke suit that exuded sophistication, he looked like the very image of the Prince Charming (the uncle version) she'd always dreamed of.

As he drew closer, Manisha's nerves kicked in. She tried to maintain her composure, but her heart sped up, making it hard to keep the calm she was desperately trying to project.

"What are you doing here, Dr. Rocky?" she asked, hoping her voice didn't betray her anxiety.

He flashed her a smile that could light up a room, and real or imagined, in that moment, everything appeared a little bit brighter. "My daughter's seeing the groom's brother, so I'm here to show my support," he replied, his dimples looking even more adorable in the sunset. They started to walk toward the banquet hall together.

"You're not going to spill the beans to my mom about our appointment, are you?" Manisha asked, half joking but clearly anxious.

"Of course not, Manisha," Dr. Rocky replied, his tone reassuring.

"Good, because I haven't even told her that I'm a ticking baby time bomb," she added with a half-hearted laugh.

Dr. Rocky chuckled, his eyes gleaming with amusement. "Is that how you see it? I hope you didn't get that impression from our appointment. If you did, then you've misunderstood."

Manisha laughed even more awkwardly, feeling a bit of tension ease from her shoulders. "Honestly, I don't remember much from that day, except for all of the, um, options you listed," she said, lifting an eyebrow in playful skepticism.

Dr. Rocky smiled reassuringly. "I certainly didn't mention anything about a 'ticking baby time bomb,' Manisha. I'm not sure where that idea came from. What I was trying to convey is that you have options, and I just wanted to make sure you know all your possibilities."

He glanced around, then leaned in a little closer. "How about you come back for another appointment? I know it was a lot to take in, but we can go over each option in detail and you can ask anything you want. We'll guide you through it all." He gave her arm a gentle squeeze. "And as I said before, there's one option I'm particularly optimistic about. Honestly, I wouldn't be surprised if he's here tonight."

Suddenly, Dr. Rocky was moonlighting as a matchmaker.

"The Prince Charming option," Manisha said. "Well, that's why I wore my best sari."

"You're a beautiful woman, Manisha, just like your mom, and I know your prince is out there."

Manisha clutched her phone a little tighter.

As they entered the banquet hall, Dr. Rocky leaned in with a grin. "Here's an insider tip: The secret to the best food is to get here early and work your way through the buffet backwards. Desserts first, then the appetizers."

Manisha beamed, feeling a warm sense of camaraderie with her doctor. She followed him into the grand hall, her smile widening at the sight of many vibrant saris. It always amazed her how much effort went into draping the perfect sari, but for nights like this, it was always worth it—especially for the food.

She waved to her dad from across the room, feeling a surge of excitement as she walked toward her family, ready to enjoy the festivities ahead.

## 33

*M*anisha stuck close to her dad as they navigated the buffet tables together. While her mom floated effortlessly from one auntie to another, charming her way through the growing crowd, Manisha and her dad were focused on the real mission of the evening: securing the best food before the line got too long.

The scent of golden pakoras and flaky samosas wafted through the air, making her stomach growl. Her dad, however, zeroed in on something that didn't belong. "Sushi? At an Indian wedding?" he muttered, frowning at the neatly rolled pieces. "What's next? Tacos?"

Manisha grinned. "It's called fusion, Dad. They're just trying to mix things up a bit."

He scoffed. "Fusion! Everything's fusion these days. What's wrong with the Indian classics?"

Manisha laughed and decided to skip the sushi, piling her plate with chaat and a generous helping of paneer tikka instead. She led her dad to a quiet table in the corner where they could eat in peace, away from the chatter and chaos.

Her dad poked at his food. "This samosa is dry, not as good as mine."

Manisha smirked. "Nothing beats your cooking, Dad."

He shook his head, chewing thoughtfully. "They probably used old oil. You can taste it. And this chutney? Too watery."

She couldn't help but laugh as he went on about the subpar quality of the wedding food. "Well, at least it gives you a night off from cooking."

Her dad raised an eyebrow. "A night off isn't worth bad food, beta."

Manisha snorted and pulled out her phone to check her messages while her dad kept critiquing each bite under his breath. She bit the inside of her cheek to stop herself from laughing out loud and drawing too much attention at her dad's very serious but comically snarky grumbling.

Manisha's dad scanned the room with a hint of disdain. The crowd of relatives and familiar faces barely registered in his mind; lately, he had made a habit of avoiding these gatherings altogether. But her mom had finally put her foot down.

"I'm tired of all the questions!" she'd exclaimed one evening, hands on her hips. "Everyone keeps asking where you are. They probably think we're divorced! Or that you're dead!"

So here he was, suit pressed and reluctantly present, fulfilling his obligation with a look that suggested he'd rather be anywhere else.

He squirmed uncomfortably as he loosened his tie. "I'm heading out for another smoke."

Another habit of his, this one adopted during his childhood—smoking cigarettes. With determined strides, he disappeared from view.

Manisha polished off the last of her crumbs when Deena's voice startled her.

"Manisha, wow! That sari is stunning!"

"Thanks, D. And your Anarkali is absolutely fire! Spin around for me."

Deena obliged with a dramatic twirl, the vibrant coral Anarkali flaring out in a blend of gold-embroidered panels. The intricate detailing on the bodice shimmered under the banquet hall lights, and the matching dupatta draped elegantly over her shoulder completed the look.

"It's actually two years old," Deena admitted, smoothing the fabric. "But it's finally getting some love tonight. We'll have to snap some pics later!"

"Absolutely," Manisha agreed, already wondering if she should share the photos with Sunil.

"By the way," Deena said, leaning closer, "there's a secret bar tucked away in the back area. Come on, let's hit it up."

They strutted through the crowd like a duo on a mission, expertly dodging the nosy aunties scanning for gossip. Once they reached the hidden gem of a bar, Deena flashed a grin at the bartender.

"Two vodka sodas, please," she ordered confidently, tossing her dupatta over her shoulder.

"Deena," Manisha said, downing her drink in one smooth motion and setting the glass on the bar with a decisive clink.

"Oh, it's that kind of night?" Deena raised an eyebrow, signalling the bartender for another round. "Well, let me catch up."

"You might want to drink up fast," Manisha said, her tone carrying a mix of humour and tension. "There's something I need to tell you. Rememb—"

Deena raised a hand, cutting her off with a playful grin. "Stop right there—you don't have to say another word. I already know what you're going to say."

Manisha froze mid-sentence, her gaze blank with surprise. "Wait . . . what? How?"

Deena leaned back confidently, smirking. "It's written all over your face."

"It is?" Manisha blinked, teetering between confusion and alarm.

"Obviously," Deena said, shrugging. "The dates have been a nightmare—I take full responsibility for that. But don't worry, I reviewed a fresh batch of applications today, and trust me, there's some real talent in the mix. Boy, do they look promising!"

Manisha let out a small laugh, shaking her head. "Oh, that's what you're talking about. Deena, I think we should press pause on setting up any new dates for now."

Deena's expression shifted to concern. "Wait, what do you mean? You're not giving up, are you? Please tell me you haven't thrown in the towel!"

Manisha sighed, glancing down at her hands. "No, not exactly. It's just . . . well, remember when I brought up being the site's 'admin' yesterday? And how I've been responding to some of the admin questions that have come in?"

Deena circled her hand in a move-it-along motion. "Yeah, and?"

"Well," Manisha hesitated, biting her lip. "It's just that . . . some of those messages weren't exactly admin-level straightforward. They were . . . let's just say, more complicated."

Deena tilted her head, narrowing her eyes. "More complicated how? Oh no. Are we in trouble? Did we break some law? How bad is it?"

Manisha laughed nervously, rubbing the back of her neck. "Well, it's not *we* who are in trouble, it's *me* who is in trouble, actually, if you want to call it that . . ."

Deena groaned, leaning closer. "Manisha, I've barely had two sips of my drink, and you're already giving me a headache. Just spill it!"

Before Manisha could answer, a smooth male voice interrupted them.

"Manisha! Deena!"

Both women turned to find Rohit approaching, dressed in an impeccably tailored suit that complemented his confident stride. "Wow," he said, stopping in front of them with an admiring smile. "You both look stunning. I'm speechless."

"You clean up nicely, too," Deena replied.

She could say that again—in a light-blue suit with a crisp white shirt and dark-blue tie, Rohit was looking good.

"You found the secret bar," he said. "I like your style. Getting a head start on things."

"How do you know Anjali?" Manisha asked after Rohit ordered a glass of wine.

"Our families are tight, so skipping tonight wasn't really an option—though, trust me, I considered it. I've been dodging those evil auntie stares all week. But my mom and Anjali's mom go way back, and it felt wrong not to show up. Besides, I think the gossip has finally cooled down a bit . . . ever since Manisha went full Tyson on Lucky."

"Careful, she's got bad aim," Deena warned, with a grin.

"So I've seen." Rohit chuckled.

Deena stared in disbelief. "You showed him the video?"

Manisha waved it off casually. "It's really nothing. He would've found it eventually."

"Probably not," Rohit added with a shrug. "I don't really go online."

"Yeah, Manisha, how would—" Deena started, but Manisha quickly cut her off.

"The Lucky thing? It was really nothing . . ." Manisha said, steering the conversation in a new direction.

"It was something," Rohit said. "She came to apologize," he informed Deena. "That's not nothing."

Deena sputtered as her drink went down the wrong pipe. She quickly reached for a napkin, coughing.

"She would've done it in due time. I had nothing to do with it," Manisha said, trying to deflect.

"I don't know about that," Rohit replied, his tone more serious now. "I hadn't heard a word from her until the city hall incident."

"Anyway," Manisha said, hoping to steer the conversation away from herself. "What I mean is, I'm glad you're here. I'm glad you don't care what anyone thinks or says anymore."

"And you know what? Forget about everyone staring," Deena added with a grin. "You can hang with us anytime. Let's give them something new to talk about."

"Yeah, totally hang with us," Manisha said. The words sounded a little too eager to her ears. Slowly so as to be subtle, she lowered her glass to the bar, not wanting to overdrink and find herself wrapped around Rohit's body again.

"How's the legal stuff for the café going?" Deena asked, looking at both Manisha and Rohit.

"Fine!" Manisha squeaked. "Why do you ask?"

Deena raised an eyebrow. "So how much more time will you both be spending together? I mean, as his lawyer," she added, though her voice lacked any real conviction.

"We don't need to do anything more for now," Rohit said with a shrug. "Once the permits are approved, we should be all set. But hey, we do have our shared love of wine to keep us connected." He flashed a smile at Manisha.

"Have you two been drinking together?" Deena asked, doing her best impression of an auntie.

"Oh, he had a new bottle of red," Manisha explained, trying to downplay it. "And after all those disastrous . . . umm . . . meetings last night, I definitely needed a drink."

"Or two," Rohit chimed in with a grin. "I had to drive her home."

"You did?" Deena's brows shot up in surprise. "Last night? In that rainstorm?"

"It was just rain, Deena," Manisha said, her voice carrying a warning. She could practically see Deena's mind racing, picturing some rain-soaked Bollywood moment between her and Rohit.

"Anyway, like you said, the permits have been submitted, so we no longer need to hang out so much. You can have all your evenings back," she said, tilting her chin at him.

"Oh," he said, feigning disappointment. "Well, that's a shame."

Just then, Bisha Auntie appeared out of nowhere, her sari showering a burst of refracted colour across the bar. With her perfectly coiled hair and gold bangles jingling as she moved, she was the very picture of authority—and not just any regular authority, but the kind that demanded you instinctively straighten your posture out of respect.

"Well, well, what do we have here?" she asked, raising an eyebrow, her eyes glinting with amusement.

"Just getting some drinks, Auntie. I mean, I am," Rohit answered smoothly, trying to cover for the cousins.

Manisha elbowed her drink closer to him. "We were just keeping him company," she said with a mischievous grin.

It felt like they were all under twenty-one again, and Bisha Auntie had transformed into the local Indian "narc" of the party.

"Chal. Rohit, come with me!" Bisha Auntie said, beckoning him with a look. "Let me introduce you to some nice girls."

"Guess we aren't nice girls," Deena whispered.

"Hurry up!" Bisha Auntie insisted, practically dragging him away.

"But—" Rohit started, trying to protest.

She pulled him along as he turned back with a pleading look in his eyes. Manisha and Deena knew exactly what Bisha Auntie was up to: setting Rohit up with a potential love interest. And they knew better than to get in the way of an auntie on a mission. Instead, they watched, throwing mocking thumbs-up and cheesy grins over to him.

In Manisha's case, they were only half-mocking gestures. The other half of her was happy that Rohit was taking the next step to finding love again. With Bisha Auntie's help, of course. And by the looks of the several other aunties tracking his movements, it seemed as if dispelling Lucky's rumours had opened the floodgates for him.

"Well, well, well, look who's been keeping secrets," Deena said, turned her attention back to Manisha.

*You have no idea.*

Manisha tried to act casual, shrugging as she sipped her drink. "What? You know I'm just helping him out with that paperwork."

"Paperwork, a.k.a. a bottle of wine and a ride home? Sounds like something more than just helping him." Deena grinned devilishly. "What exactly happened in that rainstorm, huh?"

Manisha chuckled nervously, glancing away. "It was nothing."

Deena eyed her, clearly unconvinced. "Uh-huh. You're telling me nothing happened between you two? Because that's not the vibe I'm getting."

Manisha felt herself growing uncomfortable, trying to deflect the conversation. "Really, it was just an end-of-the-day glass of wine between friends, Deena. Nothing else. I promise."

But Deena wasn't done. "Well, if it's nothing, why do you look so guilty right now?" she pressed, giving her a playful shove in the shoulder.

Manisha's thoughts raced. She could feel the suffocating weight of her secret pressing down on her. She shifted her eyes around the room, trying to evade Deena's piercing gaze, but she could still feel it burning through her mask.

"Okay, okay," Manisha finally relented with a sigh. She took a big gulp of her vodka soda. "There is something that's been going on."

Deena leaned in, her voice dropping to a conspiratorial whisper. "I knew it! Spill it. What's going on?"

Manisha leaned back, her voice lowering to a near whisper. She took a deep breath and let the truth fly. "After we launched the site, this guy emailed the admin inbox and we started talking. At first, it was just some casual messages, nothing serious. But then, things started to . . . I don't know, shift. It became more personal, and now it's like we're talking all the time. I don't even know how it happened."

Deena's eyes narrowed. "Wait a minute. You're saying this isn't about Rohit but someone else?"

Manisha nodded, watching the ice in her glass spin as she swirled it. "It's not about Rohit. We started off with small talk, but it turned into long daily emails. Sometimes, we're even answering each other immediately, back and forth, like a real-time conversation. And now, I'm in too deep."

Deena blinked, clearly confused. "Wait, in too deep? What does that mean?

Manisha sighed, feeling the weight of her own emotions. "I don't know, Deena. It started off casual, but now . . . it's complicated."

Deena raised an eyebrow. "Complicated? Wait, what's his name? Maybe I know him."

"Sunil."

"Sunil . . . ?" Deena pressed, waiting for a last name.

"I don't know. Just Sunil."

Deena reared back. "Manisha! There have to be dozens of Sunils in Baskin alone. Let me see a photo? Maybe I'll recognize him."

"About that . . ."

Deena gasped dramatically. "You're getting swept up in some stranger's words and you don't even know his full name or what he looks like? He might be a catfish!"

Manisha winced. "Don't say that."

"How have you not even asked for a photo? Manisha, that's like the first rule of online dating! You've got to see a picture. What if he's some random guy pretending to be someone he isn't?"

"I know, I know," Manisha muttered, rubbing her forehead. "But I never thought it would get this far. I just thought it was fun at first."

"That's what all the catfish victims probably say," Deena said, tapping her fingers on the bar. "Alright, let's see those emails. I need to judge this for myself."

Manisha hesitated for a moment but then passed over her phone.

Deena scrolled quickly through the exchanges as her eyes bugged out more with every swipe of her finger.

"Wow, I . . ." Deena trailed off, clearly stunned as she handed Manisha's phone back. "Manisha, you better hope he's not a serial killer or con artist, because this guy is charming with a capital C. And from what I just read, you two are totally falling for each other."

"I know," Manisha admitted, her voice low. "It's kind of crazy, right?"

Deena shook her head, still processing. "You've always been so careful, so determined to keep yourself off the radar and avoid all the weirdos out there. But in these emails, you're so open, so real. It's like you're completely letting your guard down for him. Sunil and Isha, huh?"

Manisha bit her lip, nodding. "Yeah, except for . . . well, the whole story about working for the site. Other than that, it's been totally real. So real that I'm ready to meet him, to tell him the truth."

Deena leaned in closer, her tone wary. "But Manisha, you don't even know what he looks like. For all you know, he could be here right now, at this very wedding, and you wouldn't even know it!"

"Argh! What have I done? Keeping up this facade about who I am, what I do, even my name—how could I have been so stupid? And now I've got all these feelings . . ." Manisha sighed, biting her lip in worry. "Like my mom would say, I'm such a dumbo."

Deena shook her head with a smile. "You're not a dumbo, Manisha. You're my smartest cousin. You just got caught up in someone who genuinely cares about you. I think."

Manisha let out a long breath, her mind racing. "You think. Okay, but now how am I supposed to come clean without losing him?"

Deena placed a reassuring hand on Manisha's shoulder. "We'll figure it out. I promise. It's going to be alright. He said in one of his emails that no matter what happens, he's willing to work through it with you."

The two stood there in quiet solidarity as the Indian music swelled through the banquet hall, the buzz of voices growing louder as more guests filed into the room.

"Why don't we just enjoy ourselves tonight?" Deena suggested with a soft smile. "We can talk more about it later."

Manisha nodded, grateful for her cousin's support. They made their way to the centre where everyone had gathered to enjoy the food, music, and good company.

She scanned the room and spotted Rohit awkwardly chatting with another auntie and her eligible daughter as Bisha Auntie watched closely. His discomfort was palpable, but he gave the daughter a polite smile all the same.

To her left, one couple cooed over their infant son while another sat hand in hand. Some of the older aunties and uncles were sharing a laugh. Deena was chatting with some girls and motioned for Manisha to come over. But she had no desire to join in. All she wanted to do was reread her emails from Sunil and come up with a plan to keep him in her life.

After some time, Deena walked over and gave her a gentle hip bump. "You and Rohit may as well be in a miserable digital abyss together. You both have been glued to your phones all night."

"You're right. I need to put this away." She tucked her phone back into her Gucci Marmont purse just as the DJ dropped "Jalebi Baby," and the crowd immediately flooded the dance floor.

"This DJ is on fire, and the decorations here? Totally killing it!"

Manisha hadn't even noticed how familiar the decor felt, until she realized—it was like stepping into the sexy dreams she'd had a few nights ago, only without the mystery man.

Deena whipped out her phone with a grin, snapping selfies while twirling on the dance floor. "I didn't wear this outfit not to get a few dancing pics."

"Can I join? I hate dancing, but I'm desperate." Rohit popped up out of nowhere.

Manisha raised an eyebrow. "What happened to Bisha Auntie kidnapping you and trying to set you up?"

"I'm trying to escape!" Rohit said, dramatically looking over his shoulder.

"Better keep running; she's sending reinforcements!" Deena teased.

Rohit turned to Manisha. "Manisha, dance with me."

Manisha blinked, completely caught off guard. "Me? Now? Here? How?"

"Like this!" He grabbed her hand and pulled her further onto the dance floor.

Manisha's eyes widened. "Are you trying to get us both in trouble? No handholding at an Indian wedding. You know that!"

"No one's watching," Deena chimed in, practically bouncing with excitement.

Just as Rohit and Manisha linked hands, a girl who had been eyeing him approached but immediately noticed their clasped hands. She did a double-take and quickly retreated.

Manisha let out a long, exaggerated sigh. "Someone is always watching."

"You owe her one," Deena said, giving Rohit a sly look.

"Sorry," Rohit said with a sheepish grin.

"It's fine." Manisha shrugged. "I just need a little break."

"I'll join you," Rohit said, following her to an empty pair of seats. Manisha couldn't hide her small disappointment—she'd been hoping to check her emails in peace, but that was clearly not happening now.

They sat back, watching Deena dance, surrounded by men trying to keep a respectful distance, following the strict no-contact rule of an Indian wedding. Rohit leaned back, admiring Deena. "She's such an incredible cousin—and an amazing dancer. I honestly don't get how she's still single."

"I don't, either," Manisha agreed with a laugh. "But she's definitely setting the bar pretty high for the rest of us."

Rohit raised an eyebrow. "So, what's your ideal wedding—intimate or grand?"

Manisha gave him a puzzled look and then shrugged. "Go big or go home, right?"

"I think I chose 'go home,' remember?" Rohit grinned.

"Touché," Manisha said with a grin. "I only plan to get married once, and I'm their only daughter, so I know they'd want something big." She glanced over at her mom and dad, who had made their way to the dance floor as soon as the familiar beat of the classic "O Tina O Tina" began. They were dancing playfully with a carefree vibe that had everyone on the floor joining in.

Rohit crossed his legs, a grin spreading across his face. "Your parents really know how to steal the spotlight, huh?"

A glint from his shoe caught Manisha's attention and she couldn't resist commenting. "Speaking of stealing the spotlight, nice Guccis. Very stylish."

Rohit smiled, a touch of pride in his voice. "Shoes are my weakness. The only name-brand thing I own, actually. You could say they're my vice."

"A good glass of wine is my vice," she replied with a cheeky smile. "But you already know that. I used to love shopping, too. But being back in Baskin has made me rethink all that."

As they chatted, Manisha noticed the curious stares from a few of the Gupta aunties who were eyeing them. Rohit caught them, too.

"I guess I should move over one seat," he said with feigned seriousness. "Don't want to ruin your reputation. Who knows what people will say about you hanging out with the 'awful' Rohit."

He began to shift, but Manisha mindlessly grabbed his hand to stop him, sending a tiny bolt of electricity from her skin to his. "Sorry, must be from the dance floor."

The decor, the music, the aunties, the Guccis—they all reminded her of that dream. But what about the man? She quickly dismissed the thought.

"Should we go back out there and dance?" Rohit asked, standing. He flipped their hands so hers was gripped in his and gave it a gentle tug.

"I thought you didn't like to dance?" she challenged.

Rohit grinned wider. "Well, Manisha Patel, these days you've got me doing all sorts of things I never imagined I'd do . . . like being here with you."

## 34

*L*ater that night, Manisha gazed up at her bedroom ceiling, desperately wishing that the gods her mother always prayed to were listening. She was relieved to have confessed what she had done to Deena. But it also made the problem seem much more acute. Before, she had been able to keep it contained, but now the truth was out in the open. That said, out in the open didn't yet extend to Sunil.

Uncannily, her phone buzzed with a message from him.

Did I mention I don't do patience well when I've had a few drinks?

I don't, either . . . , she replied.

Isha, there's also something I need to tell you.

Manisha shot up in her bed as his reply came in. What could Sunil have to tell her? The thought triggered her fears around relationships all over again—Oliver's betrayal had really done a number on her . . .

What is it? she hesitantly typed back, her mind racing.

Sunil replied quickly.

I've got a lot on my mind, Isha. And I'll admit, maybe the wine's talking a bit, but I've really missed your emails tonight. I want us both to be able to share

whatever it is. Maybe we can promise to hear each
other out and be supportive, no matter what comes
out. What do you think? Team Sunil and Ish? xo S

The tone of Sunil's email was surprising.

She was certainly guilty of not being truthful with Sunil, but
now she felt concern about what Sunil might have to reveal.
What were his secrets? A hidden family, a short fuse, an extra
toe . . . Manisha tried to stop her vodka soda–induced thoughts
from spiralling.

Oh, no—this was it. Deena had been on to something, hadn't
she? Manisha was about to find out that she was being catfished
after all. God, she knew better than to blindly place her trust in
people, in strangers, in men, especially when it came to her
heart. Why did everyone insist on keeping things from her?
What was it about her that said, "Why yes, I would like you to
hold back the truth, please"?

But as quickly as these cynical thoughts crossed Manisha's
mind, just as quickly, her awareness of their sanctimony followed.
Wasn't she also keeping something from Sunil? And her family?
The harsh realization left a gnawing pit of guilt in her stomach.

Deena's observation was accurate. She needed to consider the
situation carefully. For once, she would handle this maturely. She
wouldn't respond impulsively—instead, she would put her phone
away until she sobered up.

## 35

*T*he next morning, Dr. Rocky's office called to schedule Manisha's follow-up appointment for later that same day. Dr. Rocky had made it his top priority to see her, and she was grateful that he had made room in his schedule for her so quickly.

As she sat in his office, she couldn't help but wish it were a confessional, where she could spill all her Sunil sins. She still hadn't answered his last email, and it was eating her up inside. Sober or not, she had no idea how to respond.

"Manisha, good to see you again," Dr. Rocky greeted warmly as he sat down, looking effortlessly stylish in a fitted green shirt. Dolce & Gabbana, Manisha noticed, but she quickly pushed the thought aside. She was on a "designer diet" these days.

"I believe your main concern is timing, correct?" he asked, his voice soothingly professional.

"When . . ." Manisha faltered. "How much time do I actually have?"

Dr. Rocky leaned back slightly, exhaling thoughtfully before answering. "Well, biologically speaking, women's fertility begins to decline around age thirty-five, and egg quality and quantity can decrease more rapidly in your late thirties. But that doesn't mean you're out of time. You do have a window, but your results are suggesting the sooner you make a decision, the better it is for the viability of the eggs when it comes time to use them. In other words, freezing them while your ovarian reserve is still strong will give you the best chance for success."

Manisha nodded, her mind racing. She had always planned everything down to the smallest detail—career, life, even her future wedding—but now, for the first time, she was facing something well beyond her usual control.

Dr. Rocky continued, "You came to me initially to freeze your eggs, right? And we're talking about egg cryopreservation—the process where we retrieve and freeze your eggs for future use. It's a good option for women who aren't quite ready to have children but want to preserve fertility for later. The sooner we can do this, the higher the quality of the eggs."

Manisha took a deep breath. "It's just that having children is a priority for me," she said, trying to stay calm.

Dr. Rocky met her eyes with a reassuring look. "And I understand that. That's why I'm suggesting we don't wait too long. You've got a solid career, and you're very focused on your future. I have no doubt that your Prince Charming will show up when the time is right. But in the meantime, we can preserve your fertility so you're fully prepared when you do decide to start a family."

She felt a lump in her throat as the gravity of it all hit her. She had always been the polished, put-together one. But now, with her finances a mess, how could she admit she wasn't the person everyone thought she was?

Tears burned at the back of her eyes, but she rubbed at them quickly, pretending she was just fatigued.

"Dr. Rocky," Manisha began carefully, trying to keep her tone casual, "could you remind me of the cost again?" She tried to sound as though money wasn't a concern.

Dr. Rocky glanced over his notes, flipping through the pages with a practiced motion. "From our initial consultation, the estimated cost would be around 50 K."

Manisha absorbed the number. That was what she'd remembered. She gave a nod, mentally trying to calculate how she could make this work. Even though she knew she couldn't.

"Is there anything else I can help with today?" Dr. Rocky asked.

"No, I think you've covered everything," Manisha said, taking a deep breath. "You're right—it's about timing. The sooner we do this . . ."

"The better the outcome," he finished. "Manisha, I truly believe this is the right step for you. You're in great hands."

She smiled faintly, trying to keep her composure. "Thank you, Dr. Rocky."

"Fantastic! Let's get started with the paperwork," he said, standing up to walk her out. "My receptionist will take care of the details, including payment. This is a big step, and it's a sign of how committed you are to your future and to motherhood."

He cleared his throat. "How's your mother? I didn't get a chance to talk to her much at the wedding, but she looked fantastic. Really, she hasn't changed a bit," Dr. Rocky said, a hint of nostalgia entering his voice.

"Umm, I'll tell her you said hi. Thanks again, Dr. Rocky," she replied evenly, though her thoughts were a whirlwind of bewilderment and anxiety, though mostly the latter.

"It's my pleasure," Dr. Rocky replied, opening the door for her.

As she stepped into the corridor, her nerves began to bubble up. The thought of her credit cards being declined at reception, the reality that Dr. Rocky would know she was struggling financially—it all made her stomach tighten. Would she really be able to move forward with this?

"I can't do this," she muttered to herself.

It was a slap in the face to her future that she couldn't afford what she needed in the present because of her past. With a shuddering breath, she whizzed past reception and out of the clinic, trying to avoid the embarrassment of her situation.

## 36

*M*anisha stepped out of the clinic feeling like the world's weight was crushing her. Her mind was racing with all the problems she had to deal with: the fake website, telling Sunil the truth, and Dr. Rocky's outrageous price tag. Despite being in a town where Manisha knew she had people she could turn to in dire straits, she'd never felt more alone.

As the sun lowered on the horizon, she thought about how the only person she wanted to turn to right now was Sunil. But she still hadn't responded to his latest email, and now wasn't a good time, already steeped in embarrassment as she was. She felt like she was drowning in a sea of debt and despair.

She walked down the street, trying to do the math in her head again. It would take her a year to be able to pay off the egg-freezing procedure, even if she found a job immediately and cut her self-imposed sabbatical short. But did she even have enough healthy eggs to last a year?

Lost in her thoughts, Manisha walked for so long that the sun set, and she eventually found herself standing in front of Chai Time. The coffee shop had closed for the night, but she just stood outside, unable to move. From behind the glass, she saw Rohit's familiar silhouette. He was walking toward her, a warm smile on his face.

"Manisha?" he said as he unlocked the door and swung it open. "What are you doing here?"

"Rohit . . ." Manisha sniffled, trying to hold back her tears.

His face immediately filled with concern. "What's the matter? Come in," he said urgently.

Inside Chai Time, the silence mocked her as she fought to quiet her sniffles.

"Let me get you some water," Rohit offered.

"How about something stronger?" Manisha suggested, giving up the pretense and dabbing at her eyes.

Rohit disappeared into the back and emerged with a stash of booze: wine, vodka, and tequila. "What's your poison?"

"I could use a shot of anything right about now," Manisha said, trembling.

"I'll join you," Rohit said, grabbing a bottle.

As they cozied up at the counter, Rohit poured the sweet tequila into two shot glasses. Manisha didn't waste a second, downing hers and asking for another.

Rohit obliged and poured her another shot. Manisha took a long sip and let out a satisfied sigh.

"Ah, much better," she said, feeling more composed.

Rohit leaned closer, searching her eyes, and asked, "What's on your mind? Do you need a listening ear, or should I put on some tunes? Or we can sit here silently and let the tequila talk."

Manisha said nothing at first. A long stretch of silence passed before she finally spoke. "It's embarrassing. I messed up everything."

Rohit nodded sympathetically. "I get it. We've all been there."

"Have you ever wanted something so badly but knew it was out of your reach? And it was kind of all your fault?"

Rohit leaned back and thought momentarily. "I have. It's

kind of what I'm going through right now." He considered her. "So, what can we do to get it back within your reach again?"

Manisha smiled, grateful for the support of this man, once a stranger, but who, in a matter of days, had become a friend. His words were like a warm embrace, and she couldn't help but imagine that Sunil would have said the same thing.

"Thanks, Rohit, but I don't think we can." Manisha was sipping her tequila when the lights above the counter began to flicker.

"Sorry, those damn lights," Rohit said, glaring at them as if doing so would make them behave. "They act up sometimes when the dishwasher is running. I swear, they're a ticking time bomb."

A ticking time bomb. Manisha felt her tears return.

"Hey, it's okay," he said, pulling her into a tight embrace. "I'm here for you. You don't have to go through it alone."

Manisha looked up at Rohit, her eyes hazy from crying, so grateful for his presence.

"I just feel so lost," she said barely above a whisper. "I thought I had everything figured out, but now I don't know what to do."

Rohit held her tighter, his hand rubbing soothing circles on her back.

"It's okay to feel lost sometimes," he said. "Life is unpredictable, and once in a while we just have to step back and reassess our priorities. That's all it is."

Manisha nodded, taking comfort in his words. She knew he was right. She needed to take a huge step back and figure out what to do next.

*Meet Sunil.*

The thought came to her, unbidden.

"I just wish I could find someone who loves me for who I am, faults and all. Although lately I feel like I don't even like who

I am," she said, her voice trembling softly. "So, then I go and screw things up for myself even more."

Rohit pulled back to look at her, his eyes holding hers with an intensity that made her heart race. "Trust me, Manisha. There is someone out there for you who will love you for exactly who you are. You're an extraordinary woman. The way your mind works is incredible, your laugh is infectious, and when you walk into a room, you completely transform it. You bring it to life . . . it feels like your presence is sunlight breaking through clouds. I see you, I understand you, and I'm telling you, that someone is out there, and he'll count himself lucky to hold the heart of a woman as amazing as you."

Manisha was taken aback. But at the same time, a glimmer of hope flickered in her chest. Maybe Rohit was right. Maybe there was someone out there who would love her honestly and uncon- ditionally. Someone who would support her through thick and thin. And maybe that someone would forgive her for starting their relationship with a fib.

But even if that was possible, it still wouldn't undo the irrep- arable damage she'd done to her own future, her own dream . . .

The glimmer vanished. Manisha started to cry again, mum- bling between sniffles. "Rohit. Your words, I don't deserve them. It's just that I really screwed things up this time."

"Manisha, please tell me what this screw-up is." His voice was filled with empathy.

She looked down, wringing her hands in her lap, and weighed whether she should tell him. She wanted to. But with his trauma around materialism thanks to Lucky . . . what if tell- ing him changed how he saw her? Except she'd come to know Rohit as fair and compassionate. He'd proven that much over the past week.

Manisha took a deep, shaky breath. "It's so embarrassing," she finally said. "I never anticipated being in this position, and now . . . well, I need to freeze my eggs, but I don't have the money to pay for it. Because, like a dummy, I buried my sorrows in Chanel and Gucci, and for what? Now I can't even have a family, which is what I want most."

Rohit's face fell as she spoke.

Was this it—the end of their short-lived friendship?

"Manisha, is that all?" he said softly. "Freezing your eggs is a great idea, and I'm here to support you. Don't even worry about the money."

Her relief brought on a new flood of tears. "Easy for you to say—you haven't blown through all of yours."

"I can lend you money. I have more than I need and would do anything to help a friend. We're friends, right?"

Despite being touched at his offer, Manisha scoffed. "A friend yes, not a charity case."

"Yes, and I want to help my friend because I care about her. She's someone I have come to deeply respect and cherish."

Rohit gently wiped away her tears. As he lowered his hand, he stopped it midair, then trailed it down her shoulder to her fallen strap. The loose strap her mother had always warned her about. The one that would eventually lead to fireworks. He slipped his fingers beneath the fabric and righted it atop her collarbone.

The simple touch sent a rush of warmth through her, leaving her breathless. Everything else in the room seemed to disappear, as if time had paused just for them. She couldn't remember the last time she had felt something so tender, so quietly intimate in real life.

Her gaze shifted to his lips, and before she could stop herself, she found herself leaning in.

The kiss was tentative at first—soft, almost unsure—but it quickly deepened, as if the connection between them could no longer be denied. Manisha's pulse raced, her mind clouded with the sensation of his lips, warm and familiar.

But then, just as quickly, Rohit pulled away. "I'm so sorry, Manisha," he said, his voice thick with regret. "I care about you so much, but my heart . . ."

He took a step back and ran a hand through his hair. "It's just that I have feelings for someone else. I didn't mean to lead you on, and I'm sorry if you read this the wrong way. That's on me."

Manisha stared at him in horror.

*What have I done?*

*That was supposed to be with Sunil.*

*His lips. His touch. Him.*

"Please, don't take this the wrong way," Rohit continued. "I'm here for you, I really am, but my heart belongs to someone else."

She quickly shifted her gaze away, trying to steady herself. "No need to explain, Rohit," she murmured. "I'm sorry . . . it's just . . . with everything going on, and then the buzz from the shots . . ."

"Don't apologize," he said gently. "Trust me, I've been thinking about you. About this . . . for a while now. The more I've gotten to know you, the more I've realized just how much I admire you. But the timing's off, and I can't ignore what I feel for someone else."

Manisha stood there, her heart sinking. "I actually get it—"

"I don't want things to get weird between us, but I needed to be honest with you," he added quickly, reaching for her arm but hesitating just before touching her.

She swallowed hard, trying to steady her breath. "Yeah . . . of course. I understand."

"Let me explain, please . . ."

"You don't have to," Manisha said, her voice even despite the storm of emotions inside her. Slowly, she backed away in the direction of the exit. "I know exactly how you're feeling, Rohit."

With one final look, she turned around and fled.

As she stepped out the door, she couldn't help but feel a pang of guilt for kissing someone else. The thought of Sunil lingered in her mind, and a wave of regret washed over her.

Unable to stop herself, Manisha peered back into Chai Time one last time, her heart tightening as she saw Rohit pull out his phone, likely to call that *someone else*—the one who had his heart.

$\mathcal{H}$adden's, nestled in the heart of town, was a popular spot for brunch with a reputation for serving mouth-watering vegan dishes and refreshing drinks. Predictably, the place was buzzing with activity as Deena and Manisha entered. The aroma of freshly brewed coffee and sizzling faux bacon filled the air, making Manisha's stomach growl. Despite the crowd, the two cousins found a table in a cozy corner of the pub and settled in.

"So, come on, tell me everything," Deena said eagerly, leaning in. "How soft were his lips? Was it gentle or intense? Where exactly did he place his hands—on your waist, your back, or somewhere else? How did it feel? And on a scale from one to ten, how hot was it? I need all the juicy details—don't leave anything out. I'm a visualizer, so paint the entire picture for me!"

"Deena!" she exclaimed, perhaps a touch louder than she had intended. "Stop. I am not going to do that."

Their server appeared, coffee pot in hand. "Coffee?" she asked.

"Yes, please," Manisha said firmly, grateful for the temporary rescue from her cousin's nosiness.

She flipped the two mugs upright on the table and poured the steaming brew. "I'll be back to take your order," she said before walking away.

Deena took a quick, rushed gulp before turning to Manisha again. "Come on, I'm living vicariously through you. This is so unfair! Two of my friends get together, and I don't get any details?"

"One, we are not getting together and, two, there are no details to share. It was like a quick peck."

"But on the lips," Deena remarked. "And if it was just a quick peck, then why did you blush so hard when you mentioned it earlier?"

"Okay, fine, maybe it lasted longer."

"How much longer?"

"Like . . . thirty seconds."

Deena gaped at her. "That's not just a peck—that's practically a full-on make-out session these days!"

"Which he stopped before it went any further!" Manisha said, her voice shrill.

"Okay, but still, you kissed him. Even if it ended with him admitting he's into someone else. And you admitting the same. Not that you've met this guy yet."

Manisha glared at her then sighed. "I feel really bad for kissing Rohit, like I cheated on Sunil," she confessed.

Deena nodded thoughtfully, trying to understand. "I get it," she said after a moment. "But try to keep things in perspective. You're not actually dating Sunil. And I'm sure you and Rohit can move past this, unless . . ." She hesitated, studying Manisha's face. "Unless you're worried you might actually have feelings for Rohit?"

Manisha's nose twitched at the suggestion. "No, don't be silly." She quickly dismissed the idea, her tone a mix of denial and uncertainty. "Why would I have feelings for him? It was just a kiss, nothing more."

She tried to convince herself, but deep down, a part of her

wondered if there was more to her emotions than she was willing to admit.

"Well, because you've been spending time with him—a lot of time and time you've actually enjoyed. It's only natural it brings you closer together," Deena said matter-of-factly. "But let's get to other good stuff. Who do you think he's seeing?"

Manisha shrugged. "I don't know, but he felt really guilty. So did I."

There was a lull in their constant chatter as they both got lost in thought.

Manisha took a small sip of coffee, instantly regretting the move as the scalding liquid hit her tongue. She hissed, biting her tongue to numb the pain.

Deena winced in sympathy and smartly set her mug down. Not one to miss taking advantage of Manisha's injury-induced silence, she didn't hold back. "You need to email Sunil."

Manisha let out a pathetic whimper.

"The next step is to be completely honest with him, Manisha. And I think it's best done in person. Have a real conversation with Sunil about your feelings—share everything you've confided in me. Tell him how much he means to you, that you want to take things further, and . . . that you want to have his baby."

"Deena!" Manisha chided. "Putting the cart before the horse, but I hear you. It just sounds easier said than done. And—and he's been alluding to something he needs to share with me, too."

"Okay so you both have been keeping some things from each other. Look, you have to stop stressing about Rohit and focus on Sunil." Deena grabbed a menu and scanned it as she spoke. "Anyway, you mentioned that you were drinking shots of tequila, so you can lean on that as your excuse for anything that happened.

Everyone knows Tequila mistakes don't count—like Monopoly rules after midnight. It always works for me."

She nodded. "I just need a minute to gather my thoughts before reaching out to Sunil."

"Absolutely. You know, assuming all goes well, our plan to find your Prince Charming didn't fail. You just took a small detour from our initial strategy," Deena added with a grin.

Manisha shook her head, chuckling. She could only hope that Deena was right.

After they finished brunch, Manisha stayed back to craft her email to Sunil before her cowardice had the chance to overwhelm her. She took a deep breath and unlocked her phone. He hadn't followed up at all, and even though the ball was technically in her court, she had a strange feeling that he'd seemed distant the past couple of days. With that in mind, she infused her reply with as much conviction as she could muster.

> Sunil,
> Your email has been on my mind constantly. I can't stop thinking about you. I agree—I genuinely believe that we can conquer anything together. Let's do this. I don't want to waste any more time. I want to meet you. I want to be with you.

## 38

*M*anisha slowed as she neared her favourite cheesecake shop, Henriette's, a long queue of eager customers stretching out the door. She bypassed the lineup and made her way toward the bookstore next door. It was a place she used to escape to as a child, and right now, that's all she wanted to do. Nearly four hours had passed since she'd sent the email to Sunil, and still, no matter how often and desperately she checked her phone, he hadn't replied.

The mild Sunday afternoon's slight chill was tamped out as she stepped into the warm and cozy shop. She breathed in the comforting scent of book pages mixed with the faint aroma of coffee wafting from the in-store café kiosk at the back. The quiet of the shop wrapped around her like a comforting embrace as she wandered toward the romance section. Standing among the shelves of books, their bold colours lining the cases, Manisha wanted to lose herself in a story and forget about everything else.

She was reaching for the store's romance pick of the month when she caught another familiar scent wafting through the air: bergamot. Had the bookstore started using it as a fragrance, or was her nose playing tricks on her?

As she spun around, ready to investigate, her eyes landed on

Rohit. He was casually leaning against the shelves of the architecture section, wholly engrossed in his phone rather than the books surrounding him.

Even though Rohit had generously offered to pay for her egg freezing, she hadn't spoken to or seen him since their kiss. She was surprised at how happy she was to see him.

"Rohit?" Manisha called out, catching him off guard. He quickly shoved his phone away like it was contraband. "What are you doing here? Let me guess, looking for inspiration for the café renovations?"

He gestured vaguely to the bookshelves. "Yeah, I guess you could say that. What about you?"

Manisha explained that the store was one of her favourite places in Baskin. It had been ever since she was little, when Sanj would bring her here while he went to the arcade a few doors down to play with his friends. "He figured I'd be distracted for an hour here, and he was right."

They stood in silence for a moment.

"You want to grab a cup of coffee?" Rohit suggested with a smile.

"Sure, that would be nice," Manisha replied, her mind lighting up at the thought of a warm, comforting cup of coffee.

They made their way to the back where the aroma of freshly roasted Colombian coffee beans filled the air around the in-store coffee kiosk. Manisha settled into a comfortable chair as Rohit brought two cups of hot coffee, steam rising from the cups he carried over to her. He settled in across from her. "Manisha, about the other night . . ."

"I am so sorry I did that," she blurted out. She was so embarrassed she couldn't help but interrupt him before he went any further.

"No, no. Don't be sorry at all. I mean, I kissed you, too," he admitted.

Manisha was surprised by his response but relieved that he didn't seem to hold the kiss against her. "But you stopped it, as you should have," she said, showing that she respected his boundaries even if she hadn't had any that night.

"I guess I didn't realize until that moment how much I wanted the kiss to be with my lady," he said, causing Manisha's eyes to widen.

"I didn't know you were seeing anyone that seriously."

"Well, it's kind of new . . . but my heart is already hers, if that makes sense."

Manisha understood all too well. "I get it, believe me. I seem to be in the same boat—my heart is with someone else, as well, which means it was doubly out of line for me to kiss you." She sighed. "It's just a little complicated."

"Tell me about it," Rohit agreed. "But, if that person truly loves you, nothing else will matter. Right?"

Her heart swelled with emotion, grateful for the unexpected connection they had just shared.

"Manisha, I meant what I said the other night. I'm here to help you. Money or anything it is you need. I'll support whatever decision you feel is best."

"That's really sweet of you, Rohit." She smiled. "Well, look at us. From near fender-bender enemies to actual friends."

They grinned at each other, all awkwardness gone. From there, they shifted to discussing Rohit's design hopes for the café expansion. When their mugs were drained, they cleared up then made their way to the door.

"I think I'm going to head home now," she said.

"Do you want some company on the walk? I promise, no drinks tonight."

She laughed. "Sure, why not!"

As Manisha and Rohit stepped out of the bookstore, a sign caught their eye, advertising the annual "Night Under the Stars" event at the Emporium in the centre of town.

"I haven't been to that in years," Manisha remarked. "It's in just a couple of days."

"Sounds like a perfect date idea," Rohit replied.

In that moment, an idea sparked in Manisha's mind—what better way to invite Sunil on their first date? She was ready to create some in-person magic with him at last.

## 39

*W*hen Manisha got home, she hurried to the kitchen, hoping to catch the remains of the meal her dad had cooked.

She spotted Sammy standing in front of the open refrigerator.

"Isha!" he exclaimed. "Whoa, it's 7 p.m. on a Friday, and my sis is already home? I thought Manny said you had a hot date or something?"

"Not quite," Manisha replied, pulling up a chair to the counter and settling in.

Sammy grabbed a few Tupperware containers from the fridge. "Dad made his special pizza. Want some?"

"Definitely. Man, I've missed it," Manisha said eagerly, her mouth watering at the thought.

Sammy popped a couple of slices into the air fryer, the smell of melting cheese filling the kitchen. "Was that Rohit Khanna who walked you home?" he asked, glancing at her. "I saw him through the window."

"You saw him through the window? From all the way back here?" Manisha looked at him wryly.

"Okay, guilty. Older brother's prerogative," he stated with a shrug. "Anyway, what happened to that guy?"

"You tell me," Manisha said, deflecting. "You guys were friends, right?"

"We weren't super close, but yeah, he's a good guy. When he got into his tech business, we lost touch. Wait, hold up . . . are you two dating?"

"No, we're just friends," Manisha said. "Right now, I'm not dating anyone. But there's someone I really like."

"Alright, well, that's a start." Sammy grabbed the pizza slices out of the air fryer, placing them on plates. "Ouch, hot! Incoming." He sat across from her at the counter.

Manisha picked up a slice by its thick crust. "Remember when we were kids, and Dad would make us chop up all the veggies for the pizza? We'd play Pokémon to see who got the honours?"

"Yeah," he said, smiling. "I also remember winning every time."

"I won a few times!" she protested.

"Sure, sure. Keep telling yourself that." He rolled his eyes at her. "So, what's going on with this guy you like?"

"Nothing yet. But I'm meeting him in a couple of days," she said, a mix of excitement and nerves in her voice as she thought about her first date with Sunil at the Emporium.

"Look, sis, relationships are tough, and it's a jungle out there. Everyone's hunting. But I think—I know—that even in the jungle, you'll find your soulmate."

"Wow, thanks for the extra cheese," Manisha teased, gesturing to her pizza. "Manny really turned you around. My brother talking about soulmates—never thought I'd see this day."

"Alright, alright. That's enough cheese." Sammy grabbed a bite of her pizza, ignoring her protest.

"Hey, that's mine! Get your own!"

Sammy wiped his hands with a paper towel, his tone softening. "Can I tell you what I think is the secret to love? Like, the real thing?"

"Yes, please." Manisha leaned in, keeping her pizza out of his reach.

"Friendship. Be open to falling in love with someone who's your friend first. I mean, it all happened fast with Manny, but I fell in love with the friendship first. That's the secret sauce."

"Friends with benefits?" Manisha joked.

"No, you idiot. Actual friendship. Just sit with that for a bit. One day, you'll wake up and realize the person you're in love with is your best friend."

Manisha thought about her email friendship with Sunil and realized that's exactly what had happened between them.

Sammy stood up, stretching. "You may also want to lay off the drinks on your first date."

She playfully tossed a napkin at him.

"You better pick that up before Mom gets home and says that's not how they do it in the Indian shows." Sammy kissed her head before heading to the door.

"Friendship, Manisha," he called back. "That's the secret sauce. You can always add the toppings later."

"Goodnight, Sammy."

## 40

*M*anisha had picked up her favourite cheesecake from Henriette's to share with Sunil. She hoped it would be a sweet gesture, a continuation of the tradition his parents had started all those years ago when he was a child.

Walking to the Emporium, she felt the warm breeze brush against her skin, fluttering the skirt of her light-pink Reformation summer dress, perfect for the mild fall night. She'd kept her makeup simple yet effective: a burst of Fenty blush and matching red lipstick leant a boldness to her look. As she walked, she summoned her inner Rihanna. Some people might think she was overdressed for a first date, but this night meant so much to her, and she didn't care. She felt beautiful and confident, and that was all that mattered.

Manisha read Sunil's email from earlier today one more time.

I can't wait to meet you under the Baskin stars tonight.

"Over here," Deena called out as Manisha entered the building's foyer. Although Manisha couldn't wait to meet Sunil, she was still grateful that her cousin had agreed to attend the event as well. Deena's presence had a calming effect on her.

"You look hot!" Deena said.

"Not too much?" Manisha asked.

"Never too much. Are you ready?"

"I can't wait."

"And he knows how to find you?"

"Yup. I reserved the seats already. Seats 11 and 12, row J. He's got all the info, too."

They made their way into the theatre, which was a maze of people searching for their seats. Deena bid her good luck as she went to her seat in row S, and Manisha found hers below.

A few minutes later, a woman attempted to sit in the empty seat beside her in the crowded theatre. "Oh, I apologize, this seat is taken," Manisha informed her.

As the seats filled up rapidly, Manisha's anxiety grew. She checked her phone, but there was no signal in the hall. Glancing back at Deena, who offered a reassuring smile, Manisha couldn't shake the feeling that something was amiss. The theatre director announced that the show would begin in just a few minutes and urged everyone to take their seats. A child swiftly occupied the seat Manisha had saved for Sunil.

The show commenced, and as the room filled with stars and music, Manisha tried to drown her thoughts in the rhythm. But the one thing the music couldn't drown out was her heart breaking—Sunil wasn't coming.

Manisha felt crushed by overwhelming loneliness. Just days ago, she had envisioned sharing this moment with Sunil, and experiencing it alone now was more isolating than ever.

When the show finally ended, Manisha rushed out to catch up with Deena, who waited for her in the main lobby.

"I just can't believe he didn't show up. Do you think something happened to him?" Her voice filled with worry and confusion. She glanced at her phone, which struggled to hold a signal, her anxiety growing with each passing second.

"Did you take a good look around? He has to be here somewhere."

"I don't even know what he looks like!" Manisha snapped slightly. "We were supposed to meet at the reserved seats. This isn't how it happens in the movies."

"I'm sorry, Manisha. I understand you're upset. But there must be a reasonable explanation for him not showing up," Deena reassured her. "Maybe he got lost in the crowd. Or maybe he's running late. Don't panic just yet."

"You're right," Manisha replied, trying to stay positive. "Maybe he is just running late. I hope that's the case."

Deena gently guided Manisha to a quieter spot, away from the chaos of the crowd. "Let's wait here. He'll have to pass by this way eventually. Look for someone who seems to be looking for someone."

Manisha's attention was torn between the passersby and her phone screen, hoping that a message to explain Sunil's absence might come in.

Deena's attention shifted to someone approaching them.

"Rohit?" Manisha exclaimed, surprised by her friend's unexpected arrival.

Rohit's expression was one of jovial suspicion as he walked toward them. "Are you ladies following me?"

Deena hesitated before responding, "Just thought we'd check out the show, the stars and all."

Manisha sent her a look of thanks, glad her cousin hadn't outed her for being stood up. "And you, Rohit?" Deena said. "What's your excuse?"

Rohit's gaze shifted uncomfortably. "I, uh . . . I think I got stood up. It's just there was this unruly customer in the café, and I was late, so—"

Manisha, preoccupied with refreshing her inbox on her phone, took a moment to process his words.

"Wait, you got stood up, too?" Deena's voice rose in surprise.

"What do you mean by 'too'? Were you gals out for a double date or something?" Rohit asked.

Deena replied, "Not exactly. Manisha was meant to meet someone, but he didn't show up." Manisha's cheeks heated in embarrassment, and Deena rushed to reassure her. "It's quite common these days, getting ghosted."

Rohit sighed. "Ah, I see. I guess that's what happened to me, too. It's just my luck, you know? The one time I decide to put myself out there again and open my heart, this is what I get . . ." His voice trailed off, disappointment evident in his tone.

"I think I'll shoot him a message," Manisha said. "I refuse to believe that he just wouldn't show up."

"The signal really isn't great in here," Deena said, checking her own phone. "Maybe we should go outside?"

"Good idea," Rohit said. "I'll come with. She might have also tried to contact me, or maybe I mixed something up." His eyes filled with sadness.

Manisha typed as they walked through the entryway into the warm evening air. "Alright, I've sent it. Let's see if it goes through."

Rohit's phone pinged. "Looks like I have a signal out here. I just got something."

Deena's face suddenly looked shocked. She glanced at Manisha, who returned her stare, realization dawning on her.

"That's strange," Rohit said. "She says she's here, and is asking where I am."

Manisha could barely breathe as she watched Rohit read the message on his phone—the message she just sent him.

"It can't be . . ." she said, her voice barely a whisper.

"What?" he asked.

"Are you . . . Sunil?"

They stood staring at each other, and it was like the whole world around them went deadly still. Except for Deena, whose eyes jumped between the two of them like she was watching a tennis rally.

"What's happening here?" Rohit asked, tone sharp. "What are you both up to?"

"Were you pretending to be Sunil?" Manisha asked, her stomach churning. "Deceiving me this whole time?"

"Hold on," Rohit said, his brows drawing together. "You're Isha? And you have the nerve to accuse me of pretending?"

"Well, your name isn't Sunil," Manisha pointed out.

"When Deena handed me the website flyer, I checked it out using my cousin's name. I didn't feel ready to get back out there yet and using my real name felt too . . . real."

Manisha's mouth hung open. "So, you pretended to be him?"

"Who hasn't pretended before, am I right?" Deena added nervously. "Hey, I was pretending to be a fake auntie matchmaker! What's the big deal?"

"Wait, what? So, this was all a joke to you," Rohit said to them both. "You set up that site and pretended to be different people for what? For kicks?"

"No!" Manisha cried. "That's not it at all."

"Not for kicks, for dates—Manisha wanted to find her Prince Charming." Deena was trying but it wasn't helping.

Anguish flickered across Rohit's face. "Prince Charming . . . right. So, were you playing a prank on me? Is that why you pretended to be Isha, the 'admin' of some fake matchmaking site?"

"Everyone calls me Isha," she said weakly, knowing she didn't have much of a leg to stand on. She had known this moment was going to come eventually—that she'd have to admit she wasn't the admin to Sunil. She just never could have imagined Sunil was actually Rohit.

Deena put in, "Well, technically, not everyone. I don't."

Rohit's eyes never left Manisha, though. "I thought I'd made a real connection with someone. Little did I know it was all fake, for her—for you. I suppose I should congratulate you on your acting skills."

His words felt like a knife to her heart. "Acting? You think my feelings were an act?"

"That's exactly what I think," he said, his gaze hardening. "What else would you call it?" His voice . . . she had never heard that kind of edge to it. Not even during their parking lot spat. It sent a chill through her body.

"I thought we—Isha and I—had something real," he went on. But it was all fake, wasn't it?" He shook his head in contempt. "I confided in you about everything—how Lucky's betrayal destroyed me. Her lies. Her deception. They broke me. How could you— I can't believe you would do this to me, Manisha. Isha. Your emails were as fake as the website. As fake as you!"

Rohit turned and walked away, leaving Manisha in tears on the steps of the Emporium. Even Deena's embrace offered little solace as Manisha, in a daze, threw the cheesecake box into the trash, her tears falling freely.

## 41

*D*eena and Manisha sat in Deena's car in the Patels' driveway. Frozen in shock, Manisha made no move to get
out of the passenger seat. The air was heavy with silence, as if it
had swallowed them whole.

Deena shifted in her seat as she turned to Manisha, her eyes
filled with concern. "I wish I had the right words to make you
feel better. But I don't. I don't have the power to take away
your pain."

Manisha gazed out of the car window, her vision hazy and
distant. A single tear streamed down her face before she finally
turned to her cousin.

"There's nothing anyone can say," she whispered, her voice
quivering. "At least I finally know the truth. It hurts, but now I
can spare myself from further pain."

Deena reached out and gently placed her hand on Manisha's
shoulder, offering comfort in the only way she knew how. "Or
maybe, the pain will have all been worth it?"

"How, Deena?" Manisha said. "What do I stand to gain from
this experience? Will Rohit and I end up together and live happily ever after? Is this the fresh start, the new beginning that
Meena Auntie mentioned?" She shook her head, scoffing. "If
Rohit is magic, I wish he would just vanish."

"I get that's how you're feeling right now. It's all so overwhelming. But remember, the thing you loved about Sunil was his heart. His kindness. The dreams you shared for the future."

"Yeah, but little did I know he was deceiving me all along! He was never Sunil at all."

Deena's head shifted side to side as she considered. "No, he's Rohit. You weren't honest about your identity, either, but everything else you said in your emails was true. So maybe it's the same with him—he gave you a fake name, but it sounds like everything else he shared was real."

Manisha's eyes filled with fresh tears and the car fell into a heavy silence once again, the weight of the conversation hanging in the air. Manisha's voice broke through the quiet, filled with a mix of frustration and resignation.

"Maybe I wasn't cut out to be a mother after all. It's becoming painfully obvious that the universe, or whatever higher power out there, is trying to tell me something that I've been wilfully blind to."

"Manisha, please don't say that," Deena said, desperation lacing her voice. "You were meant to be a mother, and Rohit was meant to be a father. We both know the pain you've each endured in your last relationships—of course this discovery would trigger your fears. Neither of you anticipated how much love would blossom between you two. I certainly didn't!"

Manisha's voice wavered as she spoke, her emotions raw. "Deena, you don't get it. I don't love Rohit . . . I loved Sunil."

She opened the car door, her hands shaking.

"But Sunil . . . he doesn't even exist." Manisha closed the car door behind her and entered her house, leaving behind a trail of unspoken pain.

## 42

The sun was shining brightly when Manisha finally dragged herself out of bed, determined to shake off her gloom.

She sat on the back porch, basking in the sun's warmth, and felt a sense of calm wash over her. For once, she didn't care about her phone buzzing with notifications. She just wanted to be in the moment, but her mother's voice shattered the silence. Manisha rolled her eyes—of course her mother found a way to disrupt her tranquility.

Her mom stood on the porch beside her. "So quiet today."

"It is," Manisha replied.

But her mother wasn't satisfied. "No. You. You are so quiet."

Manisha rolled her eyes again. "Geez, Mom. Why can't I be quiet? Why do I always have to be on?"

"Because I want to hear something from my daughter. Tell me a story—any good dates lately?" she prodded.

Manisha's frustration boiled over. She popped up from the bench seat. "No, Mom, and you know what? I'm tired of this. I can't even talk to you without you getting in my face about dating, getting married, having a baby."

Her mother tried to calm her down. "Manisha—"

But she wasn't having it. "I'm so sick and tired of it. Why did I even bother to come back to Baskin? This place is a total gossip mill! Between all the nosy questions and your constant grilling, I'm losing it!"

Her mother looked stunned. "Isha, come sit down," she said gently.

Manisha flinched at the use of her nickname.

"I was just asking questions, like I always do—I'm sorry."

But Manisha was too angry to listen. "Yeah, well, I'm sorry, too, for thinking you could just be a normal mom for once in your life and have a conversation about my career, my friends, or maybe the fact that I need your help with stuff," she snapped.

Her mother tried to make amends. "I can help now. Tell me where to help?"

"Yeah, well, guess what? It's too late."

She slammed her teacup on the kitchen counter as she returned inside the house and grabbed the keys to the SUV. Tears streamed down her face as she drove away, not knowing where she was going but escape the only thing that made sense. After weeks of going on dates, concocting a master baby-plan full of deception, and falling in love with a fantasy, she had gotten nowhere. For once, she wanted to have no idea where she would end up. That felt safer than any plan. So Manisha drove and drove without looking back or thinking ahead.

Finally, she stopped her car in a neighbourhood that looked all too familiar. Her phone had been ringing non-stop, but she wasn't ready to talk to anyone—except for one person, that is. The one person whose house she was parked in front of, but with whom she wasn't sure how to even start a conversation.

She sat in her car, staring at the property, noting how well-kept it looked. Just like she had imagined it so many times since the last time she had seen it. A beige Toyota Corolla was parked in the driveway. Manisha rubbed her eyes, trying to banish any remaining tears. She reached into her purse and pulled out her Live Tinted Huestick, the only thing she had to illuminate her dull face. She tried rehearsing different ways to start the conversation, but none seemed right. Finally, she decided to just go for it. After all, what had planning ever gotten her?

Manisha got out of the car and slowly approached the door. She pressed the doorbell lightly, half hoping it wouldn't chime. But on the other hand, she was so ready to see her again . . .

"Grandma."

The door opened as Manisha said the word. Her tiny grandmother wore thin-rimmed glasses, her hair in a bun, and a beautifully tailored Indian suit as bright as the blue sky.

"Manisha. I wondered if you would come in or continue wasting time outside."

And there it was, the signature sarcasm that she remembered so well. Manisha couldn't help but smile.

"How did you even know it was me?"

"Your mother brings that monstrous thing when she comes to visit," her grandma said, nodding at the car. "Now come in before you change your mind and leave."

Manisha walked in, realizing she didn't exactly look presentable in her Hermès T-shirt and ripped jeans. But she hadn't known she would end up here.

Her grandmother hugged her unexpectedly, and Manisha returned the gesture, holding on slightly longer than she normally would.

"Aja. I just made tea."

Manisha sat in the large living room as her grandmother poured the tea in the kitchen. The place was simple and spare, contrasting with the eclectic Patel living room. Her grandmother's white walls weren't covered in pictures but rather houseplants that stretched through the house. On a side table, Manisha spotted a couple of wooden elephants from her parents' home-decor store. There was no way . . . had Grandma been to the store?

"It's from the store, yes. I was there the other day. I met your mother for coffee."

Manisha's head whipped around. "Really? I mean, I had no idea you were still speaking to her."

"Arrey, of course we talk, beta, she is my daughter. But seeing her and not you kids, it's not easy, you know? She always sends me pictures, and she tells me how proud she is of your career. I am so happy for your success in London. God bless you."

Manisha was surprised her mother had even remembered to mention her career among all her marriage disappointment.

"Thank you. I, um . . ."

Her grandmother handed her a cup of tea as she sat across from her.

"I don't know what I'm doing here, honestly."

"That is okay. At least you are here."

"I'm sorry I haven't come sooner, Grandma. I wanted to defer to Dad's feelings, but I don't even know what started this whole thing. I mean . . . what happened? Why doesn't Dad talk to you anymore?" Manisha felt like a little kid who'd be reprimanded for asking the tough questions she wanted answers to, but she dove right into it, knowing there would be no newspaper swats here.

Her grandmother took a long sip of her tea and reclined in her chair. With only a few wrinkles and not a touch of makeup, she was stunning.

"It is my fault. I was unfair to your father." She paused. "When your father and mother were taking out loans for their store and falling deep in debt, I . . . well, I told your mother to leave him."

"What?" Manisha said, shocked.

"Manisha, I was raised to believe a man should support his family, not put his wife under financial stress."

"But Grandma, Mom wanted the store—"

"And I wanted my daughter to be happy. I thought if she were with someone wealthy, it would provide her the happiness she deserved." Her grandma fiddled with her teacup. "So, I did something terrible; I went behind your father's back and drew up legal paperwork for a divorce."

Manisha was speechless, in total disbelief.

"I regret doing it. You see, your mother didn't want money. She loved your father—he's all she wanted. And yes, eventually they were financially stable, successful even. He had every right to be upset and angry with me when he found out what I did."

Manisha's grandmother took a long pause as they both sat in silence.

"Manisha, I was projecting my own unhappiness with your grandfather onto your parents. Your mother was always happy with your father, in love, but I . . . wasn't."

This was news to Manisha. "You weren't happy with Grandpa? You weren't in love?"

"My marriage was arranged. We were two people who simply had to make it work. We respected each other, but it would be dishonest to say that we were happily in love. Your mother's marriage was different, though. It grew from a place of love first. It wasn't arranged."

She was learning all kinds of new things today. "We always thought it was."

Her grandma shook her head. "She chose him, and he chose her. They met on a field trip with their respective schools, and in a few days, your father came to our home and asked permission to marry our daughter."

Patels didn't waste any time—no matter their generation.

Manisha sat in shock. All this time, she assumed her parents had been preselected for each other, but they'd loved each other from the start.

"Do you think Dad will ever come around?" Manisha asked, her voice tinged with sadness.

"Perhaps eventually, beta. You Patels are stubborn," her grandmother replied gently.

"That is very true."

"So, tell me, my beautiful granddaughter, why, after all this time, are you here?"

"I needed to get away. I needed to hide for a bit. Maybe forever."

"You can come here and hide anytime, beta. I am always up for company. But what, or who, are you hiding from?" Her grandmother's tone was shrewd.

Manisha hesitated before answering. "From . . . um, love . . . and Rohit-slash-Sunil."

"Two boys? Va va. Your mother was once like that, too. Peter Rocky on one hand, your father on the other." Her grandmother chuckled, a knowing smile playing on her lips, reminding Manisha of her mother.

"Dr. Rocky and *my* mom?" Manisha asked. On some level, she had known, but still, she was a little taken aback by the revelation.

"She left him for your father. Manisha, tell me—who do you truly love? Rohit or Sunil?"

"Both," Manisha blurted out, feeling embarrassed. "It's complicated, Grandma. I don't want to get hurt."

"You won't, beta, unless you deny yourself love. It is the greatest wealth in life, Manisha," her grandmother said softly, her voice filled with wisdom.

Manisha smiled, touched by her grandmother's words. "Thanks, Grandma. I really needed to hear that. I'm glad I ended up here with you."

"Come then, stay for dinner," her grandmother said with a warm smile. "You can wash up upstairs. I'll get everything ready." She led the way up the creaky oak stairs, her steps slow but sure.

"You know this 'Grandma' business is too gori pakori. You should call me Nani."

Manisha let out a little laugh. "You're right, Nani."

As they climbed, Manisha caught sight of a familiar face on the wall.

"Hey, is that Mom with *the* SRK?" Manisha looked in amazement at the picture of her mother with Shah Rukh Khan.

"Oh, yes, it is," her grandmother replied with a twinkle in her eye. "Let me tell you the story about that guy. Your mother had a few suitors back in the day . . ."

Manisha chuckled, knowing she was in for a familiar tale. One she would believe this time.

"By the way, my good friend Beatrice showed me a website with my picture on it. It says I am some matchmaking auntie. Do you know anything about this?"

Manisha smiled, nodding. "Oh, Naniji, do I have a story for you . . ."

## 43

*A* mountain of clothes surrounded Manisha, each item carrying a piece of her past—memories she was now ready to let go of. It was time for a fresh start. She wanted to shed the weight of her old life and move forward. After an evening spent with her grandmother, Manisha realized she couldn't keep avoiding Rohit, just as she couldn't keep hiding from her life in London.

The latter mess she had a plan for. She had remembered Deena's suggestion from before, to resell her post-breakup purchases to recoup some of the money. It hadn't been a viable option back when she thought she was down to the wire to summon fifty thousand dollars out of thin air. But since her follow-up with Dr. Rocky, she'd gone back to the idea a few times in her head.

Manisha called Deena to ask for her help selling most of her belongings; Deena was so excited, she came straight over. For the next few hours, they sorted through Manisha's clothes, posting them in batches on online marketplaces.

"You know, I saw something similar in a Netflix documentary—an ex selling her deceitful boyfriend's stuff online to get back the money she lost to his dishonesty," Deena said, boxing up a pair of Jimmy Choo mules.

Manisha sighed. "Why does my life always end up sounding like some dramatic reality show or doc?"

She cast a wistful glance at the piles surrounding her, a pang of sadness in her chest. She'd imagined giving so many of these outfits and bags to her children one day, but that dream now seemed like a distant memory.

Deena stopped and reached over to place a hand over Manisha's. "You sure you're feeling alright about this?"

"I am. I think selling this stuff is a good start, and then I'll figure things out in London," she replied with another sigh.

"And what about Rohit? Are you sure you can't talk to him?"

"One thing at a time, Deena, remember? Besides, I don't think so. Even if I could, where would we start?" She pulled her hand back and returned to folding.

"Manisha, I met him for a coffee, and he just looked so sad and hurt . . . He said he was sorry for hiding his true identity."

"I know, he's sent me emails saying the same thing," Manisha said, snapping a shirt in the air maybe a little too forcefully. Each one of his notes was like a slice to her heart. "I just don't think I can go there again."

"Rohit's not a bad guy, you know that. So what if he called himself Sunil? We Indians usually have a few names anyway. Deena, Derinder . . . Isha, Manisha." Deena shrugged. "Does any of it really matter? So you told him you were the site's admin. The important thing is you two found your way to each other, right?"

"Yeah, we may have found each other in this huge dating world . . . but we also found each other through deception."

"But no one's pretending anymore. Everything's out in the open now. I know you both went through tough times with your exes betraying you—"

"Exactly, Deena." Manisha's tone was growing sharper.

"But it's not the same thing. Nowhere near the same thing."

"It is to me. I don't feel right starting a relationship this way. He was right—the site was fake and so were Sunil and Isha."

"This isn't a court of law—you don't have to be so legal about everything. Sometimes, you can break the rules."

"That's all I've done, Deena. I need to draw the line somewhere, because, for the last few weeks, I haven't drawn any lines. And look where it's gotten me. I've forgotten who I am."

"Manisha, I checked the Admin folder. There are dozens of emails in there! Raw, honest, authentic conversations between two real people. There's nothing fake about the words in those emails. They'll remind you of who you truly are."

"I love you, Deena, but I have to love myself, too. And that means protecting my heart. Now, are you going to help me or not?" She shot her a stern look that clearly communicated she was done discussing Rohit.

Deena threw her hands in the air, resigned. "Yes, I am! There's just been so much mourning going on. You and Rohit and now these clothes."

"Well, it's about time. And with the money I make from selling these, I can finally start saving to freeze my eggs."

They continued to work tirelessly, sorting, photographing, and listing item after item. By 11 p.m. they had just one small pile of accessories left to post.

"Why don't you go home, I can finish up here," Manisha said, clocking Deena's drooping eyelids.

"Are you sure? Here, just let me get this last scarf—" Deena cut herself off with a squeal.

"Manisha, come look! Someone wants to buy all three of your Louis Vuitton purses!"

"All three?" Manisha scrabbled over to get a good look at the laptop screen.

"That's nearly eight thousand dollars if the offer goes through!"

"Oh my god, accept it! Quick, before they try to take it back!"

When the confirmation screen loaded showing the sale, they both jumped up, shrieking. Manisha threw her arms around Deena, giving her a fierce hug.

"It isn't fifty thousand, but it's a really good start, Manisha," Deena said, squeezing her tightly.

"I know." Manisha eased back, grinning. "Hey, can we calculate the projected total if everything we've posted so far sells for, say, seventy percent of what we listed them for? I get that's unlikely, but just to see?"

Deena scrolled through their postings on the marketplace site, quickly adding up the estimated earnings. "Twenty-seven thousand dollars!" she exclaimed.

"Deena, we're not even halfway through my wardrobe yet . . . There's still everything back in London" Manisha said, overwhelmed with gratitude. "This is exactly what I needed. I don't know how to even begin to thank you."

"I know how you can thank me," Deena said, a sly grin curling her lips.

"How?"

"By giving Rohit a chance," Deena teased gently.

Manisha raised a brow. "Go home, Deena."

With a cackle, Deena gave her one final hug for the night. "I'm proud of you, Manisha," she whispered, before taking her leave.

Alone in her now-tidier room, Manisha felt, for the first time in a long while, in control, empowered, and excited as she envisioned a more secure future.

he following morning, Manisha was greeted by yet another email from Rohit, complete with an apology and a request to meet and talk. Manisha still wasn't prepared to have that conversation, so she archived the message as she had all the others.

She wasn't sure if she'd ever be ready to face the pain of what had happened between them, and knowing that she might run into him at any second wasn't helping. So, she made the decision to do what she did best: run away from her problems. Her flight back to London was booked for later that evening. She had a closetful of items there, and Deena, being the best cousin, had agreed to fly out next week to help her list them. Together, they'd enjoy the last several weeks of Manisha's posh Marylebone rental that was conveniently located thousands of miles away from Rohit.

As Manisha began to pack up her necessities, her mother appeared at the doorway of her childhood bedroom, observing her silently.

"Mom, please come in," Manisha called out, her voice filled with sincerity and warmth.

Manisha wrapped her arms around her mother, embracing her tightly. They sat on the edge of the bed together.

"Isha, I didn't mean to upset you so much." Manisha's mother spoke softly, her eyes reflecting concern and love.

"It's okay, Mom. I was upset about something else. It wasn't you."

"I want you to know that I am always watching out for you, even if it may not seem that way."

Manisha sighed, the sound laced with exhaustion. "I know. It's just that I've been dealing with so much lately, and on top of it all, I've been trying so hard to make you happy."

Her mother's response was filled with reassurance. "Leh, why are you trying so hard to make me happy? I am very happy. I want you to be happy, too."

Manisha's voice trembled slightly. "Well, sometimes I feel like you'd be happier with me if I were married or at least close to it."

Her mother's reply was immediate, dismissing any of Manisha's concerns. "Nonsense. I may say those things like a good Indian mom should, but deep down I know that when you're ready, you'll find love on your terms and in your own time."

Manisha's expression filled with a mix of surprise and hope. "Really? You truly mean that?"

"Yes, of course."

Manisha hugged her mom again, and they both smiled.

"Sometimes it's hard, Isha," her mom said. "Once, I had three babies who all needed me at the same time. But now, I have adult children all living in their own homes with their own lives. When you're here, I cherish every moment and secretly hope you'll meet your special someone here . . . because I miss having you here with me."

Overwhelmed with emotion, Manisha's voice cracked as she responded, "Why didn't you just say that? I know I'm returning to London tonight, but things there have changed for me now. I've lost my passion for law and—"

"Okay, chal. We will find you a new passion, my dear. You are smart and hard-working—you can do anything you choose."

Manisha's heart tripped over itself at her mother's encouraging words—words she'd longed to hear her entire adult life. But she knew she wasn't done with her confessions.

"Also . . . I need to show you something before anyone else does. I wasn't exactly on my best behaviour in London, and well . . . one night, I said a few too many things to someone, and it was caught on video, and—"

"Manisha, I already know."

She couldn't have heard that right. "What do you mean, you already know?"

"Your uncle in London sent me the video."

Her heart was racing. "Oh wow. So, this whole time . . . you knew? What about Dad?"

"Your dad knows, too. But what does it matter to us? We don't need a video to tell us you weren't happy. We were waiting for you to tell us."

"So, you're not mad at me?"

"Mad? Why?"

"For embarrassing you?"

"Chup. There is no shame in this. Something to be proud of when you stand up for yourself and others."

Manisha took a beat to let her mother's words sink in. "Others . . . what do you mean?"

Manisha's mother retrieved her phone from her suit pocket. With a knowing smile, she tapped the screen to play a video, but not the one from that night in London. Instead, it showed Manisha advocating for Rohit against Lucky's accusations at city hall.

"How did you manage to get this?" Manisha asked, astonished.

"Gurshan Auntie," her mother replied.

When the video ended, Manisha locked eyes with her mom. "You know, I learned that from you. To stand up for yourself and your friends. You've always been such a great role model for me."

"Rohit is lucky to have a friend like you in his corner, Isha."

Her heart felt like it was one beat away from shattering, but she pushed aside all thoughts of Rohit to be in the moment. "I'm lucky to have you as my mother. You mean the world to me, and I love you so much."

Manisha gave her mother one more hug.

As her mom rose to leave her to pack her things, she said, "Oh, and by the way, I left a box of ladoos for you in the kitchen."

"Oh? And just how many ladoos are in there? Have you had any yourself?"

"Nope, not even one—because I got my own box, too." She walked out booming her dramatic Bollywood villain laugh.

"Mom, your phone," Manisha called after her, but she was long gone. The video was still up on the screen, and she took another look at it.

She'd be lying to herself if she didn't admit that, when she'd stood up for Rohit that day, she'd felt that their bond was more profound than simple friendship. After watching the video several times now, she finally set her mother's phone down, lost in her thoughts. She picked up her phone, which housed dozens of emails between her and Sunil. Her and Rohit.

But as she scrolled through them, she noticed other folders beyond Admin had shown up along the sidebar. Deena must've changed her access at some point. She stumbled upon a folder that caught her attention. It was labelled "Women." Curiosity piqued, Manisha opened the folder and was pleasantly surprised to find more than two dozen bios from women who were also on the hunt for their Indian Prince Charming. She smiled as she read through the bio for Payal, a thirty-three-year-old kickboxing instructor, dancing enthusiast, and coffee connoisseur who dreamed of travelling with her partner one day. Manisha remembered Paul and his wacky love for coffee—they could be a match made in heaven. As she delved deeper into the folder, Manisha realized that just because she hadn't hit it off with the Arinders of the world didn't mean nobody would. Maybe there was a woman out there who wanted to spend her life with him and his mom, and good for her.

Manisha printed out all of the women's bios, and just like Deena had colour-coded her matches, she did the same. With her whiteboard in hand, Manisha spent the next few hours creating matches for all their profiles. She hadn't felt this determined, this focused, in a long time. And with so many eligible singles at her fingertips, she knew she had the power to pair up every hopeful woman who'd submitted a bio before she got on that plane to London—and that's precisely what she did.

She carefully sifted through each woman's profile, thoughtfully selecting her perfect match, whether that was someone to cook up a storm with, a Netflix-and-chill partner, or someone ready to take another shot at love. Her heart swelled with joy knowing she had the power to make a difference in someone's life, even if it was just with one meaningful date.

She eagerly sent personalized emails to each person, inviting them to meet their match at Chai Time. It was her way of making things right after all the chaos she had caused by deceiving Rohit and all the guys she had met. And it was also her way of balancing out some of that pesky karma. There may not have been a real Leena Auntie, but Manisha was an honest matchmaker. And, at this moment, giving hope to others felt like the right thing to do.

## 45

*A*s they drove to the Baskin airport, the familiar sights of her hometown cast in the final streaks of evening sunlight greeted Manisha—each street corner, each shop, a part of her history. Her father glanced over at her with a subtle smile. But the ride passed in silence, the kind of silence that felt heavy with unspoken thoughts. They passed the familiar grocery store that she'd rush to after school to grab her Diet Coke fix, and the park where she and Deena had spent countless afternoons sprawled out on the grass, swapping secrets, overanalyzing text messages, and planning their dream vacations. A wave of nostalgia hit her and she felt a deep urge to stay, to linger—just a little longer. This place that had once felt stifling now seemed to pull at her heart, the memories of her past mixing with the present in ways she hadn't expected.

And then, there was Rohit. His presence had been bleeding into her thoughts more than she'd like to admit. She hadn't expected it to be this way, especially after everything that had happened. She'd insisted—no, convinced herself—that things with him were beyond repair. That his hidden truths, their misunderstandings, and the strange mess they'd created made any future together impossible. She had been firm in her denial, focused on moving forward and leaving behind the complications of love. But now, as she found herself standing on the edge of the familiar world she'd once tried so hard to escape, the walls she'd carefully built around her heart were starting to crumble.

She thought of the heart-to-hearts she'd had with Deena, her mom and dad, and even her grandmother. Each conversation had peeled away a layer of her defence, each one helping her see things differently. Her grandmother's words about love being the greatest source of wealth, her mother's vulnerability about missing the closeness of her children, and Deena's insistence that she be honest with herself—they had all made her reflect on what love really was. It wasn't about perfection or always having the right answers; it was about understanding, compromise, and yes, sometimes a little bit of pain. Maybe she'd been too focused on the past, too unwilling to face her own mistakes. She had spent so much time blaming Rohit for everything, but wasn't she equally to blame for never having the courage to admit what or who she really wanted?

Manisha closed her eyes for a brief moment. She thought about how often he'd been there for her, how he'd made her laugh, how he'd genuinely listened when she shared her worries and hopes. The fireworks when he slid her loose strap across her bare shoulder. And now, she realized how much she missed him— not just the version of him she'd built up in her head, but the real, imperfect Rohit who had never really stopped caring about her.

Had she been wrong about everything? Could they fix this? Her mind raced. She couldn't deny that, deep down, she still wanted to be with him. The thought of her future, the one she'd envisioned without him, suddenly felt incomplete.

"You should go in case the security line is long," Manisha's dad said, pulling her from her thoughts. "But I have no doubt that you will return soon. Always remember that we are incredibly proud of you, beta," he reminded her.

Manisha felt a lump in her throat. "I know, Dad. And I want you to know how grateful I am for everything. This visit has been . . . quite overwhelming for me, and I've learned a great deal from you these past few weeks. I feel so lucky to have a dad as awesome as you."

"A dad as sick as me, right?" Her father chuckled, his eyes twinkling with pride. "And a dad that keeps his daughter fed, no less," he teased, earning a playful eye roll from Manisha.

"Thank you for that, too," she said, her voice filled with affection.

As they hugged goodbye at the departures gate, her father offered her some Patel advice.

"I know my daughter's heart is filled with love for someone, and she'll know when it's time to open it up to him again. There's no hurry."

Manisha's eyes misted over, touched by her father's understanding.

"Thanks, Dad, and same goes for you. When you're ready to open your heart back up to . . ." she trailed off, not wanting to bring up the painful subject of her grandmother, "to anyone, you should."

They exchanged a knowing look, and her dad said, "Us Patels, we are stubborn, aren't we?"

"We sure are," Manisha said, dismayed at just how right he was.

"But maybe one day we won't be."

She kissed him on the cheek. "Maybe. I love you, Dad. Thank you."

As she went through the security checkpoint and then toward her gate, she dwelled on how lucky she was for the unwavering love her family had always shown her. She made her way to the airport lounge, her feet unconsciously bringing her to the panoramic windows overlooking Baskin as her thoughts circled back to her decision to leave. Was it the right one? Maybe it was the cowardly way out, but it also felt like the only option to get out of the mess she'd made. She could stay, try to work things out with Rohit . . . Except, could she really go back and make things right after all the hurt they'd caused each other? No, she couldn't bear all the falsehood.

A shooting star streaked across the darkness that loomed over the planes lined up at their gates outside. Manisha had one wish, and even Meena Auntie, with all her magical powers, couldn't grant it.

She replayed the events of that night at the Emporium. The memory of Rohit's face, twisted in pain and confusion, haunted her. She had seen the damage in his eyes, the pain that was surely mirrored in her own. Was it possible to come back from that? They had spent so much time together these past few weeks. They'd shared intimate conversations about their hopes, dreams, and insecurities. Even more so as Sunil and Isha.

And then there was the kiss. The passionate, electrifying kiss that had left her breathless and wanting more. It had felt so good, so right, as if they had been meant to be together all along. But had he felt that same deep, earth-shattering connection? Did any of it even matter?

Questions swirled around her as she watched one plane after another take off and disappear out of sight.

She had spent so long running, running from him, running from herself, and she couldn't do it anymore. She needed to face the consequences of her actions, own her faults, and take the first step toward fixing what she had also broken.

With a sense of quiet determination, she made a promise to herself. *I'll do better. I'll be better. No more running. No more hidden truths.*

She would go to London as planned, quickly sort through her affairs there, then come right back home to Baskin at the earliest opportunity.

But Rohit . . . he deserved so much better than to be ignored by her for any longer. She had already hurt him once by hiding the truth; now, it was time to be upfront and give them both a chance to start fresh. No more running, no more games.

She reached for her phone, her fingers trembling slightly as she typed. The message to Rohit wasn't long, but it was heartfelt. It wasn't an apology, not yet, but it was the first step toward healing.

I want to talk to you. I've been running from this, but I don't want to run anymore.

Her hands trembled as she typed the message to him. As she hit send, a weight lifted off her shoulders. She didn't know what would happen next, but she felt like she was finally on the right path in all aspects of her life.

When the announcer called out her flight number, Manisha boarded the plane and walked down the aisle to the middle of the aircraft. The red-eye flight was relatively empty, with only a few dozen people scattered throughout the cabin. She found her seat and settled in, grateful for the quiet.

As the plane taxied down the runway and ascended into the sky, Manisha reflected on her email, wondering if Rohit would have replied by the time she landed in London. She hoped he would. But her thoughts were suddenly interrupted by the charming flight attendant.

"Excuse me, ma'am," he said with a smile, "we have some extra space up front in our premium section. Would you like a complimentary upgrade?"

Manisha lit up at the thought of indulging in a few glasses of champagne while she wallowed. After all, she had several hours to kill before she could get any Wi-Fi and check if Rohit had replied to her message.

"Yes, please!" she exclaimed.

"After you." He motioned for her to lead the way to the front of the plane.

Manisha opened the curtains to the premium area, where the seats were empty except for a man at the front listening to music. Really loud music. The champagne couldn't come fast enough, Manisha thought.

As she sat down, she could swear she smelled the familiar scent of bergamot—but that had to be her imagination. She leaned back in her seat and gasped. The plane's ceiling was lit like a dazzling night sky, with hundreds of tiny stars twinkling and shimmering in a surreal display. The sight left Manisha breathless, transporting her back to Rohit's theatre, and ultimately to her first date with Sunil that never was.

*What is going on?*

"Manisha."

Manisha's heart skipped as she heard her name.

She turned in disbelief. Could it be?

Sure enough, it was Rohit's voice, unmistakable and comforting. From the front seat, he stood up, switched off the music, and walked toward her with a confident smile.

"Rohit . . . What are you doing here?" she asked breathily. Her eyes flitted across his face, taking in his every feature over and over again, as though trying to ensure that he was really here. Finally, they stopped to meet his steady gaze.

"Did you get my email that quickly?" she said it with a half-joking tone, though she wasn't entirely sure.

"What email?" he teased, raising an eyebrow.

Manisha stuttered, feeling the weight of her emotions. "I . . . I just . . . well, Rohit—"

"Manisha Patel," he interrupted gently, his tone soft but serious. "It's time you listened to me. I'm here because I brought what was meant to be our first date to you."

Overwhelmed, her eyes flooded with tears.

"Well, almost our first date," he added with a grin, reaching behind his back. He pulled out a small box, offering it to her. Inside was a slice of cheesecake from Henriette's.

She blinked back the moisture, fighting to see clearly. "You did all of this, for—?"

He nodded, his smile warm and sincere. "—you. All for you. All for us."

Rohit stepped closer, the air between them charged with something unspoken. "My mom used to say that a sky full of stars always leaves room for a wish."

Manisha stared into his eyes, and for a moment, the world seemed to disappear around them. She closed her eyes, making a wish in the silence of their connection.

"What did you wish for?" Rohit's voice broke through the stillness, his gaze tender.

She offered him a coy smile, her voice light yet full of promise. "I can't tell you if I want it to come true."

He chuckled, stepping even closer, his presence wrapping around her like a warm embrace as he balanced the box on her chair arm, then slid into the empty seat beside her. "I don't need to know the wish. I just need to be here."

Manisha's heart was racing, her breath shallow as she took in the reality of him sitting before her. "So, you boarded a plane destined to cross the ocean just to give me this?"

"I did."

Manisha could feel the warmth of his breath on her. Something she had dreamed of.

"But that's not all I came for," he said. "I'm here for you. I need to understand why you're leaving . . . why you're running away from us."

No longer able to meet his eyes, she cast her gaze down. "It felt easier."

"Manisha Patel, since when do you do easier?" Rohit asked, gently taking her chin in hand, tilting it upward until their eyes met.

"Since the truth became too hard to face. Since I got caught up in my own pretend version of reality. I—" Her voice cracked. "I've been in a relationship devastated by dishonesty before, Rohit. You know what that's like. I convinced myself that nothing good could come from a relationship that was built on half-truths."

"Manisha, listen to me. Did you hide the fact that you were the admin for Curry and Cupid? Sure. And I was shocked and upset about that at first. But as I reflected on everything we went through—both as Sunil and Isha and Rohit and Manisha— I realized that the truth we shared far outweighed the things we kept hidden."

She kept quiet, waiting for him to go on.

"Did you lie about what was in your heart when you wrote to Sunil? Did you ever share feelings with me in person that weren't true? That night you kissed me, was that kiss fake? Because it sure felt real to me. Manisha, none of this was a lie. None of it is a lie. I care for you, and I know you care for me," Rohit said, his voice steady and filled with conviction.

He cupped her cheek as he leaned in, closing the space between them. The air seemed to hold its breath, and then, as if it was the most natural thing in the world, he kissed her. His lips were soft but insistent, a kiss that spoke of everything unsaid, everything they had been avoiding.

Manisha felt her heart race, the warmth of his touch spreading through her, and for the first time in what felt like forever, she stopped thinking. The confusion, the guilt, the doubts—they all dispersed, leaving only the undeniable truth of the moment. This was real. This kiss, this connection, it was everything she had been afraid to admit, but it was also everything she had wanted.

Pulling away slightly, Rohit looked at her, his gaze unwavering. "I'm not perfect, Manisha. I know I've made mistakes, and I know you have, too. But we can't let the walls we've built to protect ourselves define us. We owe it to ourselves to be honest—no more hiding, no more pretending. Do you want to try, really try, with me?"

Manisha blinked, the words hanging in the air. She'd been so caught up in her fears, in the shame of her own choices, that she hadn't allowed herself to see the truth until now. It was never about the half-truths—it was about what they were willing to do next, how they would rebuild from here.

Taking a deep breath, she nodded, her voice barely above a whisper. "Yes. I want to try. I'm sorry for everything, Rohit. I was scared . . . I was scared of what was real."

He smiled. "I'm here, standing right in front of you. Sunil, Rohit, whatever you want to call me—I am here and not going anywhere except maybe London with you tonight. I will go wherever you want to go. I just want to be with you."

Manisha felt a surge of heat rush through her body at his words—a euphoria reminiscent of her sultry dream from all those weeks ago. Except this wasn't a dream; this was all real.

"I want to be with you, too, Rohit," she finally admitted.

As she leaned into his familiar frame, she knew it had always been him—first in her dreams, then in her inbox, and now in real life.

A sudden bout of turbulence caused them to collide even closer together. As he wrapped his arms around her, everything felt right, and she knew that she was exactly where she was meant to be—with her Prince Charming.

"I still can't believe you did all this for me," Manisha said, gazing at the stars above them.

"You know, this is how my parents met—under the stars. I always thought it sounded so romantic." He turned to her, his voice softer now. "Manisha, I'd do anything for you. For us."

Manisha wrapped her arms around Rohit. Manisha felt a small protrusion inside his jacket and pulled back. "What's this?" she asked.

"Busted," Rohit replied, a sheepish grin spreading across his face. He pulled a small baggie out of his inner pocket. "Meena Auntie. She gave me these little seeds. Don't judge me, but I took some, hoping for . . ."

Manisha didn't even need to hear the rest of his sentence—she knew exactly what he was hoping for because she had been hoping for the same thing.

"Magic," she said, and kissed him again.

She took Rohit's hand as they sat side by side on the flight to London—a city she looked forward to seeing again, despite the fact that she knew they would be returning to Baskin very soon. Together.

The flight attendant came by to pour each of them a glass of champagne.

"I love you, Manisha Patel, and as soon as we land, I can't wait to make love to you."

As Manisha gazed into Rohit's eyes, she felt overwhelmed with love, and told him so. She had to share something else with him, too.

"I finally have an idea for my next career," she said.

Rohit's curiosity was piqued. "I'm all ears, baby!"

"Let's just say it's what brought us together."

*One Year Later*

Smoothing out the surface before her, Manisha took a step back to survey her work. Her ears pricked up at the familiar footsteps padding up the stairs to her office. She turned her head just in time to catch a quick kiss from Rohit.

"They're here, babe," he said, wrapping his arms around her from behind.

She relaxed back into him, hands coming to rest over his by her collarbone.

"Mm, so what do you think?" she asked, sneaking a glance at his face, then back to the wall in front of them.

Coupled photographs covered nearly every inch of the space, and at the top, in bold lettering, was a banner that read "Wall of Fame." Manisha had just added the photos of Vikas, Paul, and their respective partners. The two men hadn't been right for her, but they were now both successfully matched and happily engaged, courtesy of Manisha. For the past year, she had made her focus helping people discover love. Soon, her passion for sharing the joy she had been lucky enough to find in her own life had transformed into a thriving matchmaking business.

"I think I love it almost as much as I love you. But I've got to say, you're one hot matchmaking auntie," Rohit said with a grin.

"Please never call me an auntie as long as you live." She turned in his arms to face him, brushing his jawline with her lips.

"No Baskin auntie is a match for my queen matchmaker," Rohit responded affectionately as he caught her mouth with his, lowering his hands to her waist.

"Oh god, so cheesy!"

"Oh, come on. Let me have it," Rohit coaxed, giving her sides a playful squeeze.

"Fine." She conceded with a smile. "Have all the cheese you want as long as it's—"

"—not blue cheese." Rohit kissed her again. "Come on, before you get me in trouble."

Hand in hand, they made their way downstairs to the café. He led them behind the counter, automatically going into server mode and putting together a trayful of chai. Manisha leaned back against the bar, surveying the bustling space.

Chai Time now hosted a vibrant community of artists, each immersed in their creative pursuits—reading, writing, drawing. In the back theatre, actors, singers, and dancers rehearsed for an upcoming production. The revamped establishment was the realization of Rohit's lifelong dream, a testament to his dedication and hard work. He'd successfully realized his mother's vision by creating a thriving studio catering to the needs of Indian creatives and artists in Baskin. It served as a sanctuary, a haven where individuals could freely express themselves without any inhibitions. Manisha knew he felt a sense of pride and accomplishment, especially whenever he saw Meena Auntie's booth outside the theatre. She had set up a charming display of her lotions, potions, and seeds, adding an extra touch of magic to the already enchanting ambience of Chai Time.

"I can't believe you accomplished all this in just a year, babe," Manisha said.

"We, Manisha. *We* made all of this happen," Rohit replied with a warm smile, his voice full of gratitude. "It's more than my mom ever could have dreamed of."

Manisha reached out and squeezed his hand, her heart swelling with pride. "I know she sees all of this, and she's proud of you."

"You wanted to make a difference just as much as I did," he said, his voice filled with admiration as he glanced at her. "And now look at you—California's top matchmaker." With a tender smile, he leaned in to kiss her forehead. Her gaze shifted to the cover of *California Business* magazine hanging beside the register, where Manisha's radiant image took centre stage. Again, her heart grew with pride, this time for herself.

Rohit expertly swooped up the brimming tray in one hand and led them to the front.

"Ah, good man, beta," Manisha's mother said, cupping the side of Rohit's face as he served her a cup of chai.

"Is there a charge for the tea? I will not pay seven dollars for something I can make at home," Manisha's father warned.

"Don't worry about it, Dad. It's complimentary," Rohit replied.

"Va, va," Manisha's mom replied. "Free for the in-laws. I like that we get our own stab."

"Tab, honey."

"How about something sweet and savoury, too?" said the third of their party.

"Come on, Maaji, I can make all of this at home," Manisha's dad joked from beside her grandmother.

"And always better, Ashok," she added, with a sincere smile.

It was a sight Manisha thought she'd never see. Last year, her dad and her grandmother had seemed locked in a permanent standoff. But after the day Manisha had found herself on her grand-mother's doorstep, and with a gentle push from her mom, Manisha's dad surprised them all by setting aside his Patel stubbornness and opening up his heart to the possibility of reconciliation. Now, they made quite the pair, Nani finding every chance to compliment and defend Manisha's dad, much to his delight.

"I'm losing business because of you," they heard a voice say from the café entrance.

"Manny!" Manisha exclaimed. Her sister-in-law stood there with hands on hips, flanked by Sammy and Deena. She hurried over to hug them, feeling a mix of joy and warmth from the famil-iar faces. Rohit signalled to Adam at the counter for more drinks.

"Wow, this place . . . it's unrecognizable," Sammy said, look-ing around with wide eyes. "You two have truly outdone your-selves. People in town can't stop talking about it."

"Now that's the kind of gossip we love to hear!" Manisha replied with a satisfied smile.

"And spread," Manny chimed in, nodding with approval. "So, what's your secret, Ish? How did you manage to attract so many clients?" she asked, leaning in.

"Well, it's a funny story," Manisha began, her eyes twinkling. "But I'll save it for another time." Her gaze slid significantly over to her parents and grandmother.

"Please don't tell me they're all your exes," Sammy teased, glancing at Rohit with mock suspicion.

"You could say something like that," Rohit replied, his grin mischievous.

"You know, I'm still waiting to hear how you two got together," Manny said, pointing between Manisha and Rohit with an eager look.

"That's another long story," Manisha said.

"I can tell you all about that," Deena put in with a wink. "But as for the café, I still think something is missing."

Everyone looked up as Deena leaned down and pulled something from the tote bag she'd brought. "Ta-da!" she exclaimed, revealing a small, vibrant plant.

"Lucky lemons," Manisha and Rohit said simultaneously, both grinning at the gift.

"I think it's perfect. All of this is just perfect," she added, as the two of them shared a knowing look.

The five of them collectively moved to join the others at the table, Deena setting the mini-tree carefully in the centre.

Greetings and hugs were exchanged, followed by much laughter and easy-flowing conversation as they all settled in. Manisha looked around at the people who had become her world—her community, her family, and the love of her life, Rohit. It all felt like the perfect culmination of everything she'd ever hoped for.

She rested her hand gently on her barely visible baby bump, a quiet symbol of the new chapter unfolding before her. There had been missteps, lessons learned, and moments of uncertainty, but they had all led her here. To this café. To this life. To Rohit. And now, a little one who would join their story, adding another layer of love to an already full heart.

Rohit placed his hand over hers. Looking into his eyes, she could see the same hope, the same joy reflected in his smile. Their journey together had been anything but ordinary, but it had brought them to a place of peace, of contentment, of belonging.

And as she looked around at the people she loved, Manisha knew one thing for certain: This was the real Patel Blessing.

# ⇒ ACKNOWLEDGEMENTS ⇐

First and foremost, I'd like to thank the incredible team at Doubleday Canada, with a special shout-out to Bhavna for her vision, guidance, and steady belief in me, and to Megan for her thoughtful support throughout this process. I'm also grateful to everyone working tirelessly behind the scenes to bring this book to life.

To Paula, for the unforgettable summer of 2025 and the laughter we'll never stop sharing. To my sister Tina, whose pride in me means more than she knows. To Joanne and Colleen, for always asking when the next book is coming out and keeping me motivated. To Husein, who reminds me that I am "unstoppable." To my friends Shouvik, Randy, Sonia, Julia, DB, and Rebecca—your hard work and perseverance inspire me every day.

To the Sikh Gurdwara in Guelph, thank you for offering me a place of peace and meditation when I needed it most. And to my agent, Carolyn—your support has meant everything.

To my readers, your love keeps me writing. And to Michael, thank you for always being in my corner with your love and laughter.

*The Fake Matchmaker*

## ⇒ DISCUSSION GUIDE ⇐

1. *The Fake Matchmaker* is filled with unforgettable characters; who would you cast in a screen adaptation of this novel? Do you think it would be better as a film or a television show?

2. When Manisha starts dating, she has a detailed list of expectations for her potential romantic partner. However, by the end of the novel she realizes that the best people may not always check every box. Do you have specific expectations for your relationships? What happens when life has other plans?

3. Manisha relies on her friends and family for advice about her personal and professional life. Is there anyone in your life you go to for advice?

4. *The Fake Matchmaker* draws on many classic romance tropes like enemies-to-lovers, secret identities, and a (two-person) love triangle. What are your favourite romance tropes?

5. If you were making a playlist for *The Fake Matchmaker*, what songs would you include?

6. When Manisha first moves back to Baskin, she has the wrong idea about Rohit's character. Why do you think she readily believed the rumours about him?

7. At the end of the novel, Manisha finds her new passion and becomes a successful matchmaker. Do you think you would be a good matchmaker?

8. Both Manisha and Rohit are dishonest about their identities when communicating over email. Why do you think they chose to do this? Should they have come clean earlier?

9. Manisha's mother tells her about the "Patel Blessing," where the family always falls in love quickly. Rohit's parents met under the stars, and he and Manisha reconnect under the star-filled ceiling of a plane. Do you think there is an element of fate in love? Has reading *The Fake Matchmaker* impacted your view on fate at all?

10. Do you think Manisha and Rohit's relationship will stand the test of time? Why or why not?

# ⇒ AUTHOR Q&A ⇐

Manisha and Rohit have such palpable chemistry both as themselves and as Isha and Sunil. What was the inspiration for their romance?

The inspiration behind Manisha and Rohit's slow-burn, can't-look-away chemistry is a spicy blend of classic Bollywood, *You've Got Mail* vibes, and all those feel-good '90s rom-coms I grew up loving. Honestly, I've felt that kind of spark before—where a single look says everything—and I wanted to bottle it up and pour it onto the page. Anyone who's ever had that kind of chemistry knows it's rare, addictive, and unforgettable.

*The Fake Matchmaker* has truly stand-out characters. Who was your favourite to write?

Manisha, hands down! She's bold, hilarious, vulnerable, and unapologetically South Asian, which made her such a joy to write. Growing up, I didn't always see characters like her in books, so getting to create one who's both strong and beautifully flawed felt really personal. Oh, and writing those disastrous dates Manisha goes on? Pure therapy. I was laughing at my desk remembering a few of my own cringe-worthy dating adventures.

You use so many classic rom-com tropes in innovative ways in this novel. How did you decide what tropes to include? Are there any tropes you'd like to explore in future books?

I'm a total sucker for a good rom-com trope, so of course I had to include some of my all-time favourites like the meet-cute and enemies-to-lovers. There's just something delicious about watching two people go from *ugh* to *ohhh*. What really inspired the tropes in *The Fake Matchmaker* was the magic of '90s rom-coms. They didn't always feature people who looked like me, but I knew those big, messy, swoony love stories could absolutely belong to South Asian characters, too. So I wrote the kind of story I always wanted to see (hopefully onscreen one day, too). But I'm also dreaming of diving into more tropes in future books: the best friend secretly in love, a juicy love triangle, or the ultimate fake dating situation where both characters agree to pretend to be in a relationship.

There is such a loving and honest portrayal of South Asian culture in this novel. How important was it for you to showcase these cultural elements?

For me, writing about South Asian culture isn't just important, it's second nature. I grew up in a house that was basically a live-action sitcom, filled with larger-than-life characters—my parents, siblings, aunts, uncles, cousins—you name it. Storytelling was how we communicated, and especially with humour. At the time, I didn't realize how special it was to be surrounded by that much personality (and drama!), but now it's the heartbeat of my books. I was raised in a Punjabi household where my mom spoke Hindi, our dinners featured everything from saag to dosa, and the soundtrack of our lives was a mix of Bollywood bangers and bhangra beats. When I write, I try to honour that blend because Indian culture isn't just *one* thing. It's layered, loud, flavourful, emotional, and full of love. And that's exactly what I try to bring to the page.

**What is your writing process like? Do you have any preferred places to write or things you need to get in the zone?**

My writing process has definitely evolved over the years, and one thing I've learned is that I have a really hard time letting go of my characters. I still catch myself looking around at my friends and thinking, "Is that . . . Manisha?" (Spoiler: It never is, but she lives rent-free in my head anyway.) It was tough saying goodbye to some of my debut characters, too. So now part of my process is gently reminding myself that once a book is done, the story lives on in readers, not in real life. I try to tie it up with a pretty little bow and move on to the next bold, beautiful South Asian heroine waiting to be written.

As for where I write? Honestly, anywhere that lets me slip into my little storytelling bubble. It could be a cozy cottage in Prince Edward County, a bustling café in Elora or Guelph, or a noisy restaurant in Toronto. I weirdly thrive in chaos. But I do try to get out of the house because when I'm home, the kitchen starts calling my name, and let's just say it's hard to write a rom-com with a mouth full of Ruffles chips.

**What was your favourite scene in the book to write? Were there any you found difficult?**

Writing Manisha's terrible dates was an absolute blast. I definitely pulled from some of my own dating disasters (and yes, a few wild ones my single girlfriends generously shared over wine) and tried to capture that universal frustration of just wanting to connect with someone. First dates are weird. Everyone's sizing each other up, nobody's being totally themselves, and half the time you're wondering how fast you can escape. So those scenes were cathartic and fun to write.

Another favourite scene was the one with Manisha and Deena throwing back shots and singing their hearts out at karaoke. I loved the happy energy of that night: just Deena and Manisha, two cousins, riding out the madness of life but still showing up for each other with so much love and loyalty. It felt real and joyful, like the kind of moment you never want to forget.

Without spoiling too much, the toughest scene to write was the moment in the book where Manisha truly feels heartbreak. Writing that moment hit me hard, and I really want readers to feel that ache, and the raw, messy, disorienting nature of it. I want them to see themselves in it, and to know that even in those shattered moments, they're not alone.

## ABOUT THE AUTHOR

**SONYA SINGH** is the author of *The Break-up Expert,* her debut novel, which became an instant hit with readers across Canada. A former entertainment reporter, she now shares her love of laughter, love stories, and South Asian representation through both books and films.